THE
CORREGIDOR
TAPE

Charles Ryan

D0970823

AN ONYX BOOK

ONYX
Published by the Penguin Group
Penguin Books USA Inc., 375 Hudson Street,
New York, New York 10014, U.S.A.
Penguin Books Ltd, 27 Wrights Lane,
London W8 5TZ, England
Penguin Books Australia Ltd, Ringwood,
Victoria, Australia
Penguin Books Canada Ltd, 10 Alcorn Avenue,
Toronto, Ontario, Canada M4V 3B2
Penguin Books (N.Z.) Ltd, 182-190 Wairau Road,
Auckland 10, New Zealand

Penguin Books Ltd, Registered Offices:
Harmondsworth, Middlesex, England

First Published by Onyx, an imprint of New American Library,
a division of Penguin Books USA Inc.

First Printing, October, 1992
10 9 8 7 6 5 4 3 2 1

 REGISTERED TRADEMARK—MARCA REGISTRADA

PRINTED IN THE UNITED STATES OF AMERICA

PUBLISHER'S NOTE
This is a work of fiction. Names, characters, places, and incidents either are
the product of the author's imagination or are used fictitiously, and any resem-
blance to actual persons, living or dead, events, or locales is entirely coincidental.

LETHAL LINKS

A corpse of a monk found in the underground corridors of the old U.S. World War II Philippine fortress of Corregidor.

A savage midnight attack by a Chinese secret army on a Russian garrison at a contested border.

A South Sea island paradise where a French scientist stoked his genius with drugs and sex as he programmed a hellish future for the world.

A floating hotel off the Great Barrier Reef of Australia that was the last word in luxury and the prime target for destruction.

What unthinkable plan linked them together—and what chance was there to stop it?

Cas Bonner and Liz Forsythe had to find out . . . as they turned from hunted to hunters . . . and from fleeing to save their lives to fighting to kill . . .

THE
CORREGIDOR
TAPE

To Robin Carr:
Wonderful writer,
fantastic friend.

On the road to Mandalay,
Where the flyin'-fishes play,
An' the dawn comes up like thunder outer
China 'crost the Bay!

—Rudyard Kipling,
Mandalay

Corregidor Island, Philippines

Manila–Corregidor ferry number 7, riding ten feet above the surface of the ocean on twin hydrofoils, banked into a shallow port turn as it aligned to the outer channel markers of Corregidor Island's North Mine Wharf. A moment later, the steady rumble of the vessel's double 1500 ST Edison diesels dropped in pitch. As speed came off, the sleek red and white hull lowered until it was once more drafting, its bow hurling spray as the hydrofoils were retracted back and under.

Up in the main passenger lounge, tourists gathered along the windows, craning their necks to get the first close-up view of the famous Rock. Only one person— a young man in a monk's habit—was not looking at the island. With feverish blue eyes he was instead intently scanning his fellow passengers.

During the forty-five-minute ride from Manila, he had cowered in the last seat on the starboard side, trying desperately to be inconspicuous. But now as the other passengers moved about, crowding against the windows, he looked into their faces, searching. Had he been followed? he wondered in an agony of fresh terror. Could one of these gaudily dressed tourists be the person who was trying to kill him?

The boat's speed dropped sharply as it approached the landing dock, and the deck trembled as the propellers were reversed. Churning water, the vessel eased into a berth beside another ferry. The other

boat's deck force lounged on the wharf, smoking ci-
gars and eating rice balls while they waited for their
passengers to return from sight-seeing excursions to
the ruins of Topside Hill, Fort Mills and the Middle-
side Barracks, all remnants of the Japanese bombard-
ments in World War II.

The gangplanks were lowered and people streamed
off onto the wharf apron where a fleet of tiny yellow
jitneys was lined up for them. Beyond were the crum-
bled remains of former warehouses and fuel-storage
tanks. On the other side of the apron were smaller slot
berths and new gasoline and diesel tanks with feeding
lines on swing arms. These were used to refuel the
fishing boats and day sailers which occasionally
stopped in.

The monk held back until the last of the passengers
had disembarked, and then he hurried down the after
gangplank. Up on the dusty roadway, the tourists were
being gathered into small groups, like schoolchildren
assembling for tours through a museum. Here and
there Japanese guides held up tiny Nippon flags as rallying points for their charges.

Loaded, the jitneys began pulling away. Some
headed up a wide coral road that would take them to
Topside. Others turned to the left, up a short, steeper
road lined with eucalyptus trees that led to the west
entrance of Malinta Hill. Within was the vast honeycomb of tunnels in which thirteen thousand Americans
and Filipinos had hidden for 128 days of continual Japanese air raids.

The monk didn't join any of the departing groups.
Instead he loitered on the wharf until they were gone
and then walked after them, up the steep incline to
Malinta. It was about three hundred yards away. The
sun came down through the eucalyptus trees and
formed dancing patterns of shadow across the coral
road. Behind him the sea stretched away, filling the
breeze with the pungency of salt and wharf tar.

As he climbed, his thick woolen habit immediately
drew sweat from his body. His fear gave it a sweet,

musky scent. By the time he reached the entrance, the tourists were already inside. The drivers of the parked jitneys were kneeling beside one of the vehicles, shooting craps. When they spotted him, they all stood and silently took off their caps as he passed.

The entrance had been left unchanged since that day in 1942 when MacArthur's force finally surrendered to the Japanese. A steel grate covered the entire mouth of the tunnel and had a swing door in its middle. The grate was badly rusted and some of the main foundation pipes had disintegrated, making portions hang disjointedly. On either side were small hillocks of bomb debris, torn rock and bricks, twisted cables, and partially burned planks and beams. Fitted into the right wall was a brass plate, tarnished to the color of dull jade, with the inscription: "WEST ENTRANCE."

He paused. He could hear little bursts of hushed conversation from the tourists already inside the tunnel. The muffled sound again drew forth a renewed sense of foreboding. God, he thought wildly, why had he chosen this place? It was like a tomb.

He glanced around and saw that the drivers were curiously watching him. He turned back, squinted again into the semidarkness of the tunnel, knowing that he *had* to go in. It was too late to change sites now. Forcing away the fear, he stepped through the grate door.

Inside, the main corridor was large, at least twenty-five feet wide, and it curved into an overhead arch like a Roman catacomb. Bare electric bulbs hung from the center of the arch, illuminating the corridor in spaced pools of light. The walls were made of gray brick, and the air was thick and smelled of cement dust and fungus. Up ahead, he could see one of the tour groups.

Following at a discreet distance, he soon came to a series of side tunnels. Wooden markers identified them as part of the Quartermaster Area. Some of the passageways were partitioned, forming rooms. Inside were desks and chairs, rusty file cabinets and one ancient typewriter.

The tour group stopped momentarily while their guide gave a short lecture, then moved on. A few stragglers lingered, sending bright camera flashes bursting up the corridor. The monk shot a look back at the entrance. It seemed a terribly long way off. Panic, clothed in claustrophobia, hit him. He pressed back against a wall. It was slightly damp and cool against his palms. Two full minutes later, he managed to calm himself enough to move on, deeper into the complex.

He reached another series of side tunnels: Harbor Defense Headquarters. From the maps he had studied, he knew he was getting close to his destination. His blood started to pound in his head. In the silence it seemed to make the air around him vibrate.

He inspected each defile, searching for markers. At last he found one shaped like an arrow. It pointed north and read, "HOSPITAL AREA." He quickly darted into the passageway. It was lower than the others, and its lights were double-spaced, which gave it a dungeon-like gloom.

Soon he emerged into a brightly lit room about the size of a small auditorium. It too was partitioned into cubicles. Some contained old Army cots, their webbing and blankets moldy. Tourists wandered among them, peering about with cautious curiosity, like people moving through a haunted house.

Across the room at one of the main entrances, a bored Filipino girl in a blue uniform and a Madonna haircut sat at a table filled with souvenirs: unfired .50-caliber rounds, tarnished insignia buttons, and bits of oddly shaped shrapnel.

The young monk stood in the shadowed passageway for a moment, studying the room. At last he spotted a small side alley, no larger than the one he was in. Above it the words *Num Three Sec* had been stenciled onto the brick in black paint. Dipping his head as if shy, he hurried to it and entered.

A few feet from the entrance, the tunnel branched off into a warren of small side rooms, each with an identifying stencil: *"OS Off," "SN Quar," "Pharmacy," "Assign DH-l."* He continued to the end of the tunnel, where the rooms formed a fan. The last one on the right was stenciled *"Autopsy Rm."*

He paused in front of it and looked in. There was a high dissection table in the center. Above it was a wide electrical fixture with two dozen empty light sockets in it. The table base had a cylindrical shaft with a hydraulic foot pump. Underneath were grooves in the floor which led to a small, open cistern near the back with a network of pipes and nearly disintegrated rubber hoses.

Recoiling at the sight, he closed his eyes for a moment and listened to the thunder of his blood. The air here seemed absolutely motionless, compacted with a vague, dark effluvium.

Bracing himself, he reached into his habit and took out a small packet wrapped in green plastic. The top had an adhesive strip. He stared at it a moment, then ducked into the cutting room. Beside the autopsy table he tore off the strip and slapped the packet onto the underside of the table. He tested it to see that the strip held, then turned and quickly exited.

As he crossed back through the main hospital ward, a woman with blue-tinted hair and a garish Hawaiian muumuu smiled at him and called him Father. He ignored her, hurrying past into the passageway that would return him to the main corridor and outer entrance.

Halfway in, a man rose suddenly out of the darkness near the floor. Startled, the monk jerked back, a cry coming up into his throat. It never reached his mouth. A thin wire had slipped over his head, and it now snapped up powerfully against his Adam's apple.

Adrenaline hit his body with the force of shorting generators. He grabbed at the wire, but it had sunk into his flesh. Kicking out, he drew up his legs, hurled his body back, felt the attacker's chest and knotted shoulder muscles.

He twisted his head. For a fleeting instant he saw

the man's face. An oriental face with a tattoo across one cheek and crowned with thick black hair swept back with grease.

The killer bent in against his ear, and the monk heard an expulsion of air, smelled sourness. Then the wire cut in like a razor. He felt blood explode out of his throat. All sounds faded, except a wild roaring inside his head that went up and up until he thought it would explode within the convolutions of his brain.

Then he was gone. . . .

1

Cas Bonner spotted the unexploded Japanese bomb a full ten seconds before his metal detector picked it up.

He quickly shut off the furious little buzzer and hovered in the water, looking down at the thing. It was nearly invisible against the reef: coral growth and reef calcite completely covered its foot-thick casing. It rested at the edge of a sand pool with its nose partially buried in the rock.

Bonner was a strapping, sun-browned man with the long muscles and powerful shoulders of a distance swimmer. At the moment he was in sixty feet of water off Corregidor's Monkey Beach. For the past hour he and two other divers from Offshore Demolition International had been working a search grid a quarter mile from shore.

From the air, Corregidor Island, which lies in the western approaches to Manila Bay thirty miles from Metro Manila and Cavite City, resembles a large tadpole with the massive bulk of Topside Hill forming its body. At the foot of Topside it narrows gently down to the North Mine Wharf, the main terminus, then rises sharply again to form Malinta Hill. Beyond Malinta the island curves out into a thin, stinger-like tail which ends at Hooker Point, two miles to the east. Monkey Beach is located halfway down the stinger, adjacent to the Quonset shells of Kindsley Field, which once housed the crews of the 199th Fighter Squadron based there before World War II.

Cas flicked his swim fins lightly and glided down to the bottom. Around him the crystalline water danced and shimmered with sun beams. His ears were filled with the constant chatter of reef life, which sounded like distant, crackling fires. Kneeling beside the bomb, he examined it closely. From its size and the tapered shape of its after housing, he identified it as a Kurasaki five-hundred-pounder, probably loaded with scatter fragments. Two of its stability vanes had been torn off by its initial impact.

Gently he brushed his glove over the after housing breech, flaking off a layer of calcite. The breech had a back plate with countersunk screw heads and a center shaft drilled for the arming wire. As he got down to the metal, he saw a streak of yellow, looking gray at depth, which had seeped from around the base plate.

He stiffened. That was explosive sweat, he knew, and the color indicated that the inner charge had deteriorated. The divers called bombs in this state "widow makers." One careless nudge, a scrape of metal on metal, even the tiny static electricity created by air moving through his scuba hoses, could instantly detonate its fragile nitro charge.

Easing away carefully, he drifted back out into clear water. As he did, the movement spooked two lobsters that had been hiding in a nearby crevice. They scooted out, tails clacking like tiny castanets, and hurdled over the bomb, throwing sand.

Bonner made a crazy sound in his throat and curled away, bracing. The lobsters disappeared into another crevice and the sand settled. With blood tapping in his temples, he took a deep pull of air and thought: "This is a damned stupid way for an intelligent man to earn his money."

He'd been working at this job for only three weeks. ODI was an American company hired by the Philippine government to clear the waters off Corregidor of unexploded ordnance from the war. The new regime in Manila had decided to build a large hotel/recreational complex on the eastern end of Corregidor Island.

Before signing on, Bonner had been wandering aimlessly through the Indonesian and Celebes archipelagoes aboard his sloop, *Napah*. He had poked into ports now and again to replenish fuel and supplies, but mainly he stayed at sea. By the time he reached Manila, he was nearly broke.

One night, by a clean stroke of luck, he'd run into an old buddy named Mark Balestera in a bar in Cavite. He and Balestera had served together in Nam with the Navy's SEAL Team One. Mark, now project head for ODI, hired him on the spot.

"You was always pretty good with HE," Balestera said, half drunk. "You still got the touch?"

"It's been a long time."

"Just keep a tight asshole, you'll be fine."

By profession Cas was a marine biologist, and a damned good one. He had that rare sixth sense for the sea, an intangible rapport with ocean life that gave his research reports a brilliance unmatched by other men.

Unfortunately, he also had a heavy streak of pure, wild independence. He hated the stuffy protocols and ego-driven brown-nosing inherent in the field of oceanic study. When put up against the clean symmetry and purpose he always found in the sea, this sort of bullshit had turned his disgust into open mockery.

His run-ins with his superiors grew more frequent. Time and again he was blackballed, locked out of assignments and research money. Occasionally friends came to his rescue, found project positions for him. And he always repaid them with incisive and innovative data reports.

But sooner or later he'd come up against more policy muddle-headedness which, in turn, usually created further abuse of the sea environment. Then his eyes would fire up and he'd go charging. The next thing he knew, he'd be out of another job.

After the last time, following an explosive confrontation with Japanese fishing trawlers southwest of Tahiti, he'd been shipped back to Auckland, where he bought a thirty-five-foot sloop off a stranded Aussie, provisioned it, and headed back to sea. He renamed the boat the *Napah,* for a very special lady he'd once known. Like her, she was solid, teak hull and up-works, with clean running gear and a Jamison heavy-weather stabilizer that could ride her through a high-number blow.

He now took another lungful of air and set about dealing with the bomb. From his weight belt he took a small plastic case shaped like a carpenter's measuring tape. It had a thin cord on a ring spool at one end. He pulled the cord out and wrapped it around a large brain coral on the bottom, then popped a rubber nipple on the unit. Instantly a small red balloon inflated and the unit began a high-pitched pinging. He released the balloon and it went jigging wobbily to the surface.

Two minutes later, one of the other divers approached him from out of the blue-green haze. From far off he could hear the slap and hum of a Zodiac boat homing to his red balloon marker. It came in, casting a shadow, and then Balestera came down carrying a bag of tools and a small satchel of explosive detonators.

Ordinarily the divers physically disarmed the bombs they found, extracting the charges and harmlessly blowing them on the reef with a detonator. The empty casings were then hauled up and carted into Cavite to be sold to souvenir shops. A five-hundred-pounder like this one could bring several hundred dollars, more than enough for a night of fun and games at Long Tommy's, a cathouse in Cavite.

Using hand signals, Cas explained about the leakage. Balestera nodded, gave a quick look, and handed one of the detonators to him. Then he and the other diver headed for the surface. They would clear the area while Bonner set the charge. That task always fell to the diver who had found the bomb.

The detonator was a small plastic box that contained a tiny contact explosive encased in a ram shaft of carbon-carbon material. It was triggered by a powerful spring which would puncture the thin outer casing of the bomb and detonate the main charge. The spring was the only metal in the unit, and it was wrapped in depolarized epoxy to prevent static electricity. It was held in by a gear timer that allowed the firing diver fifteen minutes, enough for short decompression stops to the surface, where he'd be whisked away by the Zodiac.

Cas returned to the bomb and felt along the axis weld seal to locate the precise center of the warhead. Gingerly he placed the detonator. Now came the touchy part, switching on the timer. Would the minute vibration set off the charge?

Tensed, he flicked the switch. The gear locked on with a little snap that riffled through his glove. The bomb remained inert. He drifted away from it, gave one final look, and headed for the surface.

When the detonator went, with the Zodiac idly riding a swell three hundred yards away, the five-hundred-pounder threw a balloon geyser through the surface which opened up and hurled sun rainbows. Concussion waves followed two seconds later, coming up from the bottom like the start of a magma blow. It made the Zodiac's bottom pop and jerk as if she had hit a reef.

Studying his watch, Bonner lit a cigarette and gave Balestera a reproachful shake of the head.

"What? What?" Mark said.

"You got shitty gear here, man. That sucker went off six seconds too soon."

Chiang Mai, Thailand

Jack Stanford shifted himself on the cooled sheets and ran his tongue gently in an oval motion over the young prostitute's right nipple. It was flaccid and he could feel the bunched tension in the girl's body. He glanced up at her face on the pillow. She was regarding him with a mixture of fear and confusion.

On the other side of the bed, an older prostitute idly

toyed with the girl's other nipple, occasionally dipping her jet black head to flick a perfunctory tongue over it. When she noticed Stanford looking at the girl, she snapped harshly in Thai, "Respond to him, you stupid little bitch!"

Stanford jerked his head around and glared at the older woman. "Shut up," he said in the same language. "She's doing fine."

The girl was sixteen, a virgin, undoubtedly sold by her parents into prostitution. She had light brown skin and black eyes, and her mouth trembled each time his hands touched her cheeks. He diligently kept them from moving to the top of her head. In Thai culture that was an unforgivable insult, even to an ignorant rice-paddy girl.

Stanford continued his ministrations, cooing softly to her below the rumble of the air conditioner. His hands dropped across her body now, along the symmetrical curve of her belly, down into the dark confluence of her crotch. She gasped as he allowed a finger to enter into her. "Ah?" he said, pleased. She twisted her head back and forth on the pillow, grunting softly as he probed her, increasing his rhythm.

The older prostitute disgustedly slid off the bed and went to sit by the window. Outside, there were hibiscus and bougainvillea blossoms near the glass, and the window reflected their colored patterns of light onto the whore's bored face. She picked up a bottle of gin and took a deep swallow.

Slowly the young girl began writhing. Her hips rolled on the sheets and her breathing increased. Murmuring, his own heat generating jerky, aroused movements of his body, Stanford went on.

She threw her arms around him. "Oh, yeah!" he yelled. In one quick mounting, he entered her, going suddenly deep. The girl gasped as if someone had thrashed her across the chest. He kept thrusting, thrusting, sweat beading his forehead. At last he felt the pent-up surge in his groin and, arching his back, he let it come. The girl chugged beneath him, weeping.

The phone rang.

Stanford heard it distantly, like a voice from another room. Then, as he came down out of the ecstasy, it became louder. He turned his head and stared at it. Beside it, the older prostitute was smoking a thin cigar the color of tar, disinterestedly watching a tiny yellow bird defecate on one of the hibiscus blossoms.

Jack twisted off the bed, dangling and wet, and jerked up the phone. *"Khrap?"*

A heavily accented voice said, "The disks were not obtained."

"What?" Stanford roared. "Are you certain?"

"Yue Fei is not pleased. Obtain them immediately." The line went dead.

For several seconds Stanford sat there with the dial tone buzzing in his ear. Then he slammed down the receiver with such force the telephone fell off onto the floor. On the bed, the young prostitute looked frightened again and pulled the sheet up to cover her sweat-sheened breasts.

Twenty minutes later, dressed in Levis, T-shirt and tennis shoes, which gave his lean, forty-year-old body a collegiate look, Stanford wove his way through the parked motorcycles in front of the Proong Nii Disco and entered under the dragon portico.

The restaurant was on Ratchaphakhinai Road, a block from the Thai Airways office. It was done in an orientalized Art Deco motif, all chrome and polished bars and stark white walls covered with orange poppies. The dance floor was totally black, polished to the shine of glass. Right in the center of the floor was a pit four feet across with a brass railing. Inside the pit were dozens of cobras.

At the moment a waiter was trying to hook one with a long stick that held a spring catch on the end. Some of the dancers stopped to watch. The cobra was upright, flared. The waiter slapped its hood, and the instant the snake dropped to the ground to flee, he had it. He lifted it, writhing around the end of the pole.

Stanford made his way to a table on a small balcony where a young Chinese man in wraparound dark glasses was sitting. Jack's eyes narrowed as he passed the pit. He hated snakes, especially cobras. In some unexplained way he felt they represented his own death.

The waiter, with the snake firmly grasped behind the head, came through the dancers and up the stairs. He paused beside Jack's table and held his catch up for Stanford's companion to inspect. The Chinese ran his finger along the viper's skin, then nodded. The waiter immediately produced a straight razor and deftly slit the reptile's body from throat to tail, then held it over a large wine goblet already on the table to catch the blood. Some splashed over the edge and made red dotlets on the black and white plastic. It smelled thick and raw. Believed to be an aphrodisiac, this was drunk by the diner.

With another deft flip of his razor, the waiter sliced out the animal's bladder and popped it into the goblet. Pleased, the Chinese man poked a five hundred *bhat* note into his shirt pocket. Smiling broadly, the waiter retreated down to the kitchen, where the snake would be cut up, fried, and served with curried rice.

As Jack watched, the Chinese scooped a little of the blood into a silver jigger with a wooden spoon, added a stiff shot of Hennesey's XO cognac, and tossed the concoction down. He sucked with relish through his teeth, like a man drinking his first cold beer on a scorching summer day. Then he picked up the bladder with chopsticks and dropped it into his mouth. Chewing, he grinned at Stanford and nodded toward the goblet.

"No way," Jack said disgustedly. "I'd rather eat duck shit."

The Chinese chuckled and took another shot of Hennesey's. He was a handsome man, with chiseled features, dimples and a thick Elvis-style pompadour.

Along with a perfectly tailored white suit he wore a jeweled Rolex watch and a large diamond ring on his little finger.

He was Lui "Unicorn" Sik Fu, one of the main dragon heads—councilmen—of the secret Triad society called the Green Tigers. His control area was the northern Thai–Burmese frontier, across which came tons of raw opium that was then processed into morphine in jungle labs near Mae Hong Son and Chiang Rai.

Stanford lit a cigarette and eyed Sik Fu. "What went wrong, Lui?"

"The disks no were on Forsit when my men caught him."

"What about his quarters?"

"He was at a monastery." Lui ran his tongue across the inside of his mouth, savoring the last of the snake's bladder. "Little room like shithouse. My men look but nothing."

"Dammit!" Jack took a long, thoughtful pull on his cigarette before speaking again. "Then he must have had the disks and planted 'em on Corregidor."

Lui nodded languidly.

"That means he had a pickup."

"Yes." Lui turned and watched the dancers with casual insolence. All around the floor, lounging on chairs and railings, were roughly a dozen young Chinese dressed in skin-tight white T-shirts and jeans. They were his men. People called them choppers because they were deft at slicing up a man with the long-bladed machetes called *tzutis*. Many had side enterprises, such as running "fish-ball" dens, where eleven- and twelve-year-old hill girls were used as prostitutes. Lui had once been a particularly bloodthirsty and efficient chopper.

"All right, then we go to Manila," Stanford said. "Help coordinate this damned thing."

Lui considered that a moment, then nodded.

"Can you pull one of your lab boats out to meet us there?" He was referring to the small fleet of ultramodern sport cruisers owned by the different Triad clans that handled raw opium. Once the opium was turned into morphine base in northern Thailand, it was then transhipped to ports like Bangkok and Chou on the Gulf and put aboard fishing boats. These rendezvoused with the cruisers deep in the South China Sea. The boats, literally seagoing laboratories, then re-refined the morphine into number three and four heroin, with concentrations of nearly one hundred percent purity. This was later funneled through Hong Kong for world distribution.

"There one in Manila now," Lui said.

"Good."

Lui lit a Galois and appraised Jack bemusedly. "You riding one big dragon, Stamford. Yue Fei is plenny pissed." Yue Fei was the code name for the man financing Stanford's operation, the designation taken from a mythical Song dynasty warrior.

Jack gave him back a hard grin. "We'll get those goddamned disks. You can run dice on that."

The Unicorn laughed deep in this throat. *"Ba sup tin,* baby. Den dat rocket gon' fly."

"We'll make it, Lui," Stanford said.

Ba sup tin meant eight days.

Xchiang, China

The Long March CZ-4 rocket countdown reached T minus ten before Dr. Ziyang Li, Chief Coordinating Mission Head for the Great Wall Industry Corporation's upcoming satellite launch, had to call for an abort.

The main firing room had been running a full simulation of an actual launch. Everything had gone normally until computer data started showing redundancy errors in the on-board circuit relays. Dr. Ziyang moved from his command desk down the two steps to the first of four long banks of computer terminals and studied them over the shoulders of the seated operators. Shutdown trace information was already coming in. The problem was quickly located. Somewhere a single pin in the hundreds within the umbilical electrical interfaces had misaligned its socket. As a result, the instrument unit in the guidance package of the rocket, the on-board brain of the CZ-4, had automatically switched into safety mode, stopping any further sequence.

Ziyang quietly issued orders. Instantly the operators began inputting emergency come-off sequences to de-energize the rocket. He lifted his eyes to study three huge television screens high on the opposite wall. One hundred and forty feet tall, the rocket with its gantry was poised on the launching pad some four hundred yards from the control blockhouse.

The doctor's face showed no emotion. It was a square face with a prominent nose and slitted eyes. The skin had a youthful smoothness that belied his fifty-three years. Yet inwardly he was agonizing. This had been the fourteenth stand-down in the simulation series.

Watching the television monitors closely, he saw the first crews appearing on the screens. Each shutdown created time-consuming delays while the launch technicians physically bore into the internal components of the rocket to repair the system. Worse, the propellent teams now had to go through their intricate and dangerous process of off-loading the equivalent of eighty tanker trucks of liquid oxygen and liquid hydrogen from the rocket's fuel tanks. It was a psychologically stressful situation for everybody.

Ziyang returned to his command desk and momentarily turned the operation over to his main assistant, a young engineer named Changqiao. He left the firing room and walked along a narrow corridor to the toilets. Every time a delay occurred, he found that he had to defecate immediately. He knew it was psychosomatic.

As he sat on the toilet, he brooded, gazing through the small window of the room to the low hills north of the firing complex. They were covered with pine forests which came right down to the facility's freighter dock. Often in the early mornings he had seen deer come down out of the trees to browse on the grass along the estuary shore.

The GWIC rocket complex was located three miles outside the city of Xchiang in southeastern China. Situated near the Equator, which made orbit entry easier, it was the main firing site for the Chinese commercial/military space program. Over the past three years China had been aggressively trying to enter the field of commercially contracted launches.

This particular launch was to send a half-ton space vehicle into low polar orbit. Aboard would be an American weather satellite and a small Swiss corporate telecommunications vehicle designed to monitor fishery movements in the waters off Antarctica.

For Ziyang, the launch was a matter of career survival. As a graduate of the prestigious Southwest China Research Institute of Electronic Technology in Chengdu, he was a senior member of the Beijing Space Medico-Engineering Center. A preeminent scientist in his field, he had logged time as an observer at numerous launches of both NASA and the French Ariane space vehicles.

But younger engineers were biting at his heels. During the terror of Mao Tze Dong's Red Guards, science and technology had withered. Now, as China attempted to reenter the twentieth century, her space scientists were all in their fifties and sixties. But new men, schooled in foreign universities, were on the rise. If this launch did not hold to prescribed contractual time windows, Ziyang would be on his way out.

This had been made perfectly clear to him in a recent phone call from Beijing. Minister Lee Chianghui, head of Internal Achievements for the State Council, one of China's executive bodies, had lectured him for a half hour, ending with an alarming statement: "Minister Litung is personally watching your performance." Litung Biao was the head of the Ministry for Internal Affairs, China's secret police.

Remembering that conversation, Ziyang felt his bowels coil. Minister Litung was a very dangerous man, one who would not tolerate failure. The thought struck him that perhaps the secret police had inserted undercover people into the firing site's personnel to monitor every move he made. Could they even be within his personal staff? That prospect was chilling and shoved his anxiety up another fifty clicks.

2

"What do you mean my credentials have been held up?" The beautiful young woman in an ivy green Faviani business suit eyed the Manila customs officer angrily. "Why, for God's sake?"

"I'm very sorry, missus," the officer said. "My orders say por me that you are to remain here until someone from your consulate and Manila constabulary come to spoken with you."

"This is bullshit."

"I am verry sorry, missus."

The woman stared down at the customs man for a moment. She had blue-gray eyes that now looked as frigid as the undersides of ice floes. At last she snorted and began pacing around the room. But beneath her anger a knot of anxiety was forming. Consulates? Police? What had Jerry gotten himself into this time?

Her name was Liz Forsythe, an anchorperson for the TVN affiliate in San Francisco. Thirty years old, divorced, she had earned a reputation for incisive interviews, managing to hold her own in the cutthroat world of television news. Coupled with her elegant, fiery beauty, everyone knew it was only a matter of time before New York began calling.

"How long will this take?" she snapped.

"I do not know."

She fumbled in her purse for a cigarette.

"Please do not smoke in here, missus."

"Am I allowed outside?" she asked hotly.

"Yes, but do not leave the terminal."

"Thanks a lot."

Out in the main lobby, she took up a position beside a vast orange-tinted window that looked out onto the runways. Smoking distractedly, she watched a Taiwan Airline 727 land. The long silver tube of its fuselage caught the late morning sun, flashing for a moment like an explosion. Far beyond it, the wide expanse of Manila Bay lay as tranquil as a lake.

Two days before, Liz had received a telegram from her brother, Jerry. Though cryptic, it had jolted her: "ARRIVED BROTHERS OF ST TIMOTHYS STOP MUST SEE YOU STOP IF NECESSARY GO TO CORREGIDOR PATHOLOGY STOP APPLE APPLE END."

It was confusing, typical of him. Yet the key word was *apple*. Ever since their childhood days in the horsey, super-rich life of down peninsula Burlingame, California, that particular word had been a cry for assistance, a signal between siblings.

Jerry was a highly regarded photojournalist. At twenty-eight he'd already snagged international fame covering assignments from the fall of the Berlin Wall to starvation in Ethiopia. His photos, set pieces in black and white, evoked a stark realism that could wrench the heart.

His latest assignment was to be his ultimate triumph, a photographic book covering modern China. He had been in-country now for nine months, and the few letters Liz had received from him had indicated that the Chinese government, anxious for better world press, had given him carte-blanche access to some of the most sensitive areas in China.

So what the hell was he doing in Manila? she had asked herself. And what danger had prompted his cry for help? She had immediately packed her gear and booked the first flight out of San Francisco. The snap decision had created some harsh words from her chief editor, Max Schelling, but they had managed a compromise. She was to take care of her problem in Manila, then head south to Queensland on assignment to do some on-site interviews during an upcoming summit meeting on the Barrier Reef.

A man suddenly appeared beside her. He was obviously an American, tall, tanned, wearing a light gray suit. "Miss Forsythe?"

"Yes?" she said, appraising him coolly.

"I'm Leonard Marsh, liaison officer with the U.S. consulate here. Perhaps we could sit in the lounge for a chat?"

"What's all this about? Why am I being held here?"

"Please, the lounge." He touched her arm.

The bar was dark and had padded leather walls and brass carriage lamps. They took a booth near the door and Liz ordered white wine, Marsh a Tom Collins. He waited until the drinks were brought before speaking.

"Why have you come to Manila?" he asked bluntly.

"Because my brother sent a telegram asking me to."

"For what purpose?"

"I don't think that's any of your business."

"I'm afraid it is."

Liz studied Marsh. He had a steady-eyed, clean-cut look of composed danger, like an FBI man. "I won't say any more until you tell me what's going on. First of all, where's my brother?"

"We're not certain." Marsh paused but his expression didn't change. "He may be dead."

That went into Liz like a knife. "What?"

"That's why you're being detained. Manila constabulary wants you to identify a body which might be his."

"Oh, my God!" For a moment Liz felt herself overcome with a wave of heat. It riffled up from her groin, washed through her like a rush of cocaine. She looked toward the bar, saw one of the carriage lamps flicker.

Finally she turned back to him. When she spoke, her voice seemed oddly high to her. "Why do you think it's Jerry?"

"The man was dressed in a monk's habit from St. Timothy's Monastery."

Liz stiffened. To shield it, she lifted her wine and took a large swallow. Her hand was shaking.

Marsh went on, "At the monastery they found identification papers and a passport belonging to your brother."

Her mind was whirling. She wanted to go somewhere and sink down in darkness, to be alone, to sob. She looked at Marsh and suddenly hated him, the aloof smugness, the casual delivery of news like this. She'd be damned if she'd let this cold bastard see her fall apart.

"Your brother called the consulate," Marsh said. "A week ago. I spoke with him. He was very distraught."

"What did he say?"

"He claimed that he was in danger and wanted sanctuary at the consulate. He said that something had been planted on him in China. Computer disks. People were after them and had already tried to kill him."

Liz sat forward. "Then why in God's name wasn't he safely in your consulate?"

"I told him to come in and we'd talk about it. He wanted my assurance that we would protect him. I couldn't give him that without first seeing him. He hung up on me."

"What?" Liz cried. "You mean to tell me he came to you for protection and you turned him *away?* You— *bastard!* You killed my brother!" With a cry of revulsion she started to get up.

Marsh roughly grabbed her arm, holding her down. He shoved his face in close and hissed at her. "Listen, you stupid bitch, this isn't San Francisco now. You're in the Philippines. This country is a goddamned powder keg ready to blow. The U.S. government's walking on glass here."

She struggled but he held her.

"Your brother was mixed up in smuggling. Either drugs or weapons. I knew it, I was certain of it. The fool probably got too greedy and was marked to get taken out. That's all we needed, a confrontation be-

tween the consulate and the Manila police over a fucking doper who was already dead.'' He paused, an icy
second. ''Now, I want to know what involvement you
have in this.''

Liz stared at the man with horror. Fury swept
through her. She lifted her free arm and slapped Marsh
across the face. His head jerked back and a red patch
formed under the tanned skin. For a fleeting moment
he glared at her. Then he let her arm go.

She slid from the booth and fled. As she passed
through the door, the terminal loudspeaker blared:
''Will Miss Liz Forsythe please report to the customs
desk immediately?''

Two constabulary detectives were waiting for her in
the customs office. They identified themselves and
flashed large gold badges pinned to their gun holsters.

They were very polite while questioning her. The
larger of the two sat with his big hands on the table.
Now and then he would rub his thumbs on the wood,
as if trying to scratch off the veneer to see something
underneath.

The other man spoke softly, with the rolling *r*'s and
p-fied *f*'s of Filipino English. ''You say you were
telegrammed by your brother to come here. Is that
correct?''

''Yes.''

''What was it por?''

''He said he needed my help.''

Marsh came into the office. The two detectives
glanced up but ignored him. The consulate man leaned
against a file cabinet near the door and crossed his
arms. His cheek was still red.

Liz glanced around at him. ''Does that son of a
bitch have to be here?''

''Not if you do not want him to be.''

''I want him out.''

''Marsh,'' the smaller detective said. The other
scratched veneer.

''As an American citizen, this woman has the right

to have me present," Marsh said. "As a member of our consulate, it's my duty to remain."

"Not if the lady does not request your presence."

Marsh thought a moment, then decided not to press it. With a withering look at Liz, he departed.

The detective studied her a moment. "Apparently you have already spoken to that one?"

"Yes."

"And he has told you why we need your help?"

"Yes." In saying that, she felt a fresh wave of sorrow and shock rush at her. She put her head down for a moment to collect herself. Finally she looked up. "Yes, he told me. Please, can we get this over with?"

"Yes, of course. But one other thing first." He dug into his jacket and placed a prescription bottle on the table. "We found this in your luggage. It is Seconal. Are you aware that it is illegal to bring drugs into this country?"

"I take it when I fly. I can't sleep when I fly."

The detective grunted and put the bottle back into his pocket. Both men stood up. "Please come with us."

Liz glanced at them, confused. "Am I being arrested?"

"No."

They took her by car into Metro Manila, the silent detective driving while Liz sat in the back with the other. They crossed the Quezon Bridge over the Pasig River, and then turned onto eight-laned Taft Boulevard, which skirted the east side of the ancient, walled city of Intramuros.

The constabulary morgue was at Las Concepcion Hospital in the Ermita district of the city. Once a prison, the building was a colonial structure with columns and grounds filled with tamarind trees.

Nobody spoke during the thirty-minute ride. Liz had already begun steeling herself against what she was about to see. It was going to be Jerry lying on that slab. She could feel it.

Murdered! It all seemed unreal. She looked out at

the sights of the city, the skyscrapers brilliantly washed with sunlight, the cars and motorcycles and throngs of pedestrians. But the substance of it was on the outside of her consciousness, like a travelogue seen in a cheap movie house. In her was only the dreadful silence of her own agony, exhaled into the soft whir of the car's air conditioner.

The basement of the hospital was very old and had stone walls instead of brick. The bright fluorescent lights did not dispel the impression of imprisonment. The morgue itself was a contrast, all white tile, floor, walls and ceiling. It was very cold, enough to make the men's breaths form clouds of frost when they spoke to the attendant.

The body cabinets were in square niches along one wall. The attendant went down the line to the last one. He clicked a lock and slid it out. It came out on rollers in perfect silence.

Liz felt the smaller detective's hand on her arm, edging her forward. The attendant lifted the sheet. Jerry's face was like a waxen mask, the skin shiny, the eyes closed but distended. His hair had been shaved back off the forehead, and the bristles looked stark against the skin.

Liz felt her heart wrench, an actual twisting that made her gasp in anguish. Stumbling back slightly, she immediately felt the large detective grab her around the waist from the back. She closed her eyes and felt the tears come up, her head ringing, and then she was sobbing, sobbing, the sound of it hollow and icy in the white room.

Captain Litung Lin, commander of the fifth *lyan* of the elite Sacred Pool Assault Team of the 278th Banner Division, scanned his binoculars across the opposite shore of the Amur River at the Russian emplacements lined along the bank like mushrooms growing in mud.

The river, called Heilong in Chinese, marked the Soviet–Chinese boundary in Manchuria. Like a snake, it coiled and curled back on itself repeatedly. In the fall, sections of the river became so shallow they showed sandy bottom clear across. Over one such stretch Litung watched the water sparkling in the early morning sunlight.

The captain was a lean, muscular young man of twenty-four. Like his father, Litung Biao, Minister for Internal Affairs and one of the most powerful men in China, he had the clean, sharp features of his Tang ancestors.

He swung his glasses back across the river to his own sector, letting his gaze move slowly across the rolling hills of corn and wheat, with farmers working oxen-driven harvesters. His scan roved past the fields to the fringe of the nearby forest. Out there, elements of his regiment were scattered in holes and camouflaged entrenchments under the thick pine trees and larch just beginning to turn golden.

Back the other way lay the small village of Changbai, scattered mud huts with gray tile roofs and pig stys and duck pens. Along the dirt roads rose huge stacks of wheat, and as he watched, two little girls drove a small herd of goats through the town.

He lowered his binoculars and hunkered down beside his own hole in the ground. It went down in an inverted funnel which spread out into a cavern where he and his *chinwubing*, his batman, lived. He could smell the odor of tea drifting up.

Then his eye caught a movement across the river. Through the glasses, he saw that it was a lone Russian soldier walking along the shoreline. He wore no shirt and was drinking from a bottle. Across his chest was the tattoo of a red star flag.

Litung snorted softly with disdain. The reports from his spies had told him of a sharp drop in discipline among the Soviet troops. The disintegration of the USSR had created confusion and uncertainty throughout the frontier garrisons. But as their orderliness dissipated, their belligerence had increased.

Three days before, Soviet troops had openly executed a Chinese citizen, an admitted spy. Litung had

watched from the trees as the Russians came out and
planted their string of yellow flags along the riverbank.
It was an accepted ritual. Whenever either side had a
problem to discuss, they would place these yellow
flags. Negotiations would follow, and perhaps the result would be the return of a straying fisherman or a
woman who had a lover on the opposite side.

This time the Russians had acted without parley.
They marched the Chinese man out to the edge of the
water and shot him. He fell into the reeds, and two
Soviet soldiers walked over and kicked his body into
the river. It lay there for a long time before the feeble
current finally swept it away.

Captain Litung studied the Russian soldier as he
emptied his bottle and hurled it into the water. Then,
swaying, he urinated. The captain's lips tightened. In
Chinese culture, the act of urinating where others
could see was an insult.

His batman touched his arm. "Captain, your tea."

He took the porcelain cup. It was very hot and he
sipped gingerly, tasting the sharp tang of cinnamon. He
continued watching the solder. Drunkenly the man went
up the bank and walked along a narrow road toward
the village of Kisurar, beyond the Russian bunkers.

Several women with wooden buckets on their heads
approached him, headed for the river. The soldier
stood in the road as if to block them. They went around
him. As they did, he laughed and ran his hands over
their buttocks.

The captain gathered spittle in his mouth, pressed it
against his teeth. He did not spit it out, for that was
unworthy of a warrior. But he stared and stared as the
Soviet soldier disappeared into a mud building braced
with pine limbs.

I will kill you, Litung thought with the sacred cinnamon taste in his mouth. Soon, Russian, I will put a
bullet in that flag on your chest.

The Manila constabulary captain slowly rolled the
brandy in his mouth and leaned back in the white

leather chair. He looked around appreciatively. "You got hotshot tastes, Stanford," he said.

The American nodded, his blue eyes boring into the man's face. They were seated alone in the main salon of the Green Tiger's *Flying Sun,* a sleek luxury motor cruiser presently anchored at Manila's Downtown roadstead. She was a Broward design, pure white. Running twin MTU diesels and KaMeWa waterjets, she could cruise at a steady twenty-two knots for four thousand miles. In a sprint she was capable of thirty knots.

The salon was done in autumn tones, enhanced with glass and brass polished to gleam like gold. The decking was made of teak and the lights were tinted a faint orange, which gave the atmosphere the warm glow of evening. Through the softly frosted glass the docks of Manila looked hazy, like a painting by Monet.

The captain held out his glass and Stanford refilled it. The Filipino studied the liquid a moment, as if looking for sediment. Then he drank it quickly, put the glass down, and coiled his hands together. "Why this dead Yankee boy so important to you?" His English was good enough but a bit nasal, punctuated with Americanisms learned during his hitch in the U.S. Navy as a mess boy in the Korean War.

"You don't need to know that."

"Maybe you satisfy my curiosity, huh?"

Jack shrugged. "He had something I want."

The Filipino laughed. "No shit, Dick Tracy."

"No shit."

The man sighed. "How much I get?"

"Twenty thousand U.S. for information, twenty more for assistance."

The captain's black eyebrows came down slightly. "What this assistance shit?"

"If I need your men, you supply them."

"Then the price gonna change."

"That's always negotiable."

The captain thought again, then nodded at his glass.

Jack refilled it once more. "My cousin say you okay. But I don' like some of yo' chink friends. Bad-news suckers."

"Never mind my friends. I'll handle them."

"You better. They make trouble in my sector, I gonna can yo' ass. And then I cut my cousin's lava-lavas off." He drank before continuing. "What more you want to know? We already help find him for you."

"Go over it all again."

The Filipino shifted in the chair, making the leather squeak. "Forsythe telephone the American consulate a week before he got wasted. Scared shitless, claim people want him dead." He grinned. "Pretty good prediction, huh?"

"What else?"

"He tole the consulate liaison officer he had computer disks. Didn't know how they get into his luggage. But he find them in Hong Kong, and then things get crazy and people try to bust his nuts."

Stanford leaned in. "What about the disks? Did he pass them to the consulate man?"

"The disks, huh? That what you after?"

"Did he pass the damned things?"

The captain shook his head. "No. Marsh, the consulate man, figure Forsythe is involved with drugs or gun smuggling. He try to get him to come in, but no way. Forsythe hung up."

Stanford, brows furrowed, lit a cigarette. "Has there been any other contacts?"

"A sister, television journalist from San Francisco. We had her identify the body."

"What's her name?"

"Elizabeth Forsythe." The man grinned. He had yellowed teeth and the smile curved lasciviously over his face. "Redhead pussy, look like a good lay. I like redhead American women."

"I'll bet you do. What did she say?"

"Her brother cable her to come to Manila."

"Why?"

The captain shrugged. "She claim she don' know."

"You put a watch on her?"

"What else? I don' want weapons or dope comin' through my port."

Like shit, Jack thought. Not unless you get your cut, *bijau*. He said, "Where is she now?"

"This afternoon she take the hydro-boat to Corregidor."

Jack's eyes danced. Yeah, that fit. He shoved himself to his feet and prowled around the cabin. "What time's the last ferry back from the island?"

"Six o'clock. No one is allowed on Corregidor after dark."

"You put anybody on the boat with her?"

"No, but my men are at the terminal."

Stanford glanced at his watch. It was six-fifteen. He moved to the bar, picked up a telephone, and held it out to the captain. "Find out when she came back and where she went."

It took the Filipino four minutes to get an updated report from the terminal watch. He was told Liz Forsythe had not disembarked when the last ferry returned.

At that news Stanford's face lit up with a big grin. He paid the captain the twenty thousand in five thousand dollar bills. They were wrapped in cellophane, which the policeman put into his cap. They left the salon and walked down the companionway to the dock. An Australian schooner was berthed nearby and there was a party going aboard her. The heavy thud of rock music made the dock tremble.

The captain paused, giving Jack a hard stare. "No more murder, pal. Not in my friggin' district. You unnerstand?"

"Right."

The captain drove away in a blue Mercedes XL-300 with white tires.

Lui Sik Fu was smoking a Thai stick in the salon when Stanford returned aboard. Station HJIX, Cavite, was blasting a rocked-up rendition of Duke Ellington's

"Midnight Express." The Unicorn lazily tapped his fingers against his knee, keeping time.

"Forsythe had a sister," Jack told him, grinning broadly. "Right now the cunt's on Corregidor looking for his stash."

Lui smiled sleepily. "Let's go get her, man."

"Crank it up, Lui. It'll be good and dark by the time we get out there."

3

At precisely five-thirty the main generators in the Malinta Tunnel complex had shut down. Liz, hiding in the maze of interconnecting corridors of the Quartermaster Area, was plunged into a darkness so complete it momentarily took her breath away. She stood there frozen. Around her the loss of light seemed to have sucked all sound from the tunnels, leaving only a horrible sensation of entombment, of the massive weight of Malinta Hill pressing down upon her. She actually threw her hands up, prepared to feel falling bricks.

Slowly she gained control of herself. "Idiot!" she whispered. Fumbling in her handbag, she brought out the small flashlight she had bought at dockside in Manila.

After leaving the police, Liz had registered at the Sheraton-Manila and sat in her room for nearly two hours, just staring at the soft yellow walls, her body numb. She cried several times. And then she got mad, an anger that held a potent desire for revenge.

She took out Jerry's telegram and studied it, repeatedly going over it word for word. It gave only two leads. The first was this St. Timothy's Monastery. For a moment she considered going there, but realized the police had already done that. No, she'd have to follow up the other one, Corregidor Pathology.

Pathology! The word triggered the image of the morgue, Jerry's face. It skewered so sharply into her heart, she had to sit down. Then, taking each motion

deliberately, she changed into a pair of designer jeans
and a white silk blouse, put on rubber sandals and left.

Now the little beam of her flash formed a hollow
tube of illumination. With it sound returned, a vague,
distant humming that was so close to silence that she
wasn't sure it was actually there. But from the darkness beyond the light came soft rustlings. She instantly
visualized the tunnels suddenly coming alive with rats,
pouring out of the cracks and crevices of the walls.
The vision made her skin crawl.

Finally she got moving, whispering again, staccato
swear words to steady her nerves. Trying to think log-
ically, she paused again and dug from her handbag a
tourist map of the tunnel complex. She found a desk
and spread the map out.

She knew generally where she was and where she
had to go. The hospital section was the obvious location for a pathology room. But she hadn't figured on
the complete cessation of directional sense once she
was plunged into darkness. She pivoted her head back
and forth. Where the hell was north, the main bearing
reference on the map?

For the next few minutes she wandered around,
peering at tunnel markers. But they were all just numbers or acronyms not notarized on her map. Finally
she came to a mess hall, located it on the map, and
figured her orientation. She decided that she had to go
down the main corridor within this section. That would
bring her to the entrance tunnel. Once there she would
be able to find the passages to the hospital area.

She started off slowly, her tiny light darting and jabbing. She passed more side passageways. Suddenly a
rat darted through the beam of the light. It was as large
as a cat, and Liz squealed involuntarily as every hair
on her body stood up. "Oh, you son of a bitch," she
croaked, shuddering, listening for further movement.
Nothing came back.

She moved ahead.

Ordinarily, Liz Forsythe was rarely frightened by
anything. She sailed over difficulties with that natural

aplomb usually inherent in one born to wealth. Her father was a prominent attorney in Burlingame, her mother a social butterfly of enormous charm. Thus, Liz herself had passed through the prescribed patterns of the upper class with genteel ease and self-assured grace.

At college, the University of California at Berkeley, her intelligence and private schooling had kept her always at high point levels without particular effort. And her beauty, that sultry-innocent face framed by long auburn hair, had already snagged her modeling jobs across the bay in San Francisco.

At twenty-three, after a night of moonlight and sexual acrobatics, she found herself in love with a young attorney on the staff of her father's competitor. They married in down peninsula splendor, spent a month in Nice for a honeymoon, and returned to what Liz soon found to be complete tedium. She quickly discovered that her husband was a jerk with a transvestite fetish and a mid-Victorian sense of chauvinism. Except in the bedroom, he treated her with the same superiority he showed his grooms or his golf caddy.

It took her four months, to the day, to tell him to take a hike. Then packing her gear, she left their Montclair mansion. Her parents clucked sympathy and financed a European trip which turned out to take two years. One big party from Vienna to Paris to Rome with a coterie of elegant lovers.

But even that got boring. She returned to San Francisco, took a small apartment on a hill near Coit Tower, and decided to go to work for a living. The next day she applied for a job at Channel 10 and was hired as a weather girl. Three and a half years later, she owned a co-anchor spot.

At the moment, though, she was lost. She'd run into the end of a passageway that was supposed to come out in the hospital section. "Well, shit," she groaned, playing her light on the wall. There was a phrase scratched into the brick with a nail: *"Malinta sucks!"*

She hauled out her map and tried to regroup. Ob-

viously, she realized, she'd made a wrong turn somewhere. Now she'd have to retrace, all the way back to
the Quartermaster Area and start over. She looked at
her watch. It was six forty-five.

It took her an hour to relocate the entrance corridor.
In her light, it stretched out like the main line of a
subway. She paused for a moment, studying the map,
then started deeper into the system.

Almost instantly she stopped. After being lost underground this long, a mounting sense of claustrophobia had begun creeping up on her. She had to get out
for a while, breathe fresh air. She turned back toward
the entrance, hurrying, her mind fixed on getting outside immediately.

The air at the tunnel entrance smelled like the breath
of gods: sweet and rich with the perfume of eucalyptus
and salt breeze. She walked out to where the jitneys
usually parked, feeling the dust as fine as talcum under
her sandals. Far inland, the lights of Manila and Cavite and Callocan glistened in the faint afterglow of
evening like stardust scattered against indigo. She
flicked off her flashlight.

She inhaled and inhaled and then, with a slight
shiver, she reentered Malinta.

Her watch showed 8:31 when she reached the vast
main entry to the hospital area. Its sudden hugeness
after the continuous close overhead spacing of the tunnels gave her a boost. She wandered around, poking
at things, blowing off clouds of dust. Eventually she
found the tunnel marked *"Num Three Sec."* She
stopped abruptly. Something dark, venomous seemed
to come from that particular tunnel.

Her heart pounding, she consulted the map. It
showed only a generalized reference to the tunnel.
"Okay," she said aloud. "Okay, Liz."

As she entered it, a spiderweb drifted across her
arm, faint as a whisper. She shied from it like a horse
sensing a rattler and pawed at the air in imaginary
entanglement. "God damn it!" The sound of her voice
blew into the silence and rebounded in echoes.

She found the autopsy room. A double-doored space, big as a hole into infernal things. She shivered, peered in, homing her delicate little light on dark walls. In the center a table protruded above the floor like a surgeon's operating platform.

She entered the room, moving cautiously toward the table. The icy edge of it touched her thigh. Jerry, is this where you died? she thought. She examined the table. It smelled of rank, moist decay. There were cracks in the steel surface, rivulet creases that formed shadows in her light. She played her narrow beam all around. Nothing.

Then the light caught a sliver of reflected glow from something shiny just below the edge of the table. She bent and found a plastic packet affixed to the underside. She pulled it free. Sharp edges protruded through a plastic cover. She turned it over in her hand, holding the light on it. Through the plastic it looked like a VCR tape.

A scuff sounded behind her. She whirled, her light beam swinging in a half arc. It illuminated the figure of a man standing in the doorway.

Bonner had been lounging in the helm cockpit of his sloop, now berthed at the North Mine Wharf, and had just lifted his third beer to his mouth when he spotted a tiny light at the entrance to Malinta Tunnel. He lowered the can and squinted up at the light, puzzled. No one was supposed to be on the island at night. It certainly wasn't any of the ODI men, he knew. They'd all gone whoring in Cavite with the money from the shark he and one of the other divers, named Farrel, had nailed that afternoon.

It had been a decent-sized Great White in from deep water which had periodically been nosing around the search grids for the past two days, scaring the hell out of the divers. After the demolition of Bonner's bomb, they'd spotted it again. Balestera told him to take the rest of the day off and go do his biologist thing, see if he could land that son of a bitch.

He and Farrel rigged a power winch off the stern of the *Napah*, running a steel cable for a leader with a huge hook and a slab of bacon rind. When the shark hit, the cable jumped out of its feed groove and tore chunks off the top of the cockpit locker as Cas furiously rammed back power to pick up slack.

As they finally got squared around and started winching the brute in, the shark began eating the cable. It came right up off the stern, its head as big as the grille of a Chrysler. They pumped twelve-gauge shotgun rounds into it, the blood blowing red geysers, with Farrel running around so excitedly he nearly fell off.

Afterward, they dragged the carcass up into the shallows. Using a makeshift cherry picker, they hauled it onto the foredeck of the feeder launch. Then the entire ODI crew, save Bonner, headed off for Cavite to sell it to the first Chinese restaurant they came to. The money would buy one hellacious party at Long Tommy's cathouse.

As evening came on, Cas had headed the *Napah* up island to the fueling dock at North Mine Wharf. It was dark by the time he'd refueled, so he settled in there for the night. Not long after, he saw the flashlight at Malinta Tunnel.

The tiny light now moved jerkily beyond the eucalyptus trees, paused for a moment, then disappeared. Cas uncoiled himself from the cockpit seat and jumped onto the wharf. He walked up to the dockhead to see if he could pick it up again. For an instant he caught a tiny glow illuminating the tunnel entrance, and then it was gone once more. Whoever it was had gone inside.

Curiosity fully aroused, he returned to the boat for a flashlight and went back along the wharf to the entrance road. The incline was steep. High up, moonlight bathed the tops of the eucalyptus, which threw dappled blue shadows onto the asphalt. Birds disturbed by his light chucked softly at him.

The hills of debris and the wire grate looked dark

and misshapen in the beam of his light. For a moment he flashed it into the tunnel and then went in. Just inside, he stopped and listened. He could hear the faint slap of shoes on cement. Spotting the soft glow of a light moving up ahead, he followed it.

He had a difficult time keeping it in sight. It bobbed and darted, going dark, then reappearing. He recalled hearing something about scroungers: apparently they came out at night to cut up the big twelve-inch mortars and field guns still in their emplacements on Topside. But he had been told that these robbers always stayed out of the tunnel. It had bad vibes for them. Then who the hell is this, he wondered, prowling around in the darkness?

He reached the hospital entry hall and stopped, searching for the light. There it was, going up a side corridor. He waited a moment, then went on. On the way he picked up a two-by-four lying across a desk. Holding it against his leg, he followed the light.

In the last room of the corridor, he paused and peered around the edge of the doorway. Someone was kneeling beside a table in the center of the room. In a fleeting glimpse he saw a mass of hair against the light. A woman!

As she stood up, studying something in her hand, he stepped into the doorway. Instantly, light was on his face.

Adrenaline hit Liz's body in a groin-emptying surge that literally propelled her three feet back. Out of it came a scream that exploded in the confines of the room like a Banshee screeling in the night.

Recovering, she lunged forward, trying to dodge past the man. He didn't move. Instead his flashlight came on and flared up into her face. Terrified, she lowered her head and rammed it directly at the light, felt it go into his stomach, hurling him back. A piece of wood slammed against the opposite wall.

She heard him blurt an oath of surprise before a powerful arm looped around her, yanking her body to one side. Her light went skittering across the outer passageway. She opened her mouth to scream again.

"Jesus, take it easy," the man cried. "I'm not going to hurt you."

Struggling against the strength of his arm, she felt the tautness of his massive shoulders, smelled gasoline fumes and a fishy odor tinged with the yeasty scent of beer. "Let me go," she croaked. "Damn you, let me go."

"Hold it. Just hold it, lady."

He released her and pushed her slightly away from him in order to shine the light on her face. Instantly she tried to dart past him again, but this time he completely blocked the doorway.

She shrank back, shaking. "Who are you? What do you want?"

He held the flashlight on her. "What's more to the point, honey, who the hell are *you*? And what're you doing down here?"

From his speech Liz realized this man was an American. Was he the one who had killed her brother? Her heart was beating so wildly she could feel its thud in her skin. Frantically she grabbed at an explanation, blurted it out in a rush: "I got lost off the ferry boat, and they went away and I got lost down here."

"What was that thing you took from under the table?"

"Nothing."

"Let's see it."

"No!"

His hand came through the light beam and he snatched the packet from her. He examined it for a moment, then quickly turned the light back to her face. "It's a VCR tape. What the hell is all this?"

"It's mine, give it back to me."

He let his light play over her, up, down. Then he said, "Here," and tossed the packet to her. She fumbled for a second, then held it close. Squinting suspiciously at him, she said, "What are you going to do with me?"

"Take you outside so you can tell me what this is all about."

She hung back.

"Come on, let's go."

Reluctantly she moved forward. He stepped away from the doorway and bent to pick up her flashlight, clicked it off. They went slowly back up the tunnel.

Liz was beginning to regain control. If this man wanted to kill me, she thought, he would have done it by now. Okay, okay, then who is he? A beach bum stopping for the night on the island? A stranded tourist? Or something much more diabolical?

For a moment she considered running, straight ahead down any alley that presented itself. But she discarded that idea. He had both flashlights and the thought of being totally lost in this place made her shudder.

Cas swung his light ahead until he picked up the tunnel through which they'd entered the hospital area. He motioned with the beam for her to go into it. As she did, he let the light circle play for a moment on her back. The silk of her blouse shimmered under it, and her hair looked lush and russet-colored.

She was certainly a looker, Bonner thought, with the definite trappings of money about her. The clothes were upscale chic, and her wristwatch sent off little spikes of reflected light the way only diamonds can. He could feel the class coming off her like a rich Paris perfume. He grunted under his breath. Rich bitches always evoked memories of his ex-wife.

But what in Christ's name is she doing alone down here, in the middle of the goddamned night? And that VCR tape, what's that all about? The whole thing was crazy. Still, despite his curiosity, he had a sudden, strong intuition to back off this thing. It smacked of too weird.

He had just about decided to do that—give her back her flashlight and just walk away—when he heard a tiny out-of-place sound. The click of a radio button followed by a soft *splur* of static.

Instantly he froze and snapped his light off, plunging them into utter blackness. Reaching out, he grabbed a handful of blouse and jerked her to him. "Who else is down here?" he whispered tightly.

"I don't know," she croaked back, her voice cracking. "I came alone. I swear it."

"Stay still."

They waited, their ears straining to pick up sound. After an interlude of absolute silence, something eerie happened. Things began to glow around them: dust motes in the air, Liz's fingernails, her lipstick, an earring. She could actually see Bonner's eyes glowing with a radium luminescence. Deep in her throat, she whinnied with horror.

The glowing objects seemed to dance in the darkness like drowsy fireflies. There was a scuffle of shoes and Liz heard Bonner growl something. It sounded like "Black light beam."

It made no sense to her. Suddenly he was violently shoving her downward onto the floor, his body on top. She hit the bricks with her chest and then her chin. At the impact pain exploded in her neck.

There was a click, the solid back rap of a gun breech. Then white-hot flashes illuminated the ceiling and the air was jolted by the crack of gunfire. Bullets impacted against the wall where they'd been standing, ricochets whining off as all the sound came together in one voluminous thunder that echoed and re-echoed, blowing back through the tunnels of Malinta like a dynamite charge.

Liz tried to crawl down into the bricks, become them. Vaguely she felt Bonner's weight lift off her. His foot shoved against her hip, and he seemed to go scurrying away like a crab, headed toward the flashes. A moment later she heard a heavy expulsion of air followed by something metal clattering on the floor. Throaty grunting sounds of men struggling was succeeded by a savage curse. This was followed immediately by the wet rag sound of a skull viciously colliding with stone.

Little bursts of hysteria were pumping out of her mouth. Mindless of these, she heard men shouting from somewhere across the hospital area. A screeching babble like the voices that came out of the kitchen of a Chinese restaurant. She shoved herself up, desperately trying to get to her feet.

Someone stumbled over her, quickly regained his balance. A hand grabbed the back of her blouse and pulled her upright. Crying out, she tried to pull free. She heard the man breathing hard, the air whistling through his nostrils.

A flashlight came on for an instant. In its outer glow she saw Bonner, realized there was blood on his face. He hauled her forward, half carrying her weight, dragging her down the tunnel.

They fled through the endless darkness with the crazy, distorted sensation of going downward. Now and then Bonner flicked on the light to orient himself, and then they would plunge on again, his arm around her waist, her feet sometimes flying several steps over the floor. From the inner caverns of the tunnel came bursts of furious oriental phrases.

Bonner hit a wall and Liz plowed right into him. He cursed and yanked her to her feet, flashed the light a second, then raced on. They reached the main corridor, their panting making whispers off the walls. Far away they could see a square of moonlight and went for it.

And then they sprang out into the creamy blue-white light bathing the eucalyptus trees and the air thick with the wonderful smell of the ocean.

Liz skidded to her knees, unable to go any farther. "Please," she gasped. "I can't—please—let's hide."

Bonner was so angry he was momentarily speechless. He paused just long enough to draw in a lungful of air, then wrenched her to her feet. In the shadows she saw the dark fury lining his face.

"Oh, please, I—" she started.

Bending down, he jammed his right arm between her legs, hefted her onto his shoulder. She gave a tiny squeal as he took off down the tunnel road with her helplessly hanging over his back.

4

In Washington, it was now a little after eight in the morning, a beautiful, sunlit day. The President, strolling back into the White House after a breakfast outside in the Rose Garden with several directors from the Heart Association, encountered his National Security Council chief, Frank Delaplane, on the rear porch. They usually met daily to go over latest intelligence reports from stations around the world.

The President paused momentarily in the Lincoln Library to allow Delaplane to give his update. Most of it concerned the continually shifting situation within Russia. Two items seemed particularly provocative. "Hunger riots have actually begun," the NSC chief said, "in northern Kazakhstan and Azerbaijan. Also coal miners are threatening to shut down operations in at least five republics unless pay increases are immediately implemented."

Over the preceding year, unbelievable changes had occurred within the country once known to the world as the USSR. The progressive ideals of *perestroika* and *glasnost* initiated by Yuri Markisov had released deep, long dormant dreams in the Russian people. Eventually the momentum of these dreams had led to the actual fragmentation of the nation. Now it was composed of individual republics gathered into a Commonwealth of Independent States created after an abortive and pathetic attempt by desperate hardliners to wrest control from Markisov.

But with the end of one political structure, the country was now embarked on a dangerous and highly unstable attempt to solidify another. After seventy-three years of Communist central control, it faced horrendous problems. Confusion and uncertainty were everywhere, as once minor republican leaders shifted for power. The nation's economic and industrial base was in a shambles; after four years of drought, with failing food production exacerbated by spiraling inflation, stores had plunged to ominous levels with winter approaching. Added to this, nations on the rim of the old USSR, particularly China, nurturing ancient hatreds and the hopes of reclaiming lost lands, were beginning to eye its border territories like wolves.

The President listened quietly, then asked, "How did Markisov handle the riots?"

"He ordered local troops in."

"Bloody?"

"There was some shooting but apparently everything is quiet now."

"And the miners?"

"He's personally negotiating with those in Russia and Byelorussia. The others he's leaving to the individual republican presidents."

"Smart move, spreads responsibility."

"I don't think he had many other options."

Technically, Markisov still retained his seat as head of the nation. He had been appointed chancellor of the CIS by the twelve heads of the republics at a meeting in the Ukraine three months earlier. In this capacity he continued to direct internal and foreign policies and controlled the Soviet military and its nuclear arsenal. But he was a shaky, wounded leader, picking his way delicately over a matrix of tangled lines drawn on glass.

"I wonder how long he'll have *any* options left," the President mused.

"Personally, sir, I think he'll find himself in the middle of a civil war before the next year's out. In at least six of his republics."

The President sighed. "I hope to hell you're wrong." He flopped into a green velvet Louis XIV chair, brooding. The impact of the new Commonwealth coming completely apart at the seams and plunging itself into anarchy would blow across Europe and the rest of the world like one of those west Texas tornadoes he'd seen as a boy. Good Christ, he thought, whose finger would be on the button then?

Bill Claymore, a onetime Texas senator and old personal friend of the President, strode in. With his mane of bushy white hair, he looked at first glance like Mark Twain. "Well, how'd the meet with the heart boys go?" he asked cheerily. "They lecture you on cholesterol count?"

"Endlessly," the President answered glumly.

Claymore glanced at Delaplane, who said, "More bad news from Russia."

"So what the hell else is new?"

"At least there's one thing in my favor," the President said. "I suspect old Yuri will be decently conciliatory at this conference. I don't think he'll strut very much."

The conference he referred to was an upcoming summit between him, Chinese Premier Sichen Zian and Markisov, to be hosted by the P.M. of Australia, John Frost. It was to take place on a floating hotel off the Great Barrier Reef.

The President had been pushing for just such a conference for over a year and a half. First, to establish sound treaties between the three most powerful nations on earth. Second, to forestall any deepening of the tensions which had begun to heat up on the Sino-Soviet border of Manchuria. Initially neither Russia nor China had seemed interested. But then feelers started coming from both sides. Now the meeting was scheduled to convene in eight days.

Claymore shot him a look, eyebrows lifted. "Don' be too sure about that. A sick bear is a pissed-off bear an' about as predictable as a jack-dogger fulla' corn whiskey."

"Thanks for that hopeful little gem," the President said sourly. He turned to Delaplane. "The general thinking at State concur with Bill's viewpoint?"

"No, they agree with you, sir. Markisov's too desperate for aid to create unpleasant confrontations. They feel Sichen will be the real unknown quantity at the meeting." He frowned. "In view of what's just come in, it looks like they might be right."

The President's eyes narrowed. "What's just come in?"

"I was saving this for last. Preliminary intelligence reports show some shifting of Chinese People's Liberation Army units along the Manchurian border. Primarily around Changbai on the Amur River."

"Oh, wonderful. How massive?"

"We can't really get a fix at this point. It could all merely be normal divisional rotations. But there definitely has been movement."

"Hell, maybe Sichen's just showin' some muscle before the conference," Claymore suggested. "Tunin' up his fiddle a bit to let everybody know he don' aim to be a pushover."

"The Pentagon see it that way?" the President asked Delaplane.

"Not really. Not yet, anyway. There doesn't seem to be enough strength for either an incursion or a major show of force. Still that Amur River's always been a sore spot in Sino-Russian relations. As you remember, there was that sizable artillery duel there two years ago when Chinese and Soviet garrisons opened up on each other."

The President scratched distractedly at his chin. "Well, if we've spotted movement, so have the Russians. And maybe Markisov'll want to tune up his own balalaikas. Jesus, if we get bullets criss-crossing the Amur, it'll sure as hell throw some heavy damper over that conference table."

"Yes, sir," Delaplane agreed. "In fact, an open firefight could place you in the delicate position of having to choose a side."

The President leaned back and thought about that. His NSC chief was right. If the Russians and Chinese did clash before or during the conference, he'd be in the middle of two openly hostile leaders. One of the them might be wearing a body cast, but his hand still had firm hold on some very big guns; the other, a territorial opportunist, while not commanding similar firepower, was far from unarmed.

He thrust himself to his feet and paced around the room, finally pausing at a window. The sunlight streaming through the glass made his thick brown hair glisten.

For years, ever since the Nixon trip to Beijing in '72, he had been a strong proponent of treaties with mainland China. Even after Tiananmen, he had deliberately kept avenues open for exchange with the Sichen government. In fact, he had personally been instrumental in getting an American conglomerate to sign a recent contract which would send a U.S. and Swiss weather/ comm satellite into orbit aboard a Chinese Long March rocket. This was the kind of thing which linked nations together, he felt. Still, the world's scenarios were changing with such speed that it became essential to make constant reassessments, adjust to new strategy goals and methods. He'd hoped to garner peaceful mutual agreements at this conference. But, dammit, treaties like that couldn't evolve if some of the conferees were shooting at each other.

"Okay, Delaplane, you keep on this Manchurian thing," he snapped. "I want to know the minute Pentagon sees the slightest sign of incursion strength."

"Yes, sir." The NSC chief withdrew.

The President gave Claymore a sidelong glance. "Doesn't get any easier, does it?"

The old senator laughed. "Hell, boy, that's why they pay you the big bucks."

The President snorted. "Well, come on, I'll treat you to a cup of coffee." As they walked out into the main corridor and headed for the executive offices in the West Wing, he chuckled suddenly."I just thought of something. What if I get seasick on that damned floating hotel? Wouldn't that be a helluva note?''

"Don't worry 'bout it. The Aussie consul general assures me this Seascape One's as stable as a flat rock in a field. Hell, look at it this way. In eight days you'll be soakin' up Aussie sunshine and watchin' the dolphins play.''

Off Monkey Point, Stanford scanned his binoculars across the beach, fixing on a small fire now gone nearly to embers. Beyond it, up the slope of the beach, were several tents and two Zodiac boats, their outboard motors cranked forward.

He studied the small encampment. Fishermen? Then where were they? He swung to the south for a moment. Out there, sea lights were all over the area. He returned to the camp, searching for any movement. In the moonlight he saw litter scattered about, spools of wire and thick, rope-handled boxes used for explosives.

He grunted and lowered the glasses. Beside him in the soft blue light of the *Flying Sun*'s bridge cabin was the boat's captain, a hulking Tigerman named Big Willie Chin.

"Who dem guys?'' Chin asked.

"There ain't nobody there. Looks like a construction camp.''

"Maybe the girl with dem.''

"No, I don't think so. They're probably out night fishing.'' He gave the place one more glassing.

Earlier they had dropped off five Tigermen in rubber dinghys up near the main body of Corregidor to search for Liz Forsythe. Then they'd cruised around, waiting for a radio report. On one of the down-island sweeps, they'd spotted the fire and moved closer to investigate.

Suddenly the overhead radio crackled. Chin reached out a meaty hand and keyed his mike: *"Cao chi?''*

There was a burst of Chinese from one of the two men who had been sent to Topside to search through the ruins of the old fort. The remaining three Tigers had been sent into the Malinta Tunnel complex through the south entrance. But since they were now encased within the tunnel, the boat would be unable to pick up their signal until one of the men emerged.

"What did he say?" Jack asked.

"They find nothin'."

"Shit." He studied the radar panel a moment. The *Flying Sun* had good gear, a Litton Plath auto-navigational unit and a high-speed FR-8000D Furuno monochrome radar console. The screen was now showing the scatter of fishing boats in the bay along with the big twin flares of freighters coming up the south channel for Cavite.

He told Big Willie to head back north and left the bridge. As the boat eased into a port turn and straightened, coming up to eight knots, he made his way to the sharp curve of the bow and stood looking out. Off to the northwest he could just barely make out the dark rise of Malinta Hill in the moonlight. He lit a cigarette and considered. Liz Forsythe had to be on the damned island somewhere. Or else someone with a boat had been waiting to pick her up. But he immediately discarded that possibility. It didn't feel right. This woman was working on her own. And she acted like an amateur. Going straight out to the island had been stupid, not the move of someone with plans.

Obviously, though, she knew about the disks. Somehow her brother had gotten that much information to her. But how much more did she know? What the disks contained? And if she knew that, what did she intend to do once she got them?

Stanford muttered an obscenity over it all. He hated unexpected fuck-ups like this. Some little coozy sticking her shit into it. Well, she's here, he told himself tightly, and I'll find her even if I have to scour the whole island to do it. No goddamned bitch is going to screw up *this* operation.

Yet underlying his frustration was a thread of enticement. A new problem always presented a new challenge, gave a sharper spin to the ball. Glitches angered him, but they also nudged his brain, even created a tiny, paradoxical sense of glee. It allowed him the chance to re-manipulate the fates, home to another stretch. By instinct he was a wheeler-dealer, the cool finger-snapper with a click-click mind.

As a kid it had gotten him rewards others couldn't touch. He caromed through the University of Michigan on a fake football scholarship. In Nam he finagled his way into becoming a Special Forces "mechanic" with all the luxuries of a general. And during his days with the Drug Enforcement Agency in all those crazy, dangerous places like Colombia, Sicily, Amsterdam and northern Thailand, his fast talking and joshy collegiate looks saved him many a time.

Still, he had to admit this time the stakes were higher than ever before. If his plan didn't come off, if all the scattered pieces failed to come together with a precise jelling, the Chinese would murder him without the slightest hesitation. For a moment he wondered if it was worth it. For half a billion dollars? Yeah, it was worth it.

Restive, he returned to the control cabin. Big Willie was still ensconced in his Cadillac chair, occasionally sucking on a Thai stick. When Jack asked for radio update from the men on the island, Chin merely swung his elephantine head: nothing.

At the bar the American poured himself a Hennesey's and stood staring stolidly at Big Willie smoking his joint. What a shit-ass operation these slant-eyes ran, he thought. It'd be a wonder the asshole didn't run them *into* goddamned Malinta Hill.

Reaching the sloop, Cas leaped aboard, nearly dropping his burden. Liz had regained her wind by now and was squirming, demanding to be put down. So he did, right down on her buttocks, spraddle-legged. She started to cry, "You son of—"

"Shut up," he hissed down at her. "Just shut your mouth." He stepped over her and raced down into the cabin. In a moment the *Napah*'s engine coughed into life. When he came back up, Liz had risen and was standing on the stern coaming, peering up at the moon-dappled tunnel road. "I don't see anybody," she said.

"Get in the cabin," he ordered. Loosening the stern line, he dashed forward and let the bow line go. The sloop drifted lazily away from the wharf, rocking slightly as he returned aft and started throwing switches on the cockpit panel. Seeing Liz still at the stern, he bawled at her, "Get in the goddamned cabin."

"Why?"

Wordlessly he put his palm against her spine and pushed her off the coaming toward the companionway. She nearly banged into the cabin bulkhead, glared at him, then went gingerly down the dark steps.

Bonner whirled the helm and throttled up the engine. The small sloop dipped her stern as the propeller took hold, and it headed up the entry channel, chop popping off the hull. He kept glancing back over his shoulder, looking for movement up in the shadows, expecting bullets to come zinging their way.

Within a few minutes they cleared the outer channel buoy with its tiny red and white blinker light bobbing like a metronome. Reef surf whispered off to the right as he swung the boat's bow southeast, toward Cavite. A moment later they abruptly entered the heavy chop created by the open ocean winds as they swept around the southern side of Malinta Hill. Cas eased over slightly so they were running with the chop, the wind coming in across the stern. Instantly the sloop's up-and-down lunge smoothed out, and they went with it, the after stays humming softly with engine vibration.

He bungeed the wheel and slipped down into the cabin. In the moonlight let in by the portholes he saw Liz sitting on the daybed opposite the stove. The cabin smelled of scuba tanks and netting and beer, and the sound of the engine throbbed loudly in the small space.

Bonner planted himself in front of her, his arms braced on the overhead. "All right, let's have it. Why were those people back there trying to kill us?"

"I don't know."

"You're lying."

"God's witness, I don't know. But I'll bet they're the ones who killed my brother."

"What're you talking about?"

"My brother was murdered, right up there in that tunnel."

"When?"

"Yesterday."

"Why?"

"I don't know." She brushed her hair back and it shimmered in the moonlight. "I think it's because of that damned VCR tape."

"You running drugs?"

"No!"

"Goddammit, those were Chinese back there. When you put Chinese and guns together, you got heroin."

"Look, I'm a television journalist from San Francisco. My name's Liz Forsythe. I got—"

"Oh, God, I should have known. A newsie flake."

"What do you mean, 'flake'?"

"I hate newsies. You're all dipshits."

"Hey!"

Bonner's head snapped around suddenly as he heard something. He ducked down to peer out the starboard porthole. "Uh-oh," he said.

"What?"

He didn't answer. Instead he whirled around and went flying back up the companionway.

Liz raced after him. When she reached the deck, he was already standing on the cockpit seat, squinting off to the right. She turned her head. The ocean was washed in moonlight, making little pools of illumination along the fronts of long, glass-smooth swells that were coming in from the South China Sea.

She gave a little gasp. There, a quarter mile away, the lights of a large boat were coming toward them, straight on an intercept line with the *Napah*.

* * *

Big Willie had sat forward as a blip suddenly appeared on his radar screen a mile ahead, just easing out of the shadowy bulk of Malinta Hill. Behind him, Stanford, on his fourth Hennesey's, saw it too. He lowered the glass.

"What is it?" he asked. "Your men?"

Willie shook his head. "Too much metal in the blip."

"Check it out."

Chin reached out and eased the throttles forward. The cruiser lifted slightly as her engines accelerated. Jack scooped up the binoculars and stepped out onto the port wing. He scanned the darkness until he picked up the white hull of what looked like a small sailboat bright in the moonlight. It was headed toward the inner harbor.

He poked his head through the hatch. "Willie, get your men up here. And where the hell's your blowhorn?" He tucked the glasses under his arm and slipped out a Browning Hi-Power 9mm auto from the waist band above his buttocks. He snapped the receiver back, chambering a round.

Bonner watched as the large boat approached, and he felt his skin go cold. It was coming too fast, showing too much interest in the *Napah*. Already he could make out its lines. It wasn't a patrol boat. He shot a quick glance westward, around the curve of Corregidor Bay to the dark cliffs of Battery Point. Maybe he could make a run for the reef shallows at the base, get lost in radar bounce off the cliffs.

No, it was no use. The other boat was fast enough to cut him off long before he reached the shallows. Besides, to run would immediately mark them as quarry. If this boat was part of that back in the tunnel, that'd be all she wrote. Well, he decided, I'll have to bluff my way out.

He swung the helm to starboard, the little sloop heeling slightly, and pointed her bow straight at the oncoming ship. He could make out the hull clearly now with its sleek, curved glass main house and the running lights throwing dancing patterns of light on the surface of the ocean swells.

He bungeed the helm again and ducked back toward the companionway. He ran into Liz, nearly knocked her down. "Is it them?" she cried, frightened.

He managed to get her down and back onto the day bunk. Reaching up, he slammed open an overhead cabinet and withdrew his twelve-gauge shotgun. The barrel glinted in the moonlight. When Liz saw it, she cried, "Oh, God, are you going to fight?"

He touched her shoulder and said quietly, "Stay below. Don't show yourself, no matter what happens." Then he slipped back up the companionway.

When the cruiser was about two hundred yards away, Bonner cut his motor and let the sloop drift. Both vessels were about a mile offshore. He heard the cruiser's engines drop to a throaty idle as she came up, angled slightly off his port bow.

A bright spotlight suddenly came on, the beam fixing on him. He could actually feel the heat of it. The cruiser eased up, sixty yards out, and cut her engines.

Suddenly a blowhorn shattered the silence: "Sailboat, lay to for boarding."

Cas stood up on the helm seat and cupped his hands over his mouth. "Cruiser, who are you and what do you want?"

"We intend to search your cargo."

The cruiser was now only forty yards off. Cas felt the sloop bouncing with the larger boat's surface disturbance. "You can go to hell," he bellowed back. He picked up the shotgun and nestled the butt against his right hip. "I'm in commercial transit with authority to proceed unmolested in these waters."

There was a moment of silence. Both vessels were completely dead in the water, drifting side by side on the swell. The spotlight scanned the length of the sloop. In that moment, away from its glare, Cas caught sight of several men lining the port railing. One moved forward and yelled down at him without the blowhorn. "Why are you running without lights?"

"Electrical circuit trouble."

"What are you hauling?"

He got a thought and leaped on it. "Dynamite. I'm part of a demolition crew camped at Monkey Point."

There was another slot of silence, then: "I want a look at your cargo."

"Try it and I'll blow the head off the first man who touches my boat."

The man laughed. "What's your name, jerkoff?"

"Bonner. What's yours?"

"Stanford." Two men came forward and for a moment they discussed something with Stanford. Then there was a burst of automatic fire. The rounds hit the water between the boats with heavy, jarring impacts, and the sounds of the explosions left a high-pitched ringing in Bonner's ears. Sweat popped out along his back.

Stanford laughed again. "You still want to fuck with us, Bonner?"

The adrenaline in Cas's blood felt cold, like icy needles. For a tiny moment, he continued squinting defiantly up at the larger boat. Then he lowered the muzzle of the shotgun and blew a hole in the water just off his stern. Jacking another round into the chamber, he swung the shotgun toward the cabin. "I'll put the next one through my companionway. There's enough dynamite down there to take us both out."

"You got a lot of balls on you, asshole."

"I don't like uninvited guests on my boat."

There was another silence and the light went out. Cas froze in anticipation. Were they buying it? Or were they simply going to head off far enough and then cut him down?

When the man spoke again, it was almost casual: "Hey, Bonner, you see a woman on the island tonight?"

"No," he yelled back. Then he grabbed at a sudden thought. Should he tell them he'd heard gunfire in the tunnels? If they knew about it and he didn't mention it, they'd figure he was lying since he'd just come from the wharf and should also have heard it. He played it out. "But I heard shooting in the tunnels. I don't know what the hell's going down, but I want no part of it."

There was a hurried conversation on the cruiser. Men began to scatter. Stanford came back. "Count yourself lucky, sailor. Now fuck off."

The cruiser's engines rumbled, roiling water as it pulled away. Instantly Cas restarted his own motor and swung the sloop southeast again. The cruiser's churn jacked the little boat for a few moments as he once more headed for Cavite.

Seated on the cockpit deck with her legs curled in, Liz told him what she knew, all of it. The telegram from her brother, Jerry, his murder, her trip out to Corregidor. As she talked, Cas pushed the sloop to her full eighteen knots, his head constantly swiveling from bow to stern, watching for incoming traffic. He had to continue running without lights so if the watch on that cruiser was still glassing them, Stanford would go on believing his story about the circuit problem.

Far ahead of them stretched the inner harbor of Manila Bay, a continuous blanket of lights from Navotas and the fishing towns of Malabon in the north down past Central Manila to Pasay and Paranaque on the shore highway to Trece Matires and the derricks and dry docks of Cavite, which looked like refinery cracking towers.

Cas knew it was only a matter of time before the men in the tunnel radioed the cruiser to inform them a man was with the woman they were looking for. Then it would all become obvious and Stanford would come after them. Only this time he wouldn't be bluffed.

Jesus, Cas thought disgustedly. A rich bitch newsie and people playing for blood. He jetted a bit of spittle off the stern. Whether he liked it or not, he was now a part of it, since Stanford had undoubtedly seen the name of his boat.

He studied the situation, trying to figure angles. But

first things first. To even reach shore, he'd have to lose
the *Napah* in the bay traffic. That cruiser certainly had
radar aboard which could pick him up again, lights or
no lights.

He scanned forward and fixed on a small fleet of
sampans headed out of the channel about a mile off.
Their bow lights sliced up and down through the
swells. He adjusted the sloop slightly and headed for
them.

Liz sat with her face to the wind, her hair sending
soft wisps of perfumed air toward him. He nudged her
with his foot. "Go lay out on the bow and keep your
eye open for boats coming up the channel."

Silently she obeyed, moving gingerly around the
starboard side of the cabin.

They slowly approached the sampan fleet, eight
boats coming out in a curving line. Aboard all of them,
men were working on nets laid across poles on their
cabins, and the wind was filled with the oily odor of
their exhausts. One blew its horn and blinked its running lights, warning him to keep clear. Bonner passed
just astern of the last boat in line, and the fishermen
waved and whistled, the sounds drifting like wispy
birdsong over the whine of the engine.

Bonner relaxed. Now at least the *Napah* would send
back a confused readout to Stanford's radar. For a
while. But they still had to pass directly through the
freighter lanes down channel before clearing into Cavite. Without lights. It would be dicey, since picking
out the higher running lights of a ship coming up channel against the shore glare was difficult.

Cas hunkered down in the cockpit seat and, cupping
his hand against the wind, lit a cigarette. For a moment he glanced up at the moon. It was nearing full
and he could see the shadowy crests of its mountains.

At that moment he felt a new vibration riffle up off
the deck. It seeped through his own engine's hum. It
increased, becoming the heavy churn from big propellers.

"Oh, Jesus," he bellowed. Leaping to his feet, he

scanned the ocean ahead. Instantaneously he heard Liz squeal. He jerked around. Less than two hundred yards away was the dark bulk of a freighter, looming out of the shore lights like a moving mountain, coming straight at them. The loud hiss of its bow wave sounded as powerful as steam shooting out of a broken line.

He whirled the helm and the *Napah* heeled hard to port. He heard Liz give another cry as the sloop's mast slanted across the moon. In a rumbling bass the freighter blew its horn at him. The huge, trembling blasts made the stays hum, and between blows a faint voice of someone, probably the forward watch, yelled down at him.

He held hard helm, the wheel spokes jammed into his groin. Slowly, massively, the freighter came on, slid past, the high running lights skimming up and by, its dark hull silhouetted against starlight and moon glow.

Then it was by and its propeller wash jacked the sloop violently around. The small boat rolled sharply, the mast creaking, stays trembling in the sudden change in weight. Cas fought the helm, trying to right his craft. He heard the props gouging water with a voluminous *shushing*, throwing a fine mist across the decks of the *Napah* as she floundered.

Gradually the sloop settled, though still riding peripheral turbulence. Cas regained steerage and got her bow swung around once again pointing toward Cavite. It was only then that he realized his cigarette was still in his mouth. He plucked it out and, sighing, flicked it overboard.

Liz came around the starboard side of the cabin. She was literally crawling, terrified, touching the deck as if it were made of glass. Cas eyed her sardonically. The uncertain timidity of her movements reminded him of a drunk trying to find handholds on a curb. He started to laugh.

She got to the edge of the companionway, hand-over-handed it to her feet, glaring. "What are you laughing at, you imbecile? We—we could have been killed.''

"Yeah, you got that right," he said, still laughing.

"How could you miss seeing something that big?''

"How come *you* didn't see it?''

"What the hell do I know from freighters?'' Disgustedly mumbling about ships and cursing sailors and oceans, she shakily disappeared down the companionway.

With mounting fury Stanford listened to the tinny, static-filled voice of the Tigerman informing Big Willie that they had made contact with the woman and had fired rounds at her and a man. He had been a big bastard who had thumped the shit out of one of them. Figuring the two were still inside the tunnel complex, the Tigers had spent nearly forty minutes probing corridors until they realized the two had escaped.

Speechless, Stanford stared at the overhead radio speaker, with Lui translating the incoming messages. Then he walked around in a little circle, cursing.

Lui grinned sleepily. "You fuck up, baby," he said. "Dat prick in the sailboat was the one.''

"Find him," Stanford bellowed. "Find that son of a bitch.''

Big Willie hiked the cruiser's engines into full out, and the boat tilted to starboard as he threw helm, his radar blowing signals. They headed northeast, back to where they'd cut the sloop. As they accelerated, Stanford watched the radar screen, squinting at the blips coming off the out channel. His blood was boiling; he'd been conned. Fucking *bluffed.* Bonner, heavy-balled Bonner.

Slowly he began to realize nothing was showing in the area west of Corregidor. His gaze lifted through the bridge glass toward Bataan. The sea was clear. If Bonner had gone that way, he'd be sitting out there like a supernova on the screen.

Jack laughed, and Lui turned to look sleepily at him. Big Willie frowned with puzzlement. "He's not going north,'' Stanford said. ''The dumb bastard's heading for shore. We've got him trapped.''

''We gon' lose him in traffic,'' Big Willie said.

''It doesn't matter,'' Jack answered. ''He'll head for dock somewhere and we can nail him. I read the name of his boat. It's the *Napah.*''

5

Minister for Internal Affairs Litung Biao drew himself from his meditations and glanced at the television screen. His back ramrod straight, he had been sitting on the floor in front of it for nearly two hours, lost in *jijeng,* or mental energy. But now he focused his concentration.

The television station had begun running a show from the Australian Broadcasting Network about the Seascape One, site for the upcoming heads-of-state meeting. Obviously taken from a helicopter, the picture showed the huge floating hotel from an altitude of several hundred feet. In the late afternoon sun it looked majestic, its seven-story bank of windows flashing in a glassy/chrome semaphore pattern as the aircraft swung in a wide circle.

Minister Litung lived on busy Changan Avenue a block from the gold and scarlet tiles of the Gate of Heavenly Peace on Tiananmen Square. His apartment was sparsely furnished, yet featured priceless court antiques: a red and gold Han carpet, a low, *yiywan* couch of lacquered sandalwood, and embroidered silk cushions. On the walls hung ink sketches of warriors on raging steeds painted by Gonfu in the fourth century. The bed was made of silver dragons inlaid in polished teak with a silken counterpane of sky blue and ceramic piping beneath to carry heated water. The room had a feel of time in a vacuum and seemed to give off the murmur of ancient days, of Empress Xi

Ci's whispers from behind golden curtains to her eunuch puppets.

On the couch Litung's mistress, Beijing opera star Jiang Meng, noted his eye movement and slid her legs around to look at the screen. An exquisite beauty with the smooth skin and painted fragility of a porcelain figurine, she was slightly drunk on rice wine. Yet the alcohol had not dulled the graceful motion of her body, the thrust of her small breasts beneath the thin gold cloth of her gown.

Like Litung, she had not spoken during the preceding hours, and she was restless. She would have preferred being at the cinema or in the sumptuous dining hall of the Diaoyutai Hotel, where the highest-ranking Chinese of Beijing gathered to entertain foreign dignitaries. Yet she had not allowed the slightest sign of boredom to show on her face.

Minister Litung, head of the powerful Chinese secret police, was not a man to be questioned. Although fifty-five years old, he possessed the body and stamina of a man half his age. Of medium height, with cropped hair the color of pewter and dark eyes that had a snake's steady bead, he was a rigorous follower of kung fu. Besides his strenuous daily workouts, he subjected himself to ice baths and scalding steams until through pure will he had created steel within himself.

Meng knew this power. In their lovemaking, there was at times a savagery in his hands, as if he warred with her. It always drew from her body an exquisite mixture of ecstasy and pain. Although Litung never spoke to her of his dreams, she knew that one day this man would become leader of all China.

The television announcer began explaining facets of th Seascape One, and the Chinese translations flashed on the bottom of the screen. The hotel was perched in the blue-green waters of the Maxwelton Shoals, he said, which formed a part of the northern portion of the Great Barrier Reef sixty miles from the tip of the York Peninsula. It was an ingenious technological triumph for its builders, the Southern Cross Corporation of Melbourne. Three hundred feet long, ninety wide, and eighty-seven feet high, it rested on a gigantic floating platform anchored by twin chains to the edge of the reef escarpment. It had been constructed in Singapore and then towed to the Maxwelton by two specially built "heavy lift" ships.

A rectangle with narrow flying buttresses, the hotel contained over two hundred rooms, double convention halls, two restaurants and a viewing lounge on the roof. It had its own generation and disposal facilities, a desalination plant, and enough supplies warehoused to last four months at full capacity.

On the west side, which formed the entrance facade, the announcer continued, stairs curved down to the main dock with flower beds, strips of sod, and stunted Samoan coconut trees. At each end of the dock were pontoon causeways which went out to another platform fixed to permanent columns on the reef. Out there were tennis courts and a second restaurant, built on a turntable which revolved fully every six hours.

On the outer sides of the causeways were dozens of docking slips where guests could rent small motor launches and diving gear to explore or fish the shoals. For those who wanted to view the undersea reef without getting wet, a ten-foot-round sunken plastic tube with an escalator ran from the hotel dock to the tennis courts.

The entire structure was designed to withstand winds in excess of one hundred miles an hour. The key to this capability was the structure of its eastern wall, built slightly at double angles to form a sort of ship's bow, and twin high-tech chain rooms located in the foundation platform. Within each room was a series of three huge chain drums, all computer-linked to the weather observation/control office up on the roof.

When forecasts indicated the need to "batten down," the huge pneumatic suction links of the pontoon arms and viewing tube were sealed and cut free to swing in against the tennis court/restaurant area. Then the chain drums paid out their two anchor lines, the northern one allowed to swing a full ninety-degree arc while the other acted as a pivot. Each adjusted to the shift effect as the entire hotel platform responded to the weathervaning of the wind and swung into it.

Once dead on, the slope of the wall drew the force of the wind up and over it. At the same time it lowered the foundation platform deeper into the water. Immediately, curling aerodynamic vortices on the leeward side formed a buttressing force counter to the wind's direction.

A silver-embossed telephone rang with a soft purr. Instantly, Meng rose and silently went to it. She spoke for a moment, glanced at Litung, then hesitantly called to him. "It is a man. He uses a code name."

Still motionless, Litung said, "Bring it." She did so.

The man said simply: "There has been initial failure in the design."

"Why?"

"Confusion. The artifacts are still in the Philippines. Others are involved now."

Biao stared unseeingly at the flashing images on the television. "Warn them," he said softly. "My patience grows thin."

"Yes, sir." And the man hung up.

Later that night, Meng closed her eyes and held her body up as Litung lunged and withdrew and lunged again. The strength of the penetrations was brutal, and her hip bones collided with his loin, pressing her body down onto the rug. Above her, he grunted, panting snuffles like a wild boar. Distantly she felt the soft touch of a drop of perspiration delicately land on her right breast.

She furtively curled her legs over the back of his knees and lifted her pelvis to flatten the line of her spine. Somewhere deep inside her, the faint whisper of orgasm fluttered as if confused, punctured by surges of feeling. She pushed her face into the confluence of his neck and shoulder, licking the moist skin.

Suddenly his hands grabbed her buttocks and

roughly turned her over. She did not protest but went with the movement, felt him lift her, probing. She stifled a cry of searing pain as he thrust into her anus. Litung cursed and she forced herself to open again as he drove on and on until he reached his peak with a stifled, almost agonized growl. His teeth viciously bit her shoulder as his body arched.

She convulsed, feeling his weight suddenly leaden on her, and then slowly, trembling, she lowered, felt him disengage as she merged into the rug.

She lay, her rectum and shoulder throbbing with pain. Blood pounded in her head, the alcohol making her thoughts filmy. He had never taken her in this fashion before. Why this time? she wondered distractedly. She shifted out from under him and slid away as he rose and prowled about the room.

The telephone message, she thought. Yes, that was it. It had released a new rage in him. She tried to recall the exact sound of the man's voice through the receiver. Did she know it? No, it was unfamiliar. As had been the code name the man had used for Biao. What was it? Oh, yes: *Yue Fei*.

It was nearly midnight by the time the *Napah* reached the Manila Yacht Club harbor entrance. A low breakwater curved around to the left, and the shoreline was checkered with slips and small dockways with tiny red lights at the ends of the piers. Cas wove his way through the outer channels and into the public dockage area. Chacha music drifted across the anchorage from the pavilion of the yacht club as a little man in coveralls directed him with a tiny red hand light into a berth beside two motor launches. The man helped him tie in, hooked up his power line, and walked off without a word.

Cas went below and turned on the cabin lights. Liz was sitting at the radio table beside his scuba tanks and the racked twelve-gauge. He noted, a bit distractedly, how really pretty she was in the full light, her skin glowing from the sea breeze, hair all ruffled as if she'd just climbed out of bed.

They hadn't spoken to each other since the near collision with the freighter. Now he was aware that she was watching him narrowly as he lifted the hatch that led down into the engine space. He glanced up. "In about ten minutes the harbor steward'll be around to check my entry papers. I want you gone before he gets here."

She looked jolted. "What? You're just dumping me?"

"Exactly."

"But what can I do? Where'll I go?"

"I'd advise you get back to San Francisco on the first plane out. Before these people pick up your track again."

"But they might be watching the airport," she cried. "Just shoot me down on the tarmac like Aquino."

"Then go to the police."

"Oh, yeah, sure. I'll bet they're in on it too. How else could those—those animals have known I was going out to the island? Or even that I was here?"

"Then go ask for sanctuary at the American consulate."

Liz gave him a hard look. "With that Judas son of a bitch Marsh? No way. He'd turn me over to Stanford before I got through the door."

He had to admit that she was probably right about the police. Maybe even about the consulate man too. The Philippines was a hotbed of corruption, especially here in the Metro. That jazzy, high-tech cruiser of Stanford's had told him plainly enough that this guy was running with enough cash to grease a lot of palms.

No, Forsythe would be walking through a mine field as long as she was in Manila. No matter whom she appealed to, or where she went, she could run into paid informers. But what was he going to do with a rich-bitch newsie? He'd already been shot at and turned into a marked man. Hell, he thought, I'll be lucky just getting clear of Manila and into open ocean before Stanford and his Chinese killers come gunning.

Feeling a renewed rush of anger, he wordlessly slipped down into the engine space. It was close and the engine ticked as heat came off the block. He squatted on a cross beam and, scowling, began unscrewing the gasoline line sump drain.

Liz's shadow moved across the light from the hatchway. "You're not really going to leave me, are you?" she asked anxiously.

He didn't answer.

"Are you?"

"Get out of the light."

"All right, I'm out of the light. Are you?"

"I don't know yet."

His doubt seemed to calm her. She was quiet for a while, watching him. Then she asked, "What's your full name? You never told me your full name."

"Cas Bonner."

She repeated it. "Sounds like a writer's name, trips right off the tongue."

"Who gives a shit?"

"God, are you always so ill tempered?"

"Only when complete strangers try to kill me. Or when pain-in-the-ass journalists get in my light."

"Grouch," she said and withdrew.

Fuming, he accidentally burned his elbow on the exhaust manifold. He swore loudly and nearly tore the gas line off the carburetor. Above, he could hear Liz moving around in the cabin. Then the water pump kicked in and there was the rush of a faucet. He rose and poked his head through the hatch. She was washing dishes in the small sink near the companionway.

"What the hell are you doing?" he barked.

"Cleaning your cabin. It's like a pigsty down here."

"Look, just leave everything alone."

"I'm not sailing in a garbage scow."

"Who the hell said you were sailing anywhere?"

"Oh, go back to your engine."

He started to say something, but a man's voice suddenly called softly from the dock: "Ahoy, sloop. Permission to come aboard."

In one jump Cas popped back into the cabin. As he headed for the companionway, he grabbed Liz's arm. "Listen, you're just here visiting me. You got that? Keep your mouth shut unless he asks you a direct question. If this joker gets any notion of what's going on, he'll lay a forty-eight-hour impoundment on this boat. Then we won't have any choice about the police."

She nodded.

The steward was a tall Englishman dressed in a white dinner jacket. He introduced himself as he and Bonner shook hands. He smelled of lilacs, Cas noticed, as he frowningly let him go down the companionway first.

The steward stopped abruptly on the bottom step and said, "Oh, I say." Cas glanced past his shoulder. Liz was lying on the daybed, her face turned to the bulkhead. She was completely naked. At the sound of the steward's voice, she lazily turned over, her breasts shifting ripely, showing pink nipples. She gave a little sleepy cry of surprise and coquettishly pulled the blanket up over her, not really hiding anything.

"My Lord, I'm terribly sorry, madam," the steward blurted.

"Shoot, Cas, honey," she said to Bonner with syrupy southern reproval, "why didn't you wake me? I din't know we were having comp'ny."

The steward turned and looked at Bonner. His face was flushed with embarrassment. "I say, old man, perhaps it would be better if we conducted our business topside."

Cas glared in at Liz. She winked back at him. He forced a broad grin onto his face, slapped the steward on the shoulder. "Hell, man, no problem. Don't mind my wife running around bare-assed. She always likes to show off those big gazzabas of hers. Used to be a stripper back in the States."

"Well," the steward said. "Well, I suppose it would be all right." He gingerly stepped into the cabin, diligently averting his eyes from Liz.

Cas sat down on the top step of the companionway.

"Honey, you want to get my papers out of the radio table there?"

With the blanket partially covering her, she slipped off the daybed and squeezed by the steward, allowing a naked breast to lightly brush across the man's sleeve. He instantly shuffled anxiously out of her way.

She bent and pulled open the radio desk drawer, her buttocks like twin white moons riding side by side across the blue of the blanket. The papers were in a little red envelope with "MANIFEST" scribbled across the front. She swung around. "Are these the ones?" she coyly asked the steward.

"Yes, thank you." He took the envelope, withdrew the papers and perfunctorily scanned through them. "Yes, well, I suppose everything is in order here." He handed them back to Liz, nodding jerkily. "Well, thank you, thank you. Sorry for the disturbance."

"Oh, not ah 'tall." She gave him a half-lidded smile.

He headed back up the companionway. On the after deck, he shook Bonner's hand again, two hard pumps. "Well, thank you, old man. Have a good stay."

"Will do."

Once more in the cabin, Cas silently watched Liz dress. She was not abashed by his presence, and deep inside, he felt a bright, hot surge of sexual warmth bloom in his belly. His eyes narrowed, scanning those lovely long legs, the luscious curve of spine which dipped into buttock cleavage as she bent to pull on her jeans. Finally he folded his arms and leaned against the bulkhead. "Pretty slick. You're fast on your feet."

She gave him a cold sidelong glance. "Din't yo' all know? All us strippers from the States can dip and dodge."

"It ever occur to you that the man might have really taken a look at those papers, bare tits or not? If he'd seen no jellyroll missus Bonner, I'd be sitting in impound right now."

"Well, he didn't."

"Lucky for me."

She was dressed. "So, when do we leave and where do we go?"

"I don't remember saying you were going anywhere aboard this vessel."

"Now you can't leave without me. I'm registered as your wife."

He chuckled. "They only check boats in, not out.'

She slumped. "Dammit, Bonner." She stared at him a long time. Then anger began coming up into those blue-gray eyes like clouds moving across a sunlit sky. Finally she said, "Okay, fine. Who the hell needs you?"

She fumbled in the blanket a moment for the VCR packet, turned, snapped it against his arm to make him move, and stomped up the companionway.

He followed her. She skirted the cabin and started to step up onto the wharf. Then she paused, hesitated a second, and came back. She planted herself right in front of him.

"You did save my life out there, didn't you?" she snapped. Before he could say anything, she reached up and grabbed the hair on the back of his head. Drawing him in roughly, she planted a hard, open-mouthed kiss on his lips, held it for a long moment, then pushed him away. "So much for gratitude. Now go screw yourself, buster." She whirled away.

He let her go, wanting to see how far she would play it out. He was sure she was bluffing and would come back. But it didn't make any difference. He'd already made up his mind down there in the engine space to stick it out with her. It was a stupid decision, he realized. But he couldn't walk away from this. Liz Forsythe was an innocent swimming with very big sharks.

She was halfway up the dock before he finally whistled and waved for her to return. The whistle set off a little dog to barking on one of the other moored vessels. She stopped and looked back at him, then started off again. In the end, he had to run after her, feeling as ridiculous and foolish as he knew he was.

* * *

The yacht complex was located on the bayside of Pasay City between Central Manila and Cavite. The area was also one of the hubs of the city. Beyond the yacht club were tall, glass-faced bank buildings, convention facilities, private clubs, and in the center of a vast rialto called Harrison Plaza was the orange-lit dome of the Philippine Center for International Trade Exhibitions.

After locking down the *Napah*, Cas and Liz walked on down into the rialto to discuss options. It was still and empty at midnight. They paused beside a huge fountain with a statue of Manuel Quezon, the Philippine patriot, astride a rearing charger which seemed to float on a cloud of water.

Liz watched the spray of drops making delicate patterns of orange light. "How come the sudden change of heart?" she asked.

"Let's just say I'm a fool."

She smiled at him. "Yeah, you are, you know. If I were in your shoes, I'd have really walked away from this." She touched his hand. "I appreciate it." Then she straightened. "So, what do we do now?"

"First off, we've got to get you out of Manila. And the way I figure it, the only place anywhere in the Philippines where you'd be sure of protection is at a U.S. military installation. The best bet is Subic Naval Base up north. We can make a run for open ocean as soon as dawn comes in. That way we'll be lost in the heavy morning boat traffic."

She nodded.

"That gives us about five hours to do a little investigating."

"Of what?"

He thought a moment. "Tell me, what exactly was your brother doing out here?"

"He was a photojournalist working on a book on China."

"Why was he in Manila?"

"I don't know. The last letter I got from him said that he was finishing up his four months in China with a real coup, a photo layout of an upcoming Chinese rocket launch. From someplace that started with an *X*. He said they'd given him top-priority clearance through all the checkpoints and would allow him to take pictures of everything at the launch site.''

Bonner's eyes narrowed. "He had checkpoint clearance out of the country?''

"Yes, complete.''

"Where did he intend to go after China? Right back to the States?''

"No, he wanted to do a story on postwar Vietnam before coming home. He was real optimistic about getting a Justice Department okay to go to Hanoi.''

Cas grunted and scooped up a handful of water from the fountain. He rubbed it over his face, down his neck. "Your brother ever dabble in smuggling on these photo trips of his?''

"I told you, it wasn't anything like that.''

"With those border clearances of his, it's obvious he was being used as a courier to get that VCR out of China. He could actually have been part of an operation that went sour.''

"Look, dammit, he wasn't a part of anything. I know—knew Jerry. He was too sensible to get involved in anything illegal enough to get himself or anybody else killed.''

"He ever mention this Stanford to you?''

"Never.''

Cas sat down on the rim of the fountain. "That bastard intrigues me. He's got a lot of cash and heavy Chinese *quanxi*.''

"What's that?''

"Juice, power contacts. But who the hell is he?''

"He sounded like an American.''

"Yeah, he's Yank, all right. Probably a renegade CIA man or Nam vet who didn't go home. And I'd make book that high-powered cruiser of his is either a weapons-transfer boat or a drug lab.''

"But what could be on a VCR that's so important to him?''

"Lots of things. Operation networks in China, political contacts, even stash locations."

She hugged herself. "God, this thing gets bigger and bigger, doesn't it?"

"There's one thing in your favor. It's the tape they want, not you. If you turned it in to the Manila police, it's certain Stanford's contacts would see he got it. It could take the heat off both of us."

"But what if he decided to kill us anyway, after he got the tape? Just to be certain we didn't talk about what was on the damned thing."

"There's that."

She looked at the spray again, watching its little curlicues of reflected light, then shook her head. "No, I don't want to give that scum what he wants. He killed my brother and I want to use that tape to make him pay for it."

"Well, then let's find out what's on it. It could give us some leverage. You got any money?"

"About fifty dollars and some traveler's checks."

"Good, let's go find a VCR machine."

They walked back through the plaza and across to the main boulevard, where they caught a jeepney taxi into Pasay City. The vehicle was a remodeled World War II jeep, with seats facing along the side and lots of bright dangles and rock music blaring. The driver was tiny as a midget, wore a mustache, and openly ogled Liz's breasts.

Cas told him to find an electronics store. The driver swung up Senator Puyat Avenue, crossed Taft Boulevard and entered a flashy commercial area in Baclaran. The streets, even at this late hour, were crowded. Gaudy shops and bars lined the narrow avenues with houses on the second stories. Most of the walls were painted a faded blue, and there were tables on the sidewalk where T-shirted young men wearing dark glasses drank beer and played chess. Streetwalkers stood on corners dressed in shiny Spandex pants and heels like rapiers.

They were let off at a store called the New Deal

Arcade. The front was filled with young boys playing video games. Against one wall was a small counter selling cans of Pepsi Cola and barbecued strips of meat on sticks. In a back room behind a dirty curtain were crates of Japanese boom boxes, stereos, TVs, and computer units. On a board along the side wall were three hooked-up IBM clones and a television set.

The owner was a Japanese man in a red kimono and a Western Union cap. They rented one of the VCR machines and ran the tape. Instantly a scene of a lake came on, the camcorder panning slowly from right to left. A temple rose on the opposite bank, where people were feeding black swans.

The picture changed to a city scene, flowing crowds of Chinese and streets filled with small motorcars and handcarts and thousands of bicycles. There was no sound, and it gave the images a vacuumed sense of movement, like an old silent travelogue.

Once more the scene changed, this time showing what looked like military buildings. But there were no soldiers in sight. Instead the people wore blue coveralls and some were in white frocks. As the frame panned slowly, a tall rocket gantry came into view, with the bottom stage of a missile in the pad chocks. Beyond, there were two other gantry pads resting in what looked like young corn fields.

Suddenly the television screen went black, scattered with snow. Cas waited a moment for the picture to come back. It didn't. He leaned out and ran the tape back, started it forward. This time nothing came.

He ran it back all the way to the start and switched it on. Still, nothing. He extracted the tape and examined it. The reel had become tangled inside. He tried to wind one of the sockets but it was jammed solidly.

He popped off the front flap and tried to see up into it, but it was sealed. He turned it over to the back side. He could see little wedge marks along the joint of the frame, as if it had been tampered with. Using a tiny Phillips screwdriver borrowed from the arcade owner, he took out the four screws which held the two parts of the frame together, turned it over and disassembled it.

Resting on the spools were two yellow floppy computer disks. One had caught an edge on the inside of the spool, jamming the reel. "Bingo," Cas said.

He lifted a disk. Its small metal tongue feed had Chinese characters stamped into it. He glanced at Liz and nodded toward the three computers. "You know how to run one of those things?"

"Some, mainly simple word processing."

They rented one of the IBM clones at ten bucks U.S. an hour. Liz seated herself in front of it and switched it on. The machine hummed a moment and then a program directory unfolded on the screen. She ran the cursor down the list until the DOS system was highlighted and she entered it. It went blank again and then showed a square and instructions and trademarks.

"I'll only be able to bring this up if it's compatible with a DOS system," she explained to Bonner. "That's all I know. But with those Chinese characters on the disks, I don't think it'll work."

"Give it a shot."

She inserted one of the disks into the machine's slot and punched the entry key. Nothing happened. She tried again. The screen remained blank.

"It's no use. It won't let me get into the file-allocation table to bring the data off the tape."

Cas walked back and forth behind her. "Is there a general sequence method to get into it?"

"I don't think—wait a minute." She pecked away at the keyboard, glanced up at the screen. A set of directions had come up, but they were a standard menu list for the DOS system. Again she pecked keys. The menu went off and the screen read: "INVALID SUB-DIRECTORY—CONVERT TO FILE, YES OR NO."

She hit the *y* key. The screen went blank again.

"It won't accept it."

Cas went off to find the shop owner. He asked him if he had a computer with Japanese or Chinese *kanji* keys on it. The man said, yes, he had one. It was his personal machine. Why did they want it? Cas said he had some disks from a Chinese friend. The owner agreed to let them use his unit for fifty dollars U.S. Liz used one of her traveler's checks to pay him.

The owner's computer was in a back room beside a kitchen that smelled of garbage and burnt pork. Two old women were cooking and they peered suspiciously at the Americans through a filthy curtain. The computer was a Toshiba-Datsu unit with a green screen. For another fifty dollars the owner agreed to bring up the disks himself.

He took several minutes to locate the command code to access the disk. Suddenly the screen was filled with Chinese characters and number sequences spaced like words. All three of them leaned in to see.

"You understand any of that?" Cas asked the proprietor.

"Just numbers and Chinese words." He looked at him queerly. "Dis from yo' fren?"

"He keeps forgetting I don't speak Chinese." He eased him out of the chair. "Thanks, pal." The man went off through the kitchen.

Liz sat down and began scanning down through the data using the cursor. More number sequences came up, then geometric figures and long sections of what seemed to be trigonometric arcs, algorithms, and complex graphics. Liz shook her head. "This stuff is gibberish. You make anything out of it?"

"No. Shut it down."

She homed the run back to the beginning and booted out of the system. When she extracted the floppy disk, she stared at it for a moment, then looked up at Bonner. Her eyes were glassy with tears. "My brother died for this idiocy?"

They left the arcade and stood on the sidewalk, trying to figure out their next step. Cas took her arm and they turned south, toward a small park at the edge of a river. It was filled with plumeria trees, the ground littered with blossoms, and there were gardenia shrubs with leaves as shiny as metal in the waning moonlight.

Two jeepneys were parked in the dark beside the dirt road that crossed through the park. Their drivers were standing off about fifty yards, smoking and chattering softly. In the lighted vehicles, two Australian sailors were fornicating with prostitutes.

Liz went down to the river's edge. The water was black and formed little whirlpools around rocks. It stank of refuse. She walked up the dark bank and stood alone. Cas lit a cigarette and watched her. For the first time he could really feel her sorrow in the night, like a silent sob, sharp as broken glass.

When she came back, he asked, "You said your brother was wearing a monk's habit when he was killed, right?"

"Yes, the police think he was trying to hide in a monastery."

"You know which one?"

"Yes, Saint Timothy's."

He touched her arm. "Come on."

"Where?"

"To talk to a monk."

It was a thirty-minute jeepney ride to Saint Timothy's, which was located on the edge of Makita, the huge suburban business district of Manila. The only other passenger was a drunk Filipino man in a garish yellow suit. He kept dozing, then jerking upright, mumbling apologies to no one in particular.

Liz seemed suddenly anxious to talk. She rambled on aimlessly, plucking out memories of Jerry when they were kids. Her face looked sad and pensive, her eyes misting now and then.

Cas let her talk, nodding occasionally and watching the drunk in the yellow suit. Now and again one of Liz's place references would jog his own memory. He was familiar with the down peninsula Bay Area, having done his undergraduate studies at Stanford in Palo Alto.

Back then he'd known a lot of Liz Forsythes, the products of the country club estates of Milbrae and

Hillsdale. Glowing tennis beauties who drove Mercedes sports cars and wore their snobbery with a kind of genetic elan. He had bedded his share. Ironically, years later, after he'd gotten his doctorate in ocean studies from Scripps and was still completing his hitch in the Navy, he ended up marrying one of the breed. It turned out to be a disaster.

Her name was Carolyn Silham, the beautiful and self-indulgent daughter of the publisher of the Honolulu *Sentinel*. They met at a cocktail party in Pearl Harbor. In his dress whites, Carolyn thought he looked like a movie star. They spent the rest of the night drunkenly making love on the beach out near Makapuu, and two weeks later they were married.

It was great at first, an endless whirl of parties and long, rainy tropical afternoons of slow, pot-high sex. But Bonner soon tired of this, it sat uncomfortably in him. He wanted a child, a home. Carolyn flatly refused. Disagreement deepened into open war. Then she got pregnant and without his knowledge had an abortion.

He tried to hold on, to slow her down. She hated him for the attempt. She started using coke, hard and heavy, flagrantly skimming in and out of affairs. The final cut came one day when he found a beach boy from Kuhio screwing her on the kitchen floor. He bodily lifted the beach boy off her, hurled him through a glass door, then packed and left. . . .

The Saint Timothy compound was set in a jungle of jacaranda trees and Benguet pines surrounded by a white wall of sandstone topped with barbed wire. Part of the compound was a graveyard, the tombs all aboveground like the ones on Desire Street in New Orleans. The stones were white and looked pearly in the moonlight, dappled with shadows.

The low main building was of Spanish colonial architecture. They passed through an ornate gate and walked up a cobblestone path to the main entrance. It had a tall door made of monkeypod wood, with brass

hinges and tiny dots of metal that made it look like a
samurai's breast plate.

Cas rapped the huge knocker ring, listening to the
echo resound dully through the building. Several minutes passed before a light came on and an old, thin
monk opened the door. He looked out with scowling
little eyes and snapped something in Tagalog.

"You speak English?" Cas asked.

"What do you want at this hour?"

"To talk to the monsignor."

"We have no monsignor here."

"Then who's in charge?"

"The prelate. He's alseep."

"Wake him up."

"No!"

Cas pushed against the door and stepped into the
entry hall. It was paneled in dark woods, with a high,
beamed ceiling. Two corridors broached into it, lit by
faint yellow light from fixtures made to look like
torches. The building smelled of candlewax and the
powerful odor of incense.

The monk was aghast. "You—can't come in without
permission." His slitted eyes snapped to Liz. "Women
are *never* permitted."

"Tell the prelate I want to talk about Jerry Forsythe."

The monk's mouth shut tight and he arched back,
looking Bonner up and down. "Constabulary?"

"Yes."

He went off mumbling and disappeared up one of
the corridors, his habit rustling with cottony whispers.
A chime sounded somewhere in the monastery, delicate as a struck orb of crystal. It was three o'clock.

The prelate was an extremely large Filipino in a
black habit with a red belt and a linen-lined hood. He
was seated behind a desk the size of a small boat. His
huge face looked puffy from sleep. When he spoke,
there was brusque irritation in his voice. His English
was perfect.

"Why do you come here about this man again? I've

already told you all I know about him.'' The large pouches under his eyes quivered as he studied Bonner closely. ''You don't look like police people.''

''We're not.''

The prelate scoffed loudly, waving them away. He rose.

''This is Forsythe's sister,'' Cas said.

The man stopped, stared at her a moment, then bowed his head. ''My condolences to you, madam.''

''We'd like any information about my brother you have,'' Liz said. ''Please.''

The prelate sighed and sat down. He began to speak slowly, as if picking delicately around the words. He didn't really know much, he told them. Forsythe had simply shown up one evening about a week before. Very agitated, terror in the eyes.

''I was not surprised,'' he said, shaking his head sadly. ''There are many frightened people in my country. One finds corruption and danger everywhere.''

''What did he say?''

''Simply that he wanted to become a monk. I knew it wasn't true, but I allowed him to remain. He was given a cell, clothing, and assigned certain duties. He seemed to perform them with diligence. Out of fear of expulsion, I would imagine. Yesterday he just disappeared.

''Soon after, the constabulary came and said they were investigating his murder. They found his belongings in his cell, identification and that sort of thing. After a while they went away. They returned twice, searched his cell and the grounds around it again but found nothing further.''

Bonner asked, ''Did he ever mention a man named Stanford?''

The prelate smiled indulgently. ''He would not have. You see, we are a very strict order. Speaking is kept to an absolute minimum.'' The smile faded and the huge man studied them before speaking again. ''There *was* something else. Apparently someone entered his cell before the police.''

Cas sat forward. "When?"

"We don't know exactly. Sometime in the night before his disappearance. When Forsythe did not respond to the early prayer bell that morning, one of my assistants was sent to fetch him. He found the cell open and his belongings scattered on the floor. Even the bed mattress had been sliced open."

"How could they know which cell was his?"

"I have no idea."

Bonner grunted.

The prelate rose tiredly. "I'm afraid that's all I can tell you. I'm sorry."

Cas and Liz stood up too. "Well, thank you, Father," Liz said.

"Are the police aware of your visit here?"

"No."

"Then you will understand that I must tell them. It could be . . . improvident of me to withhold such information."

"Of course."

The prelate bowed his head, and they departed.

Once more in the moonlight, they walked silently back toward the gate. The night was full of shadows, the pines dark, praying saints mourning the dead. From somewhere in Makita came the sound of a siren, rising and fading, drifting through the graves, a lost soul entangled in sorrow.

Bonner spotted the cruiser right off as their jeepney turned toward the yacht club entrance. It was sitting out there near the breakwater, lights ablaze. He tensed, slowly swiveling in his seat to keep the boat in view as the jeepney skirted buildings and stands of jacaranda trees.

Liz glanced at him. "What's the matter?"

"They're here."

"Where?"

Bonner tapped the driver's arm. "Keep going, on past the fountain."

For a moment he lost sight of the cruiser as they

passed the dark front of a sports fishing store at the head of the public dock area. He leaned out and looked down toward his sloop.

"Shit!" he growled. "Somebody's on my boat."

Liz was shifting around on her seat, squinting anxiously through the side window of the jeepney. "Let's get out of here," she said. The driver shot her a puzzled glance.

Bonner sat back, his jaw muscles working. Then he said to the driver, "Stop, right here."

The jeepney lurched to a halt with a little grab of brakes. As Cas started to get out, Liz grabbed his arm. "Where are you going?"

"You stay here," he ordered. He turned and sprinted off, running low toward one of the plaza restaurants.

"Wait! Wait!" Liz called in an urgent whisper. The driver was staring at her. She fumbled in her pockets and threw several bills at him, then climbed out the rear of the vehicle. She started after Bonner. Behind her, the jeepney made a noisy turn and sped off.

She reached the restaurant. A single green light lit the entrance and tall strands of pampas grass were growing in neat, free-form pits of wood shavings. Through the barred windows she saw polished, gleaming tables with chairs turned upside down on them. She found Cas squatting at the corner of the building, shifting his weight from knee to knee. When she came up, he whirled on her. "It's me," she hissed.

"Goddammit, I told you to stay with the taxi."

"I want to go with you."

"No!" He turned his gaze back to the docks. A hundred yards away, the *Napah* bobbed and jerked at her lines, responding to heavy movement inside her cabin. He studied the scene a moment longer, then darted around the back of the restaurant.

Once more she followed him, this time to a small garbage alcove. Cas was inside, studying the ground. He finally bent and picked up a three-foot length of pipe. Seeing her, he came over, grabbed her arm with

a vise grip. "Listen, damn you, will you stay put?"
He shook her.

"Why can't I come?"

"Because you'd do something stupid and get us killed."

"I'm not an idiot."

"Oh, yeah?"

"God, you're a nasty man."

"That makes us even. Stay!"

"All right, I'm staying."

He slipped around the edge of the alcove and moved off toward the docks, again hunched over Indian style, holding to shadows. He reached the first tied-in boat, a day sailer with a blue light on its masthead. The small dog he'd spooked earlier with his whistle started again. He froze. The dog was plainly edgy and its yips echoed like rifle shots. After a while the dog went around to the other side of the boat, making growly wuffs. He went on.

When he reached the *Napah* he saw two five-gallon gasoline tanks on the dock in front of the sloop. Had they been there before? He knelt beside them and lightly tapped a fingernail against one: it was full. Rage ignited him. The bastards were going to torch his boat.

He scurried around until he could see out into the entry channel. The cruiser was still there, her swept-back bridge lights looking like the slits of a bunker.

Heart pumping hard, he stepped lightly onto the *Napah*'s forward deck, eased his weight, and brought the other foot over. He heard soft chatter from the cabin. Going as delicately as he could, muscles straining, he moved around to the companionway. There he paused, gritted his teeth, and lunged down the steps.

The first swing of his pipe caught a Tigerman across the chest. It hit with the solid impact of all his two hundred pounds going deep into rib bone. The man let out a strangled grunt and went hurling back against the radio table.

Bonner whirled, drawing the pipe back for another swing, eyes darting. The cabin was torn apart, tanks and diving gear, clothes, dishes smashed. The radio casing was ripped open. Suddenly a second man came up through the engine hatch, his oriental face looking stupidly jolted. Cas stepped in and brought the pipe around in a wide arc. It hit the man on the shoulder, knocking him back down into the engine space.

There was a wild thumping down there, voices screeching wildly. Cas turned and leaped up the companionway, out onto the deck. He heard the forward vent hatch slam against the deck as someone's weight went onto it.

A second later, another man lunged out of the darkness and hurled himself over the top of the cabin, bringing up a short-barreled automatic weapon. Cas dropped as the man jerked off a burst. The bullets *whanged* into the metal boom. The explosions went cracking off over the docks.

There was another burst that chewed up deck a foot from Bonner's heel. He heard the little metal click of a clip being ejected, another going in. Coiling himself like a spring, he drove his leg muscles and rose up over the edge of the companionway hatch. The gunman's head jerked up. He tried to swing up his weapon, but Cas hit him with the pipe before he could. Jaw bone shattered with a wet, pulpy sound, and the man slid off the cabin, his fingers reflexively pulling the trigger.

Bullets splayed across the dock, into the gasoline carriers. A geyser of fuel went straight up into the air and then lit, a blue-orange tongue that flashed back with lightning speed. Cas heard a violent *whooomp* as tank shrapnel hurled outward and shards of flame blew, mixed with raw fuel.

The *Napah*'s foredeck erupted in a sheet of light. An instant later, the small motor launch to the left of the sloop hissed into flames. On the wharf, the tar-soaked planks caught fire.

Bonner madly tried to put out the fire on his deck. His hands slapped wildly, coming away with blue fringes of ignited fuel, burning with bone-painful surges. He heard a soft rumble in the nearby motor launch. A stream of blue flame licked out between the cabin and after deck, long as a man's arm but narrow as a needle. Shrapnel had ignited bilge gas.

Cas turned away from it, his body moving at what seemed infinitesimal increments as he went to the deck. Before he touched down, there was a hollow, jarring explosion and the *Napah* heeled sharply. Feeling the concussion through her deck, Cas found himself jolted out and up into the air, sailing.

He crumpled onto the soggy, burning tar of the wharf. Instantly he rolled and came to his feet. His eardrums still held the powerful echoes of the explosion, and spikes of pain shot up through the soles of his feet. Fire was all around him. He vaguely heard a scream, then another explosion. Suddenly the night sky was filled with shooting rockets of blue light and spirals.

He crouched and ran, broke through a sheet of flame. Up the dock he caught sight of a naked man standing on the front of a moored sampan, watching the flames with his mouth agape. Cas raced past him.

On the outer access road, some of the cars were screeching to a halt and pulling off to the side as their drivers saw the conflagration in the dock area. A few made sharp turns and came down into the plaza.

Bonner reached the corner of the darkened restaurant. The windows reflected the flames out on the dock, shifting patterns of color. He pressed against the cool wood of the wall, panting, feeling heat that only now was beginning to dissipate out of his body.

Liz's face loomed out of firelight and her hands scurried all over his chest. "Are you all right?" she cried. "Cas, are you hurt?" Her red hair looked crimson in the glow of the fires, which were now enveloping a large section of the dock and sending black smoke up into the air. The underside of the seething mass was etched with streaks of red and orange.

Wordlessly he took her arm and they hurried away. Out on the cobblestone dockway, cars were pulling up, skidding. People running, pointing. They passed a white sports car with a T-roof. A man in the driver's seat was staring through the windshield. He was thick-haired and wore dark glasses which reflected the flames in miniature.

Bonner wrenched open the door, grabbed a silken lapel and hauled him out. The man went down hard on the ground, his glasses shattering nearby. Cas shoved Liz into the vehicle and climbed in after her. Jamming his foot to the floor, he spun the car around and headed back up the entrance road, flying.

6

They crossed the river in twos and threes, twenty-five Sacred Pool assault team Rangers walking gently in the shallows, like tightrope walkers in dim light. There had been frost earlier, but then the sky became overcast and now the frost had turned to ice on the reeds along the bank. When a sandal pressed down on them, they crinkled as if the men had stepped on stiff cellophane.

Captain Litung was the second man from the point. Like all his men, he was dressed in peasant garb, lightly armed: grenades and spare clips wrapped in straw to prevent sounds, a boot knife, belt bayonet and a Shandyun assault rifle. His heart pounded with adrenaline, and yet he contained its explosive charge, instructing his mind to absorb its energy, hold it in reserve.

The point man stopped. They had reached the first of a group of eight-foot berms topped by spooled-out layers of entrenchment wire. There the light from posts ringing the inner compound made circular shadows against the reeds.

The point man came skittering back and paused beside his captain. "Two guard posts, *shangwei*," he whispered, his words frosting in the air. "One man each."

Litung glanced back down the river. Under the overcast sky it looked gray and still, like an ink sketch of a stream. His men were invisible along the bank. He turned to the second man, a lance corporal with a crossbow strapped to his back.

"Put the sappers into position," Litung instructed. The corporal melted off into the darkness. Soon he was back.

A few moments later, several Rangers moved past, hunched below the edge of the light, their sandals whispering in the hard sand of the riverbank. Litung waited, watching the luminous second hand of his watch tick off one minute.

Then he tapped the lance corporal, who instantly unharnessed the already armed crossbow and handed it over. It was very heavy in the captain's hands. Made of buckhorn braced into the tempered steel bow, it was capable of sending a thin metal shaft hurling with the power of a two-hundred-pound pull. It would strike a man like a high-velocity bullet, instantly shocking him into silence.

Litung strapped his assault rifle to his back and fell to his knees, then his belly. The ground was icy cold and felt wet. He crawled over the nearest berm until he was close to the lower strand of barbed wire where it poked out of the reeds. Forty yards away was the first guardhouse.

Earlier that evening, during his pre-assault briefing in the trench hole of his battalion commander, Litung had requested that he perform the Ring of First Blood. That designated the man in the assault team who would make the initial kill. It was granted.

Now he gently positioned his crossbow into the sand and studied the guardhouse. The Soviet guard was sitting on an ammunition box, his legs stretched out, arms folded with his head against the right wall. He wore no battle helmet. The little shack threw cross shadows from the perimeter lights, but the interior was solid light. It made the guard's face whitish, with only faint shadows formed by his eye sockets.

The crossbow shaft entered his brain through the left eye. Nearly silent, the impact caused his head to jam hard against the wall. His legs went straight out, as if he had slipped on a patch of oil, and then they trembled in a last spasm before dropping heavily.

Litung leaned back to check the second guard post a hundred yards away. He could see its guard standing in front, looking his way. Suddenly he jerked as if someone had pushed him in the center of the back and then he fell down. Litung turned and pumped his hand forward, as if beating it against a door.

A scant fifteen seconds were needed to cut a hole through the wire. Instantly a red light started blinking inside the nearer guardhouse. Litung braced, even though his informants had told him there would be no sound alarm when the wire was cut. There was silence.

Fifty seconds later, all his men had slipped into the compound and disappeared into buildings, merging with shadows. With the lance corporal at his heels, Captain Litung went into a low structure. It was made of pine posts with mud brick and a cement floor. It smelled of cabbage and sour wine. There was a lighted outer room where a man was asleep at a radio desk, his head resting on his forearms. A bank of field phones was against one wall, and there was a tiny switchboard in a canvas coverlet with all the socket lights dark.

The lance corporal cut the man's throat from ear to ear. The Russian gagged and blood sprayed across his forearms. Litung leaped past and eased open the main door. It was dim inside, just a single tiny light at the far end. The walls were lined with double bunks with footlockers and racks of rifles running down the center.

He pushed the door fully open with his boot, swung the Shandyun's muzzle toward the right line of bunks and pulled the trigger. The gun jerked in his hand, blowing powerful explosions into the enclosed space. Bullets tore through the metal bunks, whanged into footlockers.

Two men screamed, their voices coiling around each other like variations of the same sound. Dark bodies leaped up, some hurled back by the impacts of rounds. Someone at the far end started returning fire, and the doorjamb beside Litung blew apart. He paused for a moment, then swung the muzzle up the opposite side of the room, hearing the corporal's weapon going hot right beside his elbow, making his ears numb. The room was misty with gun smoke.

From other parts of the compound came more sporadic bursts: the high chatter of Shandyuns and then the throatier roars of Kalashnikovs.

Suddenly two figures loomed up near Litung. He tried to fire but his weapon was empty. The Russians cut loose at him. Their aim was slightly off and the rounds went into the wall. At the same time the lance corporal was hurled back and away. Before the two Russians could swing back, Litung had reversed his clip and cut them down.

He paused, his blood making a crazy drumming in his temples. Moans riffled through the gun smoke and something crashed down, scattering a rack of weapons. He instantly threw several rounds at it, heard the bullets go screeling off the metal.

He pulled two grenades from his belt, drew the pins with his teeth, rolled them down the center of the room, and hit the floor. The explosions came almost simultaneously, blowing the door clear across the room in a wave of fiery smoke.

Litung crawled up beside his corporal. The man was still alive, his eyelids fluttering crazily. The entire front of his peasant's jacket was covered with blood, and the floor was greasy with it. Gritting his teeth, the captain cut the corporal's jugular vein, then leaped up and dodged back out into the compound as six quick explosions erupted along the bank entrenchments: the sappers' charges were taking out the perimeter gun emplacements. Bright streaks of glowing metal arced up into the darkness.

Near the second guardhouse he could see a full firefight in progress, half-naked Russians and Rangers facing off less than fifty feet from one another. He turned and looked down toward the village. Lights had come on there, peasant kerosene lanterns and, in a tight concentration of buildings, bright electric pole lights and the headlamps of armored vehicles.

The fight near the guardhouse was dissolving into isolated shooting. He saw his men going among the fallen bodies and bayoneting them. Heavy rifle fire started from one of the inner buildings, followed by several grenade blasts. Right after them came three quick muzzle blows and then three more. Armored vehicles were charging up from the village, laying a barrage right over the compound and into the river to prevent retreat.

Litung pumped his arm, rallying his men. He raced back to the first guardhouse and squatted, waiting for his Rangers to assemble. He glanced in at the guard. The crossbow shaft protruded from his eye, dripping blood and a stringy yellow substance like mucus. On impulse he reached out and tore the man's tunic open. There was no red star flag on his chest.

Getting back across the river was hellish, what with the Soviet garrison pouring on a full retaliatory barrage: fusilades of Kalashnikovs, floating .50-caliber rounds, and 37mm shells cutting up the night into blinding white phosphorescent showers.

Once more on the opposite shore, Litung assembled his strike team and counted heads. Of his original group only six were left, two wounded. Now the Russian batteries, located four miles to the rear, began shelling the Chinese side of the river, walking their 105mm rounds back and forth at the water's edge and then farther inland. Shells started falling among the mud huts and tiny pigpens of Changbai, driving peasants up the dirt roads and across the wheat and rapeseed fields to the forests beyond.

But there was no answering fire from the Chinese batteries in Quisuing, three miles south of Changbai. As dawn arrived, the Soviet guns finally went silent.

* * *

General Yeh Son whispered to Minister Litung, "The assault mission is complete."

The two men were strolling across Tiananmen Square, the general to the left and slightly behind, as was the custom with anyone who walked with the Minister for Internal Affairs. On this cold morning the huge cement plaza was filled with men and women performing their slow-motion exercises called t'ai chi ch'uan, as hordes of bicyclists dodged past on their way to work. Here and there old men sat on cushions in circles, playing the card game called Swimming Upstream. The chilly air was filled with the yellow dust which swept each fall off the Gobi Desert and made the sun glow amber.

Son Yeh continued: "There were heavy casualties among the Russians. They initiated an artillery barrage, but it has now ceased. We lost nineteen. Your son was not one of them."

Litung showed no emotion. "And Sichen?"

"He is extremely agitated." General Yeh was Premier Sichen's personal military adjutant. "He was informed that it was peasants who had struck, over the execution of a brother. But he has ordered that the local PLA commandant be immediately brought to Beijing for explanations."

Litung paused, looking down at the pavement. On each stone was a number, put there by order of Mao so that when his army marched in the square, their lines would be perfect. Now the minister swung to his right and started off again. His strolls always formed a perfect square.

Such precision had always been a trademark of Litung's, perhaps because he had been born into chaos. The Japanese invasions of '38 and before that, the bloody campaigns between the Communists and Chiang Kai-Shek's Kuomintang, in which his father was killed when he was one. But he had learned early on to maintain mental precision, and it had given his childhood a remnant of control.

By the time Litung was fifteen, that steely manner

was reinforced when he became a PLA soldier. He fought Americans in North Korea, where his cold, precise killing capacity was noticed. In 1956, still only nineteen, he was assigned assassination missions during the Hundred Flowers purges of that year.

As a captain, he again fought in the short war with India over Tibet. Later he was sent for further tactical training to Moscow while relations were still strong with the Soviets. But then he turned their own tactics against them in the bloody border clashes along the Ussuri River. There he won his colonelcy.

During the turmoil of the mid-seventies and the subsequent downfall of the Gang of Four, he was appointed Sichen Zian's personal bodyguard by the Party Secretary Zaobang Zhao. Sichen was then vice-premier, a dedicated progressive, and Litung's true duty was to spy on him and report to the Secretary.

But Sichen consolidated his power with great swiftness and soon took over the premiership. By the early eighties, his restructuring policies aimed toward the West had alienated a solid core of hard-liners and military officers. Although Zaobang, an intransigent hard-liner, was still General Secretary, he had grown old and weak. Yet he still had enough power to get Litung appointed to Minister of Internal Affairs, chief of the Chinese secret police.

Gradually, Zaobang's conservative–militarist factions began coalescing around Litung. Secretly, insidiously he built his power base with spies, contacts and sympathizers in every branch of the government. As his own strength grew, so did his dreams. He intended to create a New Order for China, based not on mutual cooperation with the other, decadent nations, but rather through a return to pure military isolationism. When he took over the premier–chairmanship, it would mark the beginning of a new dynasty.

Still, Sichen had proven too strong to challenge openly. His adept political handling of the Tiananmen Incident, in which he had temporarily conceded to hard-line demands for martial law and the destruction of the rising spirit of democracy, had given him renewed respect among the hard-liners. But Litung knew it had all been a farce. Since then the premier had once more diligently kowtowed to world pressure for human rights, and had continued allowing what was only a slightly veiled capitalism.

Inevitably he must die. But in such a way that the masses of the nation would view his death and Litung's subsequent coup as just and correct. To do that, Sichen first had to be humiliated. The initial step in that humiliation had been the border incursion. Litung knew that Sichen, scrambling for position at the coming conference, would apologize for it. Both to the Russians and the U.S. That would be the beginning of his downfall. . . .

The two men had reached a circle of card players in their path. Litung stopped, staring down at the men. When they saw who it was, everyone instantly shifted out of his way, pulling card piles and sliding cushions. He remained motionless, studying the cards in one player's hand. Then he leaned down and plucked out a single one and tossed it onto the pavement. "Your swan card destroys your opponent immediately," he said quietly to the player.

The man glanced at the card, then turned, smiling nervously. "Ah, of course, Minister. I did not see that. Thank you, sir."

Litung and Yeh continued. Twenty paces farther on, Biao again paused to check the pavement, then swung to his right. To Yeh he said, "Forestall bringing the commander here. Make excuses. And prepare for the next step."

"Yes, Minister," the general said.

In the U.S., the President was in the middle of early dinner at the Lambarth Hotel in Cincinnati when word came of the Chinese incursion. A few minutes later in the hotel's main suite, he met with Secretary of State Joe Tichner and two senior staff officers from the Chief of Naval Operations who had accompanied him on this trip, a political swing to aid in upcoming senatorial elections.

His first question was "How bad is it?"

"We're still in the dark about the strength of the thrust," Tichner answered. "Meager reports out of Beijing say it was some sort of commando foray out of Changbai."

"Commando? No armor?"

"Satellite photos show nothing that heavy."

"And?"

"Apparently the Russians repulsed it and set up a short artillery barrage of Changbai. But there was no return fire, so everything is quiet at this point."

"Well," the President said, looking at his two naval officers, "what the hell is this?"

"Could be a feeler probe, sir," Rear Admiral Jack Hoskins said. A slim, athletic officer with steel gray hair, he was Chief Adjutant to CNO Admiral Willings.

"Which means?"

"It could be the initial moves of a major thrust," Hoskins went on. He shook his head. "But with our earlier satellite pictures showing no extensive buildups in the region, I doubt that scenario."

"Then why a raid at all?"

"Anything could have triggered it, sir. The last artillery exchange in that area started over the rape of a Chinese woman by a drunken Soviet border guard."

"But this wasn't an artillery exchange," Tichner snapped. "There was an actual crossing of the Amur River."

"Yes, that is a new twist." Hoskins thought a moment. "Maybe whatever blew this thing off got an on-site Chinese commander so enraged he lost his head."

"So where does that leave us?" the President asked.

"I think the real danger is how the Russians react."

The President swung back to Tichner. "How are they handling it?"

"So far, nothing, sir. Heavy staff traffic in the Kremlin, but very little data coming out. Let's hope Markisov is trying to hold all reaction down."

The President grunted. "That's a great assumption, but is it realistic? His military people could go right through the roof on this one. Can he hold them off, or will he appease them with an incursion of his own?"

"I'm afraid we'll just have to wait and see."

"Well, hell!" the President cried. "So much for happy faces over that conference table."

"Perhaps not, sir," Tichner offered. "Like Hoskins says, it could just be a local command thing that can quickly be quieted."

There was a soft hum from the suite's telephone. The junior officer, a commander, hurried to it and lifted the receiver. He listened for a moment, then held it out to Tichner. "For you, sir, the Pentagon."

The Secretary took it and immediately said, "This is not a secure line." Then he listened, said, "Thank you," and returned to the table. "Good news and bad, sir. The Chinese claim this was a family thing."

"A what?"

"A Chinese spy was recently executed by the Russians. Beijing lower staff is hinting it was some sort of vendetta over the killing."

"Jesus, do they still carry on with that sort of shit?"

"It's possible. These border people are five centuries behind the rest of us. That could explain why there was no return fire by the PLA batteries in Quisuing. In any case, word out of the Kremlin says Markisov is holding down any violent reaction."

"Thank God. So what's the bad news?"

"He has authorized an immediate and massive troop buildup along the entire Sino–Soviet frontier."

"That sounds like a bone tossed to the military."

"It would seem so."

The President softly sucked air through his teeth. "Well, at least Markisov's still carrying weight." He thrust himself to his feet and walked around, thinking out loud. "Now's the time for talk, right now. There's been a flashpoint and everybody's still holding place. Now's the moment for face-to-face." He swung around to Tichner. "Is it at all possible to get that conference moved up a few days?"

The Secretary frowned. "I wouldn't think so, sir. Logistical plans are all in effect. It would be a mess trying to change all the diplomatic and protocol systems now."

The President sighed. "All right, but I want immediate notes sent to Beijing and Moscow stating that now more than ever is the need for these negotiations. Something like this Hatfield and McCoy crap could start a goddamned war. But make it diplomatic, no hardass tone."

"Yes, sir."

"Keep me apprised." He headed for the door as everyone stood. "I'll see you gentlemen back in Washington in the morning."

As the .32-caliber rounds fired out the muzzle of the Beretta 465 in a steady three-second spacing, the little gun hardly jerked in Aguinaldo Babiyan's delicate hand. Thirty feet away, a series of round holes appeared in a paper target shaped in the outline of a standing man. The holes were in a cluster no wider than four inches where the paper man's heart would be.

When the thirteenth and last went out, Babiyan laughed happily and popped out his clip. He turned to Jack Stanford, standing in the next firing stall of the indoor range. "How you like that, Yank?"

Stanford nodded. He was holding his Browning 9mm, cocked and ready, pointed at the ceiling. "Not bad, not bad. But the spacings are too long."

Babiyan scoffed. He was a small, dark man with clean, Arabic features: slightly hooked nose, dark curly hair, mustache. He was nattily dressed in a luminously white shirt, red tie and gray suit trousers. Under his left arm was a silver-inlaid leather holster for the Beretta. "You can do better?"

"Of course."

"A thousand U.S. says you can't."

"You're on, Aguinaldo. Time it."

With a fluid action which was almost the continuation of his words, Stanford lowered the weapon and cut loose. The explosions sounded nearly on top of one another, crackling and echoing through the indoor firing range. His target jerked and willowed as the thirteen rounds formed a large two-inch hole at the paper man's throat.

He finished and popped the clip, grinning at Babiyan. "How long?"

"Six and a half seconds," Babiyan said disgustedly.

"Shit, I'm gettin' slow. You want to go again?"

"No."

Both men reloaded and holstered their weapons, Stanford slipping his into his back waist band. He was wearing a blue and white letterman's jacket, and it just barely hid the gun. Babiyan pulled on his coat and they walked back along the firing stalls. They were filled with businessmen, most in the ubiquitous short-sleeved white shirts with flared collars, all taking their morning gun practice. In the Philippines it was always expedient for anyone with wealth to go armed with weapons they knew how to use.

The indoor range was situated on the top of the Far East Insurance and Indemnity building in Makati. From its wide windows the shooters could look down on the vast, rolling fairways of the Manila Golf and Country Club and, to the south, the precisely manicured fields of the Manila Polo Grounds.

They left the range, turned into an elaborate dining area and took a table near the west window. A waitress in a black bunny outfit with a red jockey cap took their order. Coffee for Jack, a large bowl of strawberry ice cream for Aguinaldo.

Babiyan sat back and lit a cigar. He watched Stanford bemusedly. "You have a problem."

"Right."

"And you want my help."

"Right again."

"Ah, of course."

Babiyan was a Philippine citizen of half Iranian extraction. Among his many other enterprises, he occasionally sold intelligence data to the secret police in Tehran. Born in the Muslim provinces of Mindanao, his father had been an Iranian sea captain who took him as a boy to be educated in the Near East and Europe. Now he was one of the most prestigious corporate attorneys in the Philippines and could speak seven languages fluently. He lived in a lavish, guarded compound in exclusive Desmarinas Park, and had connections that went all the way up to the vice-president.

Jack brought up that very point. "How much juice you got here, Aguinaldo?"

"Enough."

"I may need some heavy assistance."

"In what way, exactly?"

The waitress brought their orders, and the dapper little attorney immediately set to work on his ice cream, shoveling in large spoonfuls. As he absorbed the food, he gazed around at the scattering of well-dressed women and business executives in the dining area. Periodically the muffled thuds of firing came from the range.

"Possibly some military help."

"American or Filipino?"

"Filipino."

Babiyan grunted and wiped his mouth. He and Stanford had done some drug business back when Jack was still with the DEA, a series of solid smugglings that had made them both large chunks of money. He was rather fond of the American, yet was also fully aware that Stanford was ruthless and would unhesitatingly expose him if that proved necessary. "It could be touchy," he said. "And perhaps dangerous for me."

"I won't call unless there's no other way."

Babiyan returned to his ice cream. "What is this all about?"

"I can't tell you that."

"It must be very big."

"It is."

The waitress approached their table carrying a cellular phone. "Señor?" she said to Jack. "You are Stamford?"

"Yes."

She handed the instrument to him. It was Lui, his voice sleepy slow. "The police just trace the car Bonner and the bitch take."

"Fantastic! Where is it?"

"Small fishing village south of Manila Bay. Nasugbu."

"Is the constabulary captain there?"

"Yes."

"Tell him to have his people back off. We'll take it from here. Get your people out there. And, Lui, don't let 'em fuck it up this time."

"The captain want the rest of his money."

"He'll get it when we've got Forsythe and Bonner."

The Unicorn hung up.

Jack put down the receiver, grinning. Having just finished his ice cream, Babiyan took a long, satisfied pull on his cigar and through the smoke, asked, "Good news?"

"Great news. Looks like we might not need your help after all."

The lawyer delicately tapped away a round of ash. "That somehow does not distress me."

Jack rose. "But remember, you still owe me a thousand U.S."

"Next time we go for double?"

"You're on."

Stanford turned and darted back through the tables toward the elevators.

Will Cullin was as lean as a stalk of fall corn, but his muscles and tendons were wiry cables. With his skin scorched to the color of tobacco juice, he resembled Jacques Cousteau. Now he quietly leaned on a band saw under a high-roofed tin shed five miles from the sugar mill town of Nasugbu. He wore nothing but a pair of filthy yellow shorts. An old double-barrel

Manlicher ten-gauge shotgun rested in the crook of one arm.

"What the bloody hell are you doin' here, Bonner?" he asked as Cas came up the coral road, surrounded by a pack of rangy mongrel dogs. The sports car was parked back a hundred yards in deep grass with Liz asleep in the front seat.

Bonner grinned at him. "Got a bit of a problem, you old fart."

"That so?" Cullin glanced down at one of the dogs, a Doberman bitch with a muzzle sharp as a spear point. "I see Tart remembered ya, else she'd hav' cupped your tap off by now."

Beyond the work shed was a little shack made of driftwood and tar paper built on stilts out over mud flats. Along here was a desolate stretch of coastline with savannahs of high alang-alang grass and mangrove swamps where Asian cranes came to nest in the winter.

Besides the two buildings the only other structure around was a narrow dock that went out some fifty yards to deeper water. Tied to it was an old U.S. Navy PT boat, her hull and top works still painted in faded green and brown camouflage.

Cas nodded toward the boat. "Mick told me you'd bought yourself an old Elco after you got out of Toolaroom," he said, referring to a prison in Dunberry, Australia.

"Mick Fain? Ach, where'd you run into that nong?"

"A pub in Brisbane. He said you were living up here now."

Cullin jetted a stream of spittle. "Never could keep his flamin' mouth belted, that Mick." He gazed off at the car. "You ridin' ars' bastard these days, ain't ya?"

"I stole it."

"Figures."

Bonner had met Will Cullin ten years before when he was running a Scripps assignment for the U.S. Navy, dolphin experiments off the Great Barrier Reef. Will was a legend all along the Queensland coast and had been hired on as a consultant. An ex-Aussie Navy man, he'd fought on L-boats in the Mediterranean against German lighters before the outbreak of World War II, and then in MacArthur's campaigns up the Solomons. He knew high-speed engines and the coasts of Australia and the Indonesian Passthrough like the back of his bony hand. At one time or another, he'd run everything from Aborigine whores and smuggled gold to illegal guns and drugs.

"Come on inside, Casimir," Will said, pushing away from the saw stand. "You look like you could use a coldie."

The shack was a single room cluttered with empty beer bottles and fishing gear. There was a small stove made of a halved fifty-gallon fuel drum in the center, and the windows were hung with fiber curtains tied back and braced with pieces of driftwood. A large Halicrafter XB-157 transceiver sat in one corner with an antenna cable going up through the roof.

Cullin dug out two San Miguels from a small reefer, tossed one to Bonner, and squatted down with his back against the wall. He studied Cas a moment. "Who's the bird?"

"Name's Liz Forsythe. A load of rocks."

"Ah, yes, the Corregidor monk's sister."

Cas took a long pull on the beer bottle. "You know about that?"

"Aye, I've got big ears in the right places. You part of that, Bonner?"

"By accident."

Cullin tipped his beer back, then shook his head, chuckling. "You know what kind of brumbies you fuckin' with?"

"Bad asses."

"Worse than bad asses. Them's tattoo choongs, mate. Triads."

"Triads? What's that?"

"Ricehead Mafia, fer chrissake." Cullin leaned out and put his fingers around his throat, then made a choking sound. "They like the garotte. It's a bleedin' trademark. Or when they've got more time, they like the death of the thousand slices. Cut you up with little nicks and swipes till you kark it.''

Cas frowned. "Chinamen, yeah, that fits.'' He glanced up. "You ever hear of a guy named Stanford?''

"Jack Stanford? Aye, ex-DEA man gone sour. I run into some of his cargoes in the Celebes. A fast-dealin' swaggie, that one.''

Bonner hunkered forward. "Will, I need your boat.''

"Do you, now?''

Cas laid it out for him. Cullin listened, drinking his San Miguel. When Bonner finished, he opened two more beers and grinned, narrow-eyed. "Casimir,'' he said, "I feel shiddy with them dingoes firin' your sloop and all. And friendship's friendship. But I think you best by me on this 'un. I don't relish the idea of stoushing with them chinkaroos.''

"Then get me a boat. One that'll make Subic.''

Cullin thought a moment. "Aye, I might as can do that.''

At that moment they were interrupted by the insistent blaring of a car horn. In another second they heard the roar of engines out on the road.

Bonner sprang instantly to his feet and headed for the door. As he wrenched it open, he saw Liz at the wheel of the sports car tearing straight toward the shack. Coming up behind her was a Landrover, hurling coral dust.

Liz passed the work shed and swung the car around, ramming it to a stop. As she flung the door open and got out, she found herself stumbling and crawling through the dogs that had exploded off the porch of the shack. Behind her the Landrover also skidded to a stop. An instant later, three machine-gun bursts exploded from it, hurling rounds across the car and into the tin roof of the shack. One went ricocheting off with the sound of a screeching woman.

Crouched, Cas leaped to the hard-packed ground

and grabbed Liz, hauling her back to the shack. By the time he got to the porch, Cullin had cut loose with both barrels of his Manlicher. They sounded like the booms of a cannon. The windshield of the Landrover blew apart, and the three men came out of the vehicle, firing.

Cullin yelled and tossed Bonner a handgun. It was a large-bored Walther with a ring on the grip. Stretched on top of Liz—she was trying desperately to weld herself to a porch strut—he whipped it around and began firing, triggering off till the gun was empty.

Out in the yard, the pack of mongrels had hurled themselves at the men from the Landrover, Tart leading the charge. One of the men screamed and fell to the ground, his weapon splaying rounds up into the air. The other two started swinging on the dogs, their machine pistols making frantic arcs in the air. A dog squealed and tumbled to the ground.

Cullin rammed in two more cartridges and snapped the breech. Leaping around Cas, he headed toward the Rover, bellowing curses. Bonner went after him, twirling the Walther in his hand like a club. Behind him Liz collected her wits for a moment and fled through the shack door.

One of the men brought his weapon down, turned sideways, and opened up on the dogs, the bullets going in a sweep. Two dogs were lifted up into the air, screaming and gyrating crazily. One of them was Tart.

Cullin's double charge blew the man ten feet back. Blood exploded out of his chest. The others instantly scrambled into the Rover and backed up, going crazily, front wheels careening into grass. Fifty yards away, the driver snapped the vehicle around and roared off.

Bonner went down on one knee, the Walther feeling heavy in his hand, blood roaring in his head. Four feet away, a dog lay trembling on the road, blood discoloring its fangs. Beyond, Cullin was picking his way through furiously baying animals to Tart.

She lay with her belly blown open. Pink intestines

laced with purple and scarlet lay on the coral. Will, his fingers cupping and uncupping like a man about to touch dynamite, bent to her. He lifted her head, cooing softly. Her tail thumped against the ground gently, tiredly.

Bonner got up and walked over to the man Cullin had hit. He was Chinese, lying in the fetal position, blood staining the ground under him. It smelled raw and hot. He reached down and felt the man's throat. He was dead.

"Oh, the bloody barstids," Will was crying, rocking Tart's body. "Oh, the bloody, bloody barstids."

Liz came out, walking softly, high up, as if she were entering a mine field. Cas moved around and knelt down beside Will. He looked at Tart. Her eyes rolled, tongue lolling. Blood seeped softly from her belly.

The old Aussie turned and looked at Cas. His eyes glistened with tears. "You bloody bad-luck Yank, you've got your bleedin' boat."

They rolled the dead Chinaman into a sail bag and carried him down to the fork in the road, blood dripping from the cloth. Once they spotted the Landrover, partially hidden in deep grass far back on the road, but it didn't approach again. Will made a little sign from cardboard and tied it to the body bag. It read: "BURY THIS SON OF A BITCH AND PISS ON HIS GRAVE."

Then he and Bonner dug a trench beside the workshop and put the dogs down, Tart last. Tears running down his withered face, Cullin handled her gently, not letting Bonner touch her. He patted her head once and whispered, "Oo'roo, luv." Then they covered the grave over and went back to the shack.

With nothing but a case of San Miguel, the three of them went out on the walk dock and boarded the Elco. She was an eighty-footer and up close looked aged and war ravaged. There were warp bulges in her hull and the decks were spongy. The main structure had been stripped to bare essentials. Most of the triangle post was gone, and the gun turrets, once canopied, were now only shells with nets hanging on the swivel rings where .50-caliber machine guns had once pivoted. The forward torpedo racks were still intact but rusted and crumbling, and all the after vent horns had holes, some the unmistakable punctures of bullets.

Cullin watched Bonner's reaction as he prowled around, peering into dark recesses, testing decking with his bare toes. "Looks like an ol' clapped-out Sheilah, don' she?" Will said. "But don' be fooled, mate. She's as sound as when she came off the ways, and she can take ten-footers like greased shit."

He explained where he'd picked her up, in a salvage yard in Zamboanga owned by an old Brooklyn Jew named Abbie Baum, nicknamed the Junkman. She had been resting on rocker stacks, her wood as dry as bones, but the lines of her still held the same planing grace from fairlead to exhaust braces as when she'd run down Japanese gunboats and troop barges in the Mindanao Straits.

He'd stripped her and then, loaded with pig iron, ran her down the rails and sank her in twenty feet of water, where she sat for two weeks until her wood and fibers were soaked and flexible again and could take the pounding of speed. Once more in dry dock, he replaced her cross struts and bilge runners, patched and smoothed and braced her until she was sound again.

"But come looka here, Bonner," he said, eyes twinkling. He led them down through the chart room and after quarters to the engine spaces. "This 'ere's her real bleedin' glory."

She carried three gasoline-powered engines, each a sixteen-cylinder Hall-Scott W160C-IM-4600, straight out of Cosmoline. With high-flow superchargers, each plant could churn out three-thousand-brake horsepower. Like the engine room itself, the Hall-Scotts were spotless, their heads and ignition barrels and air intakes and exhaust lines all chromed and glistening with a thin sheen of oil. Abaft their bell housings was an electronic synchro-meshed transmission with indi-

vidual shaft chains that allowed the engines to be shut
down independently.

Bonner crawled over one of the main fuel tanks and
down into the engine spaces. He moved around, grunting appreciatively, gently running fingers over the
metal. He glanced up over his shoulder, grinning.
"They're beautiful, Will. Damn, I'll bet this old lady
flat rises and shines when you're running full bore."

"Fifty-eight knots on the step with her head in the
wind," Cullin said proudly.

Once more topside, Will started up the engines and
let them idle softly, the exhausts smoking and gurgling. Ordinarily on his runs, he told them, he crewed
with an old Filipino from Nasugbu who stood engine
watch for him. But sometimes he went out alone and
had rigged a bungee system on the helm so he could
periodically check below.

It was nearly three in the afternoon when they finally
tossed lines and eased away from the dock. When Cullin first set up house here, he had blasted a channel
through the shallows, and now they went out slowly,
the sides of the PT just edging the reef. The water was
murky green until they eased past the outer reef escarpment, where it changed to a pastel verdigris and
then deepened to blue-black as they reached open
ocean.

Back on the beach, they saw that the Landrover had
come back up the road and was stopped at the fork.
The men got out and lifted the dead body into the
vehicle. Then it swung around, throwing coral dust,
and sped back toward Nasugbu.

Cullin throttled up and turned north toward Subic.
The power of the Hall-Scotts rumbled through the deck
plates as the PT lifted her bow, planing, hurling back
deflection spray and cutting a wide white wake that
folded in, center peaking off the stern with the water
riffling smoke. Holding her at thirty knots, he and
Bonner rode the surging, bucking conn deck like skiers
as she attained the step, that point of skim where water

hurls out from mid hull. Beside them Liz hung on, white-faced, her red hair whipping in the wind.

Forty minutes later, Cullin, glassing the south channel of Manila Bay, lowered the binoculars and shouted to Cas: "We've got comp'ny, mate." He pointed northeast and handed over the glasses.

There were two police patrol boats, seventy-five-foot recommissioned sub chasers, cutting water just outside the bay entrance, headed toward the PT. They were colored a sun-bright yellow with red cross stripes and had the British-style open bridge. On their forward decks, each carried two 40mm pit guns and a .50-caliber on the bow.

The two men were alone on the conn, for earlier Bonner had had to help Liz below. She was horribly seasick and retching. He fixed up a mattress of netting on one of the old officer's bunks and placed a plastic bucket beside it. She crawled in miserably.

He watched her, shaking his head, feeling a mixture of sympathy and disdain. Miss bag-of-rocks Burlingame puking her guts out. He squatted and tapped her forehead. "Hey, honey, you know what helps seasickness? A greasy tuna sandwich."

"Oh, God!"

"Yeah, really. Oil dripping down, smelly as—"

She reared up, face contorted. "Get away from me, you—" The movement started another stomach spasm. She vomited bile into the plastic bucket. Panting, she glared at him, gray eyes quivering. "I'll kill you, I swear." She flopped back onto the bunk. He patted her on the head and returned to the conn deck.

Now Cullin yelled, "They look like they're huntin'." He gave Cas a grim smile.

Bonner nodded. "What can those boats do?"

"About forty knots in a sprint. We can show the nongs wake, but it won't matter. There's a station at Mariveles on Bataan Peninsula. We'd never clear through to Subic."

Cas was glassing farther into the bay. He could see

a vast, intricate network of bamboo fish traps along
the shores of Limit Point at the southern curve of the
entrance. They formed arrows and rectangles which
covered about two miles of offshore water. On the
outer fringe of the traps, its white hull shining through
the binoculars, was Stanford's sport cruiser.

"There's the son of a bitch," he hollered, pointing.
"Stanford."

Will nodded. "I see 'im. So let's test the patrollers.
We'll bear to seaward a mite, see what the bloody
barstids do." He threw a little helm and added throttle. The PT heeled slightly to port and picked up
speed. Ahead, the horizon of the South China Sea
stretched away in salt mist.

Instantly the two patrol boats altered their line of
interception. One angled off more sharply than the
other and headed almost straight out into the ocean.
The second came straight on, and through the binoculars Bonner saw men stripping canvas off the starboard 40mm gun.

"They're arming," he called.

Cullin gave him a hot-eyed grin. "I wonder how
good these flippin' *Bijaus* can handle weapon."

Two minutes later, there was a flash on the patrol
boat. They could hear the round coming over the rush
of the Hall-Scotts, a whooshing, cloth-ripping sibilance. It dropped into the ocean sixty yards ahead and
slightly to starboard, throwing up a thirty-foot geyser
that made flashing rainbows against the sun. A few
seconds later, the PT roared past the impact point,
catching a soft, misty shower and the smell of explosive.

Another round came in, this time landing astern.
Then the second patrol boat opened up, but its shot
fell far short to starboard. Cas nudged Will's arm and
yelled, "That's a good gunner on number one. He'll
bracket us sure if we hold our heading." Cullin nodded but held the PT on the same line, as if deliberately
teasing the patrol boats.

As Bonner watched, the boats began deploying. The

closer one was now less than a mile off. He saw the gunners scrambling to the .50-caliber machine gun. It made his heart jump lightly, singing. The explosive odor of the rounds, the whistling ripple as they came in, the roaring power of the Hall-Scotts, all made his body tingle with a burst of pure energy. He found himself grinning back hard at the Aussie with that crazy, undefinable bonding of men who were walking along the cold steel edge.

Will cursed with happy frustration. "Bloody damn, if I had some decent ordnance, I'd fair nick off that yobbo's forty-millimeter."

Two rounds came in almost simultaneously. One crossed directly overhead and *whomped* into the ocean, heaving water. The other landed forty yards off the starboard beam, and they felt the jolt of its impact come up through the hull.

"Time to show the barstids what a real brumbie can do," Will bellowed. He rammed the throttle to full and whirled the helm hard over. They went barreling into a port turn, the deck tilting so deeply Bonner had to grab a rail. And then the engines howled as the old PT lifted up full into the step, her deflection strakes hurling arcs of water, and a rooster tail rose ten feet in the air far astern.

Within ten minutes, they had left the patrol boats two miles behind. Both boats finally broke off the useless chase and turned back for the channel. Only the Triad cruiser kept on charging around Limit Point. But at last it too slowed and turned away.

Gazing with a belligerent, furious grin at the departing boats, Cullin eased off the throttle until they were again at cruising speed. He was hopping excitedly around the conn space like a boy who had just stolen a handful of apples and got clean away. "I'll bet them patrol skippers was chewin' spikes watchin' us shoot through like a bloody Bondi tram." He howled and waved his fist back at them.

Then, quieting, he turned to give Bonner a long, narrow look. "Well, mate, you've gone and got me in your stinkeroo full up now, han't ya? First my dog and now those bleeding constables'll be all over my diggin's like a rash. Won't be safe for me in these waters anymore.''

"I'm sorry, Will."

Cullin snorted. "Ach, it don' really matter, Casimir. My poor ole Tart was gettin' on anyhows. Besides, I'm about bored with these flamin' *bijaus* and their blinkin' *kakaraks* that muck up the shore waters."

The ocean began to smooth out in long swells as they entered the leeward calm off the Labang Islands and the great bulk of Mindoro, twenty-five miles to the southwest. The PT skimmed lightly across the troughs.

"I'll lay you and the sheilah off on the south coast of Mindoro," Cullin went on. "There's a U.S. Marine barracks there at San Jose. They'll rack you up secure enough."

"And you?"

"It's walkabout time for me, mate. Think I'll gawk out the Celebes or maybe Java-roo, see what's doin'." Then his face went stiff, the muscles of his jaw making downward curves like the honed edge of an unsheathed hatchet. "But first, an eye for a bleedin' eye. I'm gonna pick me up some decent ordnance from the Junkman, and then I'll find that pisser boat of your Mister Stanford and put the bloody thing on the bottom."

A slow smile formed on Bonner's face. "Not you, we," he shouted back. "I got a score to settle too."

Cullin looked at him and then threw his head back and laughed. "I knew you couldn't resist, you crazy Yank, ya."

7

Chan Mung was a Yellow Pole, a 525 in the Beijing cell of the Green Tigers. This designated him as an incense master, the one who presided over initiation rites and read the thirty-six oaths to new members of the clan. It was he who killed the sacrificial cock with a sword and then mixed its blood with wine for them to drink, he who subjected them to the deadly act of Crossing the Mountain of Knives.

He stood in Minister Litung's office in the Cultural Palace of Nationalities and glared at the chief of the secret police. Chan was a small, middle-aged Chinese dressed in dark gray trousers and a freshly pressed white linen shirt buttoned at the throat. He wore two gold dragon rings on his little finger.

Like Litung's apartment, his office was spartan. The teak desk, though large, was unadorned. Beside it was a bookcase containing volumes on espionage and counter-espionage, battle tactics, guerrilla warfare and ordnance, historical books on famous battles of the world. They were in English, Russian and German, all of which Litung spoke fluently. The walls were bare except for crossed Chinese battle lances over the door.

For nearly three minutes, Litung ignored Chan's presence. Behind the minister a large window gave out onto Changan Avenue, where women street sweepers were cleaning the pavement wearing surgical masks against the Gobi dust.

Two hours before, flying squads of Litung's secret

police had raided fifteen Green Tiger cells throughout China, from the jungles of Kunming in the far south, to the railhead towns of Shenyang in the north, in Shanghai and out on the far western frontier of Sinkiang, where desert caravans came up the Long Road from Afghanistan hauling processed heroin. Now over three hundred and fifty Tigers were being held in detention barracks throughout the nation.

At last Minister Litung closed the folder he had been studying and slowly lifted his eyes to Chan. He studied him evenly. "You are kin-brother to Chan Chao." It was not a question. Chan Chao was the Green Tiger vice-chieftain, directly below Chung Ma, who was Dragon Head of all the Tigers and lived in Taiwan.

Chan snorted. "You know. Why ask?"

Litung's eyes went absolutely flat. "You are also insolent."

Chan snorted again, but this time his feet shifted restlessly.

After a moment Litung said, "You will send a message to your brother. Unless our . . . arrangement is successful, all your men taken today will be executed immediately."

Chan's face stiffened but he said nothing.

"Do you understand?"

"I know of no arrangement."

"Give him the message."

"If I refuse?"

"Then you will die now, right here."

The incense master tried to hold Litung's eyes but couldn't. He had seen the threat of death in many eyes, but this man's gaze held a frigid, dinosauric intensity that filled him with fear. He jerked his head in a nod. "I will give him the message."

The little helicopter skimmed two hundred feet above the road as it wound through the rugged Halcon Mountains on the island of Mindoro. The road formed the single link across the mountain spine that divided the island, running from the capital at Victoria to the western coastal towns of Sablayan and Pandant.

Aboard the two-man chopper, Jack Stanford moodily watched the jungle below. It was late evening, but far to the west there still remained a veneer of scarlet in the sky. Below, the jungled peaks and steep, misty ravines of the mountains appeared to be covered with an impenetrable blanket of green-black fungus.

Jack's normal finger-snapping, can-do style had been dampened ever since he watched Cullin's PT racing away from him. It was heading for the Verde Island Passage that separated Mindoro from Luzon and led to the twin seas of Sibuyan and Visaya. There was a lot of water in that direction, he knew, with reef islands that could hide a boat forever.

For a while he had felt panic-stricken. Everything going down the tube because of a derelict rum pot and a jerkoff named Bonner. He could feel forces beginning to sweep out of his control. Then he settled, rode with it. There was time, he kept telling himself.

He had immediately gotten on the phone to Babiyan. He didn't mince words: "I want contact with your Muslim brothers of the Moro National Liberation Front on Mindoro."

"Not possible," Babiyan came right back. "The MNLF only operates in Mindanao and the southern islands."

"Bullshit. You had three Moro raids on Mindoro two months ago."

Aguinaldo was silent a moment. Then: "You create extreme danger for me."

"I don't give a shit, Babiyan," Jack roared. "I want a meet with one of the heavy chiefs in charge of Moro Sibuyan Sea operations. Now! And don't be fuckin' me around with some petty *barangay* captain. I want the guy who gives the orders."

Finally Aguinaldo sighed. "All right, I'll set it up. But no names. Where are you now?"

"Still on the bay."

"Come in at Naic. I'll have my personal pilot waiting for you there."

"Give me thirty minutes."

"Be cautioned, Stanford: go unarmed. These Moros hate Americans almost as much as the communists do." He snickered grimly. "Frankly, I hope they cut your penis off and stuff it up your ass."

Stanford laughed. "Yeah, I love you too."

Aguinaldo hung up. . . .

The last traces of scarlet were darkening as the helicopter dipped slightly. They left the main road, following a double oxen path in the jungle grass beneath the trees. As they traveled this route, they were enveloped among the mountains. In the increasing moonlight, feathery waterfalls cascaded hundreds of feet down steep cliffs into mist.

Finally the pilot spotted a small, open meadow with a marker fire. They hovered, and then lowered swiftly, the meadow grass whipping in the downwash. They settled and the pilot cut back the power to idle.

Stanford got out and paused, waiting for the pilot to get out too. The man shook his head. "You go alone. Up dat road with yo' hands on yo' head."

He started off, walking quickly. All around him the jungle was silent save for the even, slow slice of the helo blades. The grass was soaking wet and soon his trousers were too. As he advanced, his eyes darted back and forth, scanning.

The road dropped slightly into a ravine. Moonlight filtered by the trees sparkled on a a small stream showing rocks on the bed and strands of moss that flowed like a woman's hair. He started up the other side of the ravine and stopped. Two men were standing on the lip. In the moonlight he saw they wore turbans and each carried M-16s with chest bandoliers.

He didn't move. The men came silently down and walked around him. One probed his clothes with the muzzle of his M-16, searching for a weapon. Satisfied, he motioned for Stanford to move ahead.

The Moro encampment was on a small rise, several

lean-tos made of gayape trunks with coconut branches spread out for a floor. In one was a large radio encased in army field green canvas with a tall whip antenna. There were fifteen men in military fatigues kneeling in prayer, eyes closed, hands cupped in front of their faces. Their weapons were stacked nearby.

Beyond the lean-tos three women were cooking over an open fire which created no smoke. One was very pretty, with black slacks and a striped blue blouse opened so that a baby hiked onto one hip could suckle her left breast. The fire threw orange patterns on the jungle trees.

The men with Stanford stepped around him and stacked their weapons, then knelt beside the others. As he watched, one of the women brought a tray of cups made of palm leaves and filled with water. She placed one in front of each man, then went back to the cooking fires.

The man on the left was thin, with a sparse goatee. His dark brown face, even in prayerful repose, looked alert, like a ferret's. He alone wore a white turban. He began to wash his hands in the water, murmuring softly. The others did likewise. Three times they washed, rinsing their mouths and snuffling their nostrils in the water. Then they washed their faces, also three times, and preened their hair, mustaches and goatees.

At last they poured out the water and lifted their faces to heaven. In the Balanai dialect they chanted: "I witness that there is no god but God the Unique, Who has no partner. I witness that Muhammad is His servant and His messenger."

When the prayer was over, the women began to serve the food, a salted fish and tomato stew called *ginamos*. The men ate quietly, all except the leader. He turned and looked at Stanford, studying him narrowly for a long moment before finally snapping his hand for him to come in.

"I am Ka Lakas," the leader said. "Why do you come here?"

"To offer you a proposition."

"What will I benefit?"

Stanford glanced at the stacked M-16s. "May I look at one of your weapons?"

Ka Lakas's eyes bore into his face. Then he nodded.

Jack walked over and picked up one of the assault rifles. He slammed back the ejector, popping a round, and peered into the breech. He tilted it so he could see inside. It was rusty. He flicked a finger into the breech and ran it along the vent bevel, then held it up to the firelight. "Metal rot," he said. "These weapons will soon be useless."

The men watched him wordlessly as he released the ejector and replaced the M-16. He walked back to Ka Lakas and planted himself directly in front. "I can supply you with one thousand new M-16s and twenty-five thousand rounds of ammunition."

This announcement stirred quick glances among the men. Only Ka Lakas's gaze did not waver. "And what do I do for you?"

"Find a boat. An old American torpedo boat owned by a man named Cullin."

"I know of this man. Years ago I purchased ammunition from him in Mindanao. He had a sailboat then."

"I don't care about Cullin. I want a woman he carries into the Sibuyan. I know you have fast boats and know these coasts. If he's there, you can find him."

Ka Lakas thought a moment, then scooped some of the *ginamos* with his fingers and ate slowly. "Babiyan says you are with the Chinese."

"Not with them. I merely use their services."

"I hate Chinese. They're all thieves."

"Agreed. But they will be the means by which you get the weapons and ammunition. Babiyan will oversee the transactions."

Ka Lakas grunted and wiped stew juice from his mouth. "Babiyan's a thief too."

"But a Muslim."

The Filipino nodded. "Still, I need good faith."

"May I touch my coat?"

"Yes."

Jack withdrew a small package wrapped in oil paper. He held it out. Ka Lakas jerked his head to one of the men who had met Jack in the ravine. Rising, he took the package and opened it. It contained bound stacks of U.S. currency, in thousand-dollar units.

"That's one hundred thousand dollars, American. The rest Babiyan will give you to pay the Chinese."

The Filipino stared at the money, then smiled for the first time. He eyed Jack for another long moment. "How do you know I won't kill you and take your money?"

"First, because you're a Muslim and a Muslim's word is his honor. Second, that won't buy you what the whole of it will."

Ka Lakas's grin widened. He turned and said something in dialect to the others. They laughed.

"One other gift," Stanford said. "If you capture the torpedo boat and bring it to me, I'll take from it what I need. Only one small item. Then the boat is yours."

The Filipino's eyes flashed over that proposition. Possessing such a boat, having the speed to outrun anything the Philippine government threw at him, was an irresistible lure. He drew back his lips, showing his teeth.

"Do you want Cullin and this woman alive?"

"No."

"Done," Ka Lakas said.

Liz crawled around in dark dreams for what seemed like endless periods of time. There were long corridors and fall-off points through which she dropped into abysses that suddenly opened and came up at her, jarring as she struck into feathery cloth. She awoke and the darkness was still there: pounding, roaring, with the stink of gasoline fumes. She was covered with perspiration. For a terrifying moment she couldn't remember where she was or how she had gotten there. Abyss!

She lifted her head, tried to rise. Nausea uncoiled in her stomach like a waiting snake, and the rest of it came back with the strike. She gagged, felt the acid tang of bile rise in her mouth. Frantically she searched through the dark for the bucket, couldn't find it, and retched over the side of the bunk. She fell back, her head pounding.

A moment later a light came on and Bonner climbed through the hatchway. As he squatted beside her, his body rolled and bobbed with the lunge of the boat. He studied her a moment. "How you feelin', newsie?" he asked, eyes dancing mischievously.

"Oh God, shitty."

"Well, hang on. We'll be putting into San Jose in about two hours."

"I don't care where we go. Just get me off this damned boat."

He grinned and left, leaving the light on. She closed her eyes and listened to her body, drenched all over with sweat. Her misery made convoluted thoughts which seemed to exacerbate the nausea, like a drunk with the world spinning off at crazy angles. Scared, she opened her eyes again and looked around.

The cabin was as small as a closet, full of brace work and tar patches and the wet-paper smell of old wood. Everywhere was the steady rumbling of the engines, a thunder echoing down through high canyon walls. But then the sound abated, trailing off into a gentle, throaty rumble. The violent lifting and pounding of the hull softened, dropping into a momentary hiss that came through the bulkheads as the PT's bow drifted off the step and once more drew water.

Liz inhaled the acrid air thankfully, felt her body being massaged delicately now by the bunk springs. Then, suddenly, over the thrumming growl of the engines came the powerful crack of gunfire and wood splintering. Someone cursed, the sound seeming distant and outraged. She bolted upright, grabbing for the bulkhead.

The Moros had come at them in a lightning strike, three twin-hulled canoes with powerful stern outboards running without lights. The PT had just passed the finger peninsula of Bulalacao on the southeastern tip of Mindoro. Bonner was on the conn, and at Cullin's instructions had closed the throttle to idle as he navigated through the tricky reef shallows which extended between the peninsula and Libagao Island. Will was below, running an engine check.

The first burst took coaming and side plate off the control space, hurling splinters of plywood. Cas felt a tiny shaft slice across his deltoid muscle, cutting into his skin. He jerked back against the backrest and heard the canoes gunning past in the darkness.

Another burst of automatic fire zipped over the conn deck and he rolled forward, feeling stickiness on his shoulder. In another instant he realized the rounds were coming in high, avoiding punctures to the hull and engine room. Their target was the helm watch. That meant they wanted the boat intact.

He reached up and jammed the throttles full forward. There was a moment of hesitation as the Hall-Scotts' superchargers lit up. And then the PT leaped forward, her bow swinging crazily as she surged into power without solid helm.

A moment later Cullin scrambled up between the protection shield and the conn hub. He crouched over, squinting at Bonner. "You hit, mate?"

"It's nothing. I think they're after the boat."

"That they are, the bloody rotters. Swing heavy to port and bring her up."

In the next burst of gunfire, the bullets sizzled overhead, sounding like droplets of water dripped onto a hot grill. The helm was jumping and swinging violently. Cas braced his elbows and steadied up. By now the PT was screaming over the water, her rooster tail erupting astern as the propeller surges came up off the reef.

He lifted his head slightly to peer over the jagged edge of the coaming. Just as he did, there was a violent jolt and things began flying back off the bow, silhouetted against starlight. Chunks of wood and metal and one solid impact that was the body of a man. It wheeled off and away, skidding over the side. He had rammed one of the canoes.

On they flew. From astern the gunfire became sporadic, finally diminishing altogether. Cullin pulled himself up onto the control panel. "Here, mate, I'll take 'er," he shouted over the engines.

Cas eased aside, feeling the sticky, hot touch of blood rolling down his shoulder. Wiping it away, he felt around for the wound. It was small but it burned. He glanced at Will. "Who the hell were those pricks? Pirates?"

"No, Moro *paraus,*" Cullin shouted back. "Pirates don't work these northern waters."

Something scraped loudly along the bottom of the PT's hull. A soft, crunching sound as the boat crossed over forming coral pinnacles and trailing seaweed. They were entering dangerous reef upthrusts.

"Bloody hell," Cullin cursed. Hands flying over the control panel, he instantly killed the two outboard engines, rammed the transmission chains into single-idle, and hauled off the throttle on the center engine. Coming out of power, it popped and rumbled throaty bubbles from the stern. The boat dropped off the step immediately, trembling slightly as they glided forward on nearly pure momentum. At last they were almost dead in the water.

Both men squinted out at the dark water, trying to spot coral heads and channels. If they rammed into a large one now, it would only be a matter of minutes before the Moro canoes reached them. Moon glow made the ocean shimmer and tremble, and it was difficult picking out flow lines across the shallows.

Slowly, Will eased the PT around until they were

headed northeast. They went on that way for ten minutes. Then, over the steady, isolated hum of the single engine, they could hear the distant, high whine of the Moro boats coming again. Cullin kept turning around and cursing, then he'd pause, his head tilted, listening to the rebound sound of the prop coming through water.

Cas darted below. When he returned, he was carrying Will's shotgun and the Walther. Liz, her face pale and strained, came up with him, asking questions. He ignored her and went around to the port side, where he hunkered down next to the curving barrel base of the old .50-caliber gun pit. Liz crawled after him and squeezed up against his back. "Is it—my God, you're bleeding! You've been shot!"

"A wood sliver. Get below."

She was dodging her head, trying to see over his shoulder out over the stern. "Is it Stanford?"

"Get below."

"What if we sink? I don't want to be down there if we sink."

"We won't sink."

"I hear motors."

"Shut up."

The whine of the engines drew closer. Two powerful lights suddenly flashed in the darkness, the beams jerking and jacking across the water. They were about a mile away.

"Oh, look, look!" Liz cried.

Cas shrugged his shoulders angrily. "Will you get off me?"

Liz didn't move.

Cullin was playing the engine now, giving throttle, easing off, hitting again. Slowly the sound of the propeller changed, from the spread-out, hollow return as its turbulence rebounded off the reef to a deeper, more isolated resonance, the water absorbing the wash.

Gunfire erupted. "Oh, shit," Liz cried, digging her head into Bonner's spine. Still, the sound of the firing was far away, no more than the popping chatter of fiercely burning logs. Several rounds ricocheted off the surface but fell short.

Cas extricated himself from her hold and scooted aft along the engine coaming. He paused near the stump of an old 37mm mount, head cocked, listening to the single prop. It was still deep and throaty. Suddenly it pitched up again as they crossed over coral heads right under the surface. That lasted for only a few seconds and then the sound deeped once more, this time indicating very deep water. Cullin instantly restarted the dead engines and all three, superchargers blowing, roared up into full power.

They quickly left the probing lights far astern.

Finally Cas, with Liz right behind him, returned to the control space. Will was grinning away and yelled in his ear, "A close cock-up, that one."

"Who were those people?" Liz shouted.

Bonner moved up beside Cullin. "Can we still make San Jose?"

The Aussie shook his head. "We'd have to run the Ambulong Channel. They could stoush us firm in those shallows."

Liz grabbed Bonner's arm. "Will somebody tell me who those people were?"

"Moros," Cas said.

"Moros? Who's that?"

"We've got fuel enough to reach the Semirara Islands off Panay," Will shouted. "I know a bloke who's head ratchet on a drilling rig off Tinabooc. We can refuel there."

"Who are Moros?"

Cullin answered her: "Muslims, missy."

"But why would they want to harm us?"

"Them was Ka Lakas's boys back there. I know him, the thievin' swinkie. But he'd never run on me unless he had a deal."

"Stanford?" Bonner said.

Cullin nodded, his face lean and dark in the glow from the panel lights. "That king dick's got more squeeze than I figured. We're gonna have to watch our arses from here on out, mate. Them Moro *paraus* is thick as flies on a dead rat from here to the Celebes Sea.''

He cut the power to cruise speed and swung the head of the PT until she lined up toward the southeast. They ran smoothly now, for the ocean leeward of Mindoro was almost glassy.

An hour later, they spotted the occulated bursts from the Buenavista light station on the southern tip of Tablas Island. Cullin adjusted so they would clear well east of Tablas. The PT's bow pointed due south now, straight for the Semiraras, deep in the Subiyan Sea.

8

When Ka Lakas radioed the *Flying Sun* to report the unsuccessful attack on the PT, Stanford's frustration was so fierce it sent him steaming around the cabin. Good Christ in heaven, he thought furiously, the whole fucking world is inept. Chinks, Fils, and now the Moros, all dumbass incompetents not worth shit.

He hated inefficiency, missed cues and imperfect timing. The whole beauty of a well-planned operation was how slick it went. Unexpected glitches he could handle, but not total screw-ups.

In the captain's chair, Big Willie watched him lugubriously while the Unicorn sat at the bar, looking stoned-bemused. Jack glanced at him. He'd known the man for over a year, and he couldn't remember ever seeing anything but that cool, distant grin on his face. He seemed to find everything absurdly humorous.

Yet Stanford knew there would be more growls from the Tiger heads over this latest example of Keystone Kops shit. And when Yue Fei got wind of it, what then? How much patience would that one have?

Stanford had never forgotten his first and only meeting with the man he knew only as Yue Fei. It had been an eerie encounter, in an opium den in Hong Kong. During the entire meeting he hadn't seen the Chinaman's face, but he felt the ominous power. This was not the butcher shop aura of the Tiger warlords. No, Yue Fei's power was decidedly purer, surgically lethal.

His initial contacts on this particular operation had

been Tigermen, people he'd gotten to know back when he was still with the DEA in Chiang Mai. At the time the place was still boiling with competing drug lords. Ex-officers from Chiang Kai-Shek's Kuomintang who had been pushed out of southern China with their field armies still intact. American deserters from Nam with operations in Bangkok. And contending Triad gangs, the Yellow Suns and Night Knives and Tigers, with their convoluted ceremonies and numbers used for names and status, all the digits evenly divisible by the number nine. Everybody challenged everybody while a deluge of heroin packets bearing the Double U-O or 999 or Lion trademarks flooded out into all of Southeast Asia and through Corsican connections into the markets of southern Europe and Amsterdam.

Stanford had rejoiced in the heady atmosphere of *fongehe*, the spinning wheel which the Chinese called their dealing. It energized his mind, created continual opportunities. He took advantage of them, just as he had when he had been DEA in Colombia and the barrios of southern Florida, or back with American Intelligence in Italy and Holland. By possessing a dead-eye knack for ferreting out the real sources of power, coupled with the ability to read trends, he had chosen to align himself with the Green Tigers. He'd been correct: they were now the dominant force in the Golden Triangle drug business.

So when he'd gotten the first mind-blowing glimpse of the present operation, he'd gone directly to Lui, who passed him on up the Tiger line. Eventually he got to the Dragon Head, a lawyer from Hong Kong named Chung Ma, who had been deported to Taiwan. He lived in a palatial home on a hill overlooking T'aitung Bay and controlled billions of dollars in illegal drugs, women and weapons.

They drank cinnamon tea on a terrace with carved cement dragons forming the coils of the railing. The sun was warm and an ocean breeze wafted over them. At last Chung lit a dark, gold-tipped cigarette and said, "What is it you want from me?"

"Your help in getting high-up introductions to your contacts within the Corsican Red Brothers organization." The Red Brothers dominated Mediterranean drug traffic, and Stanford knew the Tigers did business with them.

"To what purpose?"

"I want their access to the terrorist heads in the Middle East." He went on to explain his plan in detail, drawing astonished glances from the drug lord. In return for Chung's help, Stanford pointed out, he would turn over his powerful contacts in America, who could supply secret DEA data on the Colombian drug cartel and its lines of movement into the western United States. With such information the Tigers could take over Colombian control and eventually supplant its network of cocaine supply with their own China White heroin.

Chung Ma eased himself out of his chair and prowled around the terrace, studied the wake forming behind a fishing boat far down on the sea. At last he turned slightly. "You go back to Chiang Mai. I will call you."

A week later, the call came. It was right to the point: "Go to Hong Kong, stay in the Mandarin Oriental hotel."

Stanford did, sat around for another two days until a short, very fat Chinese man showed up. He called himself Sammy. He was dressed in a green silk sports jacket and snakeskin loafers.

He took him to Ladder Street in the heart of Hong Kong. The street was all steps, chiseled out in the 1800s so sedan-chair bearers could traverse its short length to the English mansions on Caine Road above it. It was packed with tiny shops filled with porcelains and blackwood furniture and incense.

They turned down an alley. It led to Hollywood Road and the Thieves Market, and smelled of feces and garbage and tar. They stopped at an ancient house with a balcony and delicate carvings on the door. Inside, Sammy took him up a flight of stairs. A young man with a shaven head was standing guard before another door.

He and Sammy spoke a moment, then he let them into a dimly lit room with curtains pulled over the windows. There was a single red light bulb hanging nakedly from the ceiling. Wooden bunks covered with dirty mats lined the walls. Old men were stretched on the platforms, smoking opium with long-stemmed pipes and holding their gurgling bowls over tiny lamp flames. The air was smoky and smelled sweet like rotted roses.

Sammy nodded toward a dark corner. Stanford could see the dim outline of a man sitting upright in a chair. He walked over. He couldn't see the man's face, but the erect, shadowy body told him it wasn't Chung Ma. That didn't surprise him. He had expected someone from the Mideast.

He waited silently.

At last the man said, "You have a scheme?"

Jack was surprised at finding the voice Chinese. "Yes."

"Explain it to me."

Jack thought: Who the hell is this guy? One of Chung's men? No, the air of authority was too strong. This wasn't a flunky. "Who are you?" he asked.

"You need not know that. Explain your plan."

Stanford studied the twist here. If this joker wasn't Chung's man, then he must be somebody higher up. But who the hell was higher than a top Tiger head?

He considered the ramifications. If he dealt with this man, it would mean some alterations in his plan, primarily in funding sources and coordinating parties. But then he realized that this obviously more powerful man could make things run smoother. Well, hell, he thought, did it really matter who the paymaster was?

So he laid the plan out again, even going into more detail than he had with Chung Ma. The man listened without interrupting. When Stanford finished, there was a full two minutes of silence.

Then: "What would be the percentage of success?"

"With the proper help, a full hundred."

"This Frenchman Gallaudet, who you are relying on so heavily. I have looked into his background. He's in disgrace."

"Exactly. And, as I said, a cocaine addict. That's why he'll do it."

"Such a man could prove unreliable."

"He won't. I'll be holding his stash, so he'll do anything I tell him."

Again the man fell silent. Jack could feel his gaze coming through the smoky red mist like invisible beams of pure light. Finally the Chinaman shot another question: "How much do you want?"

"Five hundred million, U.S. Unmarked bills."

The man shook his head slowly. "Like all Americans, you are greedy."

"This is a big bag."

There was another stretch of silence. Stanford felt perspiration slipping down the small of his back. He was starting to become lightheaded from the opium smoke. He shifted his feet. Come on, buddy, he thought.

The man said, "Agreed."

"Will I still have complete Tiger assistance?"

"Yes."

"How do we handle the cash?"

"It will be deposited in a Swiss bank. Activation of the account will begin after the successful culmination of your efforts."

"Fair enough." He paused. Then he thought: Let's see if this guy really is as big as he seems. "I'll need one other thing, Chung Ma's personal word."

The man snorted contemptuously. "Chung obeys me."

There it was.

"Okay," he said.

The man leaned forward slightly, just enough to shift the red shadows on his face, making it appear like a ghoul's mask. "Remember one thing, American. They die, or you die." Then his hand flicked, dismissing him. Jack hesitated a moment, thought better of it, and turned back to Sammy, who was standing near the door, fanning the opium fumes out of his face. . . .

Stanford's thoughts homed back to the *Flying Sun* and with them came a sudden burst of energy and renewed hope. He moved quickly over to Big Willie. "Keep heading south," he said. "We'll find that Aussie cocksucker if we have to search the whole goddamned archipelago for him."

Angus Porter, the barrel-chested, pugnacious head operating engineer for the Seascape One, had had his fill of foreign security people. "Bloody wonks prowl around the hotel like dingoes," he muttered, "poking into everything and swilling up free slops as if they owned the bleeding place." To top it off, the government had ordered that the hotel staff wear name tags. Like kindergarten kiddies, he thought. And soon he'd be getting KGB men and chinks from Beijing. Christ only knew what they'd be like.

At the moment Angus was standing just outside the main entrance of the hotel, morosely watching the last boatload of paying guests depart from the main causeway slip. The SS Corporation is certainly getting the short end of the pineapple on this one, he thought disgustedly. A whole week donated away for a bunch of hoons who'd get nothing done.

His gaze lifted and he studied the whipping branches of the low Samoan palms out on the concourse. Beyond, the waters of the Maxwelton Shoals were already quivering with white caps, and the wind carried the chill tang of rain.

Back in the huge main lobby, done all in imperial blues and silver, he moved to the front desk and called Control. "What's the forecast?" he barked, bitterly eyeing two Americans in newly bought Sydney shorties stroll past with drinks in their hands. Their legs were as white as the bellies of dying fish.

"Projected winds south-southeast, running forty knots in about six hours, Angus. She's already pushin' twenty knots. We'd best start cleanin' her up now instead of waiting for dawn.''

"Aye."

"As soon as the jockey boat's clear, we'll seal the tubes and vacate the outer deck.''

"Aye."

Fifteen minutes later, he was in the main chain room, sweating in scuba gear. The room and everything in it was painted a frothy sea green. The drum casings and panel boards were polished until they gleamed in the overhead fluorescents. Faintly he could hear the steady *wa-wa* of the clearance horn on the outer deck.

He instructed the watch operator to stand by for repositioning clearance, and then walked down a narrow corridor to a heavy steel door. Beyond it was a network of catwalks and a small landing on the outer side of the main flood tanks which formed the hotel's foundation. Two other divers were waiting for him. He slipped on his mask, and all three dropped into the water.

As they did, a series of high-powered floodlights strung along the entire bottom of the hotel's base came on. Angus stroked for the bottom thirty feet below. The other divers headed away, one to monitor the main anchor, the second to check wharf and tube disengagement.

The sounds of the reef came up to Porter, a vast scattering of clicks and soft, throaty *thungs* mingling with the ripple of surf. All of it rebounded off the massive underside of the hotel, which deepened the sound. He reached the bottom and skimmed along, pulling himself by coral heads. Above him the hotel floated, its concentric rings of floodlights making it look like the spaceship in *Close Encounters of the Third Kind*.

Directly ahead was the after-anchor foundation column. It was a shaft of cement twenty feet in diameter that had been sunk deep into the reef, down to basalt. Around it were three steel bands, each a yard thick, to which the anchor chain was triple bolted. The chain itself was gigantic, each link taller than a standing man and as thick as a twelve-pounder cannon. It was made of titanium-impregnated steel which had been forge-tempered fifty times. It, like the cement column, was encrusted with barnacles and lichens and draped in tendrils of sea moss.

A powerful, hollow whoosh rolled through the water as Control set the compression seals through the viewing tube and main dock fitting, preparatory to full disengagement. Porter squeezed his throat buttons, activating his radio. "Control, One, how's it look?"

"Everything on Green, One." The sound came down tinnily through the small speaker inside his mask. "Pressure standard on T and W fittings. Standing by to full disengage."

He heard the other divers reporting in, then keyed again: "Control, One, everything looks dinky-di down here. Go for full D and S."

"Going for full D and S," Control repeated.

He could hear the soft rumble of the chain drums riffle through the water, and then the aft chain went slightly slack, metal screeching against the main bolts as tension came off. A wispy cloud of crushed barnacles and sea moss dusted the water.

Angus moved around, watching the drop of the slack. He keyed: "Control, you've got 'er bang on. Now let 'er weathervane a bit." He saw the slack loop stiffen with tension again as the hotel shifted to the wind, coming up slowly, throwing another cloud off the bolt fittings.

"Good—good. Stand by." While the other divers reported the status in their sectors, he swam over to the bolt head and examined it closely. Everything was fine. He backpedaled and hovered, keying: "Control, give 'er another go."

For the next forty minutes, they worked the hotel around, giving increments of slack and then letting the wind pull the structure taut again. Topside, Control reported that the wind velocity had increased to twenty-six knots and that the Seascape was weather-vaning nicely.

At compass position one hundred sixty-five degrees, the hotel revolved dead into the main thrust of the wind, and they locked her snug. Angus made one final inspection of his sector, then headed for the out platform.

As he pulled himself up, he noticed two men watching him, the same two he'd seen upstairs. He noted that their name tags pinned to their shorts identified them as American Naval Intelligence. They tried to help him up, but he shook them off angrily.

"Damn!" one said. "This is one slick operation you got here, Porter."

Angus ripped off his mask. "What the bloody hell are you two dingoes doin' down here?"

"We came to check things out."

"Listen, when your bleedin' president arrives, then you can come pokin'. Until then, bugger the hell off!"

The heated shower water was like ambrosia as it rushed over Liz's face, down the length of her body. She turned, luxuriating in it, felt her skin come alive under the steamy flow, dissipating the nausea of seasickness. The smooth, lubricated sensation of the soap was almost sexual.

Twenty minutes before, Cullin had brought the PT alongside the Celebes Oil Company's offshore drilling rig number 348, four miles from the main island of the Samiraras. A huge platform full of lights, it looked like a carnival in the middle of the ocean.

The rig's tool pusher, a loud, red-haired Irishman named Tom Connelly, welcomed Cullin with a huge guffaw. "Well, looka what the sea's thrown into mi lap."

Liz came off the PT as unsteadily as a recuperating accident victim, testing the metal decking of the drilling rig with a sigh of relief. She'd misplaced her shoes, so Connelly brought her a pair of rubber tennies. "You don't walk on bare metal here, lass," he cautioned.

"A power short could blow your lovely titties right through your ears."

Wincing at the memory, she shifted under the shower. That was the sort of obscene, wiseass remark Bonner would make, she thought. Well, soon she'd be rid of that one and glad of it. Or would she? With a little jerk of surprise, she realized she wasn't sure. Why not, for God's sake? she wondered. The man was a barbarian.

Yet she had to admit he was big and gloriously sexy with a kind of manhood she'd never encountered before. Guys like him and Cullin ran on trip triggers, deliberately sticking out their chins to challenge the world. They were nothing like the corporate hyenas who prowled the corridors of Channel 10.

But that didn't make Cas any less irritating, she thought. She recalled their last conversation, when he'd informed her that they would be leaving her on the drilling platform. As usual, it had been infuriating.

"Connelly says you can hitch a ride on his supply boat in two days," Cas said. "It'll take you to Roxas City on Panay Island. You can charter a plane from there to Australia."

"Wonderful. But what am I supposed to use for money?"

"Call your daddy," Cas said, deadpan.

Bristling, she snapped, "God, what do you do, take lessons on being obnoxious?"

"The target draws the arrow."

"What the hell does that mean? No, wait, don't tell me." She glared at him. "Why don't you just say it outright? You don't like me."

"I don't like you."

Surprisingly, that hurt. "Why not?"

"You're an albatross."

"I see, okay, so you'll be free of me now. That make you happy?"

"Ecstatically."

"Get away from me."

She opened her eyes again and with a shock saw

someone standing just outside the open shower stall.
It was a woman in grimy work coveralls, her blond
hair imprinted with the ring of a hardhat liner.

"Oh!" Liz said and smiled, faintly embarrassed.
"Hi."

The woman tossed a bundle of clothes onto a nearby
toilet seat. "I brung you a change, luv." Then she
folded her arms and looked Liz up and down in slow
appraisal. "Well, you're top sort, ain' ya? You'll make
the blokes ogle, you will."

Liz retreated behind the flow of water, feeling suddenly exposed. The woman snorted with vague con-
tempt. "Bloody good thing you won't be with us long,
aye, luv?"

"Who are you?"

"Connie's the name."

Liz turned off the shower and reached for her towel.
Connie handed it to her. As her hand pulled back, she
lightly flicked her forefinger against Liz's right nipple,
stinging it.

"Ow, dammit," Liz snapped.

Connie gave her a hard grin. "Don' like that, luv?
Well, the *bijaus* likely to give you a bleedin' sight
more." She turned and walked out.

Liz dried quickly, hand brushing her hair tightly onto
her head. Connie had left her a pair of shorts and a
light sweater. She dressed and started out the door,
then remembered the tennis shoes and came back to
put them on. They were too big and smacked absurdly
against the steel deck.

Outside, she wandered around for a few minutes,
lost in metal corridors and endless side rooms filled
with machinery and drilling gear. At last she found a
large mess room with tables covered with sheets of
stainless steel. Bonner and Cullin were eating, with
Connelly watching.

The tool pusher turned and flashed her a wide Gallic
grin. "Ah, here's the lass." He took her hand and
ushered her gallantly to a seat beside Bonner, then
signaled a sweaty little Tonganese with a head like a

wrinkled melon, who immediately brought her a large bowl of stew.

She attacked it, shoveling it in heaping spoonfuls. It was tart, curried, and hit her stomach with pleasant fire. After a while she leaned over to Bonner and whispered, "There's something not right here."

He dipped his head. "What?"

"Some steely-eyed broad named Connie just talked to me. She said something that—well, sounded funny."

"Forget it."

"No, I'm telling you—" She stopped in mid-sentence, noticing that Connelly's eyes had darted to her. Then he quickly turned back to Will, who was in the middle of a story about hauling a boatload of whores to New Caledonia. She put the spoon into her mouth and chewed thoughtfully. She went back over what Connie had said, trying to pinpoint what had struck her as odd. *The* bijaus *likely to give you a bleedin' sight more.*

"What's a *bijau?*" she asked Cas softly.

"Mm?"

"A *bijau,* what is it?"

"A Filipino."

Her eyes slid over to Connelly's face, and suddenly her sixth sense went *bing!*

The three men were laughing at the finish of Cullin's story. Then Bonner and Will rose, Connelly jumping up, and Cas put his hand on her shoulder. "Well, good luck, sweetheart. See you around."

"Wait," she whispered harshly. "Don't go yet." Again she saw Connelly staring at her and she shut up instantly. The men went out, leaving her with a dire sense of aloneness and vulnerability. She turned around to face the little Tonganese. He was washing dishes in a huge sink. "Excuse me, is there a telephone around here I can use for a long-distance call?"

The dishwasher looked up. "No calls unless cleared by foreman."

She gave him a bright smile. "Oh, he wouldn't mind, would he?"

The man shrugged and pointed a soapy finger toward a side hallway. "Radio room that way."

She left the mess room and went into the hall. It was narrower than the others and had conduit lines up on the ceiling, each painted a different color. The floor trembled softly with the vibration of distant machinery.

At the end of the hall were several small rooms. In one she saw radio equipment and a very tall, shirtless man sitting before a large transceiver, his feet up on the console table. His head snapped around as she stepped in.

"Hello," she said, smiling. "They said I could make an overseas telephone call from here?"

He shook his head. It was covered with thick, shiny black hair that curled over his neck. "Sorry, the blower gear's down."

"How about the radio?"

"That too." He continued to stare coldly at her.

She shrugged and went back into the hall. Halfway to the mess room, she turned and saw the radioman standing in his doorway, watching her. Finally he stepped back into the room.

On an impulse she snuck back up the hall and paused a few feet from the radio room door. She could hear the man talking inside: ". . . right, she was in here wantin' to make a bleedin' overseas call."

Connelly's voice came back hard from a belt radio. "Dammit, who the bloody hell let her in there?"

"Beats me. I tole 'er the gear was down."

"Good lad, good lad. What about Ka Lakas? You raise him yet?"

"Aye, but that *bijau's* havin' a pink fit. Cullin plowed one of his boats, flat took out three of his mates."

"Jesus H. Christ!" Connelly cried. "That little Aussie shit never said anything about killin'. You make certain Ka Lakas understands we're none of this?"

"Aye. I said we couldn't hold Cullin but had the girl. Beyond that, we was standin' clear."

"Is his people comin'?"

"They're on their way."

Connelly cursed. "That's all we need, havin' the likes of that bloodeye pissed at us. Well, you keep that little bitch under lock and key. Knock her out if you have to. You hear?"

Liz turned away, fear gripping her throat like hands. Connelly had betrayed them. No, not them, *her*. She fled back through the mess room, the little Tonganese's head jerking up. Across the room two corridors led out. She chose the first and hurried down it. Find Bonner, she told herself, get the hell off this death trap.

Behind her, she heard someone shout.

She burst through a bulkhead door into salty breeze. Lights were everywhere, making false sunshine on the main deck. High above her on the derrick floor, a crew was pulling pipe, the chain men snapping the roll chains and the tongs swinging in on their swivel cable with the blocks cracking loudly.

Liz stopped, confused. A man strolled past her, cooing an obscenity. She rushed by him, found a stairway, and plunged down. It curved around and came out onto a lower deck some thirty feet above the water. Below, the ocean shimmered and danced, the derrick lights looking like sunbursts down under water.

Then she heard the quick engine roar of the PT. She dashed to the edge of the deck. Directly below her was the landing dock, and the PT with Cullin and Bonner on the conn was drifting slowly away. Will was gunning the Hall-Scotts intermittently, warming the blocks. Connelly was standing on the float dock watching.

Liz screamed, the sound erupting out of her throat in sheer terror. Below, heads snapped up. She screamed again: "Wait! Oh, God, wait!"

Frantically, like a crazed mouse in a maze, she searched for the stairway down to the floating dock.

She ran into solid bulkheads, turned back, clawing railing, stark metal. She returned to the edge of the deck and with a jolt of her heart realized the PT was standing off about a hundred yards now, Bonner waving stupidly.

She glanced down at the ocean. It seemed a horribly long way down, and the light reflections intensified the distance. With one icy, crazy burst of adrenaline, she vaulted the railing and went soaring out into space. She barely noticed the lights flashing past her before her feet knifed through the surface of the water. It slammed her arms painfully as she sliced down into water filled with twilight.

Kicking feebly, she pulled herself toward the surface. Finally she broke through and could do no more than flounder. She tried to yell, but water was in her mouth. Faintly she heard men shouting, and beyond that the steady climbing roar of the PT's engines. Then they were cut suddenly, leaving only a throaty rumble with the shouting voices punching through.

She started to swim away from the drilling platform, just lashing out, going, riding the fear that Bonner and Cullin would leave her. The water was warm and came at her in long, rolling swells, their tops sheened with light.

Something grabbed her around the chest. She let out a scream as she felt the arms close around her, a face up close, breath pumping. She raked her fingernails across the face, heard Bonner curse, "God dammit, Forsythe, it's me!"

"Oh, Cas," she whimpered, letting her body go limp so he could pull her through the water.

"What the hell's the matter with you?" he gasped between breaths. "Why'd you jump?"

"Connelly was going to turn me over to Ka Lakas," she cried. "I heard him talking to the radioman."

Cas cursed and his strokes became more powerful, dragging her. Soon she could feel the PT's propellers through the water, the vibrations touching her skin like fingers. Then the bow came toward them and the huge hull slid softly by on momentum.

Within a minute, Cullin had hauled them both aboard with a boat hook. Liz lay there, looking back at the drilling rig. Several men were down on the float dock now, yelling and waving as the PT drifted back and away, engines still idling.

"That Irish bastard turned us," Bonner shouted to Cullin. "He was gonna give her to Ka Lakas."

"Bloody hell!" Will growled, shaking his head and eyeing the rig lights menacingly. "That ocher paddy, I shoulda known he'd cover his own arse."

Liz turned over and sat up. Cas checked her, peering into her eyes. "I'm okay, I'm okay," she croaked.

"Yeah, but you're back," he snapped disgustedly.

A moment later, the engines climbed into power, the bow swung in a tight turn, and then they were racing away. Off the stern the circus lights of Celebes platform 348 faded gradually into darkness.

9

Through the rest of the night, Cullin pushed the PT toward the southeast, out of the Sibuyan into the vaster reaches of the Sulu Sea, the nearly landlocked ocean bound by the Palawan Islands to the west, northern Malaysia to the southwest, and the great bulk islands of Negros and Mindanao south of Panay in the east.

Bonner, who hadn't slept for over two days, went below and curled up on one of the forward bunks. He was gone almost instantly. Liz tried to sleep for a while, too, but the constant lunging of the boat made that impossible. Besides, she was still wired. Finally she crawled back through the charthouse and went topside.

After the rush of engine warmth that constantly swept through the lower spaces, the outside air felt chilly. Cullin was hunched over the control panel. Every time the bow pitched into water, frothing spray erupted off the deflection runners and over the conn deck. Liz hunkered down behind the fire wall, where it was warmer.

She was pleasantly surprised at how quickly her sea legs were developing. The nausea was still there, but her stomach seemed to be holding together, leaving just a heavy knot down inside. Moreover, her body was beginning to absorb the pounding of the deck with a natural riding motion of her knees.

Cullin ducked his head. "How you feelin', missy?" he yelled.

She nodded, smiling slightly at his attention.

He reached under the control panel and took out a thermos bottle, poured her a half cup, and handed it down. "Next time I see that paddy barstid, I'll take his flippin' head off. But for now we can drink his bleedin' coffee."

It was hot and very strong and seemed to her, oddly, the perfect drink for this time and place. She looked up at the wiry, diminutive Aussie on the conn seat and felt a sudden gentle rush of emotion for the older man. "Where are we headed?" she called up.

"The Mindanao peninsula. Zamboanga."

Such romantic-sounding names, she thought, made of story book magic. It struck her that a year ago, a month ago, perhaps even a week ago, she could never have imagined herself in such places. At least not like this.

She came out of her reverie to find Will watching her with a little smile playing over his face. "What?" she said.

"Just thinkin'. You and ole Casimir keep playin' nip-and-tuck wi' each other, don'cha?"

"The man's an insensitive clod."

"Aye, he's a crazy brumbie, fair enough. But a bloody good cobber all 'round, always game as Ned Kelly."

"How long have you known him?"

"Eight, nine years." He told her how they'd met, of some of their adventures together through the bars of Sydney and Timaroo, the dives and fishing expeditions off the Great Barrier Reef. "I never seen a bloke so in love wi' the sea. It's like a bleedin' mistress to him. Still, she does get 'im into slops now an' again."

"Oh? How's that?"

"Bonner has a fast boil when some bloke comes messin' around wi' the ocean. Fires up blue-hot, he does." He chuckled. "The last time, I hear he bloody near started an international stink."

Cas had been chief biologist on a Woods Hole project, Will explained, tracking migrating whale pods in the deep South Pacific aboard the research vessel *SS Tanigent*. They'd been following a particularly large pod of gray whales, mostly females with calves fresh off the birthing grounds of the Ross Inlet of Antarctica.

Then it happened. The pod ran headlong into a twenty-mile-long drag net set by a fleet of three Japanese fishing trawlers. The whales became disoriented and tried to break through the netting but instead became entangled. Cas and his divers went into the water to help. But by then the frenzied animals instinctively began sounding, pulling down over a half mile of the net. Eventually a third of the pod, mostly calves, had drowned.

"I guess Bonner jus' flat lost the strop then," Cullin continued. "In one o' them Zodiac boats, he went out and started cuttin' buoy floats, droppin' the whole bleedin' netline to the bottom. The Nips hove in and began bangin' away at 'im with rifles. So the captain of the *Tanigent* gets into it and rams one o' the trawlers." Will laughed happily. "Oh, it must 'ave been a sweet flamin' mess out there."

"My God, what happened?"

"Eventually the king-dicks in Washington and Tokyo got things smoothed out. But ole Casimir got the boot."

Liz fell into thoughtful silence. Another dimension had just been added to Bonner. She had to admit that what he had done seemed almost noble. Yet he was still such an ass, she told herself. What woman would put up with a combination of nobility and macho bullshit? Then she swiftly pulled back that statement. She knew a lot of women who could go head over heels for Cas Bonner. Just looking at him was enough to make a female think heated, possessive thoughts.

"Is he married?" she asked.

"Nay."

"Ever?"

"Aye, once." Cullin shook his head. "But a bad go it was."

Again she withdrew into her thoughts as they bore on, deep into the Sulu. After a while Liz's head lolled and she fell asleep. It seemed only a few moments before she felt Cullin shaking her. When she looked up at the sky, she could see a faint softening of the darkness and realized she'd been asleep for several hours.

Will had covered her with a blanket. She pulled it close, shivering, and stood up. About two miles off the port side, she saw the faint outline of mountains and lights here and there along the shoreline.

"Where are we?" she asked. They were using only a single engine now, and the bow sliced gently through smooth offshore swells.

"That's Sindangan Point, on the west coast of Mindanao." His face looked grim in the panel lights as he jerked his head around. "Best roust Bonner. We've got a bit of rat shit up here."

Cas opened his eyes the moment she touched him. For a second or two, he glared at her, then sat up, rubbing his face. "Where are we?"

"Off Mindanao. Cullin wants you up top, there's trouble."

Without a word he slid off the netting and hurried through the charthouse hatch. When Liz joined them on the conn, Cas was already glassing the horizon off the stern, his binoculars braced on the antenna triangle. She touched his arm, feeling her fingers starting to tingle with apprehension. "What's out there?"

Without lowering the binoculars, he said, "Motorized canoes, gaining fast. Will made 'em about thirty minutes ago off the tip of Negros Island."

"Moros again?"

"Yes."

"Then why's he going so slow? Why don't we run?"

"He's conserving fuel. We're damned near sucking fumes."

"Oh, no! What're we going to do, sit out here till they catch us?"

He didn't answer.

Cullin suddenly killed the remaining engine, and the deck tilted slightly as the friction of the water slowed her momentum. In a moment they were sitting dead, the PT lifting and dropping easily on the swells. In the silence they could hear tiny buzzing sounds way off, the whines of outboard engines as the canoes closed.

Bonner slipped back behind the conn barrier as Cullin pointed south along the Mindanao shore. Liz looked out and saw a cluster of bright lights about five miles away.

"That's a pearl station," Will said. "They're all over this coast. The brother of the Philippine president runs 'em. Gacky bloke, crooked as a butcher's hook. Each station has a private security force armed to the flamin' eyeballs. And these shonkies shoot to kill if anybody messes with their pearl beds."

Liz cast an anxious glance astern. The sound of the canoe engines seemed closer now, rising and fading. But she still couldn't see the boats. She looked back at Cullin in confusion.

He was watching her. "You see, missy, the Moros hate these stations. Attack 'em every once in a while. They consider 'em insults because this is their ocean and their bloody pearls."

"We're going to use that little fact," Cas explained to her.

"Aye," Will added. "I figure if we time this just right, we maybe can stir up a decent stoush between these nongs and get them Moros off our arse."

As they waited Liz moved around on pins and needles, watching the dawn light deepening in the east and the mountaintops of Mindanao coming up out of darkness like a fade-in on a stage. At last she spotted one of the canoes, then another and another. There were six in all, skimming over the surface with spray scudding off their bows.

Finally Cullin nodded to Bonner. "Stand engine watch and relay dial readings to me. When we jump, I'm gonna push her hard."

Cas paused a moment. "You better go below, Liz," he said. "Stay in the chartroom, it's got the thickest framing."

She shook her head. "I'll stay up here."

"I'm telling you, we'll be under fire soon."

"I've already been shot at."

Cas looked at her for a long moment, struck by this show of bravado. Then he dodged away, skittering back to the hatchway.

Will reached under the control panel and brought out the Walther. He handed it to her. "You know how to use that?"

"I'll figure it out," she answered uncertainly. The gun was very heavy and cold. She had to put both hands around the grip.

"When I tell you, just start firin' astern. Gauge the distance and compensate for it by shootin' high," he said, squinting over the boat's transom. The Moro canoes were in clear view now, coming in but still too far back to pick out features. He swung back and keyed his intercom: "Bonner, you ready?"

"Go."

Will flicked switches and tilted his head slightly before hitting the starter buttons. "When we make the headland of the pearl station, go flat on the deck and hang on," he instructed Liz. "The security force'll open on us, but I'm hopin' those swaggies aren't used to leadin' a boat this fast."

She nodded, gripping the Walther. When Cullin hit the starters, the Hall-Scotts whined slightly and then rumbled up into life. In the next moment Liz heard the distant staccato rap of gunfire. Bullets went zinging through the air overhead.

She lowered the gun and blindly pulled off a round. The recoil shocked her, ramming the grip back against her thumb. She pulled off another, smelled the tart, acrylic odor of cordite.

The PT was picking up speed, digging her stern deep as the propellers grabbed water. She felt the acceleration shoving her body against the after coaming. She pulled off two more rounds and wondered, in the roiling exhilaration and near panic of battle, if she was killing men. The thought stunned for a second and she froze. Then more bullets snapped past. One cut into an antenna strut and careened off with a scream.

The sound shook Liz from her momentary torpor, and she fired again and again until the hammer fell on an empty chamber. She felt a hand on her shoulder and jumped. Cullin shoved a box of ammunition at her. She took it and slid down the bulkhead until she was sitting and began reloading the Walther, shaking out the spent cartridges that went still warm against her legs. Her hands were trembling so violently she was having difficulty getting the rounds into the cylinder. She finally managed four bullets, straightened up, and began shooting again.

While reloading once more, she became aware that Cullin was playing the engines, dropping power for a few seconds, then gunning out. He seemed to be teasing the Moros, letting them get fairly close, then spurting ahead, always drawing them closer to the pearl station.

They took nine minutes to reach the main headland of the station, yet to Liz the time passed in a blood-pounding flash. Finally the PT was going wide open and Cullin held it there, water hurling. He yelled at her, palming his hand downward, his voice lost in the roar of the engines.

The boat tilted sharply to port as the Aussie put hard helm to it. Liz grabbed a bulkhead strut and hugged the deck, actually feeling the rush of the water going across the hull with the boat up high now, planing, and the pounding all gone.

Over the engines she heard a sudden explosion, far away but powerful, and a host of smaller detonations strung out in it. Several heavy rounds splashed into the water somewhere behind them. She could feel the jarring impacts.

She lifted off the deck and peeked over the forward coaming. They were in a small bay perhaps a mile wide. All across the water, now reflecting the silvery-yellow light of dawn, were hundreds of small floats, each with a tiny light like a pen-sized flashlight. Pearl pots. The PT slammed across the outer line of them, thudding harshly and flinging floats and their bottom networks of oyster trays off to the side.

Inland, there were small hills covered in jungle which thinned out into mangrove swamps. Right in the center of the bay, a village of wooden huts on stilts spread out into the water, with interconnecting walkways and small boats tied down in the stilt pilings. She could see smoke drifting over the huts and the small, crinkled glow of cooking fires. Men were lunging out of doorways, some still naked and pulling on shorts.

She snapped around. Behind them a barrage of gunfire opened up from the headland, throwing up geysers on the surface that looked stark white in the dawn. Here and there tracer bullets made lazy arcs, some bouncing off the water and popping straight up.

Far astern she saw that four of the Moro canoes were still outside the bay entrance, scattering crazily in all directions. The men in them were standing up on the braces between the double hulls, firing their weapons toward the headland. As she watched, one canoe seemed to suddenly go flat in the water. A moment later it was surrounded by a small forest of geysers.

When she looked forward again, her heart leapt into her throat. Less than two hundred yards ahead, the hut village loomed. She saw the flashes of gun muzzles and heard bullets whizzing past, a few impacting on the forward deck and coaming.

Cullin threw hard helm and Liz was slammed down against the deck again. She lay there, looking up at the Aussie. His lips were drawn back joyously, baring his teeth. There was more firing. It seemed just beyond the port side, the sounds swallowed by the rebound of the engine roar as they passed within twenty feet of the huts.

Then they were level again, flying full out. She

crawled up the bulkhead and looked across the bay.
The security force in the headland station and the Moros were fully engaged, their firing coming in broken,
intense exchanges. She could see only three canoes
left now.

As the PT crossed noisily through another section
of pearl pots, the hull thundering over floats, more
rounds from the headland crossed, now ahead of them.
Cullin stood up on the conn seat, yelling loudly and
giving everybody the extended finger. Liz came to her
feet, feeling the blood surging in her, feeling the tremendous power of the Hall-Scotts vibrating up through
her legs. The mangroves on the south side of the bay
rushed past, their leaves looking like orange-tinged
pewter. Then they were free of the bay, momentarily
bumping over a series of small wave chains forming
in the shallows. Once out into open water again, the
propeller sound changed to a solid, deep churn.

Liz let loose a high-pitched screech, releasing pent-
up energy and fear. She hand-over-handed to the conn
seat and hugged Cullin, feeling his small body like
steel cables coiled in her arms.

"We buggered the barstids," Will yelled happily.
"Look at 'em! They're cutting each other to ribbons."

She saw Bonner appear out of the charthouse companionway, grinning broadly. He made a fist in the air.
For a moment she wanted to rush to him and kiss him
frenziedly. But he disappeared below again, and she
disengaged from Cullin, leaning against the after conn
bulkhead, mind whirling, confused and hot-triggered,
as the PT fled south.

Dr. Ziyang crept softly through the gray light of
dawn and paused at the front door of his cottage. Behind him sounded the gentle snores of his wife and
daughter-in-law. He eased the door open, stepped out,
and quietly closed it.

There was a small garden beside the step, stunted
blossoms of rapeseed, shriveled heads of *batsai* cabbage, and a few spindly stalks of corn. It fumed with

the sour stench of the night soil, their own excrement, used to boost growth. The cottage was on the southern rim of the launch complex near the river.

He passed on through the little wooden gate, climbed onto his bicycle and headed toward the Control Building, a mile away. He pedaled slowly along a dirt road between cornfields as feeble as his wife's. Far off he saw a man "walking" a water belt near the western rim of the complex. Closer in, there were goats in the cornfield to his right, escapees from one of the barrack pens.

At the Control Building, he parked his bicycle in the back and entered through a rear door. A discordant, screeching music assailed his ears immediately. In a small recreation room he found several young technicians dancing to the song "Chidao" by the first Chinese rock star, Zhang Hang.

For a moment he was overcome by the scene. The room was windowless, its walls painted blue, and sparsely furnished with chairs and a single table on which rested a portable radio. The technicians were sweating, their eyes closed as they gyrated to the wails of an electric guitar.

"What is this nonsense?" Ziyang finally roared.

Instantly the men stopped dancing and looked up sheepishly, like schoolboys caught smoking in the toilet. Ziyang strode to the portable radio and snapped it off. "Is this how you spend your free time?" He swept the radio to the floor. "With this—this Western lunacy?"

For a full five minutes he lectured them. No one dared hold his glare. Oddly, Ziyang was surprised at the vehemence of his outrage and felt a pang of guilt. He finished, making the final point that the sole purpose for these young technicians was to achieve *chi,* that basic force which projected one to his goal. Not to lose themselves in the corrupt *ti-yong* trappings of the West. Then he stalked out of the room.

On his way to the main Control, he wondered at his lack of self-discipline. It was not like him to show that much emotion. Yet something was gnawing at him deep inside. It was the chilling fear of failure, he knew. He inhaled deeply and cautioned himself to be more careful of such outbursts in the future.

The Control Room was already alive with engineers and technicians working at their consoles. For a few minutes he was updated on the night's work and the rocket's status by his assistant controller.

The aborted simulation run had proven to be more serious than first thought. An entire bank of control systems had been overcharged due to the heavy humidity around the pad. The resulting blowouts had caused the Control Center to lose several telemetry loops. Ziyang had at first instructed the launch crews to make repairs with the rocket still in its gantry, but that proved too cumbersome. Finally, agonizing, he had ordered it taken back to the Test Building for a thorough overhaul of its control circuit boards.

After wandering around, talking to some of the Control technicians, he left the building and rode over to the Assembly Bay. It was called the Di Haiwan, or Low Bay, and consisted of a single large hangar painted all in white. The Long March 4, minus its nose section, which would carry the actual satellite packs, lay in the center of the room on eight large dolly cradles.

Each cradle rolled on heavy steel railroad wheels and ran on a track which led to the pad derricks. Scaffolding had been mounted along the sides of the rocket, and the entire assembly was ringed off behind fifteen-foot Fiberglas partitions. Crews of technicians in coveralls were working on the various components of the rocket, the inspection panels off, showing raw wiring systems.

Ziyang walked down the full length of the shaft, then came back slowly, consulting with individual section chiefs. These men had been working all through the night and looked haggard, but their forecast seemed good. The rocket could be re-gantried within forty-eight hours, they claimed.

Ziyang grunted thoughtfully. This new problem would leave them with less than four days for the integrated final testing before launch: fifty hours of tests and thirty of planned holds. It would be tight but acceptable provided that a few shortcuts could be implemented and further unseen delays did not occur.

After his inspection, he and the chief test coordinator, a short, fat engineer named Cuchow, walked together toward the main entrance, discussing possible shortcuts. With his hands behind him, his eyes closed in concentration, Ziyang reeled off viable procedures.

"We'll first align stages here in the bay rather than on gantry," he said. "I don't like doing it that way, but it will cut several hours from the countdown."

Ordinarily the launch pad engineers did the aligning and linkage of the rocket's stages at the gantry itself, using ten-inch pins and high-strength fasteners at six-inch intervals around the periphery of the stages. But the operation took eight hours to complete. To align and link in the test building created narrower safety parameters and an altered transport procedure. Still, Ziyang felt the situation necessitated such changes.

"I think we can also ground test the valves, cables, pumps and hydraulic lines in here," he went on. "The fire-detection circuits, too. We'll be able to back-check those through the telemetry system later."

Cuchow looked uncomfortable. "But, sir, if we ground check, we run a greater risk of circuitry malfunction. It would create a longer time lapse for disassembly."

Ziyang whirled on him. "There will be no malfunction this time. You will see to it that every system check is perfect. Do them a thousand times if you have to, work your crews twenty-four hours. But they will be perfect when the vehicle reaches the gantry. Is that clear?"

"Yes, sir."

They passed through the high arch of the building's entrance and stood in the morning sunshine. It was warm, and a soft breeze from the river rustled through the cornfields. Across the river, the mist in the valleys looked as thick as smoke.

"I want your gantry crews running their own tests now," Ziyang went on and realized, with a tinge of embarrassment, that his voice was high and tight again. He forced it back to normal. "Remember, I want all crews at work until the vehicle is ready. Feed them at their stations, no more free time for anybody." He started to turn, stopped. "And get someone to chase those goats out of the corn."

Cuchow's eyes darted to his face for a moment, then he nodded.

Ziyang climbed onto his bicycle. "I'll be at the Antenna Test Building if you want me." He started to pedal away.

"There's one other thing, sir," Cuchow called after him. "The civil police were here last night."

Ziyang stopped. "Why?"

"They were checking on the identity of Tzinxu." He referred to a lower-echelon engineer who had turned up missing two weeks before. He had been a recalcitrant man, prone to heavy gambling, who had gone into the nearby town one evening and never returned. "They found his body in the river. They think he was murdered."

"Ah!"

"He had been strangled with a thin wire. I sent Tzinxu's section chief with them to identify the body."

Ziyang shook his head and gazed thoughtfully out at the corn. Once more he felt that strange sense of hopelessness grip his heart, only now it was darkened with foreboding. The thought of a young engineer of his being murdered crept malignantly through his thoughts. Was this an omen of what lay ahead?

The ducks came in little echelons of fast-moving wings, but they didn't drop to the decoys. In his blind, the President shifted his legs around. They were cramping and he swore softly at them and the ducks.

Beside him, Bill Claymore gave a snort and handed over a silver flask of brandy.

The President's hunting party included Claymore, Secretary of Agriculture Weston Eberhart, and a coterie of security people. They were on the edge of the Moyock Marsh on Currituck Bay in North Carolina. It was Eberhart's favorite hunting spot, and the blinds and decoys were his.

The previous evening, the President had decided to take a final moment of recreation before preparing for the Great Barrier meeting, now six days away. He gazed out across the evening-tinged waters of the bay to the distant lights of Knotts Island and thought it had been a shitty idea. He leaned back against the icy metal frame of the blind and took a sip of the brandy. At least it felt nice.

The sudden blast of a shotgun sounded off to the right, then another. He turned just in time to see a duck wheel over crazily in the leaden sky and, folding, plummet into the marsh. A second later, he heard Eberhart's two Labradors plunging into the water to retrieve it.

He leaned over to Claymore and said with cold humor, "Isn't there supposed to be some sort of firing precedence here?"

Claymore laughed. "Hell, no. President or not, this is life in the raw, every man for himself."

"Well, there ought to be," he mumbled.

They sat out there for another thirty minutes, watching the sky deepen from orange to crimson with the ducks up as high as jet fighters. Finally the President stood up, stretching his back and legs. "The hell with this," he said.

A moment later, a small, flat-bottomed marsh boat swung out through the reeds to pick them up. Aboard was Eberhart with one of the President's personal security men at the electric motor. Eberhart held up two ducks, their neck feathers looking acrylic green in the fading light. "Got two," he shouted.

"Terrific," the President said glumly.

As the boat eased up beside the blind, Eberhart's mouth fell open. "Oh, my God, Mr. President. I—I shouldn't have shot before you, should I?"

"Don't worry about it," the President said and climbed into the little boat. Claymore followed, carrying the shotguns.

Eberhart looked distressed. "Jesus, I'm sorry, sir. I just reacted."

The President laughed and slapped him on the shoulder. "They were good shots, Wes."

They disembarked and waded through thick marsh grass and banks of pussy willow whispering in the offshore breeze. A radio truck was pulled up some ways ahead, with other vehicles and security men in dark suits milling about the entry road. Someone had set up a small electric warmer for the President, and it sent up shimmering waves of heat that were quickly carried away by the breeze.

The President, Claymore and Eberhart squatted around the stove, warming their hands. As coffee was brought, a captain from the radio truck approached. "Excuse me, sir," he said to the President. "It's Mr. Delaplane from the NSC on your secure line, sir."

The President shook his head and growled, "Frank undoubtedly has news that'll round out a shitty day." He rose and followed the captain back inside the truck. He sat on a jump seat and took the phone receiver one of the two operators handed over.

"Good evening, Mr. President," Delaplane's chirpy voice said. "How's the hunting?"

"I've seen better. What's up?"

"A few items I thought couldn't wait. I just received a red op from Cheyenne Mountain Satellite Analysis. Doesn't look good. Apparently the Chinese *are* showing heavier troop concentrations along the Amur."

"Damn!" the President snapped peevishly.

"There's still no armor showing up on the readings. But Pentagon says it's possible they could be moving between satellite sweeps and then hunkering down in the forests."

"Russian reaction?"

"Nothing so far. Apparently their satellite coverage is as predictable as ours."

"I don't like the direction this is taking, Frank. God dammit, why aren't we getting harder intelligence from there?"

"Our satellite recon over the area is just too catch as catch can, sir. As I've always said, we should never have phased out the SR-71 program. We need in-depth over-air reconnaissance to pinpoint movements this delicate."

The President thought a moment. "How long would it take to reactivate that program?"

"I don't know for sure, sir. I believe the only still functioning supply-and-operations base anywhere near status is Beale AFB in Marysville, California."

"Jump on it. I want SR-71 operations functioning within forty-eight hours. I don't care how much red tape you cut."

"Yes, sir."

"All right, what else is happening? Are the Russian coal miners out?"

"Markisov's gotten a reprieve there. The miners have agreed to a fifteen-day cooling-off period. But reports over the last twelve hours indicate several more food riots have erupted. It's the potato harvest over there right now, and apparently early winter's rotting the damned things in the fields. He's authorized conscription, everybody out to pick potatoes. If this doesn't come off, there's likely to be starvation this winter."

The President sighed. "All right, get on this SR-71 business. I want some hard-copy recon and fast. I'll be back in Washington in about four hours. Set up an NSC meeting for, say, eleven. And start getting some feelers into Beijing. I may end up calling Sichen, let him know *we* know what the hell's going on."

"Very good, sir."

He walked back to the warmer stove deep in thought. As he squatted, someone handed him a fresh cup of coffee. For a long time he stared into the brown liquid without speaking. Seeing this, the others fell into respectful silence.

Finally he turned to Eberhart. "Wes, how are our wheat reserves holding up?"

"We've got bulging storehouses, sir."

"I want two million metric tons donated to the Russians. Now. I'll have an executive order to that effect when I get back to Washington. No negotiations, this is a gift. And I want the first boatloads going out within four days."

The men exchanged glances. Eberhart said, "I'll see it's done, sir."

The President tossed his cup of coffee into the grass and rose. "Let's get the hell out of here and leave it to the ducks. They deserve it."

Stanford didn't like the look of this thing, sitting off the coast of Negros with Moro canoes all around the *Flying Sun*. There were fifteen boats in all, some with bullet holes across their hulls and crewmen wrapped in bloody bandages. As he peered down at the dark faces looking up at him, he distinctly sensed heavy native hostility down there.

Lui sauntered to his side. He had on a silk shirt that was the color of raw blood. He smiled down at the canoes. "Dees god'dam *bijaus* look piss."

"Keep your men alert," Jack whispered. "These shitheads are liable to try for our boat."

The Unicorn snorted disdainfully and sauntered off.

A canoe approached through the others. It was painted black and had three brand-new Evinrude 80s off the stern. A short, stocky Moro stood up on the center brace, glaring up at him. He was naked save for a loin cloth and a Kalashnikov assault rifle slung over his shoulder. The canoe's bow thudded against the *Flying Sun*'s hull.

"You Stamford?" the Moro called.

"That's right. Who the hell are you?"

"Ka Lingaya. I want aboard."

"Talk from there."

"I want aboard."

Jack swore under his breath. "All right. But just you." He nodded to one of the crewmen, who lowered a rope ladder. Ka Lingaya came scampering up and over the gunwale. Behind him came five other Moros, all armed with assault rifles and Malaysian bolo knives called *krisps*.

Stanford glanced over his shoulder. Lui was standing beside one of the anchor winches, his hands in his trouser pockets, grinning icily at the Filipinos. He turned back to Ka Lingaya. "What the hell happened? Ka Lakas radioed that you didn't score."

The Moro looked at him arrogantly. "Score? What the fuck means score?"

"Where's the goddamned PT boat and Cullin?"

Ka Lingaya didn't answer. Instead he strolled around the forward deck, examining the gear, walking high up on the balls of his feet, hands fisted on his hips. Cocky little shit, Stanford thought.

The Moro chief finished his circuit and planted himself directly in front of Stanford. He wasn't more than five feet tall, but the muscles of his body were round and thick, as if he had been pumping iron. "No PT," he said defiantly. "No fuckeen PT." He slapped his palms together, making a sound like a shot. "Cullin run away like mongoose. But my men get killed."

"What happened? Where did Cullin go?"

"Fuck Cullin." Ka Lingaya seemed fond of that particular obscenity. He smiled, his tiny dark eyes slitted. "I don' like my men killed. You pay me."

"Where the hell did Cullin go, dammit?"

"South. You pay me now."

"Pay you for what? You didn't score the PT."

"You pay me now or I take this boat."

Stanford casually eased his hands around behind his back, feeling for his Browning Hi-Power. "Fuck off, asshole," he said slowly.

Ka Lingaya's eyes went wide, flashing fire. Then they narrowed again and the little Moro walked back and forth in front of him, his gaze flicking up, down. "Who you?" he barked. "Who you? Fuckeen Yank shit." He skewered a finger into Jack's pectoral muscle. "I eat yo' fuckeen heart."

As the man's finger sank into muscle, Stanford's left hand jacked back the receiver of the Browning, chambering a round. In the same smooth motion he drew the weapon free of his pants and swung it around in a small, tight circle.

As he put the muzzle against Ka Lingaya's mouth, the Moro's eyes snapped wide open. Before the man could react, Stanford pulled the trigger. A burst of blood and skull tissue blew out the back of Ka Lingaya's head, the round and bone fragments striking one of the Moros behind him.

Instantly Stanford dropped to one knee, firing wildly. As he did, there was a furious fusillade from Lui and his men on the cabin wings. The bullets slammed over his head, impacting against the Moros. Their bodies were violently hurled back against the gunwale.

The instant the firing stopped, Jack bounded to his feet. Running to the gunwale, slipping on blood and tissue, he began firing down into the canoes. Lui's men were doing the same. The hail of bullets chewed canoe hulls to pieces and flung men out into the water.

Up in the cruiser's cabin, Big Willie hit the engine throttles, and the cruiser lunged forward. Stanford hit an empty chamber, flipped out the used clip, rammed in another and started firing again.

A large discoloration of blood formed around the canoes. Responding to the pull of the revolving props of the cruiser, the redness was sucked in toward the hull along with floating dead bodies. A moment later, the propeller sound dropped to a thick, chopping tone as the bodies were churned through the whirling blades.

By now the cruiser was lifting with full power, and Jack had to grab a gunwale to keep from falling. His weapon was empty again. He tucked it back into his pants, ignoring the stinging heat of the barrel, and ran aft. The Moros were now opening up, bullets thudding into the cabin and gunwales.

Six canoes came after them, engines whining, prows cleaving the offshore swells. But the Moros were firing wildly, most of their rounds going every which way, kicking up water astern or singing far overhead.

Stanford gathered Lui's men along the stern, going along their backs like a sergeant major directing a British square. "Take aim and lead the sons of bitches," he bellowed.

Gradually the Moros pulled back, nursing their wounds. They bobbed on the swells, so frustrated that they started firing their weapons straight up in the air. Jack whooped and went around joyously grabbing Lui's men by the shoulders as they gave him Chinese grins.

The blood was burning in his veins as he went forward again. Clearing the starboard side of the main cabin, he halted in astonishment. Up on the forward deck, Lui was methodically decapitating the dead and wounded Moros and tossing their heads over the side like so many melons. The headless bodies were jerking in spasms, and Lui's silk shirt was dripping blood, invisible against the scarlet material.

Gagging, Jack turned away and went around the companionway stairs into the control deck. Big Willie was sitting in the conn chair, watching dials with indifferent calm. His thick cheeks drew up into a lazy smile. "You pay me now," he mimicked Ka Lingaya's voice. "You pay me now. Huh, Stamford?"

Five minutes later, Lui came in. He had taken off his silk shirt, but his trousers were drenched with blood. His body looked slim and bony, and the streaks of blood on his chest looked like smears of crayon against wax. Jack poured him a glass of Hennesey's, handed it over. The Unicorn looked as placid as always. He drank the whiskey slowly, then put it down. "Now what you do, Stamford? No more Muslims."

"It don't matter. Ka Lingaya said Cullin headed south. I know what the prick's doing. He's heading for the Celebes and Australia.'' He paced a little. ''But now we got him. Sooner or later he's going to run out of fuel. Call out your drug-runner boats. They can box him in till we catch up.''

He walked up beside Big Willie and peered out through the glass. On the forward deck, crewmen were hosing the blood into the scuppers. A thought suddenly struck him. He started to chuckle, then began laughing out loud, the laughter fueled by the adrenaline of battle still twitching in him. Big Willie turned and looked at him, puzzled. ''Aguinaldo,'' Jack said.

''What?''

''Aguinaldo Babiyan. That poor bastard's gonna be in deep shit tryin' to explain this to Ka Lakas.''

10

On the tip of the Zamboanga Peninsula in western Mindanao, the Junkman's yard was on the edge of an estuary backed by sand dunes. It covered ten acres and possessed a natural deep-water channel that gave access to inter-island freighters in from the Sulu Sea.

The PT boat arrived off the yard a little before eleven in the morning, and Cullin took it in. There was an old heavy-docking facility built during World War II by American Seabees which jutted into the channel. Where the Junkman's yard now stood, there had once been a huge staging area for MacArthur's push up through the Philippines in 1944.

Will slowed the engines and eased the boat up against the dock so that Bonner could jump off and tie up. The dock was covered with tar and old oil, and an ancient sea dredge, its superstructure completely rusted, was berthed on the opposite side. Up in the yard, a small Filipino crew was working with a cherry picker among crates.

The yard itself looked like the original staging area after a typhoon had passed through. Equipment lay everywhere: stacks of crates forty feet high, old military truck bodies deteriorating in the tropical humidity, engines and cranes and derricks resting in pools of oily water. Toward the back were mountains of tires and haphazard piles of old, used war material under greasy tarps. Four U.S. Marine assault boats were beached beside chopped-up military aircraft, their empty engine mounts looking like scabby eye sockets. Over everything hung the smell of Cosmoline and diesel, mingling with a thin pall of oily smoke.

A beat-up Chevy pickup truck weaved its way through the debris and pulled up at the head of the dock. The door opened and Abbie Baum, the Junkman, got out. He was very fat, dressed in a filthy khaki shirt and trousers with a greasy garrison hat on his head, the brim turned up in the front.

"Ah, Cullin," he growled, coming up, his broad, jowly face breaking into a grin. "My old friend, Cullin. *Sholem aleichem.*"

Cullin jumped to the dock and stood there, grinning back. "Ah-lay-khem yoself, you Hymie nong, ya."

The two men embraced, then the fat man stepped back, frowning at the new bullet holes in the PT. "So? So? Why is this?"

"The bleedin' Moros paid a visit."

"Ach, those *suk-suk* gonifs. But just look at my precious boat." Abbie walked out to the edge of the dock, examining the PT, clicking his tongue and shaking his head.

"Just a few rounds," Will said.

"Just a few rounds, he says. On this dock I could bleed my heart out with such few rounds."

"Abbie, we need ordnance."

"Ordnance you already got. There, in your hull."

"Heavy stuff."

Baum swung around and eyed Cullin narrowly. "Ordnance you want? So the Moros can, God forbid, put you in a sea grave?"

"You still got that crated Mark 10 torpedo?"

"Ach!" Baum turned and planted himself in front of Bonner and Liz. "Torpedoes he wants. What am I, du Pont?"

"And some automatic weapons," Cullin went on. "And magnetized smoke gear."

The Junkman's eyes narrowed again, and he studied Bonner and Forsythe. "Who are these people I'm talking to?"

Cullin introduced them.

"This madness you're part of?" Baum demanded of Cas. "This William crazy man will put my precious boat on the bottom."

"And a couple of AK's, a fifty, and some gelegnite," Cullin concluded.

Baum shook his head and started off toward the pickup. "We'll talk, we'll talk."

The Junkman's house, perched on a little sandy rise at the southern end of the yard, was a replica of a Nebraska farmhouse, complete with porch and swing. It looked as if it should have been surrounded by miles of wheat instead of wispy sea grass and dunes. It was lorded over by Abbie's wife, Maria, three hundred pounds of Filipina female flesh who had given Abbie eleven children, most of them still living with him.

Maria followed them through the house, glowering at Cullin and hurling Tagalog invective at him. Apparently, Will was known to periodically get Abbie crying drunk on wine. At which point the Junkman would sit on his swing and soppily reminisce about his days in the Wild West.

As a young man, he had spent a summer as a rabbinical student in Grand Island, Nebraska. There he discovered the great truth that the expansiveness of wheat fields engendered a rapport with the Lord of Things. Sometime thereafter, he found that the sea produced the same effect. Plus he realized that military surplus was a more viable way of earning a living than being a rabbi.

He led them into his study, a huge room lined with books and technical manuals. Five of the younger children flooded in, curly headed half-breeds with sweet, oriental eyes. They sat on Abbie's lap, climbed onto Liz's. Bonner and Cullin they left alone. Gently, Baum shooed them out. At the door he called to his wife: "Daling, bring bagels and coffee."

He was met with another explosion of Tagalog. Wearily he closed the door and returned to his desk. "Ah, sometimes we seek, but the Lord does not always answer." He sat down and leaned forward, tenting his fingers. "Now, William, what is this about?"

As Cullin explained, Baum's heavy eyebrows occasionally darted upward with distress. When Will finished, he shook his head. "Oy, Triads. And this Stanford, I know of him, a real schlepper."

"Well?" Cullin said. "You got what we need?"

Abbie held up a fat finger. "One question. At this moment you should be fleeing south. Why you're not doing it?"

"The bleedin' barstids killed my dog," Cullin said. "I intend to kark off a few of these dingoes in return."

Baum threw up his hands. "Your dog they killed! Ach, that explains all." He shook his head. "A meshuggener I'm dealing with."

"Come on, Abbie. Let's iron this out."

"I have what you need."

"Ripper."

Baum studied him for a moment. "These computer disks you talk of, what do they contain?"

"They're in Chinese," Bonner said. "Nothing but groups of number sequences and Chinese characters."

"I may see them?"

"Sure." He turned to Liz. "Go get 'em."

"I've got them right here in my pocket."

"You carry them around with you? That's stupid. You get close to those running engines, and the magnetic charge from the coils'll wipe the damned things clean."

"Then I won't get around the engines, okay?" She glared at him narrowly, then dug the two disks out and handed them to Baum. He fingered them a moment, obviously perplexed, before heading into a side room. The others followed.

The smaller room was filled with an astounding collection of electronic units, data panels and three computer consoles. There were wooden toys scattered around, and some of the computer screens had food smears on the glass.

Baum settled himself heavily before a computer and inserted one of the disks. For the next few minutes he ran scanning and bring-up procedures, hitting dead ends and reversing, going up other approach alleys. At last the computer brought up the sequences Bonner and Liz had found in the electronics store.

The Junkman leaned forward, squinting his puffy eyes at the screen, running the cursor down as the machine brought up a continuous rolling readout. Now and then he would grunt and back away, only to lean in again.

The first disk reached its end and the cursor blinked on the empty screen. Baum thoughtfully rolled his fleshy cheeks between his fingers.

"Do you understand any of that?" Bonner asked him.

"Oh, yes, I read a little Chinese," the Junkman said. "Now I understand this schlepper Stanford's concern. These are guidance data for a Chinese rocket launch."

"Well, I'll be buggered," Cullin cried.

"Damn, that fits," Bonner said, glancing at Liz. "You said your brother Jerry was doing a layout of a rocket launch. And those VCR pictures showed launch gantries. Obviously somebody at that base planted the disks on him while he was there."

Liz frowned. "But I don't understand. Why would anybody want data on a Chinese rocket launch? As I understand it, their technology is far inferior to ours or the Russians or even the French."

Baum suddenly twisted his chair away from his panel, scooted to another terminal and switched it on. With stubby fingers flying over the keyboard, he brought up more data, spotted something. "Yes, yes, I thought so. A Chinese rocket from Xchiang is scheduled to put a U.S. and Swiss satellite into orbit in four days." He leaned back in the chair, thoughtfully thumping his belly. "For very high stakes this Stanford plays."

"Xchiang, that's where Jerry was," Liz said. She

frowned and turned to Baum. ''Are you saying Stanford wants to destroy that satellite?''

''Probably not.''

''Then what?''

''Steal it.''

''My God, is that possible?''

''All things are possible. But first he must have these disks to do it.''

''Then erase them,'' she cried. ''Wipe the damned things clean.''

''Erase them!'' Baum said, shocked. ''No, no, that is foolish. You must keep them. Someday they could be worth your life.''

The drug-runner crews lived in the trees, like monkeys. Tents and straw beds were braced in *hao* branches, where they would be free of the nightly invasion of crabs up out of the Tambisan Estuary located on the Sandakan Peninsula of northern Malaysia, three hundred miles southwest of Zamboanga. The trees came right down to the estuary, actually hung out over it, forming a thick canopy where spiders and snakes trembled on branches, feeding off the insects collected on the swampy water.

Under this canopy the drug boats were hidden. There were three of them, high-speed versions of the U.S. Navy's LC-11 attack boats. Called mediums, they were forty-footers abandoned in Nam after the American SEAL Riverine Force deployed out of country. Cat-bottomed and constructed of aluminum, they drafted less than two feet and were powered by twin 460-cubic-inch big block Chevy engines which could make them plane up to forty-five knots.

Once they had been heavily armed with twin .50-caliber machine guns forward and an M-60 fixed, clip-linked, high-explosive gun aft. Now the after gun space had been replaced by fuel tanks for a wider range. The boats were used by the Triads to run raw opium out of the fields of Sulawesi, the large northern Indonesian island, and then carry it to the lab boats which plied the South China Sea.

At precisely 11:04 A.M., Philippine time, their force captain, Lee Sap, received a radio message from the Unicorn. He was ordered to head for the Zamboanga Archipelago in search of a PT boat which would be transitting into the Celebes Sea. He was to capture it, with special attention to a redheaded woman aboard. Rendezvous with the *Flying Sun* would be made sometime the following dawn off the western coast of Jolo Island, the largest in the archipelago.

Lee Sap cracked a whip and his men tumbled out of the trees to run fuel-loading lines out to the mediums from floating tanks anchored in the mangroves. Lee was little more than four feet tall but had a voice like a raging lion. He hurled insults, plowing back and forth through the knee-deep estuary mud, a red bandana on his head with his upper body naked. It was completely covered with tattoos, like a Japanese Yakuza's.

Hand pumping, the men needed nearly three hours to load the auxiliary tanks on two of the mediums. The third had been having engine trouble and was to be left behind on this run. Finally everything was set, each boat carrying seven men. Mooring lines were released and the helmsmen started their engines. Wisps of vapor erupted off the churn of the twenty-inch propellers as they eased into deeper water and then gunned up, heading east, into the Celebes Sea and the Sulu archipelago.

It took all afternoon to load ordnance aboard the PT, Cas and Will and Liz sweating in the heat and drenching humidity. Abbie wouldn't allow his crews to help; this was special cargo which they need know nothing about.

The big problem had been the Mark-10 torpedo. The PT's firing tubes had long since rusted, and Cullin had to reweld the frame and then mount two new compression tanks and a firing box on the aft section. Or-

dinarily a Mark-10 setup required a torpedo man to
fire manually from the tube. So to achieve conn deck
firing, he also had to jury rig a circuit and fit a fire
box on the conn panel, using a throttle box from the
cockpit of an old Marine Douglass TBD attack
bomber.

While he was doing this, Cas and Liz made and
hauled sandbags aboard. They stacked them on the
port side of the PT in order to counter the weight of
the torpedo, and then laid some out to protect the
engine-room house and vents.

At last, Abbie brought up the Mark-10 on the old
pickup, its fifteen-hundred-pound weight making the
truck's axles screech. Using one of the cherry-picker
rigs, they laboriously winched it up out of the truck
and into the firing tube, which Cullin had already
greased. Earlier, Baum had checked the explosive
warhead and re-pinlocked the screw caps. The external metal of the unit was badly rusted, but its engine,
contact circuits and prop bushings were still in good
shape.

This particular series of torpedo was World War II
ordnance and had no electronic guidance system. It
was sight-run and self-arming. Once launched into the
water, its small high-octane gasoline engine could hurl
it at forty-eight knots. But its impeller blades had to
turn 3,500 revolutions before the warhead was automatically armed. At that point, even a five-pound impact on the nose would explode the main charge.

Meanwhile, Maria Baum had relented and brought
out blintzes and coffee. She stood around disgustedly
surveying the torpedo and then stalked off, the children following in a clot. It was mid-afternoon before
they finally got everything seated and hooked up, and
the air tanks charged from an old painter's compres-
sor.

The rest of the weaponry was personal gear. Baum
drove Cas and Will four hundred yards out into the
sand dunes to a camouflaged bunker dug under the sea
grass. It was cool down inside, smelling of gun grease

and cement and the sour, bony stench of dead crabs which had penetrated the vent slits.

The bunker had a single electric light and was filled with crates of small arms: M-16s and AK-47 assault rifles, bins of Colt 45s, Browning Hi-Powers, Walther P-38s and Tokarev TT-33s. In the back of the bunker was heavier killing power. M-60 machine guns and Springfield .50-calibers with brackets set to swivel-mount like the old dum-dum guns. And newer M-16/XM-148 grenade launchers running 40mm percussion rounds, their wooden crates marked with Nam designation number sequences.

Bonner stood in the middle of the bunker, awed. "This is a goddamned arsenal."

"But only for a select clientele," Abbie admonished.

Will selected twin Springfield .50-calibers to mount on the starboard turret beside the conn barrier. He also took a flare gun with several phosphorous illumination flares. Cas chose an Armalite AR-18 assault rifle since he'd used one when he was with SEAL Team One. It carried a 3,500-foot-per-second muzzle velocity which literally exploded its small 5.56mm rounds on impact. Moreover, it had a five-hundred-yard usable range, a much longer reach than the AK-47 or M-16.

The heft of the weapon instantly felt familiar in his hands. For a moment he paused. These were heavy-heat killing machines. Visions of the deaths he'd seen in Nam flashed in his mind, terrible, bloody pictures that had burned themselves into his soul.

He put the weapon down, doubt assailing him. Where are we going here? he thought. He glanced back at Will, at the little man's dark hands handling armament with the click and snap of an experienced fighter. And Cas's mind drew up the sound of ricocheting bullets in a dark tunnel and marker rounds arcing over them on the sea from killers on the loose who didn't give a shit about someone else's life. No, only a fool would meet this breed empty-handed.

Picking up the rifle again, he cracked back the re-

ceiver and listened to the sharp *chunk* of metal it made.
The sound was so specific that it instantly evoked that
first, sharp tingle of coming combat, brought that faint
copper taste to his mouth which he remembered from
other battles.

The next stop was the powder bunker a hundred
yards away. Everything was neat as a pin, set on
wooden pallets and separated according to good storage procedure. A small generator, running on a ther-
mostat, kept the bunker cool. They picked several
MK-26 Model O HBX haversacks, each loaded with
eight 2.5-pound cubes of gelignite. The haversacks had
wire triggers which activated an internal battery-
operated detonator running on a graduated scale between a ten-second to a full minute lag time. They
were all hydrostatic, which meant they could be exploded underwater.

As everything was hauled back to the PT, Abbie
stopped at one of his delapidated storage houses and
brought out three flak jackets. "For crazy people a
gift," he said.

Back on the boat, Cas immediately set about mounting the .50-caliber onto its turret plate, greasing the
runner sheaves and clean-oiling the hydraulic foot
pump which swiveled the gun. Cullin set up twin
smoke cans astern. They were battery driven and used
oil impregnated with minute filings of iron. The oil,
pumped across heated exhaust ducts, would create
clouds of blue-white smoke which would billow low
on the ocean and could also confuse radar probes like
chaff.

Meanwhile, Liz hauled up the other weapons and
haversacks, storing the explosives in the forward crawl
space so that the wash of the ocean under the hull
would keep them cool. She also carried more sandbags
to place around the conn deck. It was grueling work.
Worse, Bonner had ordered her to wear the flak jacket
so as to get used to its weight.

"From now on that never comes off," he said.

"God, it weighs a ton."

"You got the chest to carry it." His eyes twinkled. She shot him a hard glance, but then noticed the twinkle held something deeper inside it. "Will told me how steady you handled the Walther back there," he said. "They teach you that in journalism school?"

"Hell, yes. We trained at Fort Benning on weekends."

He chuckled softly. "Well, you did fine."

She watched him turn away and realized that her body had just warmed ridiculously. She felt a rush of giddiness, like a little girl who had just won the gold star for spelling and had it pinned to her blouse by the cutest boy in school.

The sun was beginning to drop toward the western horizon. The estuary water seemed to smoke with oily vapors and looked as thick as liquid mud with whorls of color as the diesel scum caught the slanted rays. Seagulls, attracted by the activity, came in and roosted on pilings, looking for handouts.

Abbie drove an ancient tanker out onto the dock. Cullin strung out his static ground lines and waved Liz back and away as they began to pump the 100 octane fuel down into the PT. For a while she stood at the dock head, watching. Then, bored, she turned and strode off toward the Junkman's house.

Two of his children were playing in the hard-packed yard, swinging on a truck tire hanging from a cherry-picker rig. When they saw her approach, they came running to meet her, chattering in a strange patois of Tagalog and Yiddish–English. She sat on the porch and took off the flak jacket. A flock of Rhode Island Red chickens pecked for bugs under the porch. She ran her hand through her hair. It was salt-caked into a matted mess, and her scalp itched horribly. The skin of her arms and legs was sunburned, looking red and dry, and her face felt hot.

Machine-gun fire erupted from the dock and Liz jumped, squinting against the glare of the sun. Bonner was up in the PT's turret, firing out at a floating barrel in the channel, apparently testing the weapon. The rounds impacted the surface with solid *whomps* which threw high geysers of oily water all around the barrel.

Baum's wife came to the screen door and stood staring at her.

"Hi," Liz called cheerily.

The woman didn't answer for a moment. Then she said, "What dat crazy Cullin do now?"

"It's not him. I think Bonner's checking the gun out, the jerk. He scared the hell out of me."

Maria snorted and came out onto the porch. She glared toward the dock, then looked at Liz again. "What you name?"

"Liz."

"How comes pretty gurl like you with dat bastid Cullin?"

"It's a long story."

"You whore?"

Liz chuckled. "No, I'm afraid not."

"Good. Your hair very pretty. I never see color like dat."

"It's not so pretty now. The salt's making me crazy."

Maria reached out and fingered her hair. "You like wash?"

"Oh, God, that sounds wonderful."

Baum's wife went back into the house. In a moment she was back with a large porcelain basin filled with warm water. She set it down on the porch and handed Liz a thick bar of brown soap. It smelled like newly shelled almonds.

The water felt exquisite, and when she put the soap in, it formed a thick, rich lather, releasing its pungent odor of almonds even more. It tingled slightly on her scalp, feeling good. The two children, joined by two others, came and stood around, silently watching her. They had chubby brown bodies. One apparently had a cold and periodically snuffed mucus up her nostril.

Liz closed her eyes and luxuriated in the feel of the water, the slick, squeaky friction of the soap. In the darkness behind her lids, her thoughts began to flow gently, like a soft sea breeze over dunes. She thought about where she was and how she'd come to be here. Random images came to her and darted away: the house in which she and her ex-husband had lived, Burlingame cocktail parties as vapid and prescribed as faked orgasms, studio lights and the clack of high heels down plastic-shiny corridors. All of it seemed so very far away, like places she had once visited as a tourist.

Then other, more powerful, images came. Terror and death so close she felt the crazy tumult of her heart all over again. The sounds bullets made as they ripped the air, the smell of cordite. She saw again a Moro's body flung upward by the horrible rending of high-velocity steel, blood making a pink fan in the dawn light. It came with such vividness that her hand clamped down on the soap so forcefully it spurted out into the air.

A bit unnerved, she opened her eyes and quickly rinsed, lifted herself from the basin. Maria had retrieved a bottle of oil, which she now handed over. The bottle was made of stone and contained a thick oil the color of red wine. When she uncorked it, there was the heady scent of gardenias.

"Rub in," Maria ordered. "Rub in. Make your hair soft."

"What is it?"

"I make from sea grass." She took the bottle. "I rub in."

Liz closed her eyes again and gave herself over to the woman's hands. They were powerful yet gentle, fingers streaking back, massaging her scalp.

Again assorted images came, but this time they were grotesque. The chill of a morgue room, the soft whisper of roller bearings as they drew Jerry's body into view. She was staring at him again, seeing all their years together collapsing in a whorl that coiled down into his tormented face. Suddenly she was crying, all reserve crumbling. She sobbed, curling over until her stomach ached with it. She vaguely felt Maria's arm around her shoulder, faintly heard the woman's surprised, confused murmurs of consolation.

When Liz returned to the PT, her hair swept back into a French braid, the tanker truck was gone. Cas was standing on the forward deck, smoking a cigarette and drinking a beer. He watched her come up the four-by-four plank from the dock. She walked right up to him and looked up into his face.

He said, "I like your hair that way."

"We're going to kill people, aren't we?"

He lowered the cigarette and his eyes searched hers for a moment. "You don't have to come, Liz. Frankly, I'd prefer you stay with the Junkman."

"I'm going. But we *are* going to kill people, aren't we?"

"Yes. Unless they kill us first."

"All right, I accept that," she said. "God forgive me, but I accept it." With a lightning chill she realized her world, she herself, had just passed into a new dimension and nothing would ever be the same again.

A soft, warm smile came up into his face. "I understand. I had to deal with that myself."

Looking up at him, she felt the chill melted by a wave of heat that came first up through her legs, then enveloped her entire body. A moment passed between them, unspoken and indefinable, yet powerful with a sudden bonding. She started to reach out, put her fingertips on his face. But she hesitated, lest the touch sunder the moment. Instead she turned and headed for the companionway.

A few moments later, the three of them hunkered down on the forward deck as Bonner explained to her the plan he and Will had worked out. They'd go slowly through the night toward the islands of the Sulu Archipelago, which lay due southwest, and then cross into the Celebes Sea to the south. That side of the archipelago consisted of a vast scattering of tiny islands and motus, mere specks of rock with vegetation. All lay in tricky reef shallows, but Cullin knew them, even without maps.

As they transited, Stanford was sure to pick them up on his radar. Both men figured that cruiser of his would be equipped with good enough gear to scan at least a hundred miles out. The PT would stand out like a light because in these waters very little traffic moved, save for marauding pirates out of Malaysia and the southern archipelago islands. When Stanford spotted them, he'd chase. He'd have to, time was running out on him. But as soon as the fool brought his hotshot cruiser into the scatter islands, the fight would be on their terms.

As the Aussie cranked up the Hall-Scotts, the engine rumbled powerfully in the still evening air. They backed away from the ancient dock, out into the main channel of the estuary. Abbie Baum, standing on the dock, shaking his massive head at the foolishness of men, waved good-bye. And up on the porch of his home, Maria and the children waved too.

Will brought them around and shoved up the throttle a little. The light in the western sky washed away slowly, like a blotted watercolor. At the estuary entrance, Cullin put heavy power on, and the PT, a colt freed of its harness, lifted her head and ran for the open ocean.

11

When Jack Stanford was nine years old, his father had given him a .22 Magnum rifle, a Winchester with a tube feed and a pump action. With it, for two autumns he had stalked a particular buck deer, up through the wooded glens at the edge of the Whitman National Forest in east-central Oregon. But the animal eluded him. He tracked, he made stand blinds, he holed up along watering trails—without success. He raged with frustration over the buck. It became a symbol of something he was as yet too young to comprehend. But his gut understood, and it drove him on. Finally, on a snowy Halloween evening, he got the buck with a Magnum round right through the eye and into the brain. And that vague something in his consciousness clicked and set.

Now the PT was his buck deer. His frustration had reached the point that the capture of the boat and the scum aboard her even transcended the possession of the guidance disks.

He brooded on the forward deck of the Triad cruiser as she bore south in the Sulu. He glanced back at the cabin, saw Big Willie observing him through the blue glow of the control lights. Fucking Chinamen, he thought. He had begun sensing an intensifying restlessness among the men. Lui, endlessly stoked on pot or hash, retained his glassy-eyed equanimity, but underneath, he was starting to harden. Big Willie had taken to frowning with the rest of the Unicorn's men, lounging around, fingering their weapons and giving him narrow oriental studies.

These people were obviously scared of Yue Fei. A pack of wolves frightened by a bear. He was going to have increasing difficulty keeping everybody in line, he knew. With the PT eluding them and his time frame growing ever narrower, sooner or later tempers would blow.

He went up into the control cabin. Big Willie ignored him, so he went to the bar and poured himself a drink.

"Them Cullin gone," Big Willie said finally. "We never find 'im now."

"We'll find them."

The Chinaman turned slightly. "You one big fuck-up, Stamford."

To keep from saying anything, Jack downed his scotch.

The night rolled past in a steady drone of engines, the moon outside the cabin window like a Kashmir sapphire. Far to the west he could see the running lights of a freighter, looking as isolated as an astronaut's encampment on the moon. Big Willie's first mate, a diminutive Chinaman named Chin Au, came to the bridge. Willie lifted his great bulk out of the command chair, turned over the helm, and went aft to whatever paddock he slept in.

Automatically Chin Au turned off the radar sweep. Stanford was right on it. "Goddammit," he bellowed. "Turn that thing back on."

Chin Au jumped at his vehemence. "No need . . . moonlight bright."

"Turn it on!"

As the screen came back on, Jack planted himself behind Chin and watched the swing arm. It flashed as it picked up the distant freighter's position. He blew air through his nose, noting that the first mate stank of fish and rotted cabbage.

On they skimmed over the moonscape. Time clicked away with the white churn of the *Flying Sun*'s props.

And then he saw it. At first a tiny blink under the radar's light arm. Around the beam came and again the light blinked, only stronger.

Stanford leaned in. The blip, clean and sharp now, was moving south. "That's him," he cried.

Chin Au studied the screen and shook his head. "Pirates."

"Pirates, my ass! That boat's too big. That's him!" He watched the light swing through four more revolutions. "What's the range?"

The first mate studied the screen intently, then punched a few buttons. "Eighty kilometers."

"Go after him."

Chin rattled off something in Chinese and shook his head.

"What'd you say?"

"He headin' fo' bad shallows. We no can follow."

"I don't give a shit. Go after him."

"Captain have to make order."

"Then get his fat ass up here."

Reluctantly, Chin rang down for Big Willie.

Stanford watched the radar screen. Faint smears of light were beginning to show on the far fringes of the beam's sweep: islands. Jesus, where the hell are we? he wondered.

"Where's the charts?" he demanded. Chin flicked a thumb toward the port side of the control deck. They were laid out under a wide fluorescent lamp with a swing-arm compass marker.

"Where are we now?" Stanford asked.

The first mate leaned over and pointed out their position. It was approximately a hundred miles northeast of Basilan Island, which rose off the tip of the Zamboanga Peninsula. Stretched in a curving line which ran southwest was the Sulu Archipelago, a collection of tiny islands, the largest of which was Jolo. The map showed that the entire arc lay in extremely shallow water.

Satisfied, he glanced at the radar, trying to superimpose the map contours on the screen. The blip of the PT seemed to be heading straight for the eastern coast of Jolo Island.

I knew it, he thought. The bastard's running for the Celebes Sea. Where the hell are Lui's drug runners? Once the PT got into that ocean, it'd be gone.

Bonner was alone on the conn. For the past four hours he'd been guiding the PT steadily southward, going at a smooth fifteen knots to preserve fuel and to lay out an easy target for Stanford's radar. Cullin and Liz were below sleeping, so he had the night and the moonlight and the sea all to himself.

He loved the ocean at night. During the day there were always horizons marking off boundaries, ports of call, people. At night these disappeared into a single vastness which swallowed him and his boat, creating an elemental whole in which he found comfort.

As his thoughts drifted, he found himself thinking of Liz Forsythe. He remembered how pretty she'd looked that afternoon with her hair in a braid. With that picture came the realization, clothed in surprise and reluctance, that his attitude toward her had changed. He had caught a glimpse of something in those gray-blue eyes which he hadn't thought existed. Apparently she possessed hard rock down under the Burlingame glitter.

Cas lit a cigarette and thought about that. He had always been a man who felt his way cautiously into relationships. There had been times, of course, when he had opened himself freely, even to love. Unfortunately, fate had always intervened in those times, knifed him, drew away the objects of his love. The result was the creation of more caution the next time around.

Now, remembering the look that had passed between him and Liz that afternoon, he felt his instincts go *wham!* He turned and gazed off at the moon, grinning. So absorbed was he in the memory that he was startled when the real Liz touched his arm.

"Hi," she called over the steady rumble of the engines.

"What're you doing up here?"

"I made you some coffee." She held out Will's thermos.

"Thanks, I can use it." Taking it from her, he uncorked the top and took a sip. It was very hot, sharp as gall, wonderful.

She huddled beside the conn seat. "That damned galley jumps around like a roller coaster. Hope the coffee's not too strong."

"It's great." He took another sip. "What's the matter, couldn't sleep?"

She shook her head, her hair riffling back in the wind coming over the coaming. "Full of bad dreams." She turned and gazed out at the light on the ocean, yellowed slightly with the moon lying close to the horizon. "It's really beautiful, the sea at night." She turned back, smiling. "When nobody's shooting at you."

He chuckled. "Yeah, gunfire does have a way of screwing up a mood."

"I can see why you love it out here, though." She paused. "Will said he'd never met anyone who loved the sea as much as you."

Cas tipped the thermos, then nodded. "It's the only thing I know that has nothing phony about it."

"Not like people?"

"Definitely not like people."

"Two days ago I would have said you were being cynical, but now I'm not so sure. The ocean, these islands, it all does something to you. Changes your perspective." She brushed back a coil of hair which was fluttering over her eyes. "When did you first discover that fact?"

He laughed warmly. "Oh, a long time ago, when I was a kid. I remember the first time I ever saw the ocean, or at least really got out on it. My dad took me out in this old used sailboat he'd bought, a little fifteen-footer with patched sails. We went out to Catalina and on the way back we cut a school of porpoise. They came up and rode just under our bow wave, humping up in the sunlight. I put my foot over the side and they nuzzled up against it. What a wonderful day that was.''

Quickly he glanced over at her, faintly embarrassed.

Liz watched him. "Is your father still alive?"

"No, he was killed a long time ago in an archeological dig in Baja."

"I'm sorry."

They were both silent for several minutes. Cas leaned down to make a small adjustment to the helm, and was very aware of the light touch on his skin when his arm brushed against hers.

"Cullin said you're a marine biologist," she offered at last.

"From time to time."

She laughed suddenly. "You know, I just realized something. Until this moment I'd completely forgotten where I'm supposed to be."

"Where's that?"

"Australia." She explained about her assignment to cover the upcoming summit meeting on a floating hotel and how she'd had to maneuver her boss into letting her come to the Philippines. "I'll bet old Schelling's having a fit right now, wondering where in the hell I am."

"The Seascape, I know that hotel. I came past it when I transited the Coral Sea."

She hadn't heard him. She was frowning, shaking her head in wonderment. "It's funny, but I really don't care about all that anymore. Isn't that a helluva way for a hotshot anchorperson to act? But out here that stuff just doesn't seem important somehow."

"Maybe it never was."

"Maybe." She shifted around, nestling closer to his leg. "Still, you gotta admit that what I'm doing is right off the wall. Here we are about to get into a damned naval engagement with the Chinese mafia in a beat-up boat in the Sulu Sea. I mean, my God."

When he failed to respond, she tilted her head,

rested a cheek on her palm and studied him. "You and Cullin are strange people. I've never, ever met anybody like you two before, willing to risk your lives like this. Why?"

"If you don't already understand, I'd never be able to explain it."

"That's the really nutso part. I think I do understand."

The conversation, plus her nearness, had caused Cas to ignore the compass needle, and he discovered that they had drifted nearly ten degrees off line. He brought the PT up again, the engine roar shifting slightly until they were once more steady.

Liz waited for him to sit back. Then she said, "You were married once, weren't you?"

He shot her a glance. "Old Will's full of information, isn't he?"

"What went wrong?" Then she shook her head, shocked at herself. "Oh, Lord, I can't believe I just asked you that."

He looked down at her and said simply, "Carolyn wanted something that didn't include me."

Liz studied his face for a long moment before speaking. When she did, her voice was barely audible over the engine drone. "She must have been a fool."

He experienced a powerful urge to reach out his hand, touch her hair, run his fingers over her mouth. But he didn't. Instead he fell into silence, as she did. Both of them remained motionless, achingly aware of the night and the moon's glow on the sea and each other.

Some minutes later, he said, "Well, here we are."

She roused herself and glanced over. "What?"

He pointed ahead. She moved forward and stepped up onto the panel bracket to see over the coaming. Far out there were lights on the ocean and the dark silhouettes of islands against the faint, silvery horizon.

"Better get Will up," Bonner said. "We'll be in the shallows pretty quick."

* * *

Cullin took them slowly down through the Lahing-Lahing Channel between the east coast of Jolo and the small, cone-shaped island of Bangalao. The islands looked gray-black in the dim light of dawn, and they could make out the torches of fishermen in their dugout canoes working nets along the inner channels. A few small fires glowed from isolated beaches.

Will told them he was certain Stanford and the Triad cruiser were somewhere near. Just flat smelled them in the wind. Cullin, like Bonner, had a seafarer's instincts. When at sea, he never relied on electronic gear; the PT had neither radio nor radar. But by using an occasional antiquated map, dead reckoning, and that sixth sense for reading sea sign, he always knew precisely where he was and what was around him.

Two hours later, they exited into the Celebes Sea. Cullin shut down the engines as he and Bonner discussed their next move. The Sulu archipelago was made up of five distinct island groups, the largest of which was the Basilan off Mindanao. In the center of the arc lay the Jolo and Tapul groups, with the Tawi Tawi extending farther southeast along the curve. The fifth, the Pangutaran, was far to the northwest.

If the Triad cruiser really was on their tail, Will pointed out, it would be coming through the channel islands with the onset of full light. That would mean both boats would be in the Celebes during the day. As an old PT fighter, Cullin wanted to make their attack at night when the darkness and crazy-quilt pattern of islets and motus close to Jolo would give them the advantage of surprise and maneuverability.

They decided to hole up until dark in a small bay on the island of Pata, eight miles off the south coast of Jolo. Cullin said that these remote inlets and bays were often used by pirates, raiders out of northern Malaysia who preyed on inter-island freighter traffic and transiting yachts in the Celebes. "They're bad ockers who'll nip a bullet up your arse for a candy bar. But at least they'll keep Stanford's Moro friends away," he added. "The Moros are scared shit-runny of pirates."

Pata bay was about a quarter mile wide with jungle growth overhanging the eastern shore, where they could hide the PT. A sixty-foot headland rose above the jungle, and the approach channel was very narrow, with exposed reefs on either side. Ranged to seaward were at least forty small islets and upthrust rocks forming twisted, hidden channels.

It was a little after seven when Cullin brought them into the bay and let the PT coast gently into the bank of thick *hao* and *balik* trees. The leaves and branches snapped across the coaming and the mounted .50-caliber machine gun until the boat eased to a stop, totally hidden under the canopy. The water was very clear about twenty feet off the bank. The bottom was sandy and they could see small sting rays like black bats moving close to the bottom, feeding on shrimp.

While Cullin sprayed the trees over the PT with gasoline to drive out insects, Bonner went over the side and made an inspection of the hull. There was a long, shallow gash on the starboard side near the keel, probably from coral, but it was holding all right.

Afterward he went probing along the bank, searching for *wili-wili* crabs in deep holes dug into the mud and sand down under the submerged *hao* roots. Liz came down and swam until he found one and held it out to her. It was a foot across with a single gigantic pincer. She squealed and swam way out into deep water, threatening to kill him if he brought it near her again.

They cooked the *wili-wili* in a big pot while Liz washed the salt off her with a hose from the water tank. Later they had crab meat and beer for breakfast, and Cas playfully poured foam down her back. He then took the Armalite and glasses and went off through the trees to the headland to keep watch.

The truck was an Australian Zephyr which looked a hundred years old. It had no fenders and the front wheels threw up a steady cloud of dust which blew back into the cab, engulfing Stanford. Heat poured through the wooden floorboards, exacerbating the stink of the load of pigs behind him.

Earlier that morning, the *Flying Sun* had docked at the north Jolo coast town of Patikul, a collection of ramshackle fishermen's huts with a narrow wharf covered with bird guano. It had taken Stanford nearly an hour to find someone with a mechanized vehicle, a pig "collector" making his pickup rounds like a mailman. For twenty dollars American, he agreed to carry Stanford to Jolo City, where there was a small airport.

Wings was what he needed now, increased search capability. Through the early darkness of dawn they had tracked the PT until it started into the Lahing-Lahing Channel. At that point Big Willie had flatly refused to take his boat into those waters until daylight.

At first Stanford had ranted at him, but then an adjust plan formed. Their maps showed a tiny red plane indicating an airport at Jolo City. He figured if he could hire a seaplane to sweep the Celebes waters south of the archipelago, he could scan a tremendous stretch of ocean while Lui came slowly into the Celebes. Once the PT was spotted, he could direct Big Willie and the runner boats in for the capture.

Lui thought that was a pretty good idea too. He radioed his incoming runner boats and ordered them to veer south to execute searches along the Celebes side of the arc. During the transmission Sap Lee informed him that one of the LC-11s was down with engine trouble in the Tawi Tawi group. Repairs would be made and then they'd join up.

It was nearly ten in the morning when the pig truck reached Jolo City. The airport was just outside the town, alongside a foul-smelling swamp where tall-legged black birds wandered the shallows.

The owner/operator of the facility, and its sole pilot, was an Indian named Sewajeen Ibul, a sweaty, vociferous man with pox scars. He possessed three aircraft, he informed Stanford. A tiny Cessna 150, a French twin-engined Mystic, and, anchored in the swamp, an old American PBY seaplane with patches on its wings and shattered side observation ports.

"Ah, yess, yess," Ibul said effusively, his words gliding up and down like a fast car crossing hills, "I can cover the entire ocean and find many little things."

Stanford gazed at the PBY through the dirty windows of the tin shack that served as Airport Operations. "Can that goddamned thing actually fly?"

"Fly? Fly?" Ibul said, wide-eyed. "My mistress can soar like many angels. She can carry one to where the sun rises and where the darkness comes like—"

"Let's do it."

"Yess, yess. We will perform execution of flight verry quickly."

Twenty minutes later, the PBY lifted her antiquated hull out of the muck of the swamp and turned south, struggling for altitude.

Near midday, Cas, stretched on his belly on the headland with binoculars, spotted one of Lui's LC-11s. It was coming fast along the out waters of the scattered islands off Pata. It was totally black and its twin molded hull bows cleaved the ocean, throwing a choppy pattern of spray.

He moved to the edge of the rocky cliff and whistled. Then he went back to the binoculars, watching the boat approach. A few minutes later, Cullin came up the hill, pulling himself up by exposed vines. He squatted beside him, breathing hard.

"Who's company?" he asked. "I heard the engines."

"Pirates, I think." He handed over the glasses.

Will studied the incoming vessel for a moment, then sat back on his haunches. "Pirates they are."

"That's an LC-11 they're riding. The Riverine Force used those suckers in Nam. They carry heavy weapons and good deflection plate."

"Aye, at least a couple of fifties on the forward

mount. We definitely don't need a dust-up with them bush nongs.''

As they watched the boat pass about a mile off, the sound of its engines and the slap of the hull came in little pockets of sound across the distance. It gradually faded away as the LC-11 disappeared beyond the closer islets.

Will sucked air through his teeth. "I think we best lay some charge in the channel, mate. They've used this snug-away before. Their bleedin' chunder's all over the shoreline. If they decide to come in with them fifties, we'll be up the drainpipe for sure.''

Cas nodded. "I can swim a haversack out and anchor it on a floater in the channel. We could detonate from here with a few rounds.''

"Good-oh, mate. But I'll swim 'er out. You keep an eye open.''

"All right.''

Without another word Will headed back off the high ground, wiry muscles bunching as he pulled his way down.

All through the afternoon, the PBY ran in-and-out, hundred-mile search loops off the southern Jolo islands. The interior of the seaplane was a mess, cluttered with tools and greasy spare parts and bits of food and empty Coca Cola cans. Ibul kept up a shouting commentary on everything from women to the proper cooking method for squid. Occasionally he'd cry, "Ah? Ah?'' and make some minor adjustment to the droning Pratt-Whitney 650-3 engines. From the rear came the constant rush of wind through the shattered dome bubbles.

Finally Stanford had had enough and told Ibul to shut the hell up and just fly the plane. The Indian pouted for a while but finally settled on whistling the first few bars of a song over and over again, tapping his dark fingers on the yoke.

By four in the afternoon, Stanford was certain that Cullin had not transited deeper into the Celebes, but instead had gone to ground somewhere among the scatter islands. Undoubtedly he was waiting for darkness to make a run for it. Stanford ordered Ibul to descend and skim over the entire southern side of the Jolo group. The PBY dropped heavily until they were at two hundred feet and the tiny scatter islands flashed past the windows.

They made the sixty-mile run twice, swinging a one-eighty on the first leg at Tapul Island beyond Jolo. Ibul, chattering again, adjusted course and they came in slightly from the south over Pata Island.

Suddenly Jack jumped and leaned into his binoculars. "Swing back! Cross over that bay again."

Ibul brought the PBY around in a long banking turn with Stanford stretching to see past his shoulders. Two minutes later, they floated over the small bay, engines throttled back slightly. Jack was glassing the eastern edge of the estuary when he caught a glint of metal, then the port hull curve of a boat nearly hidden beneath foliage.

"There it is!" he bellowed. "Son of a bitch, there it is!" He swung around to the Indian. "What island is this?"

"Pata."

"Pata, right, Pata."

Ibul smiled happily. "Ah, we have found your little boat. How nice. You see, I guide my mistress with verry good hands."

"Shut up and get our asses back to my boat."

Twenty minutes later, the Indian brought the seaplane down onto the ocean a half mile from the Triad cruiser. The sea was gentle, yet the aircraft jolted and leaped through the tops of a southern swell before skidding to a stop, engines idling noisily. Lui immediately dispatched a dinghy to pick up Stanford.

As Jack unbuckled from his seat, he paused a moment, studying the grinning Ibul. He was wondering if he should kill him, just to be sure he wouldn't run all over hell talking about finding the PT for a crazy American and maybe getting Ka Lakas's boys on them again. Finally he thought: Screw it. "Go home, Sewajeen," he said, slapping the man's shoulder. "And thank your gods for good things."

Ibul went on grinning, nodding his head enthusiastically. "Ah, yess, I am most lucky to have flying with such good-paying gentleman."

The sun was nearing the eastern horizon as the ancient PBY lifted off the sea. Her engines sent sharp, growling echoes over the water as she bore laboriously into the sky and then turned north. Before she was out of sight, the *Flying Sun* was already under way, headed for Pata Island.

Bonner had jerked right off his belly when the PBY soared overhead. He had been dozing, his head across the Armalite's stock. Now he rolled over into a thicket of *ti*-leaf and watched as the aircraft banked and came back around, the whirling blades catching a flashing reflection of light from the sun low on the horizon. As it came in for another pass, he looked through his binoculars at the cabin but couldn't make out anything but the opaqueness of windshield. Then it was over him again, this time less than a hundred feet above the headland, the roar of the engines thundering down into the trees. Immediately after it passed, the sound vanished, lost against the far side of the cliff.

He lay, his heart pounding an echo of the engines. Who the hell was that? he wondered. Coastal police? Or had Stanford pulled in reinforcements, air spotters? He listened for the aircraft's engines, bracing for another pass.

Gradually his ears picked up the engine sound again, but it had become distant, riffling and fading. He stood and moved to the edge of the precipice. Down in the estuary, the mangroves were throwing long, thin shadows across the water, and seaward the combers beyond the channel were shiny in the slanting sunlight, as if polished with wax.

A few minutes later, Liz came up, her face red with exertion. She made the top and flopped down, cross legged. Breathless, she said, "Will says . . . to keep a sharp eye. He thinks that plane . . . spotted us."

"He figure who it was?"

"Either a coast patrol or Stanford."

"Shit!"

Her eyes were wide and bright. "It scared the hell out of me. I was asleep on deck."

Cas glassed the ocean. It too was darkening and he spied flocks of seabirds lifting off the closer rock upthrusts and swooping along the inner channels, searching for feeding fish as the sea breeze died, smoothing the surface. Otherwise, there was nothing out there.

"Will says we'll leave as soon as it gets dark," Liz said. "He's jumpy. Makes me jumpy." She shook her head. "God, why doesn't Stanford just leave us alone? How important can these damned disks be to him, anyway? Killing and more killing, for what? A stolen satellite?"

"There's big money in it somewhere."

"No, there's something else to this, Cas."

"What?"

"I don't know, but I sense it." She fell silent for a long moment, her fingers picking up sand, letting it drain through her fingers. "Cas?"

"Mm?"

"We're going to die, aren't we? Just like Jerry."

He lowered the glasses. "No."

She hugged herself. "I can't stop shaking. That plane, it scared me. Oh, Jesus!" She put her head down. "This is insanity."

He reached out and touched her hair. It was still damp and felt like sable. He ran his fingers lightly over it. Liz looked up, then put her hand on his, squeezing.

And suddenly she lunged upward and threw her arms around him. He felt the force of her impact, the full line of her breasts under the flak jacket, her pelvis and thighs, bone and smooth flesh. She found his mouth, mashed her own against it. Teeth banged teeth. He put his right arm around her waist and pulled her in. They clung together awkwardly, shifting by degrees until Liz released her hold and hung limply against him.

"It's okay, it's okay," he kept saying. "We'll be all right."

Finally she tilted her head and inhaled deeply. Drawing back a little and shaking her hair, she smiled sheepishly at him. "Big-time reporter comes unglued."

He chortled. "Big-time reporter almost broke my teeth."

She laughed, tossing her head again, her eyes in the fading light alive and moist and filled with gray wonder. "You smell," she said quietly.

"Whoa."

She laid her head into the curve of his neck and shoulder. "But such a real smell. I never realized a man could smell so good."

Suddenly Cas stiffened.

Liz said, "What's the matter?"

"Engines!"

He pulled away and scooped up the binoculars. A minute later, she heard a distant buzzing as well. Then it faded and disappeared.

"Get back to the boat," Bonner snapped. "Something's coming."

Liz shoved herself to her feet, but stood there in confusion.

"Go! Go!"

Wordlessly she turned and started back down the cliff, grabbing roots and swinging to footholds.

Cas scanned the darkening ocean. In the binocular view the faded light made distortions on the surface. A single seagull flashed through the oval picture, its wings flaming red. And then he saw a ship's lights on the crimson sea, coming in. The Triad cruiser.

The buzzing engine sound came again, louder now. He swung the glasses to his right. A half mile to the west, he saw first the creamy bow wave of a fast-moving boat, then the black hull of an LC-11 creasing through the scatter rock upthrusts and islets which stretched on the downside of the estuary.

They're here! he thought wildly. He dropped the binoculars and scooped up his weapon. He advanced to the edge of the cliff, dropped to one knee, and braced the rifle barrel on it. Over the sight, he tried to pick out the tiny float charge down in the channel. But all he saw was darkness, with slivers of white surf looking like moving feathers on the reef.

"Goddammit!" he bellowed, scanning the rifle back and forth.

The LC-11 burst out of scatter rock and made an orange-white ribbon of wake as it curved inward, aiming for the estuary channel. A brilliant beam of light suddenly snapped on from the craft. For a moment it swept crazily and then it homed to the channel, illuminating the feathers of surf to fluorescent white lines.

Cas lunged to his feet, the rifle pressed tightly against his shoulder. Swinging the tiny dot of the muzzle sight, he searched frantically for the float charge. Where the hell is it? his mind screamed, knowing he had only seconds before the LC-11 came boiling into the bay, guns blazing.

12

The hail came down in sweeping deluges that hurled through the bunched locomotives and flatcars strung along the tracks of the railhead at Quanzie, thirty miles south of the Amur frontier. Although it was still evening, the storm clouds forced the use of spotlights. The beams made the icy drops of rain sparkle like jewels as the tank crews of the 512th Lasting Thunder Armored Division, 17th Corps of the Northern PLA Army, loaded their vehicles onto the flatcars.

The frigid, wet air was filled with the sound of revving engines and the metallic clank of treads as the Model 15 Spearthrust tanks, patterned after the small Russian T-54's, rumbled up and into their chocks. Once they were positioned and chained down, the soldiers began covering them with bales of straw and bunches of cabbage to camouflage their movement north from crossing Russian or American satellites.

In the small communications hut of the train yard, First General Trai Bon, commandant of the 512th, held his chin on his chest as he listened through a field phone to the screaming of General Hsien Tu, Chief of Staff of the Central Military Commission in Beijing. Despite the cold, Trai was sweating.

Hsien was outraged. The deployment of the armored division was fully five hours behind schedule. It should have been already up on the Amur frontier, taking bunker positions in the pine and maple forests outside Changbai in support of the Sacred Pool Assault Team.

The chief of staff paused to take a breath. Then he roared: "You will have your vehicles entrenched by dawn. Is that understood?"

"Yes, General. I have already discussed the situation with the yardmaster, and he has cleared—"

"Discussed? You imbecile, you will order him to clear the tracks all the way to the river. Is *that* understood?"

"Yes, sir."

There was a pause, more frosty than the air. "General, you are tempting the crows."

Trai's face blanched. *Tempting the crows* was a phrase that meant possible execution. He wiped a finger across his damp forehead, nodding frantically as if the COS could actually see him. "I understand fully, my general."

There was no answer, simply a crack in the line and then a buzz. Gingerly, as if he held a snake, Trai replaced the field phone receiver. He turned and looked at the railroad telegrapher. The man was staring diligently at his switchboard.

Infuriated, General Trai whipped his baton across the man's back. "You dare smile?"

The man cowered, arms lifted. "Oh, no, my general. I merely study my lines."

"Get the yardmaster up here."

"Yes, sir." The telegrapher's hands flew across his switches.

Out in the yard, the Spearthrusts churned over the ground, cutting the frozen mud as they aligned with the up ramps. Above them the soldiers, their tunics soaking wet, hurled bales of straw. Out at the edge of the spotlights, the faces of peasants, drawn out of curiosity to the activity in the yard, glistened in the rain.

General Trai, with nothing else on which to vent his rage, again slashed his baton across the back of the telegrapher. The man winced with pain and closed his eyes.

* * *

Cas held the tiny bead of his muzzle sight on a small comber that had just broken on the exposed reef. The spray exploded into drops that looked pure white in the glare of the boat's searchlight. He scanned back, reached the nearer surf, returned.

For a split second he caught a glimpse of the float charge, bobbing in surf runoff in the center of the channel. Then he lost it again. But he held the bead to the spot where he'd seen it, freezing his position. He lifted his eyes slightly and looked directly into the bright oval of the searchlight. Its beam tunneled out and washed brilliantly against the rocks at the base of the headland. In the side glare he could make out men standing and the darker bulk of the boat.

It was a hundred yards from the float charge.

Down below, Liz reached the PT. With her heart thudding crazily in her chest, she skittered out onto a thick *hao* limb and dropped to the foredeck beside the mounted survival raft. Cullin already had the engines going, their throaty exhaust rumble muffled under the trees, with faint smoke drifting through the leaves.

Flaring light was coming from somewhere toward the ocean. In the speckled shadows she made out Will up in the gun turret. As she watched, regaining her breath, he rapped back the bolt of first one .50, then the other, arming them. She went around the starboard barrier and up into the conn.

"Where's Bonner?" he shouted down at her.

"Still on the cliff."

"Bloody hell, I hope he can see the charge!" He deftly slipped under the guns and dropped behind the starboard conn barrier. His face was tight, eyes hot. "Missy, you'll have to take the helm," he snapped. "Those karkos're comin' straight in. If Bonner can't take 'em, I'll have to go for their bleedin' fifties as soon as—"

His words were cut off as the rapidly darkening air was suddenly blown apart by the powerful muzzle bursts from one of the .50-caliber machine guns aboard the LC-11.

Both he and Liz hit the deck.

Hearing the gun open up, Cas jumped. The staccato roar went rolling into the estuary and rebounded off the cliff as the gun muzzles, side by side, threw long candleflame-shaped bursts into the darkness.

The LC-11 was sixty yards from the float . . . forty . . .

Cas cut loose with the Armalite on full auto. The weapon jerked back against his shoulder, its sound hollow and puny beside the roar of the .50's. He saw his rounds throw up a line of small geysers in the channel. He swore and swung back, crossing through his own bursts.

The boat came on without slowing, but one of the .50's swung on the cliff. Bullets stitched up the side of the headland with violent, heavy impacts. For a tiny second it stopped firing, then started again. This time the rounds went over Cas's head, their velocity splitting the air twenty feet above him with a vicious rushing sound.

With his whole body tensing into a single taut unit, he swung the Armalite for another try at the float charge. His first tracers went out and the LC-11 crossed into the distant geysers. He pulled off another burst. Almost simultaneously a small explosion crackled as the haversack's detonator took a round.

Instantly the entire charge went up. Twenty pounds of high explosives boomed with a deep, water-absorbed thunderclap. For a split second Cas watched as the bow of the boat lifted nearly straight up in the air, like a dragster with too much power turning itself upside down. And then it blew apart in an orange-white explosion as its tanks ignited.

He dropped to the ground. Shrapnel flew through the air overhead, shattering rocks, slicing through the taller *ti*-leaves, the objects whirling with the whipping sibilance of boomerangs. He hugged the rock. Slowly, fading into its own echoes, the tumult of the explosion finally dropped back into silence. He lifted his head. The rocky edge of the cliff flickered with orange light from burning debris down in the channel.

Faintly he heard the engine of another LC-11 approaching.

It took him precisely three minutes to reach the PT, coming down hard over rocks in the dark, hauling on vines, the Armalite banging against his back on its harness. He went thrashing through the *hao* trees, momentarily sank into mushy water, and finally hauled himself onto the port deck. He knelt there a moment, panting for air.

Will came up with a tiny flashlight. "Casimir, ya bloody ripper," he bawled happily, slapping Bonner's shoulder. "Ya copped the dingoes beautiful. For a mo there, my arse was suckin' wind."

"Another one's coming in," Cas gasped. "Maybe more. And the cruiser's sittin' out a couple miles. We better shag ass, mate."

Cullin went on grinning in the dim light, an icy, tundric smile. "Well, now," he said with soft, almost gleeful menace, "let's see we can give the bloody dill and his choongs first cab off the rank."

As Cullin took the conn, Cas wiggled up into the gun turret. Liz was standing around, looking confused and anxious. Already the distant sound of the second LC-11 was clearly audible over the bay. Cas noticed her and came back down to the conn platform. He touched her arm. "Come aft." He led her back to the smoke canisters Will had installed near the stern.

Quickly he instructed her how to operate them. She was to first open a tiny petcock in the line and then manually pump the oil down onto the exhaust jackets. "You can lie flat between the after engine coamings till Cullin gives you a double flash," he said. "Then hit smoke for the count of ten and go back to the coamings. Can you do it?"

"Yes," she whispered. "All right. God!"

"We'll lay four bursts of smoke. But hang tight when you move around, we'll be flyin'."

Liz nodded and nodded. " 'Kay, 'kay."

He grabbed her arm, squeezed, grinning hard into her face. "You're gonna do okay, luv." And then he slipped swiftly across the after cabin roof and down into the conn barrier.

A moment later the engines came up into power with an ear-splitting roar. Liz, stretched between the vent coamings, felt their jarring, intensely concentrated potency directly below her. Through the after openings, air blew up hot and thick with oil smell.

Branches cracked and scraped across the boat, leaves raked her back. Then they were free. She lifted her head slightly, hearing the change in pitch as the engine sound stopped rebounding off the trees. From between the coamings she could see the water thrown off the bow, first slanting straight out and then angling upward, the white of it faintly tinged with the glow from the moon, which also silvered the leaves of the mangrove.

They tore through the night, straight for the channel. . . .

Jack Stanford had experienced a moment of stunned disbelief as he saw the first LC-11 go up in a horrendous explosion. He had been glassing the boat from the cruiser's starboard cabin wing, homing to its searchlight. He searched for an explanation. Maybe it had been the PT? But all the time he knew better. Now Cullin and Bonner had weapons!

Finally hurling himself out of the momentary jam of his thoughts, he lunged through the hatchway and bellowed to Big Willie to kill his engines. He had to shout twice before the lumbering Chinaman obeyed.

The *Flying Sun* was now about a mile off Pata Island, still in fairly deep water. The boat gently eased to a gliding stop and lay, rolling slightly. Jack sprinted to Big Willie's side. "Where's the second boat?" he barked. "Raise him, now."

Before the captain could comply, the radio blew out a roiling splay of static, and then the voice of Lee Sap came through, shouting Chinese as raucous as a crow. Big Willie listened a moment, said something. Lee came back with another stream of words.

"The PT comin' out," Big Willie said flatly.

"Tell Lee to intercept him. Goddammit, if that PT gets past us into open ocean, we'll never catch him."

"Lee say he's too far away."

"Fuck!" Jack ran across the cabin to the starboard wing and peered out. In a moment he was back. "Home your radar on him."

Big Willie did so with cumbersome slowness. The radar screen shifted through two levels of focus . . . click, click. And there was the PT, making a blip the size of a nickel. It was moving so rapidly that each swing of the light arm showed a positional deflection of nearly an inch. A quarter mile to its left was the LC-11, also racing flat out.

Lui entered the cabin. He had just been smoking hash, and he seemed to float over the deck, coming loose-limbed, his eyes moist. He hovered behind Stanford like a momentarily tethered balloon.

"God Almighty!" Jack bellowed, on the edge of frustrated hysteria. "Tell Lee to go after him before he gets into deep water."

Big Willie's gaze swung to him, fixed stonily. He didn't key.

Stanford whirled around to face the Unicorn. "Order him to do it. Son of a bitch, order him."

"Where we are?" Lui asked dreamily.

"The PT's coming out," Jack screamed. "He's tryin' to break out. We've got to stop him!"

Lui swayed, flipped his hand up at Big Willie, and snapped the wrist in an imperious gesture. The captain keyed his mike and said something to Lee.

Suddenly a third powerful blip appeared on the screen. It shimmered greenly, its edges stationary but flicking needles of light.

"What that?" Big Willie said. "One more boat?"

Jack leaned in and studied the screen. "No, the prick's blowing some kind of magnetic chaff." He focused on the PT blip. "But that one's him." As the light arm swung through its revolution, it showed that the LC-11 was snapping a hard turn to port, homing to the PT.

"All right!" Stanford yelled. "He's on him. Willie, swing to port and we'll have the son of a bitch bracketed!"

Lee Sap was an old hand at the chase and subsequent bloodletting. Born into the Wo Ching Wo, the traditional sea bandits of the southern China coast, he had lived most of his life on the fishing grounds off the Luichow Peninsula and the islands in the Gulf of Tonkin. He was thirty-one years old and had killed fifteen men in personal combat. When his blood was up, his skin twitched, making the tattoos all over his body writhe.

They were doing so now as he squinted over the coaming of the LC-11 at the moonlit glimmer from the PT's bow wave three hundred yards to the west. He could see that it was laying patches of smoke. The patches were filled with tiny specks of something which glinted in the moonlight like thousands of raindrops.

As he watched, the PT made a slight turn away from him, releasing another smoke cloud. He instantly corrected his own course and went straight after it. Fifteen seconds later, they blew through one of the clouds. It smelled oily and made his eyes burn.

As they exited it, he caught sight of the PT again, this time doing a wide one-eighty starboard back toward the island. Again Lee adjusted, going hard over in a tighter turn in order to intercept it.

For a moment the boat was broadside to him, less than three hundred yards out, the hurling spray of its bow defining it sharply against the dark sea. He screamed to his gunmen. Instantly both .50's opened up. Their spent casings went clattering all around him. Beyond the PT, geysers erupted in the ocean.

Immediately there was return fire—short, quick bursts containing tracers which went into the water ahead. But each successive burst was closer than the previous one.

Lee's men began firing their assault rifles, canting the muzzles high. But they were losing ground on the PT, falling back out of the curve. Its speed was too much for Lee's boat. He glanced to his right and saw the dark line of Pata and the nearer offshore islets coming up fast. The PT crossed in front of him two hundred yards distant. Easing off the helm slightly, he merged into its wake as they both shot toward the scattered islets, his men still firing.

Another flood of smoke roiled up off the stern of the PT, billowing up against the moon. Within seconds it rolled over them. Lee blinked his eyes, wiped away burning tears. Save for the pounding coming up through the deck, all sensation of the LC-11's speed had disappeared within the cloud. It was as if it were moving and they were stationary on a misty mountaintop.

Just as Lee's hands leaped to the throttles to pull off power, the LC-11 momentarily broke out of the smoke. He caught a fleeting glimpse of something huge and dark directly ahead. He bellowed, ramming back on the throttles and throwing the helm hard to starboard as they went into another thick cloud of smoke.

Two seconds later, the LC-11 ran over a stretch of exposed reef with a violent metallic rending. Lee heard a man scream. It sounded far away, as if the voice came from a deep ravine. He had the odd sensation of weightlessness, heard the boat's propellers still whirring in midair, and then the boat crashed head-on into a fifteen-foot upthrust of rock.

Lee was hurled forward into the control panel with such force that one of the throttle levers jabbed into his chest. Skewered on it, he felt horrendous pain for

a flashing moment before the stern of the boat cart-
wheeled and smashed full length against the cliff.

Lying flat between the engine coamings, Liz was
whimpering softly in her throat. She had never experienced such terror before. The entire world was coming apart with mad sound. Fifty-caliber bullets sizzled
overhead with the sounds of cracking ice. The PT's
engines screamed beneath her. And then she cringed
at the horrible crash of the LC-11 somewhere astern.

She lifted her head, feeling waves of nausea, her
eyes stinging. The forward momentum of the PT had
created a vacuum astern which sucked smoke off the
exhaust jackets right over her. Mistily she saw dark
chunks of rock and reef and fairly large islets hurtle
past on either side of the boat.

They started into a hard turn to the right. Cullin
came off the engines slightly as they rocketed past another islet, so close that nesting birds were driven into
the sky like a sweep of bats lifting from a cave entrance. The boat leveled out and up went the engines
again. Stretched out ahead was the sea, long, reaching
swells washed with moonlight. As they breasted them,
the PT pitched slightly until she was once more on the
step, her forward hull free, the swells pounding into
her a third of the way back along the hull, blowing
explosions of water out on either side at the cabin.

A mile away, Liz spotted the lights of the Triad
cruiser, moving off at a slight angle toward the southwest. . . .

When Stanford saw the PT returning fire against the
closure of the LC-11, he felt an instant headache coming on. Now the bastards not only have explosives, he
thought furiously, they also have heavier firepower than
the cruiser.

He haunted the radar set, his eyes narrow slits as he
paced back and forth. Actually, the unit was nearly
useless because the drifting smoke bursts, scattering
on the wind, were throwing all sorts of crazy reads.

And though the solid blips of the LC-11 and the PT did pop into view occasionally, they were then gobbled up by the massive rebound off Pata and the scatter islets.

Big Willie had eased up as they approached the shallows. They were now skirting along where the bottom dropped off into deep water, close to a mile out.

Stanford finally left the cabin and went out on the starboard wing, again trying to pick up wake visually in the moonlight. He was peering outward when the LC-11 struck the rock cliff. Over the cruiser's slowed engines he heard what sounded like a wreck on a nearby freeway. For a moment his spirits went spiraling upward. One of the boats had hit rock! But which? A fifty-fifty proposition.

He leaned his ear into the night breeze, listening for engines. There! He caught the low thunder of high-speed units, coming intermittently as they passed behind rock outcroppings. Then he hissed through his teeth as he recognized the heavier, rolling peal of the PT's power plants.

He saw something flash across a stretch of open water, and then spied the hurl of spray as the boat came around in a sharp turn. He watched it straighten, its bow wave cascading on either side, coming straight toward them.

He let out one explosive curse, then dodged back into the cabin, hollering: "Go to power! He's on our tail!"

Before anyone could react, they heard the staccato rap of machine-gun fire. Through the cabin's side portholes, Stanford watched tracer bullets go lazily past them on either side and into the water, deflecting straight up like Roman candles bouncing off ground.

The center Hall-Scott suddenly began running rough, heaving in powerful vibrations that shook all the way up into the control panel. Cullin started swearing, stopping just long enough to yell up to Cas: "Take the conn."

Cas hunched out of the machine gun harness and slipped over the barrier down into the passageway. When he got there, Will had his head cranked around and was staring at their wake. Black smoke was fuming off one of the exhaust clusters, banking back in the suction wind.

"The center engine's eatin' raw fuel," Cullin shouted. "She'll shake herself off the mounts." He slipped away from the control panel and Cas took his place. He grabbed Bonner's arm. "Go in for the torpedo run anyway. We'll finish the barstid once and for all. But remember, we've dropped ten knots on 'em, so figure your distance tighter."

Cas nodded as Cullin scurried back through the passageway. He swung forward again and picked up the lights of the cruiser dead ahead, about six hundred yards away. They were bearing slightly to starboard.

The PT was still vibrating viciously from the misfiring engine. Cas began gauging the closing rate and realized he'd need help. He leaped onto the conn seat and started yelling and waving his arms for Liz to come up.

A moment later, she skittered around the curve of the barrier passageway, hunched over. In the panel lights her eyes were wild. He grabbed her waist and pulled her up to the panel.

"Take the helm," he bellowed.

She stared dumbly at him.

He cupped his hand at the confluence of her jaw and throat. "Take it, Liz," he shouted. "It's just like a car. But feel for the hull movement and try to anticipate it so you can recover before she swings too far."

Liz put her hands tentatively on the wheel. Easing around her, he yelled again, "Hold to this course. When I tell you, flip up the safety cover and hit that button." He indicated which one on the firing panel. There were four of them, with red flip covers. At that moment the vibrations in the deck stopped completely and the sound of the engines thinned slightly as Cullin cut off the center unit.

"Once the torpedo's away," Cas continued, "throw the wheel around hard to the left and go straight out. You got that?"

Liz, both hands clamped on the wheel, nodded wordlessly. As Cas leaped up onto the barrier and crawled back into the turret harness, she felt the surge of the boat through her fingers and thought: Oh, shit! Then when Bonner opened up again with the .50's, she let out a little cry, feeling the recoils coming down through the decking. But she held on grimly, hearing his spent rounds scattering back and away. She watched the tracers go out, dismayed at how slowly they floated.

Gradually they closed with the Triad cruiser. Seeing little flashes of light coming from the stern, she knew they were shooting at her. She imagined bullets hurtling through the moonlight, envisioned one impacting directly into the middle of her head. She ducked slightly but held on.

In the gun turret, Bonner was firing short bursts—first to the right of the cruiser, then to the left. His purpose was not to hit it but to keep the fleeing boat on a steady course straight ahead so they could put the Mark-10 torpedo, as Cullin had said, "right up the bugger's arsehole."

He and Will had worked out the firing-run procedure earlier. Since the cruiser was capable of rapid evasive maneuvers, the touchy part was holding the target in a steady forward course until the torpedo caught up with it. That was the reason for Bonner's bracketing fire, hoping that the cruiser captain would be scared enough to hold a steady course. But with the PT's speed cut ten knots, closure time had dropped. That meant they'd have to get in closer with bracketing fire before launching the torpedo.

Cas watched the lights of the cruiser slowly approach. It was running full out. He threw a burst to the left, and then scanned across to the right, still blowing caps, attempting to stop the small-arms fire off the stern. Through clenched teeth he kept telling the cruiser: "Come on, you prick! Hold steady, don't veer on me!"

Nearer and nearer they came.

Three hundred yards . . . two-fifty . . . two hundred . . .

He yelled to Liz at the top of his lungs to fire. Then he cut loose with a prolonged burst. A moment later, he felt a heavy jolt come up through the turret seat and heard the faint blast of compressed air in the torpedo tube. He stopped firing and glanced to his right.

There'd been no launch!

Over the scream of the engines, he heard a smaller, whirring sound. He swung around. The torpedo was jammed in the tube, its forward section hanging limply while the three sets of propellers went on whirling.

Holy Jesus! he thought wildly.

Cullin screamed through the intercom: "Bonner, we got a hot run! Jam the torpedo's props before she arms!"

Cas shrugged out of the gun harness and dropped to the barrier way at a full run. He caught sight of the stern of the cruiser coming up and gun flashes, then Liz staring open-mouthed at him as he dropped to the barrier deck.

He jumped up and took the helm, whirling first to the right, then to the left, and back again, trying to dislodge the torpedo. The PT responded with hard rolls, the bow wave hurling as the turns threw her off the step.

It was no use.

He shouted for Liz to take the helm again and darted away, headed for the firing tube. Clearing the barrier, he felt the deck tilt sharply as the PT, still caught in the roll momentum, went into another turn. On the conn, Liz was trying to stop the wheel as it spun wildly, the stern skidding.

Cas grabbed frantically for the edge of the barrier coaming to keep from sliding across the center cabin roof. "Steady her up, for chrissake! Steady up!" he screamed at Liz. A moment later, the remaining engines went dead as Cullin, realizing what was happening, stopped all power. Instantly the boat leveled out, still racing but gradually losing its momentum.

Bonner slid to his knees beside the after end of the tube, cracked the hatch open and peered in. Two bullets whomped into the ocean fifty yards off. Inside the tube, compressed air was hissing furiously and hot billows of greasy smoke blew back into his face. Dimly he could see the whirring impeller blades. Just beyond, the shaft housing was glowing red.

Normally washed by water flow during its run, the torpedo's engine and shaft bearings were overheating. If he couldn't jam the props, the heat would become white-hot and the engine would lock up violently, possibly igniting its own tanks and then the main charge.

Desperately Cas searched around the deck for something to use, saw three sandbags and scooped one up. He rammed it up the back of the tube. For a moment the sound of the whirring blades deepened slightly, straining, and then a blast of sand and bits of burlap blew out of the tube and into his face.

Rolling away from it, he banged into the charthouse hatch. Instantly he was up, his face stinging. The deck under him was pitching gently as the PT settled in the water. He was vaguely aware of distant firing.

Once more he searched for something to jam the propellers. His hand touched the metal railing that ran along the edge of the charthouse roof. He gripped it with both hands and, using sheer strength and his body weight, pulled off about six feet of it.

Still using his own momentum, he swung around and rammed the railing up the tube. There was a moment of metallic screech. A piece of the railing came hurtling back through the tube like a bullet, zinging off. Then the torpedo engine stopped.

Far to starboard, the cruiser was swinging around in a hard turn.

Will appeared beside him. Together they attempted to push the torpedo out the tube. While Bonner straddled the unit and heaved with his arms and shoulders,

Cullin shoved the end of the railing. The tube was hot and fumed with grease smoke and the stench of heated metal.

Pushing and lift-shoving, they finally budged the fifteen-hundred-pound torpedo. An inch, then another, and still another. Finally it passed its weight center and, pulled by its warhead, left the tube with a loud scrape and dropped into the water.

Cas slid off the tube and knelt beside Cullin. The skin of his inner thighs was stinging and his arms ached from the exertion. Panting, Will looked up, shaking his head. "I swear . . . I'm gonna kick that bleedin' . . . Abbie's arse from here to Sydney."

Suddenly they jerked upright at a fresh sound of heavy machine-gun fire and hot projectiles sizzling far overhead. Confused for a moment, they both scanned. The Triad cruiser was still a half mile away, coming on.

Bonner swung his gaze back toward Pata and caught sight of a bow wave just clearing the outer islets. "There it is!" he yelled. "It's another LC-11."

"Bloody hell!" Cullin growled. "That friggin' Yank's got the whole bleedin' pirate navy on us." He gave Bonner a narrow-eyed stare. "I hate to give the barstids the wog ball, but I think we best vacate the field, mate."

"We'll meet again."

"Aye, mate, that we will."

"You clear the center engine?"

Will shook his head. "She took a ricochet off the intake manifold. We run her and she'll tear the arse out of us. Let's see we can outrun the dingoes with only two."

Thirty seconds later, with Cullin at the helm, the PT came up into speed chain again. He swung them due southwest, straight across the Celebes Sea toward Manadora on the Sulawesi coast.

Stanford watched the PT receding in the distance, his thoughts a painful jumble. Ohsweetjesuswelostthemagain! Even Big Willie was cursing with frustration, pointing a ham of a finger at the windshield as if nobody else aboard knew what was going on. Out there in the moonlight the LC-11 went skittering across their bow like a ghostly projectile on the ocean, its .50's flashing occasionally but uselessly as the PT streaked out of sight.

Stanford turned slowly and looked at Lui, sitting at the bar. The Unicorn was idly scratching his testicles, still grinning vacantly. But his eyes were as frozen as ice blades, and he said: "Yue Fei no gonna like this, Yank."

13

The Chinese artillery barrage started at 12:31 A.M. Beijing time. Above Ziaushen two miles south of the Amur River, 155mm and 105mm howitzers shattered the frozen silence, their blasts raising circles of smoke that floated up before a tundric moon. The rounds fell across a half mile centered on the village of Kisurar, site of the first guerrilla strike, along with Russian artillery bunkers and storage facilities farther back in the wooded hills. Over thirty percent of the Soviet artillery was knocked out within the first eight minutes of the bombardment.

The Russians soon managed to launch a counter-barrage, but their weapons were still trained on Changbai. The shells whistled in and blasted ground within the village already torn apart in the earlier barrage. Those peasants who had been brave enough to venture back to their mud huts again fled.

Before the Chinese had opened up, Captain Litung, along with the entire Sacred Pool Assault Team, had already taken up positions on the Chinese side of the river. As the Soviet shells began falling among them, orders came down to move out, across the river. Amid the sounds of bugles and clashing cymbals, they dashed across the shallows or hopped into small inflatable assault boats to cross the deeper water. With them were elements of the 108th Flying Foot Brigade, crack infantry fighters who had challenged the Vietcong ten years before in the paddies of Bao Ha.

The first wave ran headlong into strong counter fire from the Russian shore. Partially reinforced after the earlier attack, the Soviet compound fronting Kisurar set up a ferocious field of fire. Captain Litung and his men were momentarily trapped behind the river berms. The young officer scurried back and forth bellowing, *"Gungji! Gungji!"* at his men, ordering them to attack through the barbed wire encirclements and engage in hand-to-hand fighting down in the compound. Bullets zinged and screamed overhead, one clipping the strap of his battle helmet. A fragment of it sliced his cheek, but he didn't feel it.

From the rail switching yard outside Changbai came the forward elements of General Trai's 512th Lasting Thunder. Inside the yard there was a frantic mess since train sections were arriving from the south. Amid the shelling as the Soviet gunners lifted their range, the tank crews were unloading their vehicles, scattering hay bales and plowing through peasant huts as they raced toward positions along the river.

Captain Litung heard their first volleys, the cracking reports of their 75's sending sizzling rounds into the Kisurar compound, then the sharp chatter of the 7.62mm machine guns laying a sweeping fire through the barbed wire. As the first Spearthrusts came clanking and gouging across the shallows, he paused long enough to physically whip his buglers into motion. Then, screaming, he rose up and ran over the reed-covered berms, his men following. Sappers blew openings in the barbed wire and they poured through into the compound. The Russians came to meet them.

Litung ran full-length into a Soviet soldier. Locked together, they went down onto the frozen ground. Growling wildly, the Russian turned, trying to bring up his Kalashnikov. Litung's 9mm blew the top of his head off. Another Soviet soldier rammed a small bayonet into the captain's thigh, sending a fierce pain up into his testicles. He rolled, and then again, coming up as the soldier rushed him once more. As he did, a machine-gun burst cut across the Russian's back and hurled him a full ten feet into the air. In the high arc lights his face looked open and blankly startled.

Throughout the compound, individual combat was taking place. Silhouetted against the glare of the high lights and bursting shells were figures crouching, lunging, blowing bursts of automatic fire. Behind them, up on the barbed-wire encirclements, more troops poured in.

Slowly the overwhelming numbers drove the Russians back. And then they broke entirely, Soviet soldiers throwing their weapons away. Litung, blood pumping out of his thigh, raced after them, rallying his men.

Out beyond the compound lights, a solid line of muzzle bursts erupted. Soviet armored personnel carriers had advanced through Kisurar and formed a battle line. For five nightmarish minutes, they and the incoming Spearthrusts exchanged fire. Because of the distance, all of the missiles had flat trajectories, forming a molten canopy fifteen feet over the compound.

Litung halted beside a pair of mortar men. Pain was beginning to grip his entire lower body, yet the adrenaline surging through his blood ferried the pain away. Overjoyed, he realized the two were singing a ridiculous children's folk song as they methodically set up their mortar with flat azimuth and began to lob shells at the Russian APCs. The rounds shot out with metallic *thonks* under the tank fire.

Litung was no longer aware of time passing. Minutes blended together in the chaos. But then the tanks of the 512th lumbered through the compound, going hell-bent toward the Russian APCs, whose fire had been reduced to sporadic bursts. The tanks crushed the bodies of dead and wounded, and plowed through the wire along the road. As they reached the grassy slopes to Kisurar, the Russian artillery fire began raining down on its own emplacements.

Thirty-seven minutes after crossing the river, the Chinese troops swarmed into the village. As the troopers of the Sacred Pool and Flying Foot prowled like savage animals through the ruins, killing the wounded, Litung found a Russian officer standing in front of a pigsty holding a red star banner. The man was dazed and kept staring at him, his eyes narrowing and widening convulsively. Litung shot him in the chest, took the battle flag and wrapped it around his leg.

Momentarily the bugles sounded the call for retreat. Their brassy echoes formed a tinny counterpoint to the sporadic explosions of incoming Soviet artillery. Officers began screaming, slashing the barrels of their weapons on the backs of troopers. The soldiers paused in bewilderment, their blood up so high they didn't absorb the bugle order. Beyond them the Spearthrust tanks made hard one-eighties and headed back across the slopes toward the river.

Slowly, begrudgingly, the troopers retreated, filtering back in clusters, now and then firing at some struggling Russian who was crawling around trying to find cover.

Back they went, giving up their blooded ground. Through the remnants of wire, over the reed-covered berms, and down into the river, glistening with moonlight and the lumpy, dark shadows of dead men and the sparkling sheen of drifting blood.

With his battle harness, Litung scourged his men past him, their gear tinkling softly in the icy air. He mounted a tiny rise covered with scorched chunks of earth which smoked the acrid stench of explosives. Reaching down, he hefted his wounded leg up over a tangled clump of reeds touched with moonglow.

A second later, an anti-tank AT-3 Sagger missile struck him in the center of the abdomen. He had actually seen it coming, a crazily coiling light like a whirling *byandz* firestar he had watched as a boy during the May Festival fireworks. When it struck, his entire body went numb. It hurled him twenty feet before its armor-piercing fuse registered contact and blew his body into a thousand glowing pieces.

* * *

The early afternoon sun was hot and the fried chicken greasy. The President eased a moistly shimmering wing around on his paper plate and focused his fork's thrust on the little dome of potato salad beside it. It tasted tart, full of sun-warmed mayonnaise.

He was seated on a wooden picnic table in the middle of a high school football field in Valdosta, Georgia. People were milling with paper plates and cans of Pepsi in hand, attending a fund-raiser for Georgia Senator Ephram Woody. Down near the west end goalposts, the presidential helicopter sat in thin grass, roped off from curious picnickers. Everywhere dark-suited security men prowled, getting lime from the field lines on their shoes.

The stout, sweaty lady beside the President, chairwoman of the Fourth District caucus of his party, gushed over the turnout. He nodded, smiling, and speared another chunk of potato. The woman's nervousness had dried her mouth and her breath was faintly sour.

Someone lightly touched his shoulder. It was Jim Burleson, his Chief of Security. "Excuse me, sir," he said softly, "Mr. Baker has arrived."

The President's eyes narrowed. Mr. Baker was a personal code to indicate that a high-priority message from the Pentagon had just been received. "Is Hedges aboard?" he asked, referring to Frank Hedges, Undersecretary for Defense, who had accompanied him on this trip.

"Yes, sir."

"Have him take it. I'll be down."

"Yes, sir." Burleson hurried away.

The Fourth District chairwoman made a comment on how large Burleson was. "My, my," she giggled, "ah'll bet he could wrestle a goo-rillah and come out on top." She gave a tinkling laugh that made her sizable breasts jiggle. "I don' believe I have a Mistah Bakah on my list."

"He's a personal friend," the President said. He wiped his mouth with a paper napkin and rose.

"Please forgive me, Mrs., ah . . ." He had completely forgotten her name.

"Sarah. Please call me Sarah, Mistah President."

"Yes, Sarah. I'll be right back."

"Of course, Mistah President," she cooed. "Please bring Mistah Bakah back. He'll love mah chicken."

Hedges was pacing beside the copter's ramp, looking uncomfortable in the sun. He and the President huddled a moment. "Pentagon says the Chinese have initiated another incursion across the Amur River," Hedges said.

The President looked steadily at him. "You have got to be kidding," he finally managed.

"I'm afraid not, sir."

"Jesus Christ!" He put his head down, then remembered where he was and lifted it, forcing a smile. "All right, I'm leaving. Give my apologies."

"Yes, sir."

He turned and started up the ramp steps, pausing at the landing to wave and smile. Two minutes later, the helicopter flattened the grass as it lifted into the sky.

With the brown ribbon of the Witlacoochee River cutting through pecan orchards below them, the President talked by air phone with Victor Chapman, Secretary of Defense. Chapman sounded grim.

"Satellite recon shows a stronger force this time, Mr. President. Looks like an armored crossing of the Amur."

"What do the Joint Chiefs think?"

"Could be an all-out invasion. They're giving sharper looks at earlier photos of the main railheads of Quanzie and Mangui to see if they can decipher strength."

"Why in hell didn't they already do that?"

"Everything seemed normal in those sectors. Plus there's been a storm over the area."

"What the hell are the Russians doing?"

"We don't know yet. Other than that they're trying to repulse."

"What does JCS recommend?"

"They think you should talk directly with Sichen."

"I agree. Can you tie me in from here?"

"I believe so, sir. It'll probably take a few minutes."

"Do it."

Chapman clicked off. The President sat with the phone receiver in his lap, looking out at the skyscrapers of Nashville coming up across rolling green hills. He swore, drawing up a tiny bubble of tangy mayonnaise.

There was a terrible flux of static on the line when Chinese Premier Sichen came on. His voice, a high-pitched, twangy English, said, "Yes, Mr. President, yes. You are there?"

"Yes, Premier, I can hear you. Forgive me for the bad connection."

"I hear, I hear."

"Sir, why have your troops again crossed the frontier?"

"I assure you it has been a mistake."

"Yes, it was a mistake. But why did it occur?"

"It is most embarrassing."

"Premier, I would like to know the specific reasons."

"There has been tension in the area. Russian troops have been very arrogant. Recently there were killings of farmers. My local commanders have . . ." He paused a moment before continuing. "The local commanders have reacted without orders."

"Is this an invasion?" The President flinched as a burst of static blew hard across the airwaves. "Premier Sichen?"

"I hear, I hear."

"Is—this—an—invasion?"

"No. It is simply a most embarrassing mistake."

"A tragic mistake, Premier. To all of us. Can you assure me that this will not snowball?"

"Snowball? I do not comprehend the reference."

Shit, the President thought, clenching his teeth at

his stupidity. "Can you assure me that this will not develop into a major conflict?"

"Of course, Mr. President. I have already ordered that the commanders responsible be severely punished."

The President had a fleeting vision of blindfolded officers strapped to poles and being shot. Good! he thought. "Will you pull your troops back across the river?"

"It has been done."

The President looked out at blue sky. Was the s.o.b. lying? No, he didn't think so. He relaxed. "I'm most gratified that you are putting a stop to this, Premier Sichen. It is extremely unfortunate to have had this happen at this particular time. Our coming talks are tremendously important to forming national links in which such incidents do not occur."

"Yes," Sichen said.

"I intend to speak personally with Markisov immediately. May I assure him of your intentions?"

"Yes, of course."

There was a long moment of silence. Then: "Again, I thank you, Mr. Premier. Your reasonable response will help us all prevent terrible and unnecessary conflict."

"Yes," Sichen said.

"I look forward to speaking with you again at the conference."

"Yes, I look forward also. This has been most embarrassing."

The line went dead, followed by a wave of static. The President inhaled deeply, fingering the receiver. Again he considered whether Sichen was playing for time or telling the truth. And again he chose the latter.

Twenty minutes later, he was connected with Yuri Markisov. This time the link was clear as a bell, but the conversation was in sharp contrast to the one with Sichen. Markisov spoke in low-keyed, guttural monosyllables.

The President recounted his conversation and assurances from Sichen.

Markisov said, *"Da."*

"I must beseech you, sir, don't let this become a barrier to cooperation between your countries or the world."

There was a long pause. Finally Markisov said, "I will do my best."

The line went dead.

The President slowly handed the receiver back to the chopper's co-pilot. He looked out the window. Below was another river, narrow as a snake with the sun suddenly flashing in a bright ball of light. He blinked, seeing the light on his retinas like an explosion.

Sichen, asleep in his quarters within the Working People's Cultural Palace, had first been awakened by his military adjutant, General Yeh, at 2:13 A.M. and told of the second incursion across the Amur. The premier was so stunned he sat back down on his bed and stared at the floor.

Then he exploded. "These people cripple me!" he shouted. "They're poisons that sicken my blood. Why was this thing done? Who is responsible?"

"Apparently General Trai Bon of the 512th acted on his own."

"His own? His own! Who is this imbecile who defies commands?" Sichen came very close to Yeh. Although he was a small man, his rage was such that the general actually stepped back. "I want Trai here. Now!"

"Yes, sir."

"What other forces were involved?"

"Elements of the Sacred Pools, the Flying Foot and the artillery batteries in Ziaushen."

Sichen glared fiercely. "Did all these commanders act on their own?"

"It seems so."

"Get them here. Every one of them."

"It will be done, sir."

Thirty minutes later, the call from the U.S. president came in. Sichen took it in his office, where he had been listening to radio messages coming from Changbai. He was still in his sleeping gown. The telephone conversation was agony for him. He felt emotionally bruised, betrayed. His apology to the American sounded fawning, and he was filled with humiliation.

Following the call, he convened a small meeting in the adjoining council room, a windowless place as cold as a tomb, with a huge portrait of Mao looking blandly down from the south wall. Present was the Senior Member of the Standing Committee of the Politboro, Chen Jann; the three ministers, Wahan, Geung, and Litung; and Commander of the CMC, General Hsien Tu. Everyone sat around a large black wooden table covered with a red velvet sheet.

Sichen didn't waste words but immediately went after General Hsien. He raged at him for a full five minutes, excoriating the commanders on the Amur, demanding explanations for their insubordination. He didn't stop long enough for Hsien to answer.

The general was a fat man with moist eyes and a slight goatee that looked miniscule on his jowly face, which grew ever more closed. Beyond him, ministers Geung and Wahan looked distressed, while Chen and Litung listened intently, watching with cold, obdurate stares.

Finally Sichen paused for breath. Distractedly he jerked forward and took a cigarette from a silver box and lit it. As the smoke drifted out into the cold room, he again turned to Hsien. This time his voice was more controlled. "How have the Russians reacted to this imbecility?"

Hsien roused himself as if from sleep. "They have reinvested the battle site. At the moment there is no firing."

"Will they counter-attack?"

"Our informants say there is heavy military traffic at the railheads of Vlokstan and Irridai. But they are over a hundred miles inland, and they would need several days to bring up adequate troops and armored equipment to counter-strike.

Sichen turned to Minister Geung. As presiding chief over the Ministry of External Studies, he was a close personal adviser to Sichen on foreign relations and de facto head of all diplomatic affairs. He was one of the premier's strongest supporters within the lower Central Committee.

"What do you think Moscow will do, Liau?"

Geung wiped his chin distractedly before speaking. "I don't believe Markisov will authorize a counter-strike. Russia is in too much turmoil for a war. But he will make a show of force along the Amur frontier to appease the militarists."

"You see?" Sichen shouted at General Hsien. "Your disobedient commanders have made a mess for me."

"What of the Americans?" Chen Jann asked quietly. He was nearly eighty years old and carried an air of imperial serenity. "Will they side with the Russians?"

"I've already spoken with the American president, *dzufu,*" Sichen said, using the term for honored grandfather.

"Ah?" Chen said and sat forward, putting his bony fingers gently together. "And what did he say?"

"He was distressed and fearful that an all-out war would develop. I calmed his fears." Eyes met other eyes, exchanging silent questions.

"How?"

"I explained that this incident was an unfortunate mistake."

"Did he accept that?"

"Yes. He intends to speak to Markisov personally and also quiet him."

Chen nodded.

"But something more than reassurances is needed here," Sichen went on. He returned his attention to General Hsien. "The four commanding officers involved in this will be publicly stripped of their rank."

He glared at the general, as if hoping for a countering statement. But Hsien remained impassive. "You have heard me?"

"Yes, sir."

All the others save Litung frowned. To dismiss high-echelon PLA officers was always humiliating for the entire Army. To do it publicly would be a dangerous move which could possibly undermine the central government's hold over the military.

Minister Wahan, vice-chairman of the Party Congress and also a personal friend and ardent supporter of Sichen's progressive programs, spoke up. "Premier, do you think that is truly wise?"

"A lesson must be administered," Sichen snapped back. "A powerful lesson that will not be forgotten by recalcitrant officers in the future."

"But it could be perceived as a gesture of obeisance to foreign pressure."

"I agree with Wahan," Chen said. "Some punishment must indeed be administered to these officers. Realistically for foreign consumption as well as for in-country structuring. However, such a drastic measure would be detrimental to you internally."

Sichen was silent for a moment. He always attached great weight to *dzufu* Chen's advice, since the senior minister was one of the main pillars on which his power rested. He considered, smoking furiously. At last he nodded. "Yes, perhaps that would be rash." He turned to General Hsien. "There will be no public stripping of command. But you *will* administer severe punishments. Further, you will see to it that both Soviet and American intelligence contacts are made aware of them."

Hsien nodded. "Yes, Premier."

"Geung, issue a diplomatic communiqué to Markisov at once. Do not show open appeasement, but merely point out that this has all been an unfortunate incident. Indicate that it will be discussed at the conference. And hint, only hint, at the possibility of reparations."

"Yes, sir," Gueng said. Across the table Chen nodded again.

Sichen dismissed everyone except the *dzufu* and Minister Litung. He ordered tea brought. As the men drank in silence, Sichen studied his Minister for Internal Affairs over the rim of his cup. He neither liked nor trusted Litung. The man was too cold, always watching with that deadly stare. Still, he had tolerated him within his government. First, because he did not want to challenge the cadre which had formed around his mentor, Zaobang. Second, the man was a ruthlessly efficient commander of the secret police. But most important, with Litung inside the government, Sichen could watch him more effectively and thus control his moves.

He was well aware of the minister's tentacles spreading throughout the government, plus his affiliation with certain disenchanted generals. Sichen's own intelligence network, hidden within the Ministry of Foreign Relations, had reported that much. But so far reports indicated that Litung still lacked any real power within the inner sanctums of the Politboro and Central Committee. Until he obtained those, he was no threat. And before he did garner such sympathizers, Sichen would depose him.

Now, watching Litung, he wondered if this man was behind the dangerous lunge across the Amur. No, he decided, he would not dare create such an open challenge. And to what purpose? Yet an idea which had come to him during the meeting expanded. Perhaps he might utilize this situation to explore Litung's power base, possibly even pinpoint those officers in the military who were on his side.

"Minister Litung," he said finally, "you have said nothing in all this. How do you perceive these events?"

"They are, as you pointed out, stupid and ill-timed."

"Do you believe they were instigated to embarrass me?"

"Perhaps."

"And what should I do to discover the truth?" Sichen asked, lighting another cigarette. Across the table, Chen had turned and was watching Litung like an old teacher observing a particularly annoying student taking an exam.

"Put certain generals under surveillance," Litung answered.

"Ah? Which generals?"

"That can't be known until all are observed."

"A complete surveillance, then?"

"Yes."

"One that is secret, of course."

"Of course."

"Are your people capable of such a surveillance?"

"Yes."

"Begin it immediately. I will look at your reports when I return from Australia."

Litung nodded.

Sichen smiled, puffing on his cigarette. Good, he thought, now I'll let the man expose himself. With the data from his own secret investigators, along with those from Chen's in the Central Committee, he would have the ability to compare Litung's reports against the others. Discrepancies would then indicate those specific generals the minister was attempting to protect.

"You may go," he said at last.

Litung rose, made a slight bow, and left.

In the outer hall, he was stopped by General Yeh. "I have distressing news."

Litung stared evenly at him.

"Your son was killed during the incursion."

Not a muscle moved in Litung's face, nor did the dark intensity of his eyes change. After a moment he said simply, "Walk with me."

The two men exited through a small door in the rear of the Cultural Palace and walked down the western promenade. It ran along the moat in the central portion of the Forbidden City. There were lines of *lichi* trees along the moat, their branches barren of leaves. Dawn was beginning to show in the east, and its faint light looked crimson through the perpetual layer of fall dust.

"I am very sorry about your son," Yeh said.

Litung remained silent.

"I remember when he was a little—"

"You talk like a woman," Litung snapped.

Yeh fell silent.

As they neared the Meridian Gate, the minister asked, "When does Sichen leave for Australia?"

"This afternoon. He has chosen to travel by train to Kunming."

"Then you will act tomorrow morning."

General Yeh nodded but looked anxious.

Litung glanced back at him. "I see fear in your face."

"No, my comrade," Yeh said quickly, "it is merely impatience."

Litung stopped abruptly and Yeh almost ran into him. Reaching out, Litung gripped the general's ear between his thumb and forefinger and viciously pulled his head down. "I advise that you not fail me," he whispered menacingly.

Yeh grunted with pain, then nodded crookedly. "No, I will not fail you, comrade."

Litung released him. "Leave me."

General Yeh obeyed, pulling at his ear.

Several hours later, the early morning sunlight sifted through the apartment window, shedding a soft glow over Litung Biao. He was sitting cross-legged on his bed, totally naked. He was in *jijeng* and his breathing was so deep that it seemed to come from his soul.

Before him was spread an odd assortment of martial artifacts. On a small, ancient battle drum painted with tigers, snakes, birds and dragons rested a tiny golden drinking bowl half filled with yellow wine. Beside the drum was a warrior's breastplate made of lacquered hide from the ancient Sage Kings. The last item was a knife with a slightly curved blade. The handle was made of rhinoceros horn, shaped into the head of a dragon. The blade itself was pure white, fired by the famous sword makers of Wu in the third century B.C. It was a sacred relic and possessed the name Kan Chiang: the male knife.

At last Litung emerged from the energized darkness of *fangchin,* or abandonment. After a moment he raised his hand and took up the golden bowl. He spoke the name of his son and drank once, again, and a third time until the bowl was empty. Then he turned it upside down and replaced it on the drum, slightly to the side.

Next he lifted the white knife. He placed the blade lightly against the third joint of the little finger of his left hand. With a quick slice he severed it. So great was his self-control that not a muscle twitched. He replaced the knife on the drum as the stump of his finger began pumping blood.

He bent forward. Using the flowing blood, he drew a symbol, first on the breastplate, then on the drum head, then the handle of the knife, and finally on his own chest. The blood slipped down the line of his abdomen. The symbol he had drawn was a small rectangle with a line running vertically through it: the ancient pictographic character for China as the center of the Earth and the Nine Layered Heavens.

"I promise that you have not died in vain, *Hwangdiejai,*" he said softly, addressing his son with the formal term for Son of the Emperor. Then, using a sacred strip of yellow gauze, he stanched the blood from his finger.

14

It had taken a long time for Liz Forsythe to stop shaking completely. The sea fight, now seven hours behind them, had left an icy wind inside her belly which popped goose flesh onto her skin and made her teeth chatter. Now, sitting alone on the conn deck, she was fighting off exhaustion, a powerful desire to lie down somewhere and sleep for a very long time. They had been running smoothly on two engines, and Bonner and Cullin were below in the engine room working on the damaged Hall-Scott. Liz shook her head to clear off the sleepiness, stood up on the conn seat and held her face to the wind.

This tactic helped. The breeze was chilly and made her ears cold. She glanced down at the small illuminated dome of the magnetic compass in front of the helm. Its degree card dipped and jiggled beneath the course line of green phosphorescence.

As she regarded it, anger and outrage replaced her sleepiness. What in the name of God am I *doing* here? The sea engagement with the LC-11's and Triad cruiser had shaken her so thoroughly, she now desperately wanted out.

Once more she ran back through her mind the hellish chaos of exploding weapons, disintegration and terror. She recalled how afterward Cas had come up onto the conn, his body alive with energy, checking her out. As he threw his arm around her shoulder, she noticed that the masculine musk that had so recently excited her was now heated with the overlay of adrenaline and grease smoke and scorching metal.

Near hysteria, she'd screamed at him: "We're all crazy! We're all absolutely, completely crazy!"

"Take it easy, Liz," he said. "It's over."

"You're goddamned right it's over. I want off this boat. Now! Put me on an island, put me on a goddamned sand spit. I want *off!*"

She started crying, too furious to care if he was staring at her and probably thinking that she was cracking up. So what? she thought, I don't care, the hell with you.

He put his arm around her, but she pushed it away and gripped the wheel, suddenly determined to drive this hulk of a stupid PT boat up onto the first beach she came to and then she'd goddamn *swim* to Australia if she had to.

The lights of the trailing cruiser and LC-11 grew gradually smaller and smaller and finally disappeared completely. Still she clung to the helm, refusing to relinquish it. After a while Bonner informed her that he and Will would have to work on the downed engine and was she all right?

"I'm fine," she snapped.

Shaking free of the memory, she lifted her eyes and scanned the moonlit convergence of ocean and sky. The moon was past full now and seemed slightly lopsided. Its light made the sea look unbelievably deep, as if the boat were gliding over depths that went all the way down to the center of the earth.

The image sent a new shiver through her. For a moment she felt herself suspended between moonlight and chasm. With it came the powerful realization that that was precisely where she was: trapped lower than the moon, higher than the bottom of the sea, a nowhere place from which she could not escape.

She cursed helplessly and rubbed her hands over her thighs as if they had started to inch fiercely. As she did, her fingers touched the slender hardness of the computer disks in the pocket of her shorts. Angrily

she drew them out and held them in her palm. The
square yellow objects caught a glint of moonlight in
their metal tabs, looking malevolent.

"Damn things," she hissed, about to heave them
over the side of the boat. But she didn't. Instead she
gazed down at them, remembering her vague feeling
earlier that more was involved than merely the theft of
a weather satellite.

Her thoughts focused on Stanford. She tried to draw
up a mental picture of him, but the face kept looking
like the embassy man, Marsh, back in Manila. Same
arrogant, clean-cut lethalness. Why were these bits of
electronic memory so valuable to him? His chase for
them had become blind, driven.

She was well aware of the large stakes involved in
the international market for stolen high-tech gear. In
fact, she'd even helped write a story on the subject
back home. But a simple U.S. weather satellite? What
technology could that possibly hold that anybody
would pay such a price in blood for?

Besides, if Abbie Baum had been correct and they
did want to recover it, not destroy it, that would entail
a flotilla of ships and a vast array of electronic equipment for an intercept. Only a major power could bring
that into play. But who would that be? Russia? France?
Britain? No, none of them would risk the immense
world condemnation for something of such small
value. Nor would they use a man like Stanford to do
it.

She had been so lost in her thoughts that she had
allowed the PT to fall off course. Finally realizing it,
she brought it back, easing the helm slowly until the
compass line was once more fixed.

The intrusion had scattered her thoughts. She dipped
her head, feeling terribly tired all over again. Returning the disks to her pocket, she stretched her neck,
rolling it gently from side to side, feeling her vertebrae
creak softly. In her vision the sky revolved, stars and
the lopsided moon and—there, the quick, silent streak

of a falling star across the southern curve of the heavens.

She paused to watch it plunge and flame out. It left the needle-thin scratch of its tail for a fraction of a second against the sky above where Australia lay. Like the trail of a forlorn tracer bullet lazily arcing through space, she thought. Or like a satellite that had drifted out of orbit and been sucked back to the earth.

She felt a tingle riffle over the skin of her scalp. Images interlocked: Australia, a fiery, plunging satellite. She experienced a moment of stultifying horror. Could Stanford actually be attempting the assassination of—?

No, she scoffed, that was too far out. James Bond stuff fit for a Saturday matinee. She sighed, a little embarrassed by her own absurd thoughts. She checked the compass again, adjusted slightly, and hunkered down in the conn seat, her legs drawn up.

She gazed upward again, noticed how close the stars looked now with the moon's light fading. Close enough that she might have reached up and plucked them down with her fingers.

Cullin snapped back his welder's mask and swore, the words lost in the roar of the engines. He was cramped between the center engine and the bell housing of the starboard unit. The engine room was sweltering with the stench of hot metal and acetylene fumes. Sweat poured off his face. Forward of him, Bonner was stretched across the engine, cleaning the fuel-intake screens.

"Bleedin' crack gets bloody wider the deeper I go," Will shouted over the roar. He took a few deep breaths, flipped the mask down and went back to it.

For the past four hours, he'd been working on the intake manifold of the center engine. The incoming round had blown through one of the after hull struts, caromed off the transmission housing, and sliced across the manifold, creating a hairline crack. As it widened, the engine had lost intake pressure and was drawing raw fuel down into the cylinders.

It was a laborious job correcting the break, a constant sequence of heating the cast iron with a rosebud tip on the acetylene torch, cooling, then grinding with a power wheel. Only to go through the whole procedure again and again so that the eventual sealing weld would hold properly to the crystalline structure of the metal.

After a minute or two, Cullin again straightened, pulled off the mask, and cut the flame on his torch. He sank back on his haunches, glaring. Then he came forward and leaned close to Cas. "How're them screens lookin'?"

"Rust-clogged," Bonner hollered back.

"Sweet bugger all! I knew we should 'ave strained Abbie's bleedin' fuel." He shook his head. "We'll have to go to ground soon, full shut-down to clear lines. Sooner or later, that rust'll muck up the entire system."

Bonner cranked around on the engine. "How much fuel we got left?"

"Enough for another hundred miles if we coax her."

"Where we gonna get gas?"

"The easiest place would be at Manado on the Minhasa Peninsula in northern Sulawesi. That's probably where the dingoes'll take them riverines to refuel." He winked slyly. "But we'll cock the buggers, strike for Tualandang in the Sangihe Islands instead."

"What's there?" Cas hollered.

"A New Zealand copra station. The bleedin' manager's a hulkin' bludger name of Robbo Hungerford." Will's lip curled. "I hate the barstid and 'im me. But he's got high-octane aviation fuel."

Cas was silent for a long moment, studying him. Then he asked, "What do you intend to do afterward?"

"Oh, I'd love to have another go at them jimbos. Put that bleedin' cruiser of theirs on the bottom even if we had to ram her."

"So would I, Will. But I think we'd best pack it in and get the hell out of these waters. There's been enough killing."

Cullin blinked sweat from his tiny dark eyes, then whipped some off his forehead with a finger. "Aye, mate, I agree," he said and thought a moment. "After Tualandang we can make due south for Buru in the Seram Group. There's a major airport at Namlea where we can put the missy on a flight to Sydney."

"Fair enough." Cas slid off the engine. "You want me to spell you?"

"Aye, my bones are flat crackin' me."

After they exchanged gear, Will stretched, then grinned. "Think I'll go topside and see if the missy'll let go the wheel now."

"Watch out she doesn't throw you overboard."

Cas went aft and hunkered down, figuring the best approach around the engine mounts and cross struts. He finally flipped down the mask and squeezed in, knocking elbows and nipping skin. He fired up the torch and adjusted the flame until it was a blue point through the mask glass.

For days Jean Gallaudet, waiting for Stanford to appear, had been lashed by boredom of epic proportions. It was a common state of mind for him. His brain functioned at breakneck speed, and even in a city like Paris, the rest of the world moved at a pace too lethargic to challenge his thoughts. On the tiny island of Tayandu, part of the southern Ceram archipelago of eastern Indonesia, cocaine was banking his horrific ennui.

The two-square-mile island sat in the wastes of the Banda Sea and was inhabited by a few scattered subtribes of Ceramese natives. The blockhouse where Gallaudet was ensconced had once been the headquarters compound of the long-dead Japanese colonel given the responsibility of monitoring shipping through the Indonesian Passthrough during Japan's Greater Southeastern Sphere thrust in 1942. Now it was Jack Stanford's outpost to glory, stocked by clandestine shipments of equipment brought in aboard fast-moving drug-smuggling boats owned by the Green Tigers.

Five months before, Jack had located Gallaudet in a filthy slum of Bombay, living in exile with an Indian prostitute named Saran Karajan. He had made the Frenchman an offer he couldn't refuse.

Once Jean Gallaudet had been the wonder boy of French rocketry. Brilliant, moody, arrogant, his mind had arced with theoretical visions that dismayed his colleagues in the Ariane Space Agency. But he was also a flagrant voluptuary and a suspected drug addict. Eventually that got him kicked out of the French Académie de La Science, and he became a pariah within his own country. Naturally spiteful, with a heavy habit to feed, he immediately sold rocket secrets to the Germans and fled to Mozambique and then India.

When Stanford found him, he was wasted, broke and on the run. Jack said simply, ''Do for me what I know you can do, and I'll put five million dollars worth of the purest Colombian coke in your needle.'' He only had to offer once.

On Tayandu, Gallaudet had been continually injecting himself with the first of the big stash Stanford had brought. Within the drug's rush, he would close his eyes and watch fantastic mental graphics form. Surrealistic geometrical forms, whirling apparitions of pure color. Caught within this altered state, he would study the intricate patterns, calculate their parameter barriers and algorithmic coordinates, determine functional path relays and binary searches. These, in turn, created new, more exciting neuron graphics.

Sometimes, in childlike titillation, he would deliberately tease his mind with mundane calculations before taking the hit. He'd walk off the dimensions of his room and then rapidly estimate its volumetric pressure factor. Or he'd probe the curvature of the chocolate-colored breast of one of the three Ceramese native girls he'd coaxed with his drugs, and align it with precise trigonometric divergence to her other one. Often he'd study his erect penis—which held a glorious fascination for him—and then calculate the velocities of blood flow through the distended veins.

The blockhouse was filled with a vast array of electronic equipment: monitors, computer banks, relay terminals, telemetric printers and weather data consoles, looking absurdly out of place in the moldy, moisture-stained room. A single window in the building looked out onto a beautiful coral beach with coconut palms and *hao* thickets edging the shoreline.

But at this precise moment, Jean's boredom was banked. He had decided to initiate prep procedures on his own since Stanford was already two days late. Now he was on a blood scent, his weapon electronic signals.

Fifteen minutes before, solidly stoked on drugs, he had fired up his tracking and communications antennae and receivers. In his little part of the world, it was nearly dawn, the time of day best for scanning signals.

His antennae were homed to the International Telephone and Telegraph satellite CommStar in geostationary position over Java. A four-ton unit put up by a French Ariane rocket which he had helped launch, it was designed to coordinate telecommunications in the Western Pacific and Southeast Asian quadrant. He was recording all use transmissions through the CommStar originating from the northwest: Cambodia, Malaysia and Sumatra. His target was the main telephone network based in Singapore. He was running a logic watch on the transmissions, trying to isolate the sound password from the Singapore net.

Arrayed directly in front of him was an expensive collection of computers and analysis panels, all with blue sides and black glass faces. As he worked, the cocaine sent riffling waves of energy through him, made him tap his feet, drum his fingers. Softly he hummed scattered snippets from the soundtrack of a pornographic Indian movie.

A tiny bell went off. The logic-analysis unit had just isolated the Singapore signal. Gallaudet instantly pulled it off the tape, reproduced it, and inserted it into his main computer terminal's data log. Step one complete.

Next he created an identification tag for himself: Star-Hook. Using the password signal, he gained immediate access into the vast Singapore telephone switchboard system via the CommStar. Once in, he clocked his entry time and tapped in a request for a breakdown scan of the system's data bank.

Several seconds passed, then several more. He stopped humming, waited, fidgeting. He knew the Singapore net was notorious for its outdated switching equipment and slow response time. More seconds dragged by. Finally the request clearance came and his terminal screen was filled with the endless listings of particular circuits out of Singapore. Total entry/exit time: 16.3 seconds. He logged it.

Since he knew that any satellite launch from the commercial pad at Xchiang had to be coordinated through the military network in Beijing, his next assignment was to isolate the particular trunk line to the mil-net in the capital.

First, he scanned for all the trunk lines into Beijing from the mass of circuits out of Singapore. He ended up with three. But which was the military-network trunk line? He was certain that it would be protected by a special code-entry barrier. That fact he could use since it would isolate itself.

Gallaudet couldn't speak fluent Chinese, but with his phenomenal memory he had managed during the preceding four months to familiarize himself with all Chinese military, scientific and computer patois based on the standard Wade-Giles romanized phonetics which the Chinese telephone system used during intercontinental transmissions. With this information, a Chinese phonetic dictionary, and the most updated Coors-Hashigawa translator unit, which transposed the *kanji* characters common to Chinese and Japanese languages into English equivalents, he was able to communicate with the system through his computers.

Going back to Singapore, he logged in an artificial

request for verify into the Beijing network. The first line he used was linked through Rangoon–Chongqing–Xi'an–Beijing. It cleared quickly. Scratch one. The next line was Rangoon–Nanning–Wuhan–Beijing. That also cleared. Scratch two. That meant the remaining line was used by the military network.

He tested it, sending the identical artificial request. It was along a hookup via Rangoon–Guiyang–Bengou–Beijing. It immediately came back with an intercept asking him for the specific entry-code password. He had found the mil-net trunk line.

The next problem was to find the entry password. The only way to do that was to extract its sound signal from an actual transmission out of Beijing along the Bengou line. He activated his logic watch again and waited.

He walked around the bunker, then went outside and urinated. He shot up again, and the drug drove him to do endless push-ups until his wiry arms trembled. At last he reseated himself and waited. Although he was being sloppy in covering his data tracks throughout the systems he was entering, it made no difference. He knew the Chinese nets didn't possess the advanced security procedures of the Western nations, and it could take weeks, if ever, for anyone within the networks to realize someone had broken in. By then it would be too late.

The call along the mil-net came some thirty minutes after he'd set watch. The bell rang and the equipment automatically recorded the sound signal. Following the same procedure he had used on the break-in of the CommStar, he again sent his artificial request, this time clothed in the code signal rather than the verbal password.

Within five seconds he was into the Beijing Military Master Intelligence network. Immediately he cancelled the artificial request and tapped in a command in Mandarin phonetics: "Make me director."

It took only as long as the signal circuit to be completed before he was given full access to the data banks of the Master Intelligence network. Total logged time, once the Singapore link had been formed, was 3.56 seconds. Now he began scanning the MI network for the loop to the launch site at Xchiang.

That's when he hit a glitch. The Xchiang loop out of the MI in Beijing was blockaded by a plethora of outgoing transmission circuits, none of which bore specific location IDs. Any link with a specific site was carried on an operator-only circuit. As a result, transmissions were time-logged to a definitive desk panel so that trace functions could be obtained through specific corps operators. Its purpose was to isolate all outgoing/reception data through a single command base.

For a few minutes the overlay of command structure stumped him. He had already tried several tentative break-in probes without success. On one he'd ended up in a field garrison on the Manchurian border, another in some hell-and-gone outpost at Skhezi in the deserts of northwestern Xinjiang.

For a while he paced around the bunker, his frustration singing with coke flight. Then he stopped. Wait, of course! he thought. He could pinpoint the Xchiang loop by tracking the signal time of the transmissions out of the MI in Beijing.

He raced back to his computer and brought up a secondary map of China and quickly calculated the ground distance between Beijing and Xchiang. From that, using the speed of signal transference, he calculated the time it would take for a round trip between the two sites. It came out to precisely 1.04 seconds.

Now he had the timing fix. But what other garrisons held the same time coordinates? He threw an electronic compass sweep of everything at an equal distance from Beijing. He found that terminus sites were in the Qingzang Gaoyuan Mountains in southeastern China, secret outposts in Soviet Mongolia, and a sea position in the east China Sea off Taiwan. The only plausible loop left, therefore, was the Beijing–Xchiang one.

Once more riding his director status within the MI, he sent out a probe, a mundane request for inventory data of rice stores at Xchiang utilizing the signal time as identity fix.

He waited. Six point four seconds later, his computer screen gave him the columns of warehouse stats on food supplies at the Xchiang launch site.

Alors! He was into the Xchiang computer data base.

15

The copra station on Tualandang squatted on a spit of land covered with neat rows of coconut palms. It was nearly dawn when the PT eased up to the company loading dock, an old stone affair with stinking piles of copra stacked around in drying pans, smelling like dried dung.

Apparently Hungerford had heard their engines, for he turned on the dock lights. While Cas was tying in the stern line, he came walking down in a rolling gait. "Well, what the bloody hell do you want here, Cullin?" he yelled.

"Aye, Robbo," Will called back with mock cheeriness. He shut off the engines and came down to the foredeck. Deliberately he tossed over a bowline to Hungerford. " 'Ow's the snakiest nong in the Moluccas?"

"Just got snakier, mate." Hungerford's eyes surveyed Bonner and Liz, then his gaze swung to the PT, eyeing the bullet holes. "What're you smugglin' this time?"

"Nothin' but salvation, mate."

"Looks like somebody don't want you peddlin' it."

"Only the barbarians." Will jumped to the dock and walked up to Hungerford. The man towered above him, yet there was a hard look in Cullin's eye and an icy grin on his face. "We be needin fuel, Robbo."

"Do you, now?"

"Aye. Two thousand gallons of ninety-five oc."

Hungerford's eyes narrowed. "You got the ready?"
"What's the nick?"

Although sea etiquette prevented Hungerford from refusing a plea for fuel, nothing said he need give it away. "Half a quid a liter."

"Jesus Christ, man!" Bonner snapped.

Robbo shrugged his massive shoulders. "That's the go, take it or leave it."

The ice in Will's grin was like frozen nitrogen. "I've got it, you thievin' king-dick. Now run your tanker out here."

"Get up the lolly first, Cullin." Hungerford lifted his hand, rubbing a huge forefinger and thumb together. "Or bugger the fuck off."

While Will returned to the cabin, Cas gave the manager a long once-over. "You're a real hardass, ain't you, pal?" he said evenly.

Robbo looked him up and down. "What's with you, mate? You lookin' for a stink?"

Cas's face became stony. He braced, arms hanging loose but ready. "Come ahead, asshole."

Liz jumped in front of him. "No, stop it. Damn you, stop this macho bullshit."

Hungerford chortled.

"Leave him be, Casimir," Will yelled from the boat. He leapt back to the dock and came forward. He handed the station man a small stack of American bills. Hungerford counted it slowly, flicking the bills with his thumb. He finally finished, nodded. "All right, open your tanks." He turned and strode back up the dock, pocketing the money.

Will leaned close to Bonner. "Get the Walther. But keep it hidden." He winked. "We gonna make this prick cry."

It took two hours to fill the PT's tanks, running a single line off a tanker truck with the red and blue logo of Standard Oil. The four station hands helping were Javanese with dirty T-shirts and bolo knives strapped to their waists.

There was no need for filtering. The fuel was crystal

clean, a light blue color that smelled like nail polish. Aviation gas. The station always kept a large supply of this high-octane grade since it periodically refueled the seaplanes of East Indonesian Airlines on sub-contract.

When the refueling was completed, Will demanded a receipt. Hungerford looked surprised. "A bloody chit? What're you gon' do, wipe your bleedin' arse wi' it?"

"When I deal wi' thieves I get it in writin'."

Disgustedly, Robbo led him and Bonner up to his station house, a white bungalow with stained shutters that could be pulled down when the monsoon winds came. The house smelled of whiskey and old leather beneath the perpetual stink of copra. It was a man's house, spare and filthy.

Hungerford moved to a side room. It had an impressive bank of radio gear against one wall, and shotguns and heavy-bore rifles hung on pegs in the wall. Hungerford sat down and wrote out a receipt.

Will and Bonner stood with their hands behind their backs. Then Cullin's finger tapped Cas's hip. Bonner took out the Walther he'd slipped into the back of his trunks and handed it over. Cullin stepped forward and put the muzzle against Hungerford's ear.

"Bloody hell!" the man said, freezing.

"Put the lolly on the table," Will said.

Hungerford eased his big head around and gave him a sidelong glance. "You ain't really gon' do this?"

"On the flamin' table."

Hungerford dug the bills out of his pocket and put them down gently. "My men'll cut your grotty pissers off."

"They try an' they'll be buryin' their boss."

"Shit!"

"Wait a minute, Will," Cas said. He had been studying the radio gear. On a side table he found a small short-wave radio, a Hallicraft 300 with a tele-graph key, the only portable equipment in sight. "Maybe we can use this."

"Take it," Cullin said.

Hungerford eased his head around under the muzzle. "Oh, you nongs are gonna pay for this."

Will pressed steel. "Shut the hell up!"

With Cas carrying the radio, they went out and down to the dock, Will occasionally jabbing Hungerford with the Walther. The station workers didn't know what was going on. They milled around, staring at the weapon, touching their bolo handles until Cullin said something to them in Indonesian. The four men instantly sat down.

While Bonner held Hungerford under the gun, Will jumped aboard and started the engines. For a wild, roaring moment he let them run, clearing out carbon with the high octane. Then he waved to Cas, who freed lines and leaped to the foredeck.

As they pulled slowly away from the dock, Hungerford paced back and forth, his bulldog face flaming. "I'll get you barstids," he screamed. "Next time either of you sonsabitches sees me, you'd better come shootin'."

"Count on it!" Bonner shouted back happily.

As the shallows turned from green to blue, the stink of copra faded into the salty aroma of the ocean. Then Cullin let the Hall-Scotts loose, all three running blue-octane-hot on high chain. The PT lifted, water hurling off her chines, and found the step, running south.

Ahead lay a long reach across the Molucca Sea and then into the Ceram past Tobalai in the southern Halmaheras. They would then transit the Ambo Channel between the Ceram and Buru Islands and into the Banda Sea, where the monsoon winds coiled and gathered strength for their sweeps north, and then finally the port of Namlea.

Premier Sichen woke gradually to the gentle swaying of the train. Although it was just seven in the morning, the air was already hot in the sleeping portion of his private car, and tiny beads of perspiration had formed on his broad, high forehead. He rolled over and tapped the buzzer for his valet to bring tea.

The compartment was not luxurious. The bed was covered with pale blue brocade sheets and a straw mat which helped ventilate his body during sleep. Once there had been air conditioning in the entire car, but when Sichen became premier, he had ordered the apparatus removed. He wanted to make a point that even a premier's life should be simple. But the truth was he preferred traveling without that comfort, enjoying instead the heat and dust and sound.

All his life he had loved trains. As a boy, he remembered watching with fascination as the old steam locomotives pulled the grades along the Yangzte near his birthplace of Wuhanje. The sight of these steel monsters had filled him with a sense of concentrated power, and the image never left him.

With the Amur crisis, it might have been wiser for him to remain in Beijing until his departure for Australia. But Sichen had chosen to hold to his earlier schedule. The train trip would take nearly two days, from Beijing to Kunming in the southern part of China. From there he'd fly over to Queensland on a special flight of China Air. But the train ride was the thing; it would give his mind the serenity needed for his confrontation with the Americans and Russians.

They were past the halfway point, in the Sichuan Plain just outside Chengdu. He pulled the crushed velvet window curtain aside, sipped his tea, and watched the landscape slip slowly past. It was lush and verdant and small rivers seemed everywhere. There were farmhouses with shiny black-tiled roofs, and on the high ground, fields of rapeseed and stands of mulberry trees which separated the rice paddies. It was a sharp contrast to the barren yellow earth of the plains of Hebei and Shaanxi through which they had passed the evening before. The comparison was so stark that he thought: *This* was what all China should be. Green and peaceful, rich with the promise of modernization.

Twenty minutes later, over his breakfast of spicy

mapo doufu and ham diced in eggs, his military adjutant, General Yeh, updated him on events of the night, primarily those concerning the situation on the Amur River. Sichen ate quietly, only now and then interjecting a question. Apparently the cessation of fighting had held. The Soviets had started reinforcing their side of the frontier but had refrained from any crossing in force. Also, Yeh went on, the offending commanders from the Amur were now in Beijing under house arrest by the CMC in the barracks of the Shanguan Military College.

The general paused abruptly and Sichen glanced up at him. He noted that Yeh looked unusually nervous, with little frowns fluttering between his eyes and droplets of perspiration glistening on his cheeks.

"What's the matter?" Sichen asked. "You look distraught."

"I merely suffer from stomach upset, sir. I did not sleep very well last night."

The premier grunted and leaned back thoughtfully. His own sleep had been restless and the main reason had been his recollection of his conversation with the U.S. president. Once more he felt the humiliation he had endured. It is a good thing, he thought, that I spoke in complete privacy. The specific words and tone would have garnered a definite loss of face among his ministers if they had heard. Most particularly those reactionary fools who would undermine his efforts to bring China into the modern world.

Still, he realized he'd had little choice. To have taken even a partially aggressive posture with the American president would have created a tug-of-war at the conference, him on one side and the U.S. and Soviet on the other. That would constitute a defensive position, not conducive to the delicate negotiation tacks he planned.

He pushed his dishes away and stared out the window for a long moment. The train was slowing as it entered the outskirts of Chengdu. The streets were crowded with bicycles and buses with their huge black bags of natural gas on their roofs, and there were produce markets lining the roads, piles of vegetables and slabs of meat and eel heads nailed on racks.

At last he waved for Yeh to continue. The final item was an update on the satellite launch in Xchiang. Everything there was running according to schedule, he was told. The launch would go off precisely on time, slightly less than sixty-nine hours away.

Sichen smiled for the first time. He liked that. It meant their rocket would be entering its orbit just about the time the leaders would be sitting down for breakfast in Australia. He wondered vaguely if he could actually see it. It didn't matter, it would be there, a symbol to the world that China was ready to take her place among the technological countries. On this high note he dismissed his adjutant.

Out in the corridor, General Yeh leaned against the window and wiped the sweat from his face. His hands were shaking, and his stomach seemed on fire. For a moment he distractedly looked out as the train crossed a bridge, the girders throwing flashing shadow lines across his tunic. Then he pushed away and hurried forward, crossing into the next car, which contained his office and the small communications center which always accompanied the premier during travel. He tapped the young communications officer on the shoulder, and together they went into his office.

General Yeh handed the lieutenant a cablegram. It bore Sichen's signature which he himself had forged last night in his quarters. "This goes to General Hsien immediately," he snapped.

The young officer glanced at it, then jerked his head up in shock. The cablegram was a personal order to the CMC chief of staff that the commanders of the 512th Lasting Thunder Brigade, the Sacred Pool Assault Team, the Flying Foot Brigade, and the commandant of the artillery batteries in Ziaushen all be executed in the yard of the Changuan Military College at dawn the next day.

"General, can this be—?" the lieutenant stammered.

"Send it!" Yeh shouted.

The junior officer braced, his eyelids blinking. "Yes, sir."

"Premier Sichen has further instructed that no one on this train except you and I know of this order. And that the names of these officers never again be spoken in his presence. Never!"

"Yes, sir."

"Out, out."

The lieutenant withdrew.

For many minutes General Yeh's hands didn't stop shaking. He wanted to vomit but forced the nausea back. The train began to rock as it slowed to approach the station at Chengdu. The general finally rose, walked around his tiny office. It suddenly seemed horribly confining, yet he would not allow himself to go out.

Another fifteen minutes passed before he composed himself enough to pull open the door and pass through the communications room.

Dr. Ziyang had a blistering headache. It had come during the night while he haunted the launch site, going from building to building in the humid air, checking with crew chiefs on the progress of the rocket.

To make matters worse, a new observer had just arrived from Beijing. His name was Xinjin Wu, a Committee head from the State Council. But Ziyang knew he was a personal friend of Minister Litung and was undoubtedly here to openly spy on the proceedings.

The headache grew worse. He sought relief in acupuncture, pushing needles into his forearm and ankle, areas which controlled the energy flows of the forehead. His attempts were futile.

At 3:00 A.M. he was notified that the Long March was ready for pad assembly. The rocket engineers had beaten his order and cleared for placement a full five hours ahead of schedule. His headache immediately faded. He even managed to drink a cup of tea without vomiting.

Situating himself in the Firing Room, a bunkhouse located four hundred yards from the pad, he watched as the rocket was tracked from its assembly bay to the launch pad and stacked. The sun was well up by the time the final satellite section was hoisted aboard and affixed.

The fueling crews began loading the tons of liquid oxygen and hydrogen for a repeat plugs-out simulation firing. It took them nearly four hours to complete it. At last the rocket was alone out there, isolated and magnificent with the sun directly overhead and faint wisps of condensation fuming off its chilling tanks.

Forcing himself to ignore the prowling Xinjin, Ziyang ordered the simulation to begin.

In the Xchiang complex there were two main control centers. The first was the Firing Room, with its six banks of monitoring consoles. It was responsible for coordinating the thousands of switches and valves and pumps which would actually get the vehicle launched. The second was the Command Section, which would take over control the moment the rocket left its pad and headed for orbit.

Since all telemetry and circuit tests for actual flight had already been completed, the doctor chose to observe from the Firing Room for this test. As in an actual launch, the sequence was broken into segments starting with T-minus-60 minutes with scheduled holds at T-30, T-10 and T-3 minutes and again at four seconds before the on-board computers took over automatic control of the firing.

Everything went smoothly through the scheduled holds until T-minus-10 was reached. Ziyang was leafing through the test-protocol manual for the next stage when he was told that a particular circuit line on the lowest gantry swing arm had not logged in for standby status.

A quick check indicated that the offending circuit

had become dislodged in its twist head. Ziyang initiated a repair order, notarized it, and overrode the circuit. The countdown continued.

At T-minus-3 minutes and 40 seconds, another problem cropped up. Console readings showed that infeeding helium, which created pressure within the propellant tanks and allowed feed to the induction pumps, was showing only a twenty percent pressure gradient.

Once more they went into an unscheduled hold while the engineers analyzed the reason for the pressure drop. It turned out to be a partially malfunctioning valve in the helium outflow matrix, an easily repaired item. Again the doctor logged repair orders and the countdown continued.

At T-minus-3 minutes, the Firing Room computers took automatic control of the launch. This was the crucial part of the entire procedure. All the technological knowledge of Ziyang and his engineers was crammed into these fleeting 180 seconds. Although Ziyang was still able to shut down the sequence manually, this was the real test. Had they programmed correctly? Had every single minute detail of the final moments before the Long March fired into space been adequately affixed and correlated into functional and correctable data?

The automatic sequence ran smoothly except for one tiny glitch. Due to the humidity, there was a slight impingement angle of the propellant nozzle. This, in turn, would have created a distorted fan of the liquid oxygen into the combustion chambers and lowered the thrust potential of the engines. But it was a minor and easily rectified problem. The rest of the AS ran down to T-minus-O, at which point the Long March would have been lifted into the sky if the chamber igniters had been aboard. The simulation was complete.

For the first time in what seemed a thousand hours, Li Ziyang relaxed in his management seat abaft the rows of consoles. His headache was gone. He felt hungry. Down in the "pit," the console section, the monitormen were easing back, smiling, jabbering. One

pulled a sack from under his unit and leaned forward
to take a bite from a *bao,* a small pork-filled pastry.

Ziyang saw it. It was a breach of procedure to eat
while on console, yet he was so elated, he let it pass.
Indeed, he actually walked down to the offending
monitorman and tapped him on the shoulder. The man
swung around, eyes wide.

"You have another?" the doctor asked.

"Sir?"

"I would like to share your repast."

The technician fell all over himself offering his food.
Ziyang thanked him and went back up to his management chair. He was about to bite into the *bao* when he
caught a sight of Xinjin coming up to speak with him.

The state councilman said, "I noticed there were
slight errors during the run, Doctor. Were they serious?"

"No."

The man eyed him coldly. "Such things will not
occur during the real launch, will they?" It was not a
question.

"No, they have already been corrected."

Xinjin grunted before turning away.

Ziyang lost all interest in his *bao.*

All through the long morning, the PT headed south-
southwest, staying in the deep ocean between Sulawesi
and Halmahera and holding a steady course across the
Molucca Sea to Buru Island. The ocean was smooth
at first, all empty space and long swells. Then around
noon, high clouds began scudding across the sky from
the west. The wind picked up, sketching little patterns
of foam on the swell faces, and the PT began to breast
them with long, jarring lunges, throwing spray.

There hadn't been much conversation on board since
leaving the copra station. Will shuttled back and forth
from the conn to the engine room, while Cas set out
a trolling line using one of Cullin's marlin poles. He
baited it with a strip of leather slashed to make a Javanese *pandiri* lure, which skipped and fluttered off the

edge of the PT's wake. Liz wandered from deck to cabin and back again, feeling oddly discomforted by their silence. Earlier Bonner had told her that they were making for Namlea on Buru so she could catch a plane to Australia.

The effect of the news had surprised her. Despite her protestations of wanting to be rid of the whole affair, she found herself hurt by their easy agreement. The thought of leaving oddly saddened her. Was it really all over? Would she just quietly get on a plane somewhere and return to that other world of hers? Never see Cas Bonner or Cullin ever again?

As the day wore on, her feelings gradually changed to anger. They were getting rid of her because she had lost it back there during the sea fight. For a while she had won their respect, but now they had returned her to the category of burdensome cargo.

Okay, fine, she thought defiantly. If that was the way they wanted to play it, who needed them? Yet she couldn't help feeling slighted. They'd accepted her and then she'd lost her nerve.

Finally, sick of thinking about it, she stomped up on deck and went aft to where Bonner was gutting a four-foot fish he'd just landed. He had already killed it with a brain stab. It was brown and sleek, its mouthful of teeth gripping the handle of the pole.

She squatted down beside the fish. "What is it?" she called over the roar of the engines coming up through the stern vents.

He turned and grinned at her. "Barracuda. Son of a bitch hit like a sledgehammer."

She looked at it and one eye, big as a half dollar, looked back at her. With a neat slash Cas severed the head and flicked it over the side along with the intestines. He cut back the outer skin and sliced off a paper-thin fillet. The meat was pale white, resembling a strip of bacon fat. He held it up to her.

"Don't you cook it first?" she cried.

"No, you eat it sashimi style, raw."

"I'll pass."

He laughed and took a bite. It made his lips glisten. "I should have saved the eyes for you. The Polynesians pop 'em like grapes."

"Jesus, that's gross."

He laughed again, his teeth very white in his tanned face. "They say it's an aphrodisiac. Makes 'em horny as sailors."

"Yeah, well, I need an aphrodisiac right now like I need a third foot."

At that moment the PT bore into a particularly large incoming swell, and she had to grab one of the air vents as a blast of spray flew past. Bonner merely rode it with his legs and continued filleting the barracuda.

Irritated by his nonchalance, Liz watched him. His hands were so expert with the knife, the blade peeling off flesh like a balogna cutter in a meat market. Finally she tapped him on the shoulder. He glanced around.

"So I was scared," she said sharply.

"What?"

"I said yeah, I was scared. Last night."

"So?"

"I just don't happen to be some big macho turd with testicles down to his ankles, okay?"

He peered at her curiously. "What are you so mad about?"

"Well, I think I did fine and you guys are being jerks and you can both go to hell."

Shaking his head, he sliced off another fillet before turning back to her. "Listen, you were terrific. A damned sight better than a lot of men their first time in combat. Including me."

"Really?"

He nodded. "Hell, the first time I saw action in Nam, I couldn't stop shaking for two days. Worse than that, I didn't shit for a week. My asshole was so puckered I couldn't."

"Then why are you letting me go?"

"Because it's over, Liz. We've had enough of revenge."

She studied him and her anger melted in a wash of

sudden tenderness which sent a silly, reflexive rush of warmth up her legs. But she merely shook her head, rose and started back toward the cabin.

"Hey, stick around," Cas called after her, grinning. "I'll get another 'cuda and save you the eyeballs."

She gave him the finger.

As the afternoon wore on, Cullin gradually slowed more and more as the wind and swells grew. The sky was completely overcast now, with the sun showing weakly above swiftly moving clouds.

Liz's stomach was beginning to tremble again. She lay around, staring at the cabin's overhead and cursing. After a while Cullin came below, headed for the engines. He looked in on her.

"Gettin' a bit schinkered again?" he asked.

"A bit."

"Take your mind off it, luv." He nodded toward Hungerford's radio on the adjoining bunk. "You know anything about radios?"

"No."

"Well, give that one a go. I'll hook 'er up for you. Put some tinker to her, see if you can raise a signal."

He ran a line off his batteries back through the hatchway and brought her some tools. "She looks like she's been settin' for a while," he said. "You might have to pull the back and clean out webs. Down here in the tropics, insects can pink fit a receiver."

She didn't have to. As soon as she started whirling the dials, all sorts of signals came in, long, wavering treble voices that were undecipherable along with splurges of music warped by heavy static. She finally found a fairly strong commercial station out of Australia with a disk jockey selling Fosters beer, barbie units and an aftershave lotion called Bondi Blow, and some hard, throbbing rock. She lay back in the bunk, listening to the program, so incongruous here in the rumble of the PT. Yet to her it was wonderful to hear crass commercials again.

She dozed for a while, and then she became vaguely aware the station was having a news break. Drowsily she listened. First came local stuff: a robbery of guns from a store on a street called Dingo-Dee; a report of an attempted rape; a croc attack near Secular Island.

She rolled onto her side.

Next came snippets of international news. Another killing in Beirut, another riot in Russia. The last item was an update of the coming conference on the Barrier Reef: "Preparations continue on the Seascape One for the upcoming international conference. The arrivals of the heads of state of the United States, Russia and China are scheduled to begin over the next three days. Canberra reports that security is extremely tight for this momentous gathering." The announcer chuckled softly and added an aside, "No chance of terrorists in this barbie, aye?" and then moved on to other matters.

In the confusion of Liz's half sleep the image of the bright, plunging arc of the falling star came to her again, and suddenly she sat bolt upright in the bunk. The convergence of the vision and the announcer's words sent a shaft into her heart. It's true! she thought wildly. She slipped off the bunk and poked her head through the engine room hatch, looking for Cullin. He was down in the foundations of the starboard engine. She turned and raced for the companionway, her heart trembling.

She was shocked to realize that it was raining now, not heavy but the droplets were large, whipping into her face out of a gray, whirling sky. Far off along the western horizon, squalls marched past in segmented order, and the wind was chilly and sodden.

Bonner was on the conn, hunkered down below the coaming, wearing one of Cullin's sou'westers. It was too small for him, and his long arms poked out of the yellow, oil-stained sleeves.

"I know what Stanford's going to do," she yelled into his ear. "He wants to assassinate the heads of state on the Seascape One. He's going to put that satellite right down on it."

Bonner leaned back and frowned askance at her.

"That's why the bastard's been so frantic to get these

disks back. Without them, he can't take control of that rocket.''

He studied her hard for a moment, then shook his head. ''You're crazy.''

''Think about it, Bonner. The timing of the launch and the conference are exactly the same.''

''Coincidence.''

''But I—'' She paused, turned to the wind for a moment. The rain had eased and the drowsy jolt she'd felt began to dissipate. Another dream picture had been shaken by a chilly, real-time world. She shook her head and turned back to him. ''God, the picture was so real that I—''

He had stiffened and was looking intently over her head toward the west. Turning, she searched the gray horizon but saw nothing. ''What is it? What're you looking at?''

''An aircraft.'' He reached down for the binoculars. Bracing the helm with his hip and left arm, he scanned until he found the plane. It was out about three miles, two hundred feet above the ocean, coming directly toward them.

Liz finally picked it up, this little dot. She kept losing it against the gray-black background, then spotting it again, closer. In it came. Now she could see that it was a twin-engine. When it was a half mile out, it suddenly lifted higher, banked to the right and then to the left. She could see that the top of the aircraft was painted in a camouflage pattern of deep blue with white streaks through it. It kept banking, circling the PT.

Bonner swore and followed the aircraft with his glasses. It had no markings, but the blue-white camouflage told him immediately who it was: smugglers hauling contraband. They always painted their planes that way so patrol aircraft couldn't see them against the ocean as they came in low, below radar nets.

''Who are they?'' Liz shouted.

''Smugglers.''

''Oh, no!''

For a full two minutes the aircraft continued circling, the wings jittering in the wind. At last it leveled, swung back toward the west, and descended once more until it was barely skimming the surface of the sea. Within a few moments it was out of sight.

Cas swore again and jerked his head toward the cabin. ''Get Will. We've just been position-fixed.''

16

For the past eighteen hours, Stanford had been pacing the cruiser's bridge. Everybody kept giving him dark, foreboding looks. All except Lui, of course, who maintained his sub-arctic grin. The strain was exhausting, made the fatigue in his bones seep out like poison.

As the *Flying Sun* cleared the north tip of Sulawesi, they had taken some of the LC-11's crew aboard along with its two .50-caliber machine guns. Ever since then, the ship's radio had been alive with messages, Chinese chatter going until he thought his head would explode. Most of it was chink invective, he figured. The warlords back in China were obviously nearing their breaking point.

He and Lui finally huddled. "We gotta pick 'em up again," he said. "They're out there and we gotta find the bastards."

"*You* gotta fin' the bastards."

"Then bring everything in on it, Lui," he pleaded. "Get your people in the whole Celebes–Molucca area in on the search. Everybody, boats, aircraft, all the *guanzi* network. They're out there, somebody's got to see 'em."

"Somebody betta," Lui said and went off.

For the rest of the afternoon, more radio messages flooded in. Stanford was astounded by how vast the Triad dope network really was. The voices coming in were Aussie English and Indonesian singsong and one that was as southern-drawl American as Colonel Sanders. Unfortunately, all the reports were negative: no PT boat sighted anywhere. Shit! he thought, and went into another circuit of the bridge. Outside, the weather was rapidly turning foul, but the cruiser was still holding smoothly as her stabilizers creamed off the main thrust of the swells.

Big Willie was holding a steady southern course. At mid-afternoon, they passed close in to Bacan Island, a series of upthrust mountains on the eastern horizon, and an hour later its sister island, Oblatu. It was then Stanford got his big break.

The radio had been silent for several minutes when suddenly the speaker crackled: "DD-zero-fiver for MTN one-zero-five hundred, do you copy?"

Willie picked up his mike, spoke into it.

"Your signal scratchy as hell, mate. Say again."

Willie repeated. Behind him, Jack moved closer.

"We've spotted your bleedin' torpedo runner. He's sixty kilometers off Buru making for the Ambon Channel."

"Gimme, gimme," Jack said. Willie handed the mike over. Stanford keyed: "DD-zero-fiver, when did you see him, over?"

"Ten minutes ago."

"Give coordinates."

DD-05 complied. Jack scribbled the numbers down on the edge of a map. "DD-zero-fiver, did they see you, over?"

"Hell yes, mate. We circled the blokes for one twenty."

"What are you flying?"

"Say again."

"What's your aircraft?"

"Negative, mate, negative." He wasn't going to give away his plane's description.

Stanford swung around to glance at Lui. "Is this guy one of your drug flights?"

Lui nodded placidly.

Dammit, Stanford thought, that meant Bonner and

Cullin would know they'd been spotted. He keyed: "Are you certain they're headed for the Ambon Channel?"

"He's runnin' storm speed, mate. Common sense says he'll hole up somewhere in Buru or Seram till she blows past."

"Stand by, stand by." Stanford slapped Willie on the shoulder. "Get me a map of the area, quick."

"It right there," Big Willie said.

Jack found it, shifted it around and peered down. He ran a finger through the Ambon Channel, hesitated for a moment, then drew it across the Banda Sea, which separated Buru from the Western Daya islands of Timor and, farther to the east, the Tanimbars.

His mind was racing. They'd never shelter in the Serams now, he knew, not after spotting the drug plane. No, they'd keep heading south. But sooner or later they'd have to refuel. So where? Timor or—"Willie," he barked, "what direction is this storm coming from?"

"Due west."

Okay, okay, he said to himself. He pictured the swirl of the typhoon winds coming across Malaysia and Sulawesi right down into the Banda, trying frantically to think as Bonner and Cullin would be thinking. They'd play the storm, veer to the east. His hand lifted, came down with a finger pointing at the Tanimbars.

"That's where they're headed," he shouted triumphantly. "The fucking Tanimbars!"

The speaker blared again: "MTN one-zero-five hundred, what's the hold, mate?"

Jack keyed. "You're cleared, DD-zero-five. Good work, out." He hurled the mike aside as the drug aircraft closed transmission and glared at Lui. "We've got them cocksuckers by the balls."

"You betta hope so, Stamford," Lui said.

The main force of the storm struck the PT head-on at seven-thirty in the evening as she cleared south of the Ambon Channel, roaring in from the west with high gray-backed swells and the wind howling at sixty-five knots.

Bonner and Cullin had prepared as best they could, running safety lines along the mid housing and companionways, then battening down the engine-room and vent horns. Now unable to go to port anywhere in the Serams for fear of being landlocked by more Triad LC-11's, they had decided to go right on through the Channel and head for open ocean in the Banda.

Fuel was going to be a touchy business, however. Will figured they'd have enough to cross the Banda and score refueling at one of the Daya Islands north of Timor, maybe Serua or Nila. There were mission settlements on both, he said, where'd they'd be able to cop at least enough low-octane to get them to the big Aussie fueling docks at Dill in East Timor. Hopefully, the storm wouldn't suck up too much gas and leave them stranded in open ocean.

Transiting down through the Ambon Channel had been tense. If the main storm had caught them there, they would have had serious trouble keeping seaway, what with outcroppings of rocks and shallows on both sides. Fortunately, they made it through before the full blow hit.

Since the thrust of the storm was coming at them from off the starboard quarter, the boat was taking a hellish pounding, hurling herself into the slanted swells and blowing free in explosions of water. As she cleared, her propellers would wind up running in thin water, sending back tremendous vibrations through the shafts and chains.

Cullin stood engine watch and Bonner clamped his legs around the helm seat. Liz was in the charthouse, trying to stay put in one of the bunks and not vomit. Her seasickness had come back full bore with the violent lunging and pounding of the hull. Now and then a wave would wash down through the companionway, and then the automatic inboard pumps under the decking would whine to life like a washing machine gone haywire. Astern she could hear Cullin yelling and cursing.

Cas had all he could handle keeping the torpedo boat moving into the quartering sea. Occasionally squalls would sweep out of the darkness, and the rain would lash him like bullets and chill his insides. They'd pass and the sea, under a sky here and there faintly backlit with moonlight, would loom black again, moving mountains with wind showering gray-white lines across the foredeck like plumes of snow.

Yet he was exhilarated. He loved the elemental fury of storms at sea. Gripping the helm wheel with bungee cords strapped down to prevent runaway, his body tensing and bracing, playing the engines and faintly hearing the wind-whipped curses of Will coming up through the intercom, he was home in this chaos.

Everything else was forgotten as his senses absorbed each slamming roll, every billowing gust, the cold, sharp scent of the ocean. He gloried in all of it, standing up there idiotically laughing and whooping challenges at each new wave front that came at him.

Unfortunately, the aged PT did not have his flexible sinew. Her plywood skin, having already absorbed a thousand miles of pounding, began to strain. First hair fractures appeared in her forward spaces, and soon a steady stream of water was washing back through her innards and the pumps were falling behind. Aft in the engine room, Cullin was walking around ankle deep in water.

As the storm got worse, both men realized they'd have to do something before the waves completely breached the PT's hull. Cullin came topside, pulling himself along the safety line, and squatted near the conn seat. "We'd best lay out a sea anchor, Casimir," he yelled over the wind. "She can't take much more of this with power on."

Cas ducked his head, cupped one hand around his mouth. "We got any timbers aboard?" he shouted back.

"I can lash up beams from the charthouse."

''What about oil?'' A perforated can of oil was usually tied to a sea anchor. When deployed forward of the boat, the oil seeped to the surface, creating a slick which prevented the waves from forming into crushing combers. ''Can we spare enough?''

''Aye, we'll do.''

While Cas continued bulldogging the PT into the wind, Cullin returned to the charthouse to jury-rig the sea anchor. The wind was increasing and the gauge on the gun turret climbed to seventy knots. All along the eastern horizon, lightning was now blowing across the sky in bright flashes.

Thirty minutes later, Cullin returned topside. With a safety line around his waist, he began hauling the lashed timbers and a five-gallon oil drum up the companionway to the starboard deck. Liz appeared, trying to help. Will waved her back and Cas hollered down for her to get below. But she stubbornly refused until Cullin gave in and put a line around her shoulders.

Crawling on hands and knees, the two of them pulled and shoved the makeshift sea anchor toward the edge of the deck. Now and then a huge wave blasted across the bow, sending a deluge of water cascading over them and knocking them flat.

At last they managed to get their load over the side. Instantly the lashed timbers slammed back against the hull, tearing off the low gunwale railing. Cas immediately shoved the throttles off to stall the boat's forward movement enough for the sea anchor to lay out. The PT dropped deeper into the water, rolling violently and causing Liz and Cullen to grab for handholds. Then the anchor line sprang taut and Cas saw that the incoming waves were losing their crests, smoothing out as the seeping oil formed into a slick. The PT shook itself and then the heavy rolling motion died away as she breasted bow-deep through the swells.

Liz and Cullin came scurrying along the safety line and dropped to the conn deck. By now Bonner had eased on low power again to maintain seaway. He locked the throttle and pulled off his sou'wester, gently wrapping it around Liz's shoulders. She was trembling from the cold and managed to give him a feeble smile.

A powerful flash of lightning suddenly crashed out of the sky, illuminating the deck and the sea for a blue-white second. Behind it instantly came the furious, rolling crash of thunder. It made the tiny helm lights jiggle. Liz shied away from it, huddling close against Cas's leg, as the PT pitched and lunged into the night and the face of the storm.

Fifteen hundred miles to the southeast, Teddy Weaver leaned away from his computer and made a notation on his watch board. The latest reports from his computer-linked weather stations at Surabaya in Java and at Ujung Pandang and Butung on Sulawesi were showing that the storm was beginning to veer northeast. Soon its front would pass over northern New Guinea, leaving the Australian north coast clear.

Weaver, a young assistant meteorologist for the Australian Weather Institute at Smithton Station Four on Tasmania, sighed with relief. The storm, designated BQ-12, wasn't going to be a problem after all. A high was moving into its wake with open sky and lots of clear weather.

This meant he'd have the chance to turn his attention back to his real passion, tracking satellites. Though only a hobby, he had spent many nights following the paths of orbital vehicles as they crossed into his area of the sky. And now he was looking forward to tracking a Chinese rocket which would soon be launching a satellite into southern orbit.

Someone slipped an arm around his neck and he heard the breathy voice of his girlfriend, Angie Wilkes, whisper into his ear, "Hello, luv."

He turned and gently knocked his head against hers. "Aye, you smell good." Angie was the receptionist at the weather station.

"Aren't you finished yet? Your watch ended ten minutes ago."

"Just keepin' a glimmer on BQ-12 to see she doesn't cock-up on us."

"Well, come on or we'll be late for Nicko's party."

"Be right with ya."

He quickly finished his report, signed it, and turned the watch panel over to the late-night man. He paused at the main window and glanced down. Station Four was situated on a rise that dropped a thousand feet into the Bass Straight, where the fast water was outrun by faster sharks. It now lay peacefully in moonlight.

He glanced at his watch, noted the time on his pay chit, and then he and Angie headed for the door, with him thinking that it was now only forty-one hours and sixteen minutes before the Chinese rocket was set to lift off.

The PT finally broke out of the eye of the storm with her engines roaring and her hull exhausted. For four hours she'd ridden her sea anchor with endless chains of swells engulfing her, only partially soothed by the oil. But gradually the wind dropped, shifting slightly to the south, and the sky began glowing more brightly.

That was what Bonner and Cullin had been waiting for. They cut the sea anchor loose and began adding power. The old boat responded, shaking defiantly as she started up into motion. But it was impossible to know how far the storm had blown them off their Daya Islands course. With no stars to shoot from yet, they had to rely on instinct. Cullin and Cas wandered around the conn deck, smelling the wind, watching the direction of the overcast tainted by moon glow, and trying to estimate divergence. They compared notes and set a new course of 188 degrees true.

Bonner held the conn while Cullin went around below, patching leaks and bracing frame struts. Liz made coffee, again thick as gelatin, and drank it thankfully, sitting on the base of the engine hatch, looking as frazzled as a bag lady. Her seasickness was rapidly fading. She was proud of the fact that she'd just come through a tropical blow straight out of Conrad with her stomach under control, her ass soaking wet, and outward bound for the Dayas.

The night ground past in an endless run across swells and long, reaching moments in valleys with the engines echoing back in the wind. But slowly this lessened too, and then they slipped completely beyond the edges of the storm, and the lopsided moon broke free, lighting the ocean with silver.

Bonner took a bearing fix off the Southern Cross and disgustedly realized they had miscalculated. The storm had blown them much farther east, nearly eighty miles. He and Cullin huddled.

"We'll never make the Dayas," Will said. "It's now either the Kai Islands or the Tanimbars. And both're a bloody toss-up."

Cas thought a moment. "I was on a dive mission once off Namwaan in the Tanimbars. If I remember correctly, there's an Aussie logging outfit there." He laughed. "The bullbucker and I had a few drinkin' bouts down island at Yamdena. He'll at least have machinery octane we can use."

Cullin nodded. "Right-o. But you'd best run only the outboards to conserve what we've got. It's gonna be iffy."

With backed-off power, the PT swung her head to a new course, 167 degrees true, straight for the jungle island of Namwaan.

Shanguan Military College had once been a Buddhist monastery. It was situated on a beech-covered hill near Yuqiao Reservoir, twenty-five miles from downtown Beijing. Surrounded by a high wall, it was composed of galleries which surrounded a central courtyard. In the center was a temple hall called the Pavilion of Precious Winds. At each corner of the wall stood four smaller pavilions, each with curving tiled roofs and walls decorated with elaborate bas-reliefs made of bronze castings.

The cadets lived in wooden barracks constructed farther down the slope. There were no fields for marching, or artillery parks. This was a school for exceptional junior PLA officers who had been chosen for advanced tactical studies and strict physical training. Every morning and evening they could be seen in full battle gear double-timing it on the dirt roads to Pinggu or to the ancient ruins of the Qing Tombs deeper in the hills, where they conducted field problems.

But this morning was different. Now the one hundred and ten cadets, dressed in their formal uniforms of black and red, were lined along the upper-level gallery, silently looking down into the main courtyard. It was cold and windless, with an overcast sky which, combined with the desert dust, gave the dawn light a tainted gray, somber pearliness.

At the precise moment the sun cleared the eastern horizon, a coterie of men entered the courtyard through a moon gate. First came twelve soldiers and a lieutenant of the elite 17th Great Wall Force, the contingent assigned to protect the buildings and personnel of the central government in Beijing. Each was an ex-commando and sharpshooter. They formed a precise line with their backs to the leafless, stunted plum trees which rose beside the west wall of the courtyard. The lieutenant's orders echoed through the dawn silence, followed by the solid rap of palms against stocks as the soldiers brought their rifles down into a parade rest position. The rifles were Hwabo bolt-actions, patterned after the U.S. Springfield ought-6 sniper's weapon. They had chromed breeches and glass-shiny black leather harnesses.

Four more men entered the courtyard, accompanied by the commandant of the college and his two personal aides. The four were dressed in coveralls, pure white, the Chinese color of death. They were generals Trai Bon of the 512th, Xianlu Yuan of the 108th, Shijou Du of the Sacred Pool Team, and Jinhua Ho of the 51st Field Artillery of Ziaushen. They were lined opposite the sharpshooters, against the east wall.

A rustle of shocked whispers scattered through the

watching cadets. Below them, in a ground-level gallery, other murmurs came from a second group of observers. These were civilians, twenty-three in all, high officials of the Central Committee along with reporters for the *Peoples Daily* and the more powerful, internal organ called *Reference News,* which carried the official directives of the State Council.

The commandant stood before the condemned men and read the charges against them: insubordination and actions against the state. Then came the execution order with Sichen's forged signature. The papers shook slightly in the commandant's hand. As the four men listened, all except Shijou Du had their heads bowed. He stared with icy arrogance at the officer.

The commandant finished reading, rolled the papers, and handed them to an aide. Then he nodded to the second aide, who immediately stepped around him, marching stiffly, and braced before the first general, Trai.

He spoke softly to him. Trai was sweating profusely, his coveralls soaked under the arms and at the neck. He nodded. The young aid withdrew a blindfold from his tunic and tied it around Trai's head. Then he pinned a small yellow ribbon to the general's chest where his heart was. Trai flinched as he did it.

Next was Xianlu, a tall man. He was visibly trembling, but he held himself very erect and refused the blindfold. He closed his eyes and did not look as the aide pinned the yellow ribbon to his coveralls. The third man in line was short, compact Shijou, the coverall material stretching over muscular shoulders. He glared at the aide, snatched the ribbon from his hand, and pinned it on himself.

The last man, Jinhua, fainted. Went right down to the ground in a heap. The aide turned and looked back at his commandant, perplexed. The second aide hurried forward. Both men lifted Jinhua. He was fat and very heavy, and his legs wouldn't hold him.

Beside him, Shijou glared contemptuously. Then he reached over and grabbed the front of Jinhua's coveralls, pulled him upright, and held him there with only one arm. To the stark-faced aides he growled, "Get on with it." They withdrew. At the other end of the line, Trai was weeping softly, his throat muscles tight, his mouth trembling in an effort to keep it still.

The crash of the rifles was like enclosed thunder, and the bullets, two rounds per man, tore the yellow ribbons apart. The men were knocked against the stone wall. It was mossy and they slid down it, leaving a garish mixture of blood and green slime which smoked softly.

Trai's body twitched for an entire minute before it finally ceased. Beside him, Xianlu's head was down on his chest, as if he had fallen asleep. Slowly, inching, he fell to the side. The bullets had spun Jinhua totally around, and he lay with his forehead against the wall. Only Shijou's eyes were still open, still staring hotly.

Everyone in the twin galleries released their breath. The silence in the courtyard had become painful. The lieutenant of the firing squad shouted an order. Palms slapped straps, the weapons were shouldered. The soldiers, pivoting as one, marched out as other soldiers with litters entered through the moon gate.

Three officers of the Great Wall Force herded the civilians from the lower gallery. Some, those cognizant of what lay ahead, were allowed to leave. But the others, including the reporters and known followers of Sichen, were taken to a central meeting hall. There they would be held throughout the day and given indoctrination lectures in which Sichen's order, and thereby his entire leadership, would be excoriated. Not until long after dark would they be released. In this way, word of the executions would not reach Premier Sichen until he was already in Australia.

In the Pavilion of Precious Winds, Minister Litung had impassively watched through a slit window of a tiny room filled with stored statuary. He had remained motionless as the executions were carried out, as the bodies were hauled away, as the cadets were silently marched off. Now the courtyard was empty. Birds returned to the bare plum tree branches. On the sandy ground, the pools of blood had coagulated and looked black. A single crow landed near one and pecked at the edge.

At last Litung roused himself. He exited the tiny room, crossed a corridor completely barren of ornament, and went into a garden beside the pavilion. There was a small pool in the center with goldfish and reeds. As he passed it, a single shaft of sunlight pierced the overcast and touched the water, made it glow. Litung noticed but did not pause.

17

The small-gauge railroad track ran straight into jungle on a constant, gentle rise. The rails were laid out on a low gravel embankment and were rusted save for the top surfaces, which were steel-shiny. On either side the jungle lay steamy and breathless, soaring *kanari* trees overgrown with *dalakorak* vines and moss, and beneath, thickets of ginger and *soriang* ferns. From it came the buzz of insects and now and then the chirping clicks of a fever bird as Liz and Bonner, the Armalite rifle slung over his shoulder, trudged slowly along the track, stepping on the creosoted ties and sweating in their flak jackets.

The Namwaan timber operation had turned out to be abandoned. The docking facilities were still extant, built on a deep-water estuary, flanked by high cliffs on the far side and a terminus area cleared out of the jungle. Huge piles of teak logs rotted in the sun near the dockhead alongside empty tanks and a small tin-roofed repair shop devoid of gear. The place looked as if it had been left in a hurry.

Farther in, a river broached the estuary. There was thick jungle on both sides, but the east side went up into steep *palis* which joined the estuary cliffs. The river water was the color of milky coffee, and where it gurgled and swirled under the trees, it left a dark, foamy veneer on any exposed roots, indicating that somewhere upstream there were rapids.

They had reached the island just after sunrise and

tied up on the river side of the long dock. Previously it had been used for loading the teak logs onto lumber freighters from Sulawesi.

With their fuel tanks nearly empty, their situation had become desperate. If by some chance Stanford and his riverines stumbled onto them here, it would be all over. Their only recourse would be to abandon the boat and go to jungle, trying to make their way to the tiny fishing villages on the east coast of the island.

Cas suggested he hike up to the main lumber camp. Perhaps in its haste the company had abandoned sufficient fuel stores to get them at least to Namdena or even across the Arafura Sea to the north coast of Australia. With nothing for her to do on the boat, Liz decided to accompany him. Cullin stayed with the PT to work on the engines.

It took them over an hour to reach the camp, a pathetic collection of tin shacks and wooden tent foundations with their canvas sides rotting away. Everywhere the jungle was already reclaiming it, vines and creepers curling up walls and *alang-alang* grass protruding through floors.

On a siding, a small diesel switch engine sat in a webbing of vines, its wheels locked with heavy rail ties. It was covered with rust and water stains, and moss colonies were growing in the darker recesses of the drive wheels and carriage. Beside it lay coils of rusted cable and lengths of chain linked to heavy gripper jaws used to haul logs.

Beyond the camp, the upper hills had been clear-cut and were filled with timber debris, teak stumps and rotting logs, and the ground was scarred with bulldozer tracks and rain gullies. A wrecked Landrover was mired in mud up to its hood at the foot of the second hillock, its engine stripped out and wheels rotted away.

On the river side of the buildings, the ground fell sharply down through thick jungle. A wide trail had been bulldozed straight down to a small pier on the river a quarter mile away, and a cable was stretched from a jack post all the way down. They could see a stretch of the river where it swept around the dock's pilings, and from upstream came the distant rush of a waterfall.

For several minutes Cas and Liz wandered through the camp, anxiously poking into buildings, nosing into crevices for any sign of fuel tanks or drums. "What happened here? I wonder," Liz asked. "The place gives me the creeps, like it's haunted."

"Whatever it was, they sure got out fast."

In one shack they flushed sleeping fruit bats off rafters. As Liz squealed in horror, the animals, large as ferrets, dropped to the floor and went flapping around, blindly trying to find dark holes. On one of the *kanari* trees a plastic water bag was still hanging on chains. It was filled with crystal-clear rainwater, and the bottom was coated with moss that smelled like watermelons.

They located the largest of the buildings in a small gulley. A warehouse, its sides and roof were made of corrugated iron sheets covered with thick cobwebs that glistened like spun silver in the sun. Cas paused, sniffing the air. "I smell diesel." He hunted around, found a rusty crowbar, and forced the door. They took off their flak jackets and entered.

The air was hot and thick, and the odor of diesel fuel was very strong. There were stacks of black fifty-gallon drums, five high, on wooden pallets. Each drum bore the blue trademark of the Pertamina Oil Corporation of Java. The pallets were worm-eaten and some had collapsed under the weight, tilting their loads precariously. Several of the jammed barrels had leaked, dripping diesel down the sides to form pools where little islands of gray fungus had erupted, feeding on the trapped carbon in the oil.

Cas touched Liz's arm. "You better wait outside. These stacks are about ready to come down."

"No way," she said, hugging herself. "I don't like being alone here."

Cas shook his head and handed her a crowbar. "All

right, then check for filled gasoline drums. But watch it.''

He turned up one of the alleyways between the stacks, knocking knuckles against drums and peering at their ID stencils. Liz started up a different alleyway. Toward the back the light became very dim, and Cas had to bend down close to make out the lettering. As he did, he heard scurrying underneath the pallets. Mice, he figured.

He finally located a stack of gasoline drums. The stencil said it was 87 octane, regular vehicle fuel. The PT could run with it, he knew, but she'd go sluggishly, and enough of this stuff would eventually clog up her valves. But at least it was fuel.

He moved to another stack. Periodically he had heard the faint tang of Liz's crowbar on the other side of the shack. But all of a sudden he heard her shout something which was followed by a furious banging of the crowbar.

He froze. "Liz?" he shouted. "What the—" Another sound—like the rustle of dry leaves—came from the wooden pallet close to his shoulder. Startled by its nearness, he jerked back.

As he did, something skittered along the edge of the pallet. A second later, he dimly made out other things moving in jerky little lunges like large ants roused from their burrows. Two fell from the pallet to the sandy floor with a soft plop. He stared at them. The objects were black, as large as his thumb.

Scorpions!

Liz's voice had risen to an hysterical pitch interspersed with solid collisions of the crowbar against metal. He glanced toward the door. In the shaft of sunlight coming through it he saw that the floor was alive with insects. Sweet Jesus! he thought. They'd never make it out without getting badly stung. And if one of them stumbled and went down—

With his skin crawling, he started around his stack and headed toward Liz. A scorpion dropped onto his shoulder and he jerked away from it, slapping furiously. Another crossed his bare foot. He could feel dozens crunching under his flip-flops.

When he rounded the alley Liz was in, he found her jumping up and down, face contorted, swinging blindly with the crowbar. He lunged toward her and grabbed her around the waist. Lifting her off her feet, he tore the crowbar from her hand. "Hang on to me!" he bellowed. She tried to crawl up him, murmuring with an insane revulsion.

Hooking the bar into one of the nearby pallets, he ripped it out. The upper drums banged together sharply as the stack tilted. One of the top barrels tumbled down, crashing to the floor and rolling violently into another stack. He hooked the crowbar again, tore out another length of the two-by-four frame. With a soft scrape of metal, the whole stack started down.

Cas turned, curling himself over Liz. The upper barrels crashed into the floor directly behind him and tumbled away with a solid, rolling sound. Other stacks started down. The floor trembled with impacts. Like a deck of cards, all the stacks were shifting, tilting, dropping barrels.

The first drums reached the open door and went rolling through. Those behind it crashed into the framing, and their weight blew it apart. Several careened off to the side and burst through the right wall, flooding the inside of the building with sunlight. In broad daylight they saw that the mass of scorpions had become so thick that the floor itself seemed to be moving.

Cas glanced toward the door and instantly dashed toward it. The drums had squashed a four-foot-wide pathway through the insects. Carrying Liz as if she were weightless, he sprinted, running as lightly as he could, letting his feet touch and bounce.

As he reached the burst door frame, he felt a sharp sting in his right thigh. Another. They shot into him like the pricks of white-hot needles. Then he skidded in the grass outside, going down onto his knees, with

Liz tumbling off and rolling away. She came up slapping her body and shuddering.

Cas found four scorpions still crawling on him, but he managed to slap them away before they stung him. His leg was throbbing. Quickly he stood up, tore off the rifle, and undid his shorts. His penis was shrunken. Desperately he tried to urinate. It wouldn't come. Watching him open-mouthed, Liz had forgotten her own terror.

He grimaced, forced his bladder, aching. A little spurt of urine came, then a flow. He held his cupped hand under it, then slapped it onto the scorpion bite and started rubbing it in.

Liz finally understood what he was doing and hurried over. She scooped up a ball of mud splashed by his urine and smeared it over the wound. It was already turning slightly red and swelling. "Give me your shirt," she snapped.

Cas pulled it off and handed it to her. She bound it around his thigh, then stuffed more moistened mud under the strip. When it was tight, she stood up and gazed into his eyes. "How venomous is the sting?"

"I don't know." He kept shaking his head, his jaws tight. "Burns like fire, though."

"You better lie down."

Shaking his head, he limped over to the engine and leaned against it. He glanced down at the fuel warehouse. It was still rumbling with rolling barrels, and as he watched, another section of corrugated iron blew out. His thigh was slightly numb now.

Finally he looked at Liz and forced a grin. "Well, at least we found our fuel."

She closed her eyes and shuddered again, hugging herself as if she were freezing. "That's the most horrible sight I've ever seen."

From far away came the sudden roar of the PT's engines. It rose sharply, faded, then rose again. Directly afterward came the sound of automatic gunfire, thinned by distance into hollow cracks, like marbles falling on a cement floor. Then they heard the heavier-throated growl of a .50-caliber machine gun.

"Jesus, they're after Will," Cas cried. He swept up his Armalite and jacket and, limping, headed across the camp, Liz right behind him. Drowning out more firing was the roar of the PT, bouncing off the far cliffs, echoing back over itself. Will was heading up-river.

Bonner hobbled right through the camp clearing and down the road to the river, sliding on the steep incline, bracing his feet, smashing through the waist-high new growth. All around him, the jungle was filled with the approaching roar of the Hall-Scotts.

Stanford, braced against the foredeck peak of the *Flying Sun,* let go a burst from one of the LC-11's .50's. It nearly knocked him down, the bullets arcing furiously up into the air. He yelled with joy as he lowered the barrel, feeling its heat burning his hand. His next burst stitched across the water about a hundred yards ahead, throwing geysers far astern of the receding PT. Beside him, three of the riverine men were hammering away with small arms but were hopelessly outranged.

At last he dropped the weapon and sprinted back to the cabin wing, went up the port ladder and jammed his head through the hatchway. "How far up does that river go?" he shouted to Big Willie.

"Map show mile, mile and a half. But get waterfall inside."

"We got the pricks trapped. Go get 'em."

Willie shook his huge head. "No, too shallow up there."

For a moment Jack was furious. Then he considered the matter. It didn't make any difference. The only way Cullin and the others could escape was to come past them or go to bush. Well, he'd close the latter gate immediately.

"Okay, go back to the wharf and drop me and some men. Then you can take a position at the river entrance. Mount the fifties and blow that PT to shit if it tries to break out.''

The huge Chinaman accepted that. He eased the cruiser around in a slow turn and headed for the loading dock. Two minutes later, they eased up beside it, the engines backwashing softly.

After the radio call from the drug plane, the *Flying Sun* had rendezvoused with another LC-11 off Buru and taken on more crew. Then they had run the Ambon Channel and headed straight for the Tanimbars. The going had been hellish for a while out in the open ocean with the storm slashing at them, yet the big cruiser had kept headway well. As soon as they broke through, Stanford ordered radar scans and on they went southward, blowing signal. With the PT running slowly on double engines, the *Flying Sun* made good time against her. Around three-thirty in the morning, they'd picked her up—the only traffic on the sea—forty-three miles north of Namwaan.

Stanford took eight men, all armed with automatic weapons and bolo knives. They jumped onto the dock and sprinted up to the landing, the tar on the wharf scorching hot under their feet. For a moment they gathered in the clearing and Jack deployed them. He sent three into the jungle which skirted the shoreline to cut off any attempt by Cullin and the others to go to ground there. The remaining men he led up the rail track toward the timber camp.

Cullin's face was gun hard as he brought the PT upriver, now idling on a single engine, and eased her over to the small loading pier where Bonner and Liz stood waiting. Farther upstream, the river went around a bend, with the trees hugging the shoreline, making shadows where whirlpools spun. From beyond the bend came the crash of the falls.

Synchronizing the boat's forward movement to the current, Will waited until Cas jumped aboard and tossed a line to Liz. When she tied in, he disengaged the engine and let the PT trail with the current.

Bonner came up onto the conn. "Stanford?"

"Aye, the bugger come in from the north. I'm bleedin' lucky I was topside and spotted the choongs before they came in. Barely pulled away from the wharf as it was."

Bonner was covered with mud from the plunge down the trail to the loading pier. "I heard fifties. They got riverines with 'em?"

Cullin shook his head. "No, they must have dismounted weapons." He looked off downriver. A gray crane, hidden in the bank, lofted suddenly into the air, flapping heavily to gain altitude. "The cruiser dropped men at the wharf. Now it's sittin' out in the estuary waitin' for us to make a run."

Cas snorted and jetted spittle through his teeth. "Looks like they got us by the short hairs, don't it?"

"I'd say that was a fair assessment, mate."

"Well, if the bastards are coming, let's be ready for 'em." He studied the jungle on the camp side of the river, then glanced across at the cliffs and *palis* that climbed steeply away from the opposite shoreline, figuring fields of fire. "If I remember, the falls are about two, three hundred meters from here. Can you take the boat any farther upstream?"

"Aye, at least to the bend."

"If you shelter on the far side and I go up to the falls, we'd have the pricks in a decent cross fire. They won't be expecting that."

"Just what I was thinkin'. We hold 'em off till dark, we might make a run past that cruiser." Cullin's eyes were beginning to sparkle with excitement.

"What about fuel?"

"We got maybe a half hour's run, no more. But that could get us to the Ranarmoye River. I don't figure that choong cruiser'd follow us up into them shallows. When we sucked empty tank, we could cut across island by foot for either Batkas or Yamdena."

Cas nodded. He too was starting to experience the pump of adrenaline, the tingle in his fingers. This was going to be nasty, he knew, up at those falls with men coming at him through the jungle—bush fighting, the worst kind. He'd seen his share of it in Nam. But at least he'd be above: they'd have to fight him and the slope.

He quickly went below. In a moment he returned with spare clips for the Armalite taped to both thighs and two haversacks of explosives. The scorpion stings were giving him periodic throbs, but he ignored them.

"Don't let the bastards cross the river," he said. "When dark comes and they try it, blow a flare."

"Aye. How much ammo we got in the fifty?"

"Only a few bursts left."

Cullin chuckled icily. "Then I'd say we're sittin' fair dinkum."

"You're one hell of an optimist, Will."

Cullin engaged chain again and eased the PT back to the pier. Liz was standing there, looking forlorn and fearful, like a little girl lost on a dark street corner. As Bonner jumped off, she stared at the taped clips and explosive satchels. "Where are you going?" she asked anxiously.

"Up to the falls. Get up there with Will."

"Aren't we leaving?"

"Yes, after dark. Until then we'll have to hold them off." He shrugged into his flak jacket.

"I want to go with you."

He paused, frowned at her. "No, Liz, I'll be moving all over hell up there."

"I can help. Just tell me what to do."

Cas drew back his lips, showing his teeth. He studied her darkly for a moment, then nodded. "All right." He shoved one of the explosive haversacks at her. She took it and started shouldering into the strap.

"No, put on your jacket first," he snapped. Without another word he let go of the PT's line, picked up the assault rifle, and trotted back up the pier. At the edge of the jungle he paused and looked back. Liz had her jacket on but was clumsily trying to get the haversack settled. "Come on, move it," he bellowed.

She hurried after him and together they slipped into the jungle.

Climbing up the side of the falls was like scaling a greased stairway on little juttings of rock overgrown with moss and ferns that smashed under their weight. They continually slipped and floundered. Cas soon kicked off his flip-flops to get better toe holds. Behind him, Liz struggled upward, panting and frowning with concentration. After a while, he reached back and took the haversack from her. She looked up and gave him a wild look that held thankfulness somewhere down in its blue-gray depths.

The falls were about sixty feet high, a plunging cascade the color of dark coffee. It dropped into a vast bore pool, where the crashing water threw up a mist that was as cold as fog drifting over a snow-capped peak. Tiny jungle swallows darted across the face of the falls, riding the updrafts and hovering like Japanese kites.

Soaking wet, the two made it to the top and crawled into a small rock crevice. The sound of the falls filled the opening, and they had to holler to be heard. Cas leaned out and studied the terrain for a moment: the PT was partly hidden under overhanging trees on the opposite bank. He ducked back.

"I'm going over to the left," he yelled. "It drops off in a gradual slope there. If they come up, that'll be where they do it."

Liz nodded, hugging herself against the chill.

"You watch my right flank. If you spot any movement along that ridge line, give a couple of screams and then jump."

Her mouth opened with shock. "What jump?"

"Into the basin pool and ride the rapids down to the PT."

"You've got to be kidding."

"You won't have any choice. If they overrun me, that's the only way you can go." He studied her closely. "You understand what I'm saying?"

She leaned out and peered nervously down at the bottom of the falls.

"Liz?"

"Yes, all right."

He thrust himself to his feet and darted away.

"Be careful," she called, but he was already gone.

Moments later, he was crawling through jungle awash in the distant thunder of the falls. Its mist coated the tree trunks and mossy crevices with glistening water droplets. High overhead, the canopy of the trees created an evening gloom, and the air had an emerald glow to it. Here and there a clean slice of sunlight came down, highlighting the drifting mist.

The earth undulated with hillocks of lichens and foul-smelling mushrooms. He reached a spot where the slope dropped down sharply, and he spied the river and the stern of the PT. Skewering around, he pressed his back against a tree trunk ablaze with purple orchids and faced downslope.

He waited.

Minutes trooped past sluggishly, yet his concentration was so keen that he detected the subtle whisperings of the jungle beneath the pealing rumble of the falls: sibilant buzzes and hums, the drip of moisture, the rustle of leaves. Ten feet away, he caught a slight movement in the ground cover, and a snake poked its head through. It was red with a two-foot blue body. A *tualarang!* He drew back, his skin crawling. A bite from that thing, he knew, would kill him in forty seconds. As he watched, the snake silently glided off under a lichen-covered tree trunk.

A short, furious firefight erupted down on the river— Will's .50-caliber over smaller fire that quickly died away. Atta boy, Cullin, he thought, keep the bastards on this side.

Cas waited some more.

Suddenly he noticed an unnatural hush. The array of sounds around him had stilled, leaving only the pure overtone of the falls. His heart triggered up. Someone was coming. He eased to his knees, legs tensing, head tilted to listen.

Seconds passed. Stillness. Then he caught the unmistakable tinkle of metal, very close. His eyes darted around, looking for sign of movement. A branch trembled as if touched by a breeze. Another sound, like a sigh.

Then a body loomed up out of nowhere. For a split second he saw a round oriental face with a black bandanna tied across its mouth. The man's shoulders cleared the jungle cover as he lunged straight up at him.

Cas propelled himself off his coiled legs and met the charge. A bolo knife sliced past his ear, snapping down through branches. Cas twisted, feeling the man's belly and knee against him. He hurled the attacker away and in the same motion slashed the butt of the Armalite across the man's face, felt bone give.

He rolled away and came to his knees again. The man was stretched in the broken branches in front of him, blood spurting through the fingers of one hand as he held them against his mouth. For one crazy moment they looked into each other's eyes. Then the man swung the bolo up off the ground. The blade arced through the emerald gloom. Hurling backward, Cas brought up the Armalite and pulled the trigger. The rounds knocked the man back into the brush.

Instantly the jungle resounded with muzzle explosions and zinging rounds chopping leaves and branches like furious bees. Cas crawled away, frantically feeling for the haversacks. He found them, hauled them up and, cradling the weight, hugged the ground.

The firing stopped.

For a peculiar moment he heard nothing, not even the falls. The gunfire had momentarily made him deaf. Then, as clearly as a voice across an auditorium, someone called, "Give it up, Bonner, you son of a bitch. Or you're a dead man."

Stanford!

Cas twisted his head, trying to locate the man's position, but he couldn't. Gently he reached down and felt all over one of the haversacks for its trigger wire. It was under a flap, the pull ring clipped. He set the timer for a four-second delay, eased off the ring, paused, and lifted his head.

"Go fuck yourself," he yelled, then rolled away across open rock, down into a tiny gulley.

Automatic fire instantly blew the jungle apart again, the rounds tearing branches where he had been. Over the edge of a mossy boulder he pinpointed the muzzle blasts. In the gloom they looked like little bursts of lightning. In a single motion he pulled the trigger wire, twisted, and hurled it downslope toward the flashes. It crashed through underbrush like a rolling boulder. He curled over and, eyes closed, counted the seconds: . . . three . . . four.

The charge went off with a boom so powerful it blew waves of air distortion back through the jungle, echoing, whomping off through distant leafy corridors. A man's scream spiraled up, reached a top note and fell immediately away.

Cas jumped to his feet and cut loose with the Armalite, spraying back and forth until the clip was empty. Smoke drifted around him, made the gloom iridescent. He dropped to the ground again and tore off one of the spare clips. Ejecting the empty one, he rammed it into the weapon and jacked a round up into the chamber. Then he scooped up the second haversack and, furiously crab-walking, crawled farther upslope.

Down on the river, two of Stanford's men had tried to toss a line across the river. They were driven back by a violent burst from Will's .50. After an angry chatter of return fire, everything went still but the roar of the falls.

In her crevice, Liz had watched the exchange. Then firing had come from where she supposed Bonner was. Every shot pronged into her flesh, made her chest feel hollow. When the first haversack went off, it shook the rock under her. Petrified, she jumped so high she banged her head against the overhang. As the echoes riffled off, absorbed by the water rushing close by, she still heard the throbs. Finally she realized it was her own blood pounding.

She looked out and peered downslope. Nothing was moving down there save wisps of smoke wafting through the trees. As they drifted out over the falls, they were suddenly sucked upward in the updraft.

A furious burst of several automatic weapons opened up, and she threw herself back into her crevice. Two rounds actually went past her into the stream where it curled over the edge, as smooth as chocolate taffy. They made two tiny eruptions which quickly vanished.

"Bonner?" she kept saying over and over aloud, her voice shaky with terror. "Where are you? Bonner?"

The second haversack went off, this time closer. She saw debris flying out into the air in front of the falls. She clung to the rock, feeling panic beginning to take hold, that dangerous ascent of terror, drawing all rational thoughts with it.

Desperate to move, to feel her muscles functioning, she crawled out onto the overhanging rock above the falls. Sixty feet down, the column of water crashed into the bore pool.

Someone touched her shoulder. She screamed, whirling.

It was Cas. There was blood on his face and part of his flak jacket had been torn open. His eyes were dark and quivering. "I can't hold 'em off," he bellowed. "Jump!"

Bullets ricocheted off a rock three feet away, whining with the screeches of dogs struck by a car. Cas held back a moment, then lunged out and fired, the spent cartridges whanging back against the overhang. "Get outa here," he yelled over his shoulder.

Dazed but slavishly obedient in her fear, she crawled out to the edge of the rock and jumped.

She felt as though she plummeted for a long time, the face of the falls flashing past like a fast-moving train. Her mind was racing with it, imagining herself impaled on rocks as spiky as the dark pickets of a fence. There was a scream somewhere in her throat, yet she couldn't hear it.

From somewhere in the tumult of her thoughts came the idea that she should make herself as narrow as possible. Wasn't that the way divers made their Olympic dives? The thought was so overwhelmingly sensible that her body reacted to it before she consciously accepted its premise.

Just as her toes pointed, she crashed into the water with an impact that jolted all through her. She felt her arms lifted violently, felt shoulder muscles cry out as the flak jacket was nearly torn off her. Down she went into icy blackness. All around her was a massive booming, and the water thrashed and tugged at her. Desperately she tried to kick toward the surface, but she was so disoriented, she didn't know where it was.

Her feet touched polished rock, and then a current completely swept her off again, her body straightened, riding over projections on a cushion of water. A moment later, she broke through the surface, popped into the air a foot or so, and crashed down again.

The second time she came up, she was already on the far side of the bore pool, her body slithering around rocks and down into shallow channels, the jacket taking much of the buffetting. She gasped for air and looked up in time to see Bonner dropping off the upper ledge, legs together, arms at his sides like a parachutist exiting an aircraft.

Something yellow zipped past her on the surface, riding the current. Her head swiveled and she saw it was one of the computer disks. Beyond it a few feet was the other. The impact into the bore pool had knocked them out of her pocket.

She started after them, stroking clumsily over the rocks. Two tiny geysers erupted off to the right, making little *thwumping* sounds. Bullets! Instantaneously the PT's machine gun erupted from downstream as Cullin began throwing rounds up into the jungle near the head of the falls to cover her and Cas.

The disks were rapidly swirling away from her. She

started after them again. For a moment she lost sight of the yellow specks as she slid around a particularly large protruding rock. Beyond it she found herself in a secondary pool. She sculled her legs, trying frantically to relocate the disks. Across the river the .50 had stopped firing, then started up again.

The disks were gone.

A moment later, Cas appeared through the surface behind her. He grabbed her waist and together they went down over another series of small, rough rapids. Here and there were shallow channels that funneled their descent, rapping their bodies against the rocks.

A string of bullets stitched across the water less than four feet ahead of them, and Cas glanced toward the PT. Up in the gun turret, Will was frantically working on the breech. The .50 had jammed.

"Dive underwater," he yelled. "Make for the boat."

Immediately she ducked her head down and dived deeper. Faintly she could hear more gunfire and the impacts of the rounds all around her. Through the brown darkness she saw them enter the water, making sizzling trails.

She swam and swam, struggling against the weight of the jacket. Soon her lungs and arms started to burn. Terrified of exposing her head, she kept on. Finally she couldn't anymore. She rolled in the water and let her face break free just long enough to exhale and drag in another lungful.

She felt Cas's body, his powerful stroking rhythm beside her. Then he was dragging her down again, holding her by the back of the jacket. They wound again through the brown darkness.

She gagged, swallowing water that had a sour, grainy taste. She had to go up again. Once her face cleared the surface, she found herself looking up into trees only inches away. She became aware of small counter currents tugging her, and then they drifted among roots and mud as slimy as mush. The bow of the PT rose above them, its sides speckled with tree shadows.

Lunging upward, Cas gripped the edge of the foredeck and pulled himself aboard. He twisted, grabbed her and hoisted her right out of the water, depositing her, gasping, on the deck. Without pausing he turned and darted toward the conn. Nowhere near as alert, she crawled after him.

Will was glassing the jungle near the falls. As Bonner came scooting up between the barrier bulkhead, he snapped, "The buggers are movin' downslope."

Cas climbed up into the gun turret, checked the breech. Will had cleared it. "Check downstream," he called out. "The disks are in the river. I'll be damned if I'll let the pricks get 'em."

Cullin's gaze swung away from the falls, sweeping the river down toward the bend. A moment later, he yelled, "There's one! There, right at the swirl of the bend."

"I got it." As Cas swung the turret around, the hydraulics whispered softly. He blew a burst. After only three rounds the belt slapped up out of the ammo box, empty. "Son of a *bitch!*"

Downriver, he saw the disk bobbing and dipping, showing corners, its metal tab catching the light. A few seconds later, it disappeared around the curve of the river.

Liz had by now come up onto the conn and was sitting under the control panel. Bonner and Cullin turned, glaring intently up at the jungle across the river. Then Cas slipped through the turret bars and hit the conn deck already running. He darted to the charthouse ladder and went below. In a moment he came back with Cullin's Walther and the three remaining explosive haversacks. Behind the conn barrier Will was loading his flare gun.

For long, dragging moments, they waited for Stanford to come across the river. In preparation Cas laid out the haversacks in a handy line, and Will tucked the spare flares into the band of his shorts and on the control panel.

Liz crawled over to Bonner. "What can I do?"

He handed her the Walther. "Make your shots count."

She nodded, gripped the gun, watching the jungle

across the river. It looked horribly foreboding now. Is this the end of it? she thought, her blood ringing inside her head. Gory images shot through her mind of death, the pain of ripping flesh. Would the men rape her?

All round the PT, life was returning to the jungle. Across the face of the falls the swallows began darting in their long, sweeping arcs. A furtive *nip-nip* deer came to the bank to dip its golden brown head to drink, while the raucous call of a bush parrot drifted through the trees.

Cas said, "Oh-oh," and pointed downstream.

Three hundred yards away, a man had stepped out of the jungle near the bend. He stood for a moment, then stepped into the water. It swirled and eddied around his legs. He was looking toward the PT. After a moment he lifted his arms. In each hand was a tiny yellow object. The disks!

Taking the revolver from Liz, Cas walked to the PT's stern. He paused there, his body relaxed yet containing a clean, hard line, the Walther down at his side, realizing it was too far for a shot as he stared at the man that he knew was Stanford.

For a long moment the two of them regarded each other. Stanford was whirling his arms like a football player who'd just made a touchdown and was yelling something. Bonner cocked his head, trying to pick it up. The voice drifted up under the sound of the falls in wavy surges: "—ou lost, prick—hotel is—all dead as stone—you—fucking thing—"

Then very deliberately Stanford lowered one arm slightly, slapped his other hand into the angle of his right elbow, and lifted it again, thrusting a fist at the sky. One last, triumphant Fuck you, Bonner!

Hotel . . . dead . . .

The words went around and around inside Cas's head. They're dead. *They're dead!* He swung around and looked at Liz. She had heard too. Her face was white.

It was true, Stanford was going after the Seascape One!

18

Jean Gallaudet had crashed into sleep as dense and dreamless as death. Eighteen hours he slept, stretched out on the floor of his tiny electronics lab with spittle drooling from his lips and spiders exploring his inert figure.

On one of the panels of his main console, a single red light began to blink insistently. It was Stanford. But Jean slept on, his body circuits completely shut down.

Now and then two native girls entered the lab, prowled about looking for the needle-drug. Then they'd wander off to haunt the coconut groves nearby, perhaps wondering why there was such a pull in their blood.

At last Gallaudet roused. He lay for a while contemplating the faint scent of salt in the air. He felt the delicate, tremulous bounce of a daddy longlegs on a thigh. He brushed it off and stood up.

"Merde!" he gasped. Head whirling, he probed his environment until he found his stash. It was a sizable plastic bag the color of absinthe. He shot up. Body connections came alive, shot crazy splurges of energy everywhere, made him feel like the terminus of connector lines in a rocket, full of flowing fire.

The red light again blinked in a dot-dash burst.

Gallaudet, with a ridiculous nursery rhyme singing through his mind, flopped into his control seat and flicked several switches. He keyed his mike: *"Qui est?"*

The voice that came back was angry: "Where the hell have you been, asshole?"

"Visiting the gods."

"What?"

"No, not that." Gallaudet giggled, feeling the cocaine make a pure, neat cone of his head. *"Se tripoter,"* he said, using the infinitive for masturbation. It seemed adequate, almost expansive.

"What? What the fuck are you talking about? I got the disks here, man. Open your modem, I got 'em."

Got 'em? Jean wandered for a moment through essences. Ah, yes, the disks, his data. He homed onto three switches, lifted a secondary radio-receiver and delicately deposited it into its carriage. "Modem away," he crooned.

The information came through with lightning rapidity. He watched as the visual screen splayed data. The lines flashed, bright little troops of electronic insects. Phrases, numerical sequences prodded memory jogs in his mind. He nodded. "Yes! Oh, yes!"

When the data stopped, Stanford's voice came back. "You got it?"

"Oui."

"All right, get to the heavy programming, buddy boy. We'll be there in twenty hours. You got that? Twenty hours."

"Oui."

Stanford was gone. No good-bye, just gone.

Gallaudet felt a sudden, overwhelming urge to eat, like a bowel surge. But he paused long enough to check his in-feed consoles to see that everything had been taped. Then he went to his refrigerator and scoffed up peanut butter. It tasted as tart and sweet as a woman's clitoris, *la praline*, a sugared almond erect with lust blood.

Hunger satisfied, he return to his consoles. For a moment he played around with his fingertips like a giddy pianist preparing to play a complex concerto. It just seemed right to do. Then he went into his timed entry to the Xchiang launch site.

At first he wandered around in the system, observing updates. He discovered that two cases of flu had broken out within the engineering staff and requests for antitoxin were insistent. He studied the problems that had shown up during a recent plugs-out test of the Long March rocket. Minor stuff that would easily be rectified. But it pointed up how archaic the Chinese actually were in telemetric control.

Then he planted the virus. It was a meaningless number sequence that when released would instantly eat up everything within the Xchiang system, flashing through with electronic speed. It was a neat little interject that would snuggle into the system as easily as a mouse in a silo of corn.

He paused, trying to decide on the trigger phrase. What? He scooped another fingerful of peanut butter. *La praline*. But of course. He leaned forward and punched in the number *69*. As it entered the system, Gallaudet sighed, feeling a fresh urge for cocaine, a dragon lifting from the sea. He checked reception. His screen flashed two words: *lingshou-id*. Accepted.

It was a go. Now the moment he punched the trigger phrase, within 3.56 seconds the little silo mouse would begin to eat, sending the entire Xchiang control system into total decay. . . .

Back on Namwaan it had rained, a short, intense shower trailing in the wake of the main storm. When it surged into the jungle, it made a roaring sound and the branches hung down laden with runoff. It lasted a few minutes, tapered off, then came again. When it finally moved on, the jungle steamed with whorls rising through the trees like morning mist. Tiny cascades on the banks turned the river from coffee brown to a slate gray, which made the eddies look like wrinkles in satin.

It also made the job of bringing down the fuel barrels from the timber camp extremely difficult. With the PT tied to the small loading pier, Cas and Liz had gone up to the camp warehouse and began extracting barrels marked as gasoline, moving gingerly around, glancing constantly underfoot for scorpions in the grass.

Cas pulled off more of the tin siding, exposing the rear stacks. Then using a line from the boat, he lassoed the ones he wanted and pulled them out into the grass. As he did, scorpions plopped off and scurried for the shadows under the building.

Drenched in sweat, he paused, glancing toward the river. "All right, now we have to get the damned things up that incline to the dolly cable," he informed Liz.

It was rough, rolling the barrels all the way down through the camp and up the slight slope. Unfortunately, the cable dolly was missing, so they had to rig the barrels onto the cable and then back stay them with their own weight all the way down the muddy, slick trail.

Now and then one of the heavy drums would get moving too fast, its line singing along the cable, with Cas and Liz stumbling and falling down through the mud trying to get it slowed. One finally got completely out of control and went all the way to the bottom, smashing into the *jhonny* post that held the cable and tearing it and part of the pier foundation into the river. Cullin, up on the PT, yelled as the barrel with cable wrapped around it went sailing right over his bow.

When Cas reached the pier, he stomped around the slanting deck, glaring at the barrel floating downriver trailing the *jhonny* post. Liz came down panting and looked at him, then up at Cullin. Silently she sat down and wiped mud out of her eyes.

Bonner suddenly said, "Damn, look at that son of a bitch."

"Yeah, it's beautiful," Liz said disgustedly. "I love it."

"No, you don't understand. Look at it floating. Why in hell didn't I think of that before? We can roll the bastards down here and let 'em *float* out to the estuary."

So that's what they did. While Cullin got the PT turned around, playing a single engine and the current, Cas and Liz went back to the warehouse and hauled out more drums, laughing at each other because now the work had been cut in half. But they sobered as the realization hit them that now time had become precious, flying inexorably away from them, while somewhere in China a rocket sat, waiting to carry death across the sky.

At the top of the dolly trail, they sent the drums crashing down the slope, tearing through shrubbery and finally bouncing off the remnants of the pier and into the river. There they bobbed off, riding the five-mile current.

All told, they managed to locate fifteen barrels of gasoline. They lost one when its bung ring blew out on impact and spewed fuel across the surface of the river, making glassy patches on the water which glistened rainbow colors in the sunlight. But at least they had seven hundred gallons of fuel, enough to get the PT all the way to the York Peninsula on Australia, some two hundred fifty miles away.

Afterward, they made one last reconnoiter of the camp in the hope of finding more gasoline. But there wasn't any. So, filthy with sweat and mud, they started back down along the tracks.

They went about a hundred yards when Cas stopped. Barefooted, he was having a rough time on the embankment cinders. He turned and looked back toward the camp.

"What's the matter?" Liz asked.

"To hell with walking." He headed back. After a moment she followed.

He made for the small switch engine, walked around it several times, studying the wheels and sighting down the track. Finally he nodded to himself. "Yeah, it'll work."

"What are you going to do?"

"Ride this sucker back to the dockhead."

"Will it go?"

"She's on a downhill slope all the way."

"How do we stop it?"

"There has to be a manual brake somewhere." He pulled himself up into the control space. A rotted umbrella was stuck up over the operator's seat. The seat itself was made of canvas, and there were worms in the stuffing.

Cas hunted around, fingering the controls. There were two dials on the panel, their glass turned amber by moisture. Everything held that old steel, oily odor like abandoned cars in an empty lot. He found the throttle and the brake lever, tested it. It creaked, coming up hard against something.

He turned to Liz, grinning. "Let's give her a shot. Go get the line."

While she was gone, he cleared off the vines. As tough as hemp, they smelled like mucus when he snapped them. Then he pulled out the twin ties from in front of the wheels. They came away sucking softly, with maggot colonies that had been feeding off the creosote.

With Liz aboard, Bonner ran his line through the catcher fork, trailed out a little, and then fashioned a harness. He shouldered into it and, bracing his legs, began to pull.

Nothing moved except his stomach muscles. Gritting his teeth, he leaned into it. The line dug into his shoulders, made his spine tingle with the strain. Jerking and snapping against the harness, he pulled some more.

He produced an inch of movement.

"This is a waste of time," Liz said.

"Then get the hell down here and help," he hissed through clenched teeth. She did. They got another inch.

Then the line went completely slack, and he went sprawling out onto his belly. Behind him, he heard the rusty wheels of the engine crunch and then the soft sough of steel on steel.

"She's moving," Liz cried, jumping up on the catcher. "Look out."

As Cas rolled over, the blunt front of the little engine loomed, vines tearing off like snakes whipping in the wind. He let it go slowly past him, then grabbed the step-up bracket and pulled himself aboard.

It was like riding a huge turtle that had just lumbered up out of sleep. But gradually, in tiny increments, the little engine began to pick up speed. Soon its wheels were rumbling, and Cas whooped and Liz giggled, her hair whipping in the wind. Tiny insects flitted up out of rusty crevices, disturbed by the motion. They hovered in the still air and went upward, forming a softly humming canopy.

Faster and faster they went, until Cas finally had to hit the brake lever. It trembled in his hand, its bands screeching, making the wheels stink of hot metal.

They reached a section of level grade, and the engine's momentum dissipated rapidly, falling to a walk. Far off, they could see the estuary, sunlight making huge patches of glowing water. The PT was easing around as Cullin crisscrossed the mouth of the river, waiting for the first barrels to reach him.

The grade went gently over a hump, the old engine groaning softly with the strain. "Come on, baby," Cas coaxed. Then she eased up and over. Below them it was downhill all the way.

Soon the jungle was flashing past as gravity pulled the weight of the engine ever faster. Something dislodged off the locomotive, a rod of some kind that skidded into the embankment, making a flurry of dust. Bonner hit the brake, slowing their descent slightly.

Around a wide curve they went. Before them was the dockhead, four hundred yards down a sharp slope. The little switch engine was rocketing now, and Cas pulled harder on the brake.

There was a screech of metal but no deceleration.

Liz yelled, "Slow it, we're going too fast."

"Get off," he shouted back. "The brake's not holding!"

"What? Oh, God damn you." Liz stood up, grabbing for handholds among little rusty metal protrusions, as if they would give her a solid hitch to the motion.

"Go!" Cas yelled.

She squeezed between rusty bulkheads, braced her legs, and soared out into midair. She hit the ground like a sack of potatoes, rolled over and over, skinning her arms and legs. Right behind her, Bonner sailed off, curled into a ball. He landed beyond her and tumbled like a boulder leading a landslide.

They stopped rolling finally and watched the little engine hurtle toward the dockhead. It hit the stopper ties at the end of the track, blew through them, and continued at an angle out onto the dock itself. There it plowed into a stationary tank. Wood and metal flew and then the engine went over the starboard side of the dock in a small, neat arc and nosed down into the water. In a moment it was gone amid a blow of foamy brown bubbles.

Liz pulled her leg up and stared at Bonner. There was blood on her knees and her head was ringing. "Oh, that was real smart," she said angrily. But he was laughing, stretched out on the ground, the dust looking like talcum on his skin. After a moment she began to laugh too.

"We could have been killed, you asshole." She threw a handful of dust at his head.

He dodged it and winked. "But we didn't have to walk, right?"

For the next two hours, they gathered the floating drums, hitching lines and winching them aboard. After a while barrels littered the foredeck and down between the torpedo tubes. Their final count was thirteen. One had jammed somewhere upriver.

What followed was the damnably time-consuming part of it, filtering the fuel down into the PT's tanks. All of the drums held residual rust formed from condensation in the warehouse, and the fuel had slightly varnished. If that went through the feed lines, they'd be sitting out in mid ocean with clogged intakes.

Tied up to the main dock, they used chamoises with the fuel coming down to the after tanks through hose lines running on gravity feed. Cullin and Bonner were braced over the tank outlets while the chamoises filtered with agonizing slowness, pooling and giving up fumes that would send them all to hell if ignited.

Night came on, at first the slanting sunlight making deep blue shadows along the rim of the estuary, and then suddenly darkness, with the stars popping into view all over. Still they filtered fuel. Every now and then Liz spelled Cas or Will until the fumes made her sick.

Then she lay out on the stern, staring down at the dark water. It gave terrible visions in the starlight's reflection. She cursed their helplessness. But soon a thought struck her and she twisted around, scurried forward to where Cullin was leaning down into the after-engine vent hatch.

"Will," she cried, "why can't we transmit a message with Hungerford's radio?"

Cullin snapped his head up and frowned at her. "Aye, we might try that. I'd complete forgotten the bleedin' radio."

While Bonner continued straining gas, he and Liz went below. The station she had located earlier was now thick with static. Will unhooked the semaphore key from the back plate and ran its leads back down into the radio's main power unit. He tested. The key was dead.

"Bloody hell," he growled, starting to pull off the back plate. It took him an hour to clear out the trouble. Spider pockets had shorted out several transistors, and he had to jury-rig bypasses, using copper wire off spare engine coils.

Cas came down and sat on the companionway, his eyes red-rimmed. He grinned crookedly. "Those damn fumes are getting me stoned."

"How's it going?" Liz asked.

"Almost done." After a few moments he went topside again.

At last the radio was ready. Will went up and unsheathed the PT's ancient antenna, rigged a line down to the unit. He boosted the semaphore key with a connection to the battery from his cold box. Then he tapped out the standard ranging call and heard the drops of sound crackling out of the speaker.

Nobody homed to him.

"What's wrong?" Liz asked.

"Our signal's not strong enough," he said. But he kept at it. Ten minutes later, something came back—faint dots and dashes drifting on air disturbance: "Designate Cullin . . . receiving weak . . . identify again."

Cullin hissed between his stained teeth. "Bing-bloody-oh, we got somebody." He tapped: "We are small craft at Namwaan . . . desire you relay message . . . identify you."

The signal came back. He was talking with a radio operator aboard the oil tanker *Indonesian Spring* two hundred miles northeast of the Alor Islands off Java.

Cullin keyed: "Request relay message to—" He paused, fist clenched. "Where should we go wi' this?"

"Try U.S. Naval Intelligence."

He tapped: "Message to U.S. Naval Intelligence, designate Pearl Harbor, Hawaii."

"Are you in distress?"

"Negative."

"What is message?"

Cullin glanced at Liz. "How do I put this? The bloke'll think I'm suckin' icy pole."

"Just tell him."

He tapped out: "Assassination attempt on world leaders designate Seascape One off Queensland by Chinese rocket. Must notify American authorities." He leaned back. "Gawd, I can hear the barstid laughin' from here."

The return signal proved him out: "Deny request. Who are you? Designate authority."

"No authority. Must believe. Give U.S. Naval Intelligence name Jack Stanford. Repeat: Jack Stanford."

"You're bloody bonkers, mate."

Cullin ran his tongue over his lips. "The blighter's Aussie." He thought a moment, then tapped a message: "What is your home ground?"

"Newcastle, South Wales. Why?"

"Do me and I'll shout ya a coldie in Big Jackaroos."

"So you're a Digger. But what is this gander?"

"It's monty, mate. Relay for us."

A long silence followed, pierced with static. At last the *Indonesian Spring* came back: "I'll relay but will stand clear of message content."

"I owe you one."

"You owe me ten. Clearing transmission."

"He's going to send it," Will said and sank back on his haunches, his forehead furrowed.

Liz threw her arms around his shoulders. "We've done it, Will. We've warned them."

"Ach, don't be countin' cheery yet, missy. That bleedin' message'll run into some heavy disbelief on its way." He sighed. "I'd best get back and let old Casimir get some fresh air."

At long last they finally chamoised the last barrel. Cullin took the helm and cranked over the Hall-Scotts, shattering the stillness with their throaty rumble. He glanced aft at Bonner, who winced and shook his head. The engines were running ragged, the residual varnish still in the fuel making the valves stick.

They hauled in the lines and eased away from the main dock, going slowly while the engines heated to operating level, and then swung across the estuary, once more headed for the sea and their final reach.

It was night by the time the *Flying Sun* began picking up the landfall of the islands of Tioor and Kaimeer, twenty miles north of Tayandu and Gallaudet. The sea was running in long swells driven by a twenty-knot wind. Big Willie went to pure radar course, and they finally located the north coast of Tayandu. He brought the cruiser around to starboard, holding a position with her bow into the wind. His instruments showed he was now about a half mile off Tayandu at the point of land where Gallaudet's bunker was located.

He twisted in his command seat and gave Stanford a flick of his hand. "Yo' island back dere. You can get off now."

Stanford, gazing out the port wing at the night, looked over in shock. "What the hell you mean, get off? Here?" He had figured they would sail right on in, let him off, then continue on to rendezvous with drug-runner boats off Dorak, New Guinea, returning the following afternoon.

"I no go closer," Willie said. "Too many goddam' rocks, shallows."

"Bullshit! I ain't going out there in a small boat. I couldn't even find the fucking island."

"Just hold compass heading," Willie answered stolidly. "You find 'im."

Jack turned to Lui. "Will you tell this bastard to go in closer? For chrissake, I'm liable to float all the way to New fucking Guinea!"

Lui grinned, enjoying Stanford's anxiety. "No, no," he said. "I don' steer the gawd-dom boat. Willie say too shallow, then too shallow." He laughed, scratching his thigh. "Wassa matta, Stamford? I thought you say you one-time sailor."

"Sailor, my ass." Jack prowled around the wing, feeling all sorts of adrenaline surges. He turned and started to plead a little more to Lui, but the gleeful look on the man's face suddenly enraged him. He looked around at the others. Everybody was grinning. Well, he thought hotly, fuck the slant-eyed bastards. I'll show 'em!

"All right," he shouted. "Get your goddamned rubber boat out."

Transferring from the cruiser, working off the after port side, ended with Stanford with a gear bag leaping out over the railing as the little rubber dinghy rose on a wave. He landed on his face, with one of the fixed aluminum oars poking him in the groin. Grimacing with pain, he straightened around and watched as the lights of the Triad cruiser quickly receded.

Within a few seconds he was lost in moonlit darkness amid the heaving ocean. The rubber dinghy rocked up and down, sliding off swell faces into troughs that seemed as deep as valleys. Occasionally he caught sight of faint flashes from the cruiser. Overhead the moon drifted like a sailing ship dodging stretches of cloud-reef, the last remnants of the storm.

"Jesus," he kept saying over and over, panting with fear. Finally he got his gear bag open and a flashlight and compass out. The compass was a little military model with a sighting snap. He held it up close and took a bearing. The island lay directly ahead of him, right along the line of the incoming swells. Whenever the dinghy crested a swell, he could actually see its dark shadow.

Feeling a little better, he adjusted his buttocks on the inflated seat and started rowing. He was so afraid of losing the compass that he held it in his mouth, with the flashlight jammed down into his pants.

His progress was achingly slow. The swells and wind kept jacking the bow of the little boat around. It was so light, it skimmed along crests like a leaf, and then Stanford would have to reorient himself with the swell direction and stroke madly until once more thrown off course.

The more exhausted his arms grew, the more enraged he became. By the time he finally began picking up the sound of surf under the wind, he was so livid, he'd actually put teeth marks into the crystal face of the compass.

The swells began deepening along their faces as they came into the shallows. The roar of surf increased, booming periodically. The island was very close but was absolutely pitch black. At last the lightness of the rubber dinghy began to work in his favor. It bobbed easily over even the steepest wave face and then flew down the far side with the groin-dropping sensation of a plummeting elevator.

Finally, in an intermittent breakout of the moon, he

made out the line of a beach about a hundred yards ahead. He braced himself and made for it, stroking with all of his rapidly fading strength.

Suddenly a wave chain caught him, lifting the stern of the raft sharply. He saw a huge, dark shadow rise high above him like a looming hill. Then it crashed down onto him, a furious whirling, pounding ton of water that slammed him flat against the bottom of the boat. The compass and flashlight flew away from him.

Groaning with panic, he fought to find air. For a second he popped up out of the water but was instantly jammed back down again. He was no longer in the boat and the duffel bag of gear pulled at him like lead weights. Desperately he swam, kicking his legs and arms.

He hit bottom, the point of his shoulder digging into the sand. Without knowing it, he was flopping around in shallow water, the bottom dipping and rising, forming deep pools into which he plunged. After what seemed like an eternity, he managed to find solid footing, only to be immediately knocked down by a wave. Eventually he crawled completely beyond the high-water mark and sprawled on the sand, spitting water and gagging for breath.

It took him about a half hour to recover his senses and stand up. The beach led immediately to the jungle, interspersed with tall coconut palms bending in the wind, their blades clacking. He had no idea which direction would lead him to Gallaudet's bunker. He considered. Assuming the wind had blown him away from it, he decided to head north.

He walked above the high-water mark. The ground was level, forming an upper shelf before the start of the jungle. He kept stepping on crabs, and their shells squashed wetly under his tennies. Each time that happened, his skin crawled, and his mind began making images in the moon-shadowed trees.

Do New Guinea crocodiles come out to these fringe islands? he wondered desperately. Are there goddamned headhunters lurking in the bush? Walking along, he intently watched the great black wall of the jungle to his right, his ears straining through the wind for the roar of a croc.

Some three hours later, he reached the bunker. A light shone over the front steps, and he went down to the entrance. Smelling of fungus, it was low and he had to bend.

Gallaudet was lying in his bunk, naked. With him were two native girls, also naked, entwined around his body like snakes. All three were so far advanced in their drug high that they moved in rapid jerks, bellies slapping, mouths sucking, arms twitching as eyes arced across the ceiling in a kind of terrified glaze.

Standing in the doorway dripping wet, his face white with exhaustion, Stanford blew up. "What the fuck are you doing, you coke-headed frog son of a bitch?" he bellowed.

One of the girls immediately slid behind the bunk and peered at him over the crumpled sheets. The other, on top of the Frenchman and impaled on his penis, groaned and bent forward, her sweaty brown buttocks glistening in the light.

Jean, eyes like twinkling stars, turned slowly, lazily until he focused on Stanford's face. A grin spread over his own. "Ah," he sighed dreamily, *"Eh bien, mon cochon americain."*

The U.S. Naval Communications Center at Subic Bay in the Philippines was the first American unit to receive the message from the *Indonesian Spring*. The freighter's radio operator, after consulting with his captain, had been ordered to send it to his company's overseas headquarters in Hong Kong rather than go through all the procedures necessary to clear into a U.S. military base. In Hong Kong, an operational supervisor thought it was a joke. He raised the *Indonesian Spring*, got verification, debated a moment, and then relayed it on to the British consulate, under whose flag the freighter was registered. From there it was sent on to Subic under miscellaneous, non-diplomatic transmission.

Since Midway Communications was the primary clear-

inghouse for all communications throughout the U.S.
Navy's Pacific Command's WESTPAC sector, the message was routinely sent there from Subic for analysis.

At 10:23 P.M., a chief petty officer standing coordinator watch at the Midway Comm Center received the following message:

NON-CODED BULLETIN
100612Z////15134

MIDWAY COMM OP via NSA (Subic)

Message Follows:

Received 100609Z transmission des. (via British Consulate HK) from Trans-Malaysian Shipping Company of reception transmission from undesignated source in Molluca Quad (15F/File 3) of Chinese missile attack on des Seascape One in Barrier Reef (12G/File 77). Des source one Stanford, Jack. No further details.

BREAK
Evaluation: Non-analysis//des Stanford, Jack nonfile Subic NI//assigned low priority.

END BULLETIN
1006127Z

The chief lit a cigarette and thought: another freako coming out of the woodwork. It was always the same, whenever the big honchos met, the crazies always sprang out. Still, he rang upstairs to the analysis room and passed the message on to the watch officer.

Fifteen minutes later, he was informed that Stanford, Jack, showed non-file in the NI station section. The watch officer instructed him to relay the message in the normal lineup to COMMPAC at Pearl Harbor.

19

Exactly ten hours before, Aguinaldo Babiyan had been shot to death as he walked from his office in Metro Manila. Two men on a small motorcycle had sprayed him with assault rifle fire, nearly decapitating him. No one knew who was responsible yet, but Manila had seethed with emotion over the killing. Although Babiyan had been a man who played many sides, his murder became a flash point around which opposition forces of the government rallied. There had already been several demonstrations in Manila and Pasig, and scattered disturbances in the southern islands.

The Philippine president reacted with decisive swiftness. She was getting to be an old hand at suppressing these sporadic eruptions. Government troops were immediately sent into potential trouble spots, and gradually things began to simmer down. However, the possibility of violent demonstrations at the Manila International Airport prompted her to request that the U.S. head of state land instead at Subic. Since the suggestion had come from the Philippine government rather than American security units, there seemed no loss of face and the change was agreed upon.

Late in the afternoon, while Cas and the others were still filtering gasoline in Namwaan, the U.S. president had arrived at the huge, sprawling naval base north of Manila under gray skies and the drizzle from the storm that had come up from the southwest. After a short review of the force personnel, he was driven to the

home of Admiral Richard Balfour, the base commander.

At six-thirty, the Philippine president arrived. She
was an attractive woman in a formal *balagang* dress,
yellow and edged with silver beading. Under umbrel-
las, the U.S. president met her at the limousine and
escorted her up to the admiral's house, a low
plantation-type home built of *ibari* wood with green
shutters and a wide veranda that ran its full length.

In a large, rattan-furnished room with the admiral's
hunting trophies on the walls, the two leaders met pri-
vately for over an hour. The President informed her of
his aims during the upcoming meeting in Australia.
They then discussed certain aid protocols and cancel-
lations of American base contracts in the Philippines.

The President was quite taken with his guest. She
was charming, erudite, and had acquired an aura of
statesmanship since their last meeting four years earlier in Washington, when she had first been elected to
lead her government.

Later in the evening, a private dinner was given in
her honor. Afterward, the President again personally
led her to her motorcade. The rain had stopped, but
the wind was still wet and chilly, and it whipped at
her dress, pressing the delicate fabric sensuously
against her trim figure.

After a thirty-minute meeting with Balfour and his
staff for update of local and regional situations, it was
decided that the President would go directly on to Australia rather than wait for an early morning departure.
Still in his formal dinner clothes, he boarded *Air Force
One* with the strains of ''Hail to the Chief'' throbbing
in the ocean breeze. At precisely 9:57, the aircraft
lifted off the main Subic runway and turned south-
southeast for the three and a half hour trip to the Australian Northern Air Force base at Grenville on the
York Peninsula.

Nine hundred miles away, the Long March rocket
at Xchiang had just gone into its last scheduled hold

at T-minus-40 minutes in the final, plugs-out Count-down Demonstration Test before launch. The vehicle and its umbilical tower stood out on Pad 3, bathed in searchlights which intersected at its apex. In the glare its color was washed to a grayish-white, and it looked like an obelisk with construction scaffolding beside it.

Everything was going smoothly so far. The CDT had passed all previous marks without glitches. In the main Firing Room, Dr. Ziyang was quietly going through his procedures manual with the assistant firing coordinator. Around him, the people in the room were as tense as if the actual launch countdown were in effect. There was the clatter of data machines and the soft voices of men in the testing loops as information streamed into the consoles from Pad 3.

Ziyang was near total exhaustion. A bone weariness made his head heavy, his thoughts sluggish. He had not slept for forty-eight hours, and the sleep before that had been fitful and filled with dark dreams. To add to his anxiety, Xinjin, the observer from Beijing, continually hovered around the Firing Room like a hunting falcon, peering about stern-faced and silent.

At a signal from one of the consolemen indicating completion of data infeed, Ziyang authorized the countdown to continue for the power-transfer sequence. Slowly, with the Firing Room tabulating each step of the procedure, the rocket was isolated from its umbilical tower and transferred to internal power systems. This phase was completed and the CDT went into another scheduled hold at T-minus-26 minutes.

Once more the consoles and data machines ingested feedback off the Long March. In the meantime, Ziyang paced behind the machine banks, checking for himself. After a few moments he moved to the large slit window which opened onto the pad line nearly a half mile away. Through binoculars he studied his rocket. Everything looked fine except for a tiny movement which caught his eye. The wind cups at the very top of the umbilical tower were spinning rapidly.

He turned and snapped an order to one of the closer

consolemen for the latest weather update. It came back: wind at twenty knots but dropping; sky clearing; humidity at sixty percent. The forecast was that the wind would decrease to seven knots by 3:00 A.M.

He returned to his position behind the data banks, momentarily checked his manual, and then authorized the next phase to begin. This was the chill-down process for the thrust chambers of the first- and second-stage engines. Once the actual launch took place, the internal environment of the chambers would have to be tuned to the incoming fuel, which would be under extreme pressure and at sub-zero temperatures so that ignition would take place evenly. The procedure ran perfectly, with chamber temperature gradients dropping in a precise curve.

The CDT continued. T-minus-8 minutes: everything looked good. T-5 minutes: clear data streamed in. At T-3 minutes 7 seconds, the automatic sequence was initiated.

During an actual launch, the rocket would begin functioning entirely on its own. The Firing Room could still abort the launch manually, but for all intents and purposes, the Long March would have been free of the computers within the control area.

At T-14 seconds, the entire system was manually shut down as the CDT was completed. Ziyang stood watching incoming peripheral data as the thousands of circuits and monitoring connections went into quiescence. All panels were showing green overlays.

At last he walked back to the slit window and glassed the rocket. There she stood on her pad, fueled, checked out, a fully operational vehicle which had performed every intricate detail of her launch except the lighting of the chamber igniters.

Ziyang felt a rush of emotion which nearly brought tears to his eyes. His long agony seemed on the brink of ending with success. In precisely eight hours and thirteen minutes, he would send his charge into the heavens.

* * *

Stanford sat cross-legged with his back to the damp bunker wall and watched Gallaudet working at his consoles. From outside he heard the soft whine of gears of the antenna dishes as they tracked slowly across the southern sky. He had a bottle of rum and was half drunk.

Now and then he would question the Frenchman about what he was doing, and Jean would answer. But it was all electronic mumbo-jumbo to him. As nearly as he could understand, the French cokehead was now tracing the signals from the down-range Chinese tracking stations which would be monitoring the coming Xchiang rocket shot. One was at Koor on the top of a peak in the Tamrau Mountains of Irian Jaya, northwestern New Guinea. The second was a light ship running on sea anchor in the middle of the Coral Sea. Gallaudet was exploring their tracking procedures and checking his extrapolations to the tape data that Jack had modemed.

Stanford lifted his rum bottle and toasted himself, giggling impishly like a frat brother who had just scored with the prettiest girl in the sorority across the street. He peered out through the door at the stars. The storm had passed now, and they were clear as crystals of salt in the moon-white sky. He giggled again. In his drunkenness he was sure they could see him, down through the millions of light-years that separated them. In his sense of triumph he felt he too glowed. One big, bright, wheeling-and-dealing motherfucker was about to change the face of the world.

Gallaudet gave a little cry of joy, whispered the notes of a song. Stanford said, "What?"

"Everything falls into place, *mon cher.*"

"It damn well better."

"Ah, to worry makes the skin dry."

"Fuck my skin, Jean-o."

Gallaudet grinned and shook his head. *"Le trou de balle."* Asshole.

Stanford shifted around, feeling the dampness of the wall like clammy fingers on his spine. Damned frog, he thought, always throwing in Frenchie phrases. Was probably insulting the shit out of him. The drunkenness made his eyes narrow. He sighed and looked out at the stars again.

The sight of them touched him once more. "Hey, stars," he said aloud, "get ready to move aside. In seven hours you gonna have company up there." He made a tiny space with his thumb and forefinger and peered through it at the sky. "Until I steal it back."

Gallaudet chuckled and whispered his dirty song.

At 11:03 P.M., Australian Standard Time, the PT raised landfall off the small fishing village of Coomarai on Australia's York Peninsula. For the past three hours she had been transiting through the Torres Strait and Thursday Banks, and was now near the northern fringe of the Great Barrier Reef.

But her engines were still running raggedly as the bad fuel clogged lines, causing lots of power loss and strain. The best she could do was twenty-five knots with all three units on high throttle. Below, Will was sullen, wading around the engine room in water up to his calves, talking with soft apologies to the Hall-Scotts. He could almost physically feel the engines nearing their breakdown point.

On the conn, Bonner had tried his best to alleviate some of the strain by periodically easing off the throttle and letting the boat ride with the currents. But like Cullin, he felt the vessel coming apart at the seams, heard the distress in her roar.

Liz had remained below, hovering over the radio, trying to glean time fixes. But everything that came over was jumbled and scattered: tinny music and ship traffic and Morse code that infuriated her. Finally she gave it up and went to join Bonner as they motored slowly into the channel to Coomarai.

The harbor was ringed by steeply sloping hills on which houses were scattered, looking like blocks that had tumbled off the ridge. The dock was a long, narrow causeway with a loading shed at its base. A fish conveyer belt enclosed in a wooden frame ran from the dockhead up to a large tin-covered processing plant on a small hill.

An aborigine pier hand in a tattered Aussie sailor suit caught their lines as they came into the dock. Tied in on the lee side of the pier were a dozen low-decked fishing boats with lobster boxes stacked in their stern wells.

Cas shut down the Hall-Scotts. A moment later, Cullin came topside. He squinted up at the moon and then toward the town. "I think you'd best go on up and talk to the constable," he said. "Tell 'im what's up. If our message proves fizzogg, he'll at least 'ave a radio so you can relay to Cooktown or Southampton. The moon says we don't 'ave much more time."

"You know this constable?" Cas asked.

Will shook his head. "Used to be an old choom name of McCauley, but he's long dead."

"You think this guy'll buy what we tell him?"

"I doubt it, but you'd best give it a glean. I'll fuel up and see I can soothe my brumbies." He snorted, shook his head sadly. "Poor buggers, they're close to packin' it in." He swung around and hollered angrily at the aborigine pier man. "Hey, you bleedin' abo, rig your fuel lines out here."

Bonner and Liz went up the causeway and climbed a narrow street with houses perched on tall foundation braces to lessen the slope. Men were sitting on stone walls drinking beer, and there were nets hanging from drying racks. Women in summer dresses watched them approach, and the light from the houses silhouetted their bodies through the fabric. Cas inquired about the constable from a group of drinkers.

"That duffer'd be up to Tommy's about this time" came the answer. "Lay course up the 'ill to the red sign. Heeth's 'is name."

Tommy's Bar was as devoid of ambiance as an out-back paddock. A single room with an ancient billiard table and several young, bare-chested men drinking beers. The constable turned out to be a small, muscular fellow in filthy shorties and a Digger hat covered with sweat stains. He wore a heavy single-action Soursill .357 revolver on his hip.

Heeth swung around when Cas asked for him. He was half drunk, his blue eyes twinkling. "Aye, I'm Heeth. Who wants me?" He, along with everyone else in the room, gave Liz a long, studied swoop.

Bonner moved up. "Can we speak with you? In private?"

Heeth guffawed. "This dingo wants private." He looked Cas up and down slowly. "Why, mate?"

"It's important."

"Aye?"

Cas put his hand on the edge of the billiard table, his eyes hard. "It's real important."

"You a Yank?"

"Yes."

"Well, I'll be buggered. Part of the big shin out on the Barrier, are ya?"

"Yes."

"Well," Heeth said with a mocking twinkle, hefting his gunbelt, "I'd best look into this, aye, mate?"

They went outside and stood on unlevel ground. The earth had a salty sour stench to it, as if seaweed had rotted there. Constable Heeth, swaying slightly, said, "So, Yank, what's bloody hell blinder?"

Cas explained with Liz walking around the two men. Heeth heard him out, then growled in his throat, as if he were gathering phlegm. "A bleedin' Chai-neese rocket?" He tilted his head. "You're tryin' to shonk me, mate."

"It's true."

Heeth snorted. "And I'm a flamin' poofter."

"Look, at least relay it to Southampton. Let them decide."

"Bugger off!" The Aussie started to turn away.

Cas lost it. He reached out and grabbed Heeth's shirt, drew him in tight. "Listen, you besotted son of a bitch. What I've just told is no shit up. There are men out there, important men, who're gonna be gone if you don't do something.''

The hard, cold muzzle of the Soursill .357 suddenly pressed into Bonner's stomach, and Heeth's face opened into a hot grin. ''You've just nipped into some ocker shit, mate.''

Liz, unaware of what had happened, said, ''What's the matter?''

Heeth turned his silly, steamy grin onto her. ''You and your bed piker 'ave just made a misstep, luv.''

''What?''

Bonner's fingers coiled in Heeth's shirt.

''Ah-ah, mate,'' he cautioned. ''A little more of that hardass'll get you a hole in your belly.''

Cas said, ''Shit!'' and released him.

The constable snapped the muzzle of his weapon back and forth. ''Up the slope, pissweaks. You're busted.''

20

The huge HH 52A Sea Guard helicopter of the Australian Air Force hovered for a moment above the landing pad on the floodlit roof of the Seascape One. Then, giant rotors cracking in the soft sea wind, it lowered and gently alighted in the middle of the red circle on the pad. Immediately men scurried out and chocked the wheels as the engines died in a dropping whine. A small stairway was wheeled out and fitted against the hull. As the main door was opened, a group of American and Australian dignitaries moved forward, their coats flapping. A moment later, the president of the United States exited the helicopter, smiling and waving.

He was met at the bottom of the gangway by Australian Prime Minister John Frost, a burly man and ex-soccer star. They spoke for a moment, heads tilted toward each other. There were introductions and then everyone moved quickly toward the viewing lounge on the south side of the roof.

In the main room of the weather station across from the lounge, Angus Porter took a long pull of his beer and peered out at the landing pad. Beside him was Harry Miles, chief meteorologist for the Seascape One. From behind them came the steady clack of a teletype machine and sporadic bursts of radio talk.

"He's a big 'un, in't he?" Miles said, referring to the U.S. president. "The tele doesn't do 'im justice."

"He's big, all right," Angus agreed dismally, adding: "An' I'll be bloody glad to see that arse of his climb back into that helo and vacate my rig."

Miles laughed softly. "Aye, it's been a bit of a bitch for ya, han't it, Angus?"

"I'd say that."

Particularly over the past twenty-four hours, the pace had speeded up dramatically on the floating hotel as everybody started getting tense, preparing for the arrival of the four heads of state. The first to arrive, of course, had been the Aussie P.M., who had come aboard late that afternoon. Next was Premier Markisov, an ordinary-looking man with his wispy hair raised by the sea breeze. He moved around solemnly shaking hands with everybody and then paused to peer out at the moonlit sea and the distant lights of the frigates on picket duty with a kind of thoughtful sadness. An hour later came the Chinese premier, who arrived with his entourage of little men in dark suits.

Each was taken directly to his personal quarters while their chiefs of staff met in a marathon session which would continue throughout the night. The first contact between the main leaders was to be at breakfast in the main restaurant at six.

Every time another head of state arrived, the pulse of the personnel in Seascape One went up another fifty notches. The excitement was evident everywhere. Security men darted about, pausing only long enough to shout orders through portable radios. In the kitchens, the chefs fussed about and swore over last-minute menu changes dictated by personal emissaries of the governments involved. Waitresses and bellboys, desk personnel, even maintenance crews, were hyped, their eyes sparkling, elated to be part of this momentous occasion.

All except Porter. He kept getting gloomier and angrier. Most of the previous night he'd spent watching the weather reports of the storm westward in Java. Fortunately, it turned out to be a sharp but localized blow which had gone north. Still, he knew that open ocean storms were unpredictable. They could veer at any time, at least enough to give him headaches on the Reef.

Even if the storm hadn't developed, though, there remained endless little emergencies Angus had to attend to, from mismatched towels in Markisov's suite to a minor breakdown of one of the air-conditioning units deep in the bowels of the hotel. They kept him jumping with no chance for sleep.

Yet he wasn't tired. Any chief project engineer worth his salt learns early on that fatigue is unacceptable. So he carried on, crawling around in, vertically and horizontally transiting, his hotel, and generally prodding and kicking the staff to make conditions as perfect as he could. His only satisfactions were strings of lush obscenities and periodic cans of icy Fosters beer.

The weather room's intercom clicked on: "Harry, is Angus up there?"

Miles leaned back and punched his receiver button. "Aye."

"Angus, you better get down to number one kitchen. We got trouble in the main refrigerator units."

Porter swore, downed his beer, and headed for the door.

"He's on his way," Harry said.

Outside, the air smelled of jet fuel from the copter. Its crew, tall men in dark blue jump suits, was tying it down. "Aye, mate?" one of the men called after him. "Where's your bloody pisser on this tub?"

Angus silently pointed at the lounge and continued ahead. He glanced at his watch. Under the floodlights the crystal looked red. It said: 11:56.

The Coomarai township detention cell was a filthy bare room about the size of a pool table, with a single tiny window covered with a metal screen. It smelled of vomit and stale urine, and graffiti had been scratched into the dingy white walls. From another room a radio was playing softly, big band music spaced between polkas.

Bonner and Liz had been incarcerated for nearly an

hour, with Cas pacing in silent fury. Now and then he'd glare out the window. He could see down into the harbor a half mile away, the PT under the dock lights taking on fuel. Finally he came over and squatted beside Liz, who was sitting with her back to the wall. "We've gotta get out of here," he whispered. "Fast. It's near midnight already. That rocket will probably go at dawn."

"How do we do it?"

He nodded toward the window. "Can you squeeze through that thing? I think I can maybe pry the screen off a little."

She studied it. "I don't know, it's awfully narrow." She looked at him. "Where's Heeth?"

"He went back to the bar."

She shoved herself to her feet. "Let's give it a try."

Cas pushed and pulled at the screen until his fingernails were bleeding. It was thick and anchored solidly. By the time he got the faintest movement, he was drenched in sweat and wild-eyed with frustration. He walked around for a moment, flexing his arms, then went at it again.

He had just gotten one side of the screen opened a crack and was rocking it hard when they heard a door slam, then boots on the floor. Someone was unlocking the door of the cell. Bonner immediately pulled the wire back, dropped to the floor, and began doing push-ups.

The door swung open and Heeth peered in, swaying drunkenly. He grinned at Liz and then saw Bonner. "What the bloody hell are you doin'?"

"Exercizing," Cas answered through his teeth.

"Exercizin' ?" Heeth blinked as he thought about that. "What the bloody hell for?"

"Keeps me from jacking off."

The constable threw back his head and laughed. "Oh, you're bleedin' mad as a meat ax, Yank." He waved his hand. "Come on, who has to piss? Last call, I'm lockin' up for the night."

Liz was studying him intently. She reached out and

lightly touched his arm. "Tell me something," she said quietly, "do you like your job here?"

Heeth stopped laughing and focused on her face. "What's that?"

"I asked if you like your job."

"What the flamin' hell's it to you, missy?"

"Because as soon as your government finds out who you've got locked up, you won't have it anymore."

Heeth's eyes narrowed, the skin on the edges bunching. He studied her for a long moment, then snorted. "What's this bloody nonsense?"

Bonner stopped doing his push-ups and lay there, looking quizzically at her.

"I'm an American journalist here to cover the meeting on Seascape One," Liz went on evenly. "What do you think your government will do to you when they find out you've thrown a foreign newswoman into this garbage hole?"

Heeth's upper lip curled slightly and he sucked at a yellow incisor. In the outer room, the polka band came to an abrupt stop and a full-throated man's voice came on: "This is station KHIL, Rockhampton, Queensland. The time is twelve P.M., Australian Standard Time. Here are the latest items off our teletype . . . "

"You a newsie?" Heeth asked.

"Yes."

"Where's your bleedin' credentials?"

"On our boat."

Heeth thought about that, his brow working. On the floor, Cas grinned, winked at Liz.

"Ach, you're dickin' me," the constable said finally.

"Think about it, Heeth," Liz said, cool as ice. "How do you spell that? H-e-a-t-h or H-e-e-t-h? I want to be sure."

The man moved slightly, put his hand out and braced against the doorsill, his eyes darting from her to Bonner. "What about 'im? He a bleedin' newsie too?"

"He's my photographer."

Heeth stared and stared at her, then shook his head. "You lyin' to me, tart."

"Think about it."

"No, you lyin'." He stepped back and slammed the door.

Bonner made two fists in the air and grinned gleefully. Outside, the radio announcer was finishing coverage of the Seascape One meeting and moved on to other international news.

One minute later, the door opened again. This time Heeth had his .357 in his hand. "All right, you two, out." He poked the muzzle of the weapon close to Liz's nose. "I want to see them bleedin' credentials of yours."

They walked through the front office, which wasn't much larger than the cell. There was a transceiver on one wall, a small gun rack on the other, with a yellowed clock between them. In the middle was a cluttered desk with several empty beer cans lined on the edge.

The deep voice of the KHIL announcer was just concluding an item on the latest challenge to the British prime minister's government by the opposition party: "Back-bench Liberal speakers were again vehement in their denunciation of the poll tax. Political experts are unified in their opinion that this issue will eventually bring down the Conservative government."

Heeth paused at his desk to finish a beer, the .357 steady.

"Now to a scientific item" came from the radio. "Reports from Beijing indicate that the coming launch of an American and Swiss satellite from the Chinese rocket complex at Xchiang is on schedule."

Cas threw a hot glance at Liz. Heeth slammed his empty beer can onto the desk. "Let's go," he snapped.

"Wait," Liz cried.

"What?"

"Launch time is set for six A.M., Australian Standard," the announcer said. "So all you amateur astronomers, keep an eye peeled. If you're lucky and have good gear, you might see the Long March reach orbit.''

''Move it,'' Heeth growled.

As they started forward, both Cas and Liz checked the clock. The time was 12:09.

Ten minutes later, Heeth jumped onto the PT first and stood beside the engine hatch with his .357 leveled while Bonner and Liz followed. The aborigine pier hand was still out there, coiling up the fueling lines. Cullin was nowhere in sight.

''All right,'' Heeth said. ''Let's see these bleedin' credentials.''

Liz started down the charthouse companionway, with Bonner behind her. The Aussie came down stealthily, peering around like a man entering a narrow cave. Below the deck, the pumps were working, filling the cabin with urgent sloshes.

''Never been on one of these jam boats before,'' Heeth said. ''I'll bet a fiver she—''

He didn't finish. Cullin had stepped quietly down the companionway behind him and laid the muzzle of the Walther lightly against his ear. ''Far enough, mate,'' he said. ''Lay your piece on the table.''

Heeth froze, his drunken eyes snapping wide open.

''On the table. Easy, now.''

The constable obeyed. Cas immediately picked up the .357. ''We got less than six hours, Will,'' he said. ''The rocket goes off six A.M., our time.''

Heeth turned slowly and glared at Cullin. ''Will? You're Cullin, ain't ya? I know you, mate.''

''Good for you,'' Will said. ''Set your arse on the bunk.''

Heeth sat down. ''Oh, you're all in some ocker shit.''

''Shut up,'' Will said. To Bonner, ''What d'ya figure?''

''There's no more time to screw with this thing. We've got to go straight for the hotel.''

''Aye.''

''What are you going to do with him?'' Liz asked.

"We'll give the little shitass a moonlight swim," Cullin answered.

Cas nodded toward the engine room. "Will the Hall-Scotts hold up?"

"Aye, it's only forty miles to the Maxwelton Shoals. Crank 'em up, Casimir." He pushed the Walther into Liz's hand. "Shoot this rotter if he tries anything."

Heeth seemed decidedly sober as he watched Bonner go up the companionway and Cullin disappear through the engine room hatch. He turned to Liz, who was holding the heavy revolver with both hands. "You know what you're doin' here, missy?"

"Yes."

Heeth grinned, showing yellow teeth, and put his hands up, palms out. "Look, maybe we can talk about this—"

"Stay on the bunk, you," Liz snapped. "You move an inch and I'll blow your goddamned head off."

"I'm stayin'," Heeth cried. "I'm bloody stayin'."

As Cas took them up the channel, the moon's reflection glided alongside like a shimmering, lopsided silver plate. They cleared the Coomarai headland and struck into open ocean.

Twenty minutes later, the tip of York Peninsula showed dark against the horizon, and they pulled in close, running in very low chain. With the rise of land less than a hundred yards off the starboard side, they jettisoned the constable. He splashed into the dark water, cursing the PT and everyone aboard her before stroking furiously for land.

Once more they started for deep water and Cas pushed up the throttles. The PT shook violently with engine vibrations as she came up into the step. At first she blew only a sluggish twenty-two knots, and then she straightened out and the speed climbed as they headed down the east coast of the peninsula.

An hour later, the water began to shallow out, and the engine roar echoed hard off the bottom. They were entering the outer shoal grounds of the Maxwelton.

* * *

The *Indonesian Spring*'s message wound slowly through Pearl Harbor's COMMPAC communications to the San Diego clearinghouse without making any particular ripple of concern. It was understandable. Without any concrete reference base attached to it, it was continually being sidetracked for more important data. Eventually it reached the desk of Captain "Big Mike" Clifton, division head of the SD comm center. He studied it for a few moments, then extracted a map from his desk which showed the WESTPAC quadrants.

In his mind, an attack rocket meant a cruise missile, fired from either a ship or a land-based site. He visually began measuring distances from the Seascape One's position. But he was merely toying. The idea of a missile attack on the conference site was absurd. Who in hell would do it? The leaders of the two unfriendly countries capable of such a thing were both there.

Could it be some complicated coup attempt in either Russia or China? No, that was out too. The very word *complicated* precluded it. Such an attempt would involve a massive internal deception. Still, the message intrigued him. Who was this Jack Stanford? The communiqués back through the link indicated that nothing was showing on such a man, at least not in Naval Intelligence records. Well, maybe the FBI had something on him.

He keyed his intercom and ordered a Trace/Fugitive run sent to FBI headquarters in Washington on one Stanford, Jack. No further information available. He paused for a moment, considering priority. Finally he decided it warranted a minor request chit. After all, he didn't want the Bureau thinking SD Comm was flinching at ghosts.

Litung Biao's face glowed with inner energy, yet his movements were serene, his commands monosyllabic. Where he passed, people drew back instinctively, as if from a blast of heat. Everyone sensed an emerging majesty in him.

He covered a lot of ground, shuttling between the sterile headquarters rooms of the Central Military Commission in Chairman Mao Memorial Hall to his offices in the Cultural Palace. Word of the execution of the generals was now spreading through the city and even into the outlying Bureau districts. In response, CMC radios were being deluged with demands for an explanation. Outrage crackled across the airwaves. Still, General Hsien was closely guarding his military network, which was the only link with Premier Sichen, and no communiqués concerning the deaths of the generals were going south.

In Beijing, the complex networks within the government were flashing white-hot. Ministers and Central Committee members were being roused out of sleep by their aides. Confused and distraught, they flocked to their offices and into the back council rooms of the Working People's Hall, milling. Outside, on the wide boulevards and avenues of the capital, tanks rumbled through the night as elements of CMC regiments took up positions under Hsien's personal orders. It was ostensibly to quell possible riots but was in truth the prerequisite to martial law.

From his office, Litung sent out his secret police like a fire chief fighting a citywide conflagration. Out they spread, to infiltrate, listen, take notes and make lists. These would be used to designate who would be purged and who would be saved.

Then, at 1:00 A.M., Litung, alone, walked across Tiananmen to the Bajou district close to the Qianmen Temple. His destination was the spartan apartment of Chen Jann, senior standing member and Premier Sichen's mentor and power base.

He found the old man quietly sipping tea. Chen had on a silken robe and his body looked shrunken in its folds. He eyed Litung placidly. At last he lowered his cup and said, "So, it begins."

"Yes."

"How did the generals die?"

"Only one with honor."

"Shijou?"

"Yes." There was a rustle of cloth and Litung caught a glimpse of Chen's wife scurrying, silent as a shadow, into another room.

Chen snorted. "You people are wasteful of good men." He studied Litung with his narrow black eyes. "We should have known it was you who drives the dragon."

Litung made no answer. For a moment he wondered at Chen's serenity. Did the old man fully comprehend why he was here? And if so, why was he so inactive? He should have been on the phone, desperately trying to solidify Sichen's position.

The old man again sipped his tea. The room reeked of old age, a sour odor like that of discarded underwear. "We were fools to underestimate you. You have moved swiftly. Do you intend to assassinate Sichen?"

"Yes."

"How?"

"By a rocket."

"Ah." Chen nodded. "Have you fully thought out the consequences? Foreigners will die with him, powerful ones."

"It has been planned for." He nodded toward the other room. "Call your wife in here."

For the first time Chen stiffened. "You would dare kill us?"

"It's necessary."

Chen grunted. He looked at Litung for a long moment, but his ancient eyes didn't lose their equanimity. He had seen enough of life to know that this man before him would not be dissuaded from doing what he had come to do.

At last he turned his head. *"Tai-tai,"* he called softly. A moment later, his wife came into the room, gazing at the floor. She was even more dwarfish than he was. He patted the couch beside him. "Come, sit with me. But be silent." She obeyed.

The room was pervaded by her silence, broken only by the insistent sound of armored vehicles from far off. Chen watched with his hands cupped as Litung withdrew a small .25 automatic from his tunic. It was black and had a silencer on the muzzle. He knelt before the old man, the weapon resting in his outstretched palm. "You were always an honorable man, *dzufu* Chen," he said. "I will not insult you by killing your wife."

Chen's eyes quivered, but only for a fleeting moment. Then he reached out, took the pistol. His wife murmured something. He touched her gently, stroked her white hair. Then he placed the silencer against her temple and pulled the trigger.

It made a tiny *thump,* like a pebble hurled into a still pond. Chen's wife folded down, ancient bones crumbling within silk. The old man sighed but in his eyes flared a bright incandescence. He glowered at Litung, hefting the pistol in his bony hands.

"Perhaps you're the fool, Minister," he whispered.

"Perhaps."

"I could kill you."

"But you won't. Your honor prevents it."

"You're an animal."

Litung leaned forward. "Yes, but an animal that China needs, *dzufu.* Look at me! Look, into my eyes. Do you see cowardice? Capitulation?"

Chen was trembling with emotion now. He lifted the pistol and pointed it at Litung's forehead. The silencer touched the minister's skin, yet Litung did not move. The weapon shook. Then, abruptly, Chen pulled back, placed the muzzle against his own forehead and fired. Blood splayed across Litung's cheek.

The Australian frigate came at them out of the silvery-black darkness like an avenging angel, her props driving, creating a hurling white bow wave. She cut across the PT's line and lay over in a hard turn to port, coming back up sharply, her lights smeared with speed, the outline of her superstructure silhouetted against the dappled ocean.

Cas hauled back on the throttles and the PT slowed, rocking. He'd been watching the frigate for the past twelve minutes, trying to discern her course against the horizon. Now the picket boat dropped speed and fell into a parallel course two hundred yards off the starboard side.

A blowhorn blared: "Motor launch, lay to and identify yourself."

Cas let the PT's momentum drift off, then moved around the conn barrier and cupped his hands over his mouth. "We—are—inbound—Seascape One—Urgent—message."

The frigate also eased to a stop, her propellers back washing with a noisy, churning sound. She seemed huge and lethal standing off. "Identify yourselves," the blowhorn cracked.

Cullin and Liz had come topside. "Tell the bleeders we're DF-3," Cullin said.

"What the hell's that?" Cas asked.

"Aussie Naval Intelligence. Tell 'em."

Bonner yelled the message, but it was lost in the vastness. For a few seconds the frigate waited, her lights rolling slightly in the swell. Then the blowhorn came back: "Clear this area immediately. Say again, clear this area immediately. Or we will blow you out of the water."

Cullin said, "Damn the bloody gasbags."

Bonner tried again. It was no use. The blowhorn blared again: "Clear this area immediately or you will be fired on within sixty seconds."

Bonner swore and returned to the conn. He brought up the Hall-Scotts, swung hard to port, and headed back toward the distant silhouette of the peninsula. The frigate trailed them for fifteen minutes, sitting off the stern of the PT. At last satisfied, it turned away.

The PT went straight for land, fifteen miles away, cutting delicately through patches of reef that glistened with surf, feeling its way through channels and submerged coral heads. Cullin was on the conn now. He knew these waters and was heading for a strip of comparatively deep water created by tidal movement which fringed the peninsula. Once there, with the land mass right off their starboard side, they would be practically invisible to the frigate's radar, which he was certain was still lashing them. The sonar pings would also be washed by the tidal disturbance across the reefs.

The smell of the land was sharp in the air now, the hay-like dryness of savannah grass and the minty scent of eucalyptus groves. They could actually see the Seascape One, a cluster of bright lights standing off about twenty miles to the southeast. Seaward were lesser dots of light which were the picket vessels.

They hove to in a narrow harbor under a low headland. There were trees along the crest of the headland that were touched with the soft, fading glow of the lowering moon. It made them look frosted. The Hall-Scotts rumbled quietly, sending periodic vibration spasms through the floorboards.

In the conn, the three of them discussed what to do. Nobody had a watch, but from the position of the moon they estimated it was close to two in the morning. Four hours left.

Bonner studied the distant hotel, then turned to Will. "How close you think we can get before one of those frigates tries to blow us away?" he asked.

"The scullies'll first warn us off like they did," Cullin answered. "But I don't think they'd home fire until we got three, maybe four miles from it."

"What about smaller patrol boats this side of the reef line?" Liz pointed out.

"Aye, they'll be there, all right. But I figure they'll have only small arms aboard."

Bonner was walking around, squinting out at the hotel. Obviously something was working in his mind. He paused. "How many gelignite satchels do we have left?"

Liz said, "Three, but one's minus a packet."

Cullin was studying him closely. "What're you thinkin'?"

"You know anything about the foundation works on that hotel?"

Cullin shook his head. "Not really, but I've 'eard it's capable of swingin' to the wind."

"That's what I thought. That means she's chain-anchored, no permanent pilings."

Cullin tilted his head, clucked his tongue softly. "Ah, I see where you're headed, mate. I think you're skimmin' fringe."

"Maybe not."

"What are you talking about?" Liz asked.

"You'd 'ave to put in a helluva swim," Cullin said. "In shark waters."

"What? What?" Liz asked again.

"When's the tide set around here?" Cas said.

"Offshore peak at dawn, onshore at sunset."

"That's good, that means the big, pelagic sharks will be feeding on the outside of the main reef escarpment from now until after sunrise."

"What the hell are you two talking about?"

Cas turned to her. "There's only one way we can do this. We can't stop the rocket, but maybe we can move its target."

She looked shocked. "You mean the hotel? That's crazy."

"If I can blow the anchor chains, with the tide running seaward, the current'll take it away from the reef."

"Oh, my God!"

"There isn't time for anything else."

She turned and looked out at the lights of the hotel, shaken by what he was saying. She swung back. "But what about our message? Maybe it got through."

Bonner shook his head. "No, there'd be all kinds of activity on that hotel by now if it had."

Cullin nodded. "Aye, he's correct, missy. It's our strike now. Either we do it or that bluedocker Stanford'll send that bleedin' satellite screamin'."

"What's the maximum detonation delay on the satchels?" Cas asked.

"One minute."

He thought a moment. "Yeah, okay, that should give me enough time to set double charges and get out of the water."

"What if there's more than two chains? You'd never be able to place three charges in a minute. The first concussion'd kill you."

"I'll have to risk it."

Liz leaned around and looked into his face. "You're going to jump off the boat and swim to that thing?"

"You got a better way?"

She sighed, perplexed. The whole idea was insane. But then, so was everything else at this point. She swore softly, put her head down, then lifted it sharply. "Okay, I guess you're right. So how do we do it?"

Grinning faintly, Bonner shook his head. "You're going ashore." He turned to Will. "What do you think our best approach is?"

"Well, if we skirt the shore until we're as close abreast of the hotel as we can get, we might be able to make a bloody dash for it. The frigates'll pick us up on radar soon's we clear background, but they'll have to position away from the hotel's sight line before firing. Should give us a few extra minutes."

Liz said, "Why am I going ashore?" When Bonner didn't answer, she grabbed his arm. "Look, I've come this far and I intend to go all the way."

"No."

"Why not?"

"It's too dangerous."

"But it's not dangerous for you, is that it? Oh, you're an arrogant bastard."

Cullin laughed.

"Liz, listen to me—" Cas said.

"Look, you can't blow those anchor chains alone and you know it. The first concussion'll kill you and then what? The other ones will still be there and you'll have died for nothing." She glared triumphantly at him and poked a finger into his chest. "No, this time you need me, macho man."

Cas glared back, furious. Then his features gradually softened into a lopsided grin. He glanced at Cullin. "Hard-assed broad, isn't she?"

"She's earned the right to be, mate."

Bonner reached out and ruffled Liz's hair, batted her head affectionately. "All right, killer, then let's get it on."

As they moved slowly along the coastline, now and then they passed camp fires on the shore, lighting silhouettes of fishermen and aborigines. Once, over the engines, they heard the roar of a crocodile from some swampy place. It sounded like a lion in the night. Liz stiffened. "What the hell was that?"

"A croc," Bonner answered. "Don't worry, they won't be out where we are."

To seaward, the supernova of lights that was the Seascape One shifted gradually from the port quarter to amidships. A breeze had started, drifting in from the sea, and in it they could hear isolated sounds—splurges of generator hum from the hotel, a boatswain's whistle off one of the frigates.

The three gathered on the conn for one last briefing. Bonner watched the ripples on the surface a moment. "That breeze is really starting to pick up, Will. Dawn'll be here pretty quick."

"Aye, I figure two and a half, three hours at the most."

They went over the jump procedure once more. Earlier in the cabin, Cas had explained it to Liz, a standard SEAL operational technique. Will would cut the power and make a hard turn to port. At the precise moment when the bow swung over and the PT began losing forward momentum, she and Bonner would leap out over the tiny starboard rail into the water. This way the centrifugal force of the turn would propel them beyond the suck of the Hall-Scotts' propellers.

Now Bonner repeated a point: "Remember, when I

say jump, you jump, no hesitation. Wait too long and that stern'll hit you right in the butt.''

She nodded solemnly, yet inwardly her heart went spongy all of a sudden, as if something were squeezing blood droplets out of it. She glanced at the two men and felt an inordinate welling of love for both of them. They were all sharers in the same desperate mission, and that thought drew from her a sense of closeness and tenderness she had never felt before. It made her skin tingle and brought mist to her eyes.

''Well, good luck, mates,'' Cullin said.

Bonner slapped the Aussie on the knee. ''You too, Will.''

Finally Liz couldn't contain herself. She sprang up and hugged Cullin fiercely. ''You watch yourself, Will Cullin,'' she cried. ''You hear me?''

He chuckled. ''Aye, luv, that I'll do.''

A moment later they eased over helm and pointed the PT's bow toward the Coral Sea. At first their progress was slow, breaking out of the strip of tidal deep into a long stretch of flat, submerged plateau reef, the coral heads twenty feet below their keel. Then across another five-mile open channel where Will, listening to the rebound off his engines, gunned up, squeezing every last pound of thrust from the Hall-Scotts. They came up into the step with the hotel lights growing ever larger.

The outer dots began to move as the frigates, starting to pick up their radar signal, raced to take up positions flanking the Seascape One. Frantic semaphore bursts snapped into the darkness. Up on the conn, Cullin yelled over the engines, ''Look at the buggers scramble.''

More lights began appearing, two coming from the hotel itself, four others breaking free of the shoreline toward the south. They came on, sharp and clean in the night.

The Seascape drew closer. They could see the individual floodlight beams off the roof. They were eating up distance as Cullin held full throttle.

Eight miles . . .

Bonner and Liz hunkered down beside the starboard conn barrier, the satchel straps wrapped around their arms.

Seven miles . . .

Will, reading the frigates' semaphore, shouted, "They're loadin' weapons."

On they rushed. Cullin played the helm as they drove past exposed reef shelves. The sound of incoming surf thundered clearly through the darkness, then a host of sea birds screamed raucously as the PT's noise drove them into the sky off their floating perches.

Six miles . . .

They saw two quick flashes from one of the frigates about a mile out. A moment later the sibilant rip of two Mark 75 three-inch rounds hurtled through the sky. Geysers erupted in the water a hundred yards directly ahead of the PT. Before the water could drift back down, they were through them, mist coating the deck.

"They've got us on scope!" Bonner shouted. "Next burst will come in hot."

He grabbed Liz's arm and steered her around the conn barrier onto the starboard deck. They crouched there, riding the lunging surges of the PT with their knees. Suddenly a rising sound burst above the PT's engines. Cas shoved her back behind the barrier and laid across her, pushing her flat.

A moment later, a small assault helicopter flashed overhead, its spotlight illuminating the after deck with brilliant white light for a fleeting second. It swept past, making a wide turn, its blades crackling in the air.

It jockeyed around, trying to match the PT's speed. At last it was hovering off the port side about sixty yards out, and someone played the spotlight all over the deck. A loudspeaker blared: "On the boat, alter your course immediately or you will be sunk. Repeat, get out of this area or you will be sunk."

As if to punctuate the order, a splay of small-arms fire erupted from the side of the aircraft, scattering rounds across the forward deck. Wood splinters and bits of canvas whirled off into the wind. Up on the conn, Cullin was roaring obscenities at the helo, his upper body clear in the brilliant wash of the floodlight.

Then, quickly whirling the helm, he sent the PT heeling hard over toward the aircraft. The pilot, caught off guard, lifted sharply and veered up and away.

"Get ready," Cas yelled into Liz's ear.

Her hands were trembling as they clutched her explosive satchel. She couldn't see the helicopter but could hear the rap of the blades over the PT's engines. She turned and looked southward. A line of lights from the incoming shallow-draft patrol boats was homing to them about two miles away. Immediately in the foreground, Bonner's bicep was tensed into hard muscle.

Her concentration was rapidly being shattered as everything came at her with excruciatingly powerful surges: the slam of the deck, the flying spray from the bow, Bonner's arm like iron, her own body spewing adrenaline. She cursed, forcing herself to keep focused.

The PT leveled and then the engine's wild chaos seemed to pause for a moment. Once more the deck heeled sharply to the left. The boat's hull went boom-boom, smashing the surface, and Liz felt her body sliding against the barrier.

Bonner's hands pulled her upward, but her feet, calves, thigh muscles refused to move. "Now!" she heard him bellow. "Jump!"

Before she could command her body to react, Bonner lifted her bodily off the deck. There was a moment of drag and then she felt herself being hurled, tumbling, out into space. Far off to the left she saw the lights of the chopper. She felt a tiny moment of weightlessness and then she slammed against the water, bounced and hit again. The impact jolted through her as if she had been skidded across ground. For a second she was actually skiing on her buttocks. Then her right leg caught in the water and she went into it, diving down into the depths. In the process the satchel was torn away.

Her head was thundering with sound which seemed to come at her from a long, dark cavern. It whomped and hummed with a high-pitched violence. The PT's propellers!

As her plunge dissipated, the sound of the props began to fade. She somersaulted and popped through the surface, feeling turbulence whipping at her. Out of it came a hand as big as a bear paw. It gripped her with unbelievable strength as she pirouetted in the water.

Bonner's face was suddenly close, breathing hard. "You're all right," he shouted at her. "Hang onto me."

"My satchel," she gagged. "It's gone."

"Shit!"

Slowly the water around them became quiescent, rising and falling in a soft regularity. As she sculled, Bonner looped the strap of one of the remaining satchels over her head and swam away, searching for the other. In a few moments he was back.

"It's gone," he said tightly. "Get on your back, float-swim. And for God's sake, don't lose that one."

She nodded automatically, still disoriented. From somewhere out beyond the dark horizon of the swells, she heard the Hall-Scotts whining as Cullin raced away. Above him, like a furious dragonfly that darted and dipped, the helo went after him, its light probing for a new fix.

Cas's hand found the back of her head. "You okay?"

"Yes." In fact, she was shaking, more violently than before as her body began to lose heat. She focused her will, fought against it, and eased up beside him. The night and sea became one, save for the splay of stars directly overhead. He looped a narrow line around her waist and cinched it.

"Keep the line paid out but not taut." He touched her once more, a soft touch on her cheek, a reassurance. With a strong kick he leveled out in the water and glided away from her, stroking powerfully, his satchel bobbing behind his head.

The line jerked her waist and she went with it, laying her own body out flat and swimming steadily, evenly through the water. She concentrated on the movement of her muscles straining and relaxing, on the gentle flow of the ocean around her, so she would not think of the darkness below or what it might contain. Four miles away, the Seascape One, now and then glimpsed, lay on the sea like an ocean liner in the night.

She heard another distant burst of gunfire, but gradually the whir of both the helo and PT faded and then was completely lost in the waves. As she rose on a swell, she caught sight of the boat speeding toward the northwest, the chopper right on it. Far to the left the squadron of patrol craft had turned and were now racing after Cullin. More menacingly, so were two frigates.

Will held the PT with her throttles full open, his head cocked, listening to the roar of his beloved engines. They came like the thunder from locomotives, yet the dark spaces within the sound, short, choppy piston hesitations, clawed at his heart. He glanced astern and saw smoke trailing away, distorting the faint light over the sea.

Above him, the helo suddenly swept past again, its light illuminating the conn space, throwing sharp, dark shadows of himself onto the deck. Once more it synched with his speed, wobbling slightly as the pilot adjusted vertical control.

"Attention, the boat," the blowhorn blared. "This is your final warning. Lay to for inspection or we—"

Will hurled hard helm and sent the PT screaming into a port turn toward the aircraft. The chopper lifted slightly as the boat swung under it, and the spray off the hull flew up into the blades, forming a watery helix which whirled upward, looking orange-gold in the aircraft's lights. As the PT cleared to the opposite side, the helo bobbed and dipped in the air disturbance.

Machine-gun fire flashed for a moment, and a line of rounds went stitching across the coaming. The last two hit Cullin squarely in the back. The impact knocked him clear out of the conn seat, jammed him in a heap against the foot panel. Gasping for breath, he rolled over, looked directly into the aircraft's spot. It hovered there like a white sun, shards of gun smoke making little ghosts.

Rage poured through him, but right behind was pain, out of the momentary numbness of the bullets' shock, an avalanche so profound he curled into a fetal position.

Another burst of fire swept across the deck, one round pinging off something metal. Then one engine went dead. The boat, responding to the sudden imbalance of propeller drive, heeled sharply to starboard, sending Cullin skidding down against the conn barrier.

He was hissing now, like a snake driven into a hole. He tried to get to his knees, but the deck was slippery with blood. It glistened in the shimmer of the spotlight. With a pure burst of will, he reached up and gripped the control panel. His hand touched the flare gun. His fingers curled around the haft.

The PT was going in a wild circle now, the port engine screaming as its prop lifted near to the surface. For a second Cullin lost his focus on the helo's spotlight. It just went out in a blur, came back, went out again, came back. He forced himself to his feet, holding the flare gun with both hands.

The blowhorn blared: "Drop your weapon and lay to or we will open fire again."

Grinning, his heart throwing blood down his chest like a fountain, Cullin croaked, "Up yo' bunghole, you shonky ba—" He pulled the trigger. The flare gun jumped violently in his hand and went spiraling away. Through a bloody haze he saw the flare go straight out, trailing sparks. It ricocheted off the bottom of the aircraft, sparks flurrying, and then continued on into open air, making an arc that etched across the darkness like a fingernail covered with fluorescent paint.

The helo jacked around crazily for an instant, and then responded with a new fusillade of furious, determined gunfire. The bullets rained down across the coaming and deck and conn seat.

One smashed Cullin's knee, but he hardly felt the pain as he lay on the deck, glaring up at the helo and the sudden high explosion of the flare beyond it going off, floating on its parachute.

A second later, the PT disintegrated.

A single white-hot slug had pierced a fuel tank. Fumes ignited, went through lines to other tanks, creating other fumes. In a violent, sundering explosion, the released energy tore the PT in half.

The forward deck and conn section, with Cullin bouncing like a pea in a jar, rode the momentum and continued cutting water, gradually turning in a grotesque, skimming pirouette until at last it skidded to a jarring stop and floated. Will's body was jammed against the base of the seat. It twitched for a second and then went still.

21

Since midnight, Dr. Ziyang had defecated three times, straining, useless sessions which, however, left him oddly energized for his return to the main Firing Room. The place was buzzing with excitement and the constant soft clatter of consoles and machinery as the night slipped past. By two in the morning, weather forecasts had proven correct: the wind dropped to less than three knots and humidity was holding in solid green level.

Out on the rocket, one minor problem had surfaced. The fairing which housed the main solar array had shown a slight warpage and bolt holes were off a fraction of an inch. This was quickly adjusted. A short check sequence was run on the multiplexers and encoders and decoders within the telemetry packet to see if any magnetic disturbance had registered from the drilling gear. Data showed everything okay.

Throughout these pre-launch hours, Ziyang's anxiety increased, sending him back and forth between the Mission and Firing rooms, peddling his bicycle through the warm night. His fatigue was becoming eclipsed in the mounting urgency of the approaching launch, and once he had actually jogged over the sandy ground.

A three o'clock, Xchiang time, he ordered the main countdown to begin and solemnly took his place at his central console panel in the Mission building. From his monitors, formed into a half circle before him, he could observe all data loops from both the Firing Room and the Mission Control area.

Alignment of the Inertial Measurement Unit, a sophisticated system of computer-assisted gyroscopes, was initiated, precisely fixing the space vehicle's position relative to the rest of the solar system. Instantly the onboard computers checked off as its position was set at sea level along lines of longitude and latitude centered at Pad 3, which was spinning eastward at one thousand miles an hour due to the earth's rotation.

Immediately the Koor and Coral Sea tracking stations also synchronized with the position fix. Then all on-board transmission and receiving units were checked, television-frequency band widths aligned, and satellite telemetry circuits cleared for operational status.

Countdown progressed, the time clicking off as each system sequence was registered, verified and cleared. Out on Pad 3, ground crews made their final visual checks of the Long March and then withdrew beyond the safety perimeter a half mile away. In the Firing and Mission bunkers, the technicians and engineers spoke into their link loops in muted, clipped tones.

3:31:00. T-minus-90 minutes. The first sequence hold went into effect.

Dr. Ziyang felt his bowels heave. He fought it, remained at his position. The mass of data coming across his screens was absorbed by his mind with almost electronic swiftness. Everything was singing in precise parameters. He scratched a finger across his jaw, blinked his eyes.

Sixty seconds later he set the countdown clocks running again. More circuits were activated, aligned and cleared. Weather clearance was received indicating that the launch window was holding precisely to schedule. All motion within the bunkers sank into an expectant, nervous hush, as outside on the pad, the Long March came gradually up into launch state.

4:20:03. T-minus-40 minutes, 58 seconds. The second hold sequence went into activation.

Across the room, the main flight-tracking screen began showing potential tracking data as the Mission consoles began running sequence-coordinating checks with the on-board guidance systems. As back-link data flowed in, the tracking lines on the screen inched together until they were aligned. Splays of number bytes began reeling down the side of the screen.

Everything was still on go. Ziyang ordered the countdown to proceed.

The television cameras showing the Long March began picking up the faint, distorted light of dawn showing along the distant pine-covered hills. Final guidance and mission data were entered into the satellite's on-board computers, and a last launch-abort signal was run through a check.

4:41:00. The final manual hold of T-minus-20 minutes went into effect. The seconds ground past as the Firing Room first-line bank of consoles electronically reached out to the rocket, its circuits feeling through it like fingers for one delicate touch, synchronizing all systems before the final run to launch. Everything was still coming back in the green.

A tiny film of perspiration formed on Ziyang's forehead, then on his upper lip. He glanced for a fleeting second from his monitors to the men around him. Backs and bent heads, voices as if whispering secrets. In this strange semi-darkness formed of electronic visions, he felt an overwhelming kinship with the others. Like huntsmen, they had all come through the dogged groping and were now on the threshold.

He ordered the final countdown to commence. From now on there would be no further holds unless something went drastically wrong. In precisely 19 minutes, 58 seconds, the Long March would ignite and reach for the sky.

Seventeen minutes earlier, the president of the United States had lifted his head from his silk pillow at a gentle tapping on the stateroom door. He sat up instantly, rubbing his eyes. He glanced at his bedside clock. It read 5:26, Australian Standard Time.

CIA Director Milt Price entered the room looking haggard. While the President shaved, the director perched on the toilet seat and filled him in on the night's events. "We've finally gotten some solid SR-71 reconnaissance of the Manchurian frontier, sir. The incursion across the Amur River has completely settled down, but there's still extensive military movement within three miles of the border. On both sides."

The President swung around. "How extensive?"

"Fairly massive repositioning of both infantry and armored units. We expected that on the Russian side, but Pentagon's a little worried over the Chinese activity."

"God damn it!" He studied his own anger in the mirror. "What are you hearing about it from here?"

"Nothing from the Russians. But I had a short talk with the Chinese chargé d'affaires. He claims these repositionings are merely a defensive movement in case the Russians decide to initiate their own incursion. He also mentioned that the commanders responsible for the crossing are now in Beijing waiting for Sichen to return. Made a point of it."

"So what do the Joint Chiefs say?"

"Well, to put it in butter-and-egg terms, it looks like both sides are getting ready for a facedown. But they're puzzled over the pulling of the frontier commanders. On the surface it would seem Sichen is trying to show that this whole thing really was a screwup and that those commanders are going to be soundly punished for it."

"On the surface. What about underneath?"

"It could be a ploy. Maybe Sichen's showing he can play hardball to increase his clout here at the conference."

"And?"

"Pentagon's got high-level analysis on this. With the SR-71 hard recon coming in, they're trying to fit the pieces together and see what possible scenarios emerge.''

''So when do I get some solid recommendations?''

''In about two, three hours, sir.''

The President growled disgustedly and flicked off the last tiny bit of soap from his chin. ''You can bet your ass that if Markisov knows about the extent of the Chinese concentrations, he's going to start asking the hard questions before goddamned breakfast is over.''

Price nodded gloomily.

''All right, you get on the horn and tell the Pentagon I want some strong data here sooner. I'm not going into that conference with everybody knowing more about the situation than I do.''

''Yes, sir.'' Price hesitated. ''There's one other thing, sir. There was an apparent attempt to breach the hotel's ocean security net this morning.''

''What kind of an attempt?''

The director explained.

The President studied him. ''You mean that boat actually got close enough to be fired on?''

''Yes, sir. In fact, it was sunk.''

''But I didn't hear a thing. Who the hell were these people?''

''Nobody's sure yet. Aussie Naval assumes it was merely nosy fishermen, probably drunk.''

''Did they have to sink the damned thing?''

''That looks as if it was an accident. One of the patrol choppers tried to get it to hove to with some small-arms fire. They must have hit a fuel tank and it just blew.''

''Is the crew dead?''

''They've only recovered one body so far.''

''Christ!''

''Premier Frost has sent up his apologies for the incident.''

The President glanced back through the bathroom door and out the large bay window of the suite. Out there lay the Coral Sea, vast and majestic, now gray in the light from the sun, which was still below the eastern horizon. For a moment he studied its surface. How terribly deep it seemed. Eternal. It made him feel instrusive, as if he were an alien who had just landed on it and had already brought death with him.

He shook the thought away, wiped his face. Stripping fully, he stepped into the shower. It was as hot as he could stand it. Beyond the curtain, he watched Price go quietly out the door.

He sighed, going over in his mind the conference schedule. There was to be a short pre-breakfast conference with his advisers, then the formal meeting of the heads of state in the main lounge of the hotel's restaurant. This would be followed by breakfast and the first of the day's series of high-level confabs.

He wondered dismally how that first contact between Markisov and Sichen would go now. If the fireworks erupted during the private sessions between the three men, his ability to throw on controls would be vastly heightened. But if it started with everybody else watching, egos would add to the heat.

At precisely 5:58, he shrugged into his jacket, checked his watch, and walked into the small conference room adjacent to his suite, where Price, Claymore, and his military and protocol advisers were waiting.

Gallaudet was humming again, a silly little song that had soft trills at the end of each line. Every time the Frenchman's voice went squeakily up into them, Stanford, prowling around between consoles and data banks, ground his teeth. Still, everything seemed to be holding perfectly. Gallaudet, the coke flying through his eyes, was going about his duties with the serene casualness of a woman prodding melons at a fruit stand.

Stanford couldn't tell precisely what was going on, but for the past hour he had watched anyway, a fresh rum bottle in hand. From what he could see, the frog had been monitoring the Chinese rocket site at

Xchiang. All the data had been coming onto his panels as if he were sitting right there at the launch pad. He still occasionally demanded explanations from Gallaudet, but the answers were just more computerese bullshit. So most of the time he wandered around and sucked rum.

Suddenly, however, Gallaudet held up four fingers spread wide, a leisurely, almost effeminate gesture. Stanford instantly hurried over. The panel directly in front of the Frenchman contained number sequences that kept changing.

"What is it?" Jack growled.

"In less than four minutes," Gallaudet said merrily, "our little Chinese *putain* flies."

The crack of gunfire had come across the sea sounding to Bonner like the shots of hunters in distant hills. And then the flare had gone off, shedding an envelope of sodium light far off, followed by more gunfire. He had instantly stopped swimming, treading water while he watched the sharp, white-orange light of the flare drifting down with agonizing slowness. Then he heard a distant explosion and saw glowing chunks of debris hurtling upward where the flare was.

And he knew Cullin was dead.

A moment later Liz bumped into him. She had been swimming with her head down. Now, panting for breath, she entwined her arms around his waist. He pushed her off and, driving with his legs, propelled himself as high out of the water as he could to see. But there was nothing out there except the lights of the helo and the flare almost down to the water and the flying projectiles still arcing but gradually losing their glow, like dying embers thrown into the sky.

"Oh, Jesus, no!" he moaned softly.

"What's the matter?" Liz croaked. "What's that light?"

"They just killed Will."

"Oh, my God. Oh, Cas, no!"

He didn't say anything further, just turned level in

the water again and began stroking, his stomach hollow with sorrow. The line became taut and Liz came on, murmuring tearfully between gasps.

The swim proved to be agony for Liz. She was a good swimmer, but she was out of shape. Doing laps three times a week in a spa pool was no preparation for a long-distance crawl through open ocean. It didn't take long for her to start lagging, for her body weight to start pulling on the line. But Cas could tell she was giving it everything, grunting, swearing at herself to keep going. But her strokes steadily became more spastic, and he ended up having to drag her.

Inside he was raging, a cold, sharp fire as blue as an acetylene flame. Will was gone, killed by fools while madmen ranged like vultures. And that goddamned hotel, sitting out there like a city God had thoughtlessly dropped into the sea, insulted him with its nearness which he never seemed to reach. He roared and the anger gave his muscles a strength that came up from the dark, hollow place in his belly.

The miles ground away in endless chains of swells. Once a helicopter swept past a half mile to the southwest, its spotlight darting across the water. Then it veered and headed toward the ocean where the frigates were.

Sometime later, after what seemed like hours, he heard a small patrol boat coming toward him, its engine buzzing with isolated regularity over the water. It hung around for a few minutes and then it too went away.

Twice they crossed along the sides of exposed reef. These were respites, and he and Liz clung to the edge, their bodies undulating with the small surf and the crabs on top scurrying and clicking in the night. During the second time he scanned the eastern sky. It was beginning to deepen with that peculiar thickening that precedes dawn. He inched over to Liz, who was gasping softly, arms over an upthrust of coral. He touched her hair. "How you doing?"

"Okay, okay," she mumbled.

"Look, maybe you'd better stay here."

"How far?"

"About three quarters of a mile."

"I can do it."

Bonner rubbed her neck, let his fingers gently massage the tightness of her muscles beneath the T-shirt. She turned her head and looked at him. He smiled even though he knew she couldn't see it. "You got a lot of grit, honey."

"Right now . . . it weighs a ton . . . let's go."

He paused a moment to survey the water. Sharks were out there, he knew. Now and then he had spotted the tiny reflected sheen off a fin and upper body curving out of the surface, heard the soft hiss of water. Yet only once had one come in close. He'd shoved his satchel at it and felt it whirl away from the impact.

On they swam. Slowly the sky began to lighten to a soft indigo. As they drew close to the hotel, it seemed huge and thrust up so high into the air that it was visible at all times over the swells.

At long last, they reached the northern edge of the main reef on which the Seascape One was anchored. The hotel itself rose two hundred yards away. Liz was nearly helpless now, and Cas held onto her, feeling her exhaustion pumping from her mouth.

"How far?" she uttered feebly.

"We're there."

She sighed with relief.

He studied the hotel. Its lights still glared against the brightening sky and threw illumination down into the water where they were. Below he could just make out the dark shadow of the reef slightly etched with light. Beyond it was a sudden break-off where the escarpment plunged into deep ocean. The water there absorbed the light and looked black and menacing.

Moving very slowly, they approached the hotel. Cas could feel the heartbeat of the thing coming through the water. The steady thrumming of motors and pumps, the thick thud of pressure tanks, the soft, sibilant hiss of underwater release valves. Everything seemed alive, strangely organic, like a dragon resting for a moment in shallow water.

Angling against a strong seaward current, he struggled with Liz floating on her back. Minutes later, they slid under the northern tip of the structure, beneath a vast honeycomb of tanks and catwalks that intensified the sounds as if they came from a cavern. Tiny lights outlined the catwalks, and a dinghy with a sunburst on its bow was tied up to a floating dock.

He eased Liz up into the boat, where she lay still, heaving. After a few seconds she vomited, only seawater coming. She moaned softly. He laid the satchels beside her, paused for a moment to check the area, then oxygenated twice and dived into the water.

Below was a strange phantasmagoria of light and shadow and resonating sounds. At twenty feet he leveled out, swimming hard against the current. He figured it to be seven, eight miles per hour toward the escarpment and deep ocean. Some eighty yards away were the lights of the connecting tube which ran from the main hotel to the outer restaurant and tennis courts. It was a great luminous tunnel that lay on the bottom with seal rings every ten feet. Despite the distortion of the water, he could see figures moving through it.

He swung around. The huge after-anchor chain was forty feet to his left. All right, he thought, that's one. Feeling his eyes burning from the water, he blinked, squinted, and scanned in the other direction. There! The second anchor chain was just barely visible on the south side of the hotel. Two!

His chest was beginning to ache with the need for oxygen. He quickly scanned again, a complete three hundred and sixty degrees. No more chains. Releasing air, he bolted toward the surface. It danced and shivered above him with light. Just before reaching it, he slowed his ascent and came gently through the surface, a few feet from the dinghy. As he did so, a sudden flood of sharp light burst along the outer edge of the hotel as the sun's rim cleared the horizon.

Liz had recovered somewhat and was sitting up, her

face pale and strained. She was staring out at the sunrise. Beyond the hotel it made the surface sparkle with diamonds. "What time do you figure it is?" she whispered hoarsely as he came up to the boat.

"Somewhere between five and six."

"Oh, God, the rocket's coming!" she cried, starting to crawl distractedly around the little boat.

He grabbed her arm. "No, there's time. Western China's still behind us on the clock." He stared her in the eye. "Are you rested enough?"

"Yes, I'm okay."

"Now listen, there's two main anchor chains, one out there"— he nodded toward the outer chain—"and the other one on the south side of the hotel. I'm going down and place both charges. Wait here till I get back, then we'll go down and trigger them at the same time."

"How deep is it?"

"About thirty feet."

She shook her head. "Wait, that's running it too close. Let me place the second charge."

He hesitated a moment, then nodded. "All right, you take the south chain. You can probably get all the way across to it along those catwalks. But watch out for workmen down here. Don't get spotted."

"Right." She shouldered her satchel.

"Put the charge on the point where the chain links into its cement base. Wedge it solid so the current doesn't pull it out. Watch the current, it's strong. Angle down against it."

"Yes." She kept clenching and unclenching her fingers, nodding her head. Energy was blowing all around inside her now, all of it fear-driven.

"When your charge is set, trigger it immediately and then get the hell out of the water, up onto the catwalk. And don't forget what I told you: when you pull the trigger wire, jerk it hard, pull it free."

"What about you?"

"The water's clear down there, so I'll be watching you. As soon as you start toward the surface, I'll trigger mine and come up. Work your way toward the center of those catwalks and be braced for the concussions and possibly water blow. Afterward, stay put, I'll find you.''

She was rocking now. ''Oh jeez, yeah, okay.''

He reached out and pulled her face down close. ''It's gonna work. It's got to.'' He smiled at her, kissed her hard on the mouth, then pushed her to get up and out of the boat. ''Go!''

He watched her scamper off along the catwalk, those lovely legs and haunches pumping up and down, her feet leaving wet imprints on the deck. She disappeared around a slight bend.

He reached into the boat and retrieved his satchel. With it around his neck, he waited, counting off the seconds to give Liz time to reach the opposite side of the catwalk complex. Finally he took a couple of deep breaths and went under. Down he angled, feeling the satchel slapping against his back and the water, now flooded with sunlight, humming. On the bottom, the sand channels were fuming mist as the current streamed out toward the sea.

Xchiang Mission Control, T-minus-2 minutes, 42 seconds . . .

Dr. Ziyang was working on full automatic, brain impulses locked into the electronic surges going and coming through his machines. He watched as the Firing Room sent commands for the auxiliary power units—hydrazine-fueled systems which drove the hydraulic pumps that operate the engine nozzles, fixing them into gimbal positions—to come up into operational state. Data loops began clicking into the green, indicating hydraulic systems functioning properly as the first stage's main engines were gimbaled into a preprogrammed series of position checks. As the checks were completed, the engines were gimbaled into final firing position.

T-minus-1 minute, 30 seconds . . .

The rocket switched from ground power systems to its own electrical system. Vents in the tanks closed as liquid oxygen and hydrogen, in their separate chambers, began to pressurize.

T-51 seconds . . .

Management of the Firing Control system was switched to the on-board computers as the last electrical link with the ground was cut.

T-24 seconds . . .

Flooding vents around the rim of Pad 3 opened, allowing a deluge of water to cascade into the depression below the firing base. This water was designed to dampen the sound energy from the engines, which could cause vibration damage to the delicate instrumentation of the satellites high above in the payload canister.

T-7 seconds . . .

The rocket guidance-command computer signaled the opening of the valves which funneled the supercold liquid hydrogen and the oxygen oxidizer through hoses to the stage one main engine. Instantly the liquids were turned to gasses, compressed, mixed and ignited.

A vicious explosion of fire erupted out the nozzles, blowing outward, deflected by the incline of the water depression. Steam clouds instantly enfolded the Long March rocket as the engine's fifty thousand pounds of thrust shoved its base nearly ten feet laterally in a rolling, roaring crescendo.

T-2 seconds . . .

The on-board computers automatically checked engine power pressurization and thrust. As the nose of the rocket returned to true vertical position, explosive charges blew out the retaining bolts which were holding the rocket to the pad. Link lines from the service tower severed as the vehicle began to lift, inching heavily off the ground.

The clouds of steam continued to boil up and out as it cleared away. Three feet—ten—twenty— Now the flames of the main engine's three nozzles became visible through the steam, pale blue arrows of fire rising as the earth trembled with thunder.

* * *

At one thousand feet, the Long March rolled slightly, its nose pointing into an arc track. Taking advantage of the earth's eastward speed, it accelerated with a force of 3 Gs, climbing in velocity. The rocket vibrated violently in the thick atmosphere.

Thirty seconds into the flight, anyone aboard the rocket would have seen the sky turn from a deep blue to a solid black. Speed was nearing Mach 1 with altitude at eight miles. At fifty seconds, there were two violent sonic booms as it crashed through the sound barrier. Instantly the first-stage engine sounds became quiet, like the soft soughing of electric generators.

One hundred ten seconds: velocity reached Mach 4, altitude twenty-eight miles. Ten seconds later, the first-stage engine completed its burn. Holding rings around the rocket were blown, and the used stage dropped away, tumbling leisurely.

Instantly the guidance-command computer ordered valves opened into the second-stage engine. A single arrow of blue fire erupted from the stern of the rocket as the second-stage engine began hurling the Long March forward with 25,000 pounds of thrust.

Velocity climbed rapidly. At forty miles altitude, speed was Mach 9, and it continued accelerating. As four minutes, forty seconds after launch passed, the rocket had reached Mach 15 at an altitude of seventy miles.

One minute, fifteen seconds later, the second-stage engine completed its burn. Its holding rings blew along with the main forward fairing bolts. Both the second stage and halved fairing sleeves, aided by a short burst of hydrazine, drifted away and down. Velocity was Mach 23.

Now the small apogee kick motor, housed within the stern firing sheath of the satellite package, fired up. For seventy-five seconds it would burn, producing five thousand pounds of thrust. In so doing it would use two thirds of its fuel capacity. The remaining propellant would be saved for the eventual reentry alignment.

Velocity reached orbital entry speed of 17,590 miles per hour.

Seconds clicked off. At last the apogee motor began its shutdown sequence. The space vehicle, now seven minutes fifteen seconds into launch, glided smoothly into the cold near-vacuum of low orbit, 115 miles above the earth.

22

Gallaudet wasn't humming anymore. Instead he moved with the sharp, sure precision of a Las Vegas croupier, hands darting, head swiveling, his eyes hot with the flashing combustion of the coke. His machines and display screens ran with him.

As for Stanford, he walked around even more softly than before. He realized that events had reached a critical point, and he dared not make an intruding sound, offer a question. Gallaudet wouldn't have answered him anyway, for he was off by himself in an electronic universe.

Although the Frenchman had once explained exactly how he intended to take over telemetric control of the satellite, Stanford had grasped only that it would involve a high-frequency radio beam, an electromagnetic burst of radio waves up in the gigahertz range. In fact, Gallaudet had already started his gigantic generators outside the bunker to build up power for the beam, and their steady hum filled the room.

So Stanford merely skulked about the bunker like a shadow. As the minutes passed with agonizing slowness, Gallaudet became stock still, studying the numbers splaying across his displays. Jack's frustration and anxiety began to grow. Why had he stopped? he wondered. Shouldn't things be getting more intense?

Then an horrendous thought struck him: What if Gallaudet was out of control of things? A surge of nausea came up into his throat. Good Christ, he thought, the Frenchie was a goddamned cokehead. Sure, he'd once been a genius when it came to rockets and astrophysics, but what if the years of shooting up had warped his grip on reality?

With sudden drunken rage Stanford hurled himself across the bunker and grabbed Jean's arm. "What the hell's happening, goddammit? Why aren't you doing something?"

"*Ballot!*" the Frenchman roared back, viciously pulling his arm free.

Startled by the response, Jack growled, "Listen, you fuck, you better not blow out on me. I swear, I'll put your—"

"Get out!" Gallaudet shouted. "Get the hell out!"

Eyes glowing, Jack slunk off to a corner of the bunker and his rum bottle.

In truth, he needn't have worried—yet. So far Gallaudet had everything in the palm of his hand, cycles and sequences splitting hairs right down the middle. His programmed timing, despite the small loop lag out of Xchiang, was holding as precisely as a solar clock. However, the real test was still ahead. The attack of his beam and subsequent takeover of satellite command had to come in right on the button, without flare lag of even a hundredth of a second. If the firing was too early, before his killer virus could complete its destructive work within the Xchiang Mission Control data banks, the MC could conceivably negate the beam's effect. If too late, the satellite would glide out of the precise air thinness of 0.012% of sea level, and his radio impulses would be attenuated and scattered. A touchy business all around.

But unlike Stanford, Gallaudet had no doubts. Cocooned within his rare pharmaceutical atmosphere, confidence had become giddy arrogance. His theories were sacrosanct, his calculations irrefutable. The only problem was the presence of this cretin of an American with his imbecilic interference.

Drawing away from Stanford's momentary distraction, he leaned into his displays. Over the past seven minutes since launch, he had been coordinating data off his tracking dishes with the slightly time-lagged impulses from Xchiang MC. As he watched the satellite enter low orbit, his automatic command of *69*, activating the killer virus, went out. Panel numbers began reeling past, blips of digital light.

And then *wham!* 1.56 seconds later, the terminal which linked him to Xchiang went crazy. Flashes and electronic pyrotechnics exploded. This was followed by a sharp burst of display light and then the screen went dark.

His eyes quivered. The virus had just wiped out massive sections of the data banks of Xchiang's Mission Control. Precisely 1.20 seconds after the data destruction, the automatic sequence within his mainframe unleashed five thousand gigahertz of electromagnetic energy in an intercept convergence with the orbiting vehicle.

Liz had just lowered the satchel into the water and was sitting on the edge of the dock when a man came through a side door. He was wearing a yellow dive jacket, shorts and tennis shoes, and his thick, slightly bowed legs were tanned the color of mahogany.

He stopped short when he saw her. "What the bloody hell?" he barked. "Who the fuck are you?"

She instantly let the satchel go and stood up. "I'm a—a reporter," she stammered. "I'm covering the conference."

The man's eyebrows lowered. He was powerfully built with a thick, homely face and pale blue eyes. "How'd you get out 'ere?"

"I swam."

"Bullshit." He started down the stairs. "You're comin' wi' me, lady."

Liz searched frantically for a way to escape. Then, panicking, she jumped into the water, went down into a flurry of bubbles. Before she could straighten out, a terrible pain shot through her skull. The man had grabbed her hair. Viciously he yanked her back up through the surface.

"No, you don't," he yelled. His legs braced against the dive ladder, he hauled her back up onto the dock. She swore at him, the pain in her head like fire. He wrestled her around and tried to put a knee on her back. She hit him, shoving a fist into his neck. He responded by slapping her hard.

The blow blasted her temple like thunder, made her eyes water. Manhandling her again, he jacked her to her feet. "Settle down, you bloody tart, or I'll break your friggin' jaw."

As he shoved her viciously toward the stairs below the door, Liz stumbled forward, almost fell over a tarped motor. "Look," she pleaded, "you have to listen to me. We're all in terrible danger here. There's a rocket coming."

He snorted. "Aye, an' I've got a two-foot dick. Up the stairs."

She went, reached the door. Her head was throbbing. She whirled to face him again. "Damn you, you stupid bastard. I'm telling you the truth. There's—"

He reached around her and yanked the door open, shoved his face into hers. "Move it!" he bellowed and propelled her through.

They went up a narrow stairway to a room filled with generators and banks of control switches and relay terminals. The room was hot and smelled of electrical wiring and packing lubricant. A short man in dirty white coveralls peered around one of the generators. "Ocker, what 'ave we 'ere, Jocko?"

"A friggin' newsie," Jocko answered. "Arsey bitch claims she swum out. Get Angus down."

Liz was rigid with terror and frustration. Would Bonner know she hadn't placed her charge? she agonized. And if so, would he be able to cover on his own?

A new thought bored into her. What if these men spotted him too? She swung around, knowing she had to do something to draw them away from the foundations.

The generator man had moved away to a small desk affixed to a bulkhead. He talked on a phone a moment, then came back. He stood gawking at her. "She's a looker, ain't she?" he crooned.

"Okay," Liz said, "you got me, but you're both in serious trouble. I'm an American network journalist."

"Who gives a fuck?" Jocko snapped.

"Yeah? Go ahead, take me to this Angus of yours. He'll fry you."

The generator man sniggered. "What he'll do, missy, is kick your lovely arse up shitty crick."

Jocko laughed and shoved Liz toward another door.

Bonner completed setting his gelignite charge into the curve of chain and cement on the main anchor line. Then braced against the piling, he squinted through the water toward the other anchor to check Liz's progress. The water was bright with sunlight, which also threw a sharp, slanting shadow from the bottom of the hotel. He could see the south anchor chain clearly silhouetted against the brightness beyond.

Liz was nowhere in sight.

Swearing in his throat, he headed for the surface, climbing up the chain. Just as he neared the point where the huge links went up into a shaftworks, he caught sight of something in the water on the far side of the hotel. It was sunlit, floating slowly downward, twisting and gliding like a large falling leaf. It was Liz's explosive satchel.

Heart jarring, he surfaced abreast of the shaftworks. It was made of six-inch steel and covered with rust. From somewhere deeper up the shaft, he could hear the soft hum of generators and the heavy shifting of the chain in the shaft sleeve as the hotel moved ponderously against it in the current.

Twice he ducked his head to see if he could pick up Liz. Still no sight of her. By now the satchel had reached the bottom, and he couldn't make it out against the dark reef.

He eased up through the surface again and swam over to the small dinghy. In one smooth lunge he was up into it and onto the catwalk. Walking swiftly, he followed Liz's wet tracks along the walkway and up a small ladder.

On the second level, between the sides of the gigantic central flotation tanks, the catwalk showed no more moisture. She had quit dripping. Still, he kept on.

He came to a branch in the catwalk. One pathway went up through a small trapdoor overhead. It had a wheel lock in its center like that of a submarine hatch. He continued along the other pathway. Bright sunlight began flooding the end of the tunnel. All around him, the flotation tanks groaned and throbbed ponderously as the level of the sea rose and fell up through the bottom vents, causing pressure pockets up near the tops. This was what he had heard out in the water, the periodic thud and wash of pressure adjustments.

Suddenly he stopped, hearing faint voices. He cocked his head, listening. A few seconds later, a man's voice clearly yelled, "Move it," and then there was the slam of a metal door that echoed back through the catwalk tunnel.

Cas felt his back crawl. He turned his head back and forth, trying to pick up further sounds. Nothing came save the breathing of the flotation tanks. Cautiously he moved ahead. Another catwalk came down to meet his. A minute later, there was another ladder that went down to a small landing bathed in bright sunshine. It gave out onto a wide view of the sea and the curve of land far off. Auxiliary motors lay under plastic tarps on one side of the dock and a small diver's ladder flanked by pressure nozzles. Above the motors a small stairway went up to a full-sized door with a red lock box.

He squatted to study the metal decking near the stairway. It had little chits in the steel and the sun had warmed the metal. There was water all over the place. In it he could see the lines of tennis shoe soles, and here and there the imprint of a bare foot. Liz's! Somebody had caught her.

"Shit," he hissed softly. For a moment he studied the water beyond the landing, then turned and went up to the door. Easing it open, he peered up a narrow stairway to a second door. From beyond it, the sound of heavy electrical generators hummed hollowly. He started up the stairs, then stopped.

It was no use going after her, he knew. They'd both end up getting caught. With that phantom rocket coming in like a lightning bolt out of the sky, he'd have to go back, try to trigger both satchels himself.

He returned to the landing and knelt. The current was pushing the water up from under the landing smoothly, pressing out ripples. Cupping his hands against the glare of the sun, he peered down and instantly picked out the square green shape of the explosive charge lying in a small sand pool thirty feet below.

He fixed its position in his mind relative to the slant of the sunlight. Then he leaped up and ran back through the catwalk tunnel, going swiftly, silently, high on the balls of his feet.

When Gallaudet's electromagnetic beam hit the satellite, a concentrated electrical field was instantly created within the concave structure of the vehicle's SHF receiver antennae. In the thin atmosphere the field caused molecular acceleration within the air's charge carriers, hurling them into instantaneous collisions with neutral particles. The result was a total electrical breakdown called "avalanching."

With the speed of light the avalanche formed a plasma sheath around the antennae. This plasma, a soup composed of free electrons, ions, neutral atoms and unshattered molecules, generated a blast of kinetic energy which started oscillations radiating outward from the center of the antennae dishes. So violent were they that the upper metal surfaces of the arrays became etched and minuscule pieces of the coating flaked off.

Deep within the guidance-command platform of the satellite, the environmental sensor director system registered these tiny reactions of high-energy smear, oscillatory vibration, and a minute gravitational decrease due to the layer peel. Immediately it attempted to analyze the data to find a coherent cause and form a response.

Focusing on the weight loss, which was the most programmed exigency, it assumed that it was flying too high and had to perform a tilting maneuver to decrease altitude. But then the gyro and inertial reading showed that it was not out of tracking altitude.

Again it attempted analysis to come up with a second answer to explain the weight loss. It was flying too fast, which could also account for a decrease in mass. It would have to compute and execute a short burn of its maneuvering motors to decelerate. But once more secondary systems indicated that velocity factor was on proper fix.

Confused, the guidance command went to its programmed three-level redundancy system for resolution and reaction command. The purpose of the system was to analyze unexpected and unprogrammed problems. As each level independently worked on the data and came up with possible resolutions, the last level—called the modifier or arbiter—would scan infeed from the other levels and decide on a final response. But unlike the more complex redundancy systems in American guidance-command modules, which carry five density-analysis levels, this system contained only three.

The arbiter, lacking analysis density, was unable to arrive at a coherent solution. It therefore automatically sent an inquiry to the Xchiang Mission Control and clicked itself into shut-down mode to await resolution command.

But Xchiang MC was no longer there.

* * *

At the CIA headquarters in Langley, Virginia, where it was a little before four in the afternoon, everybody was coasting, waiting for the five o'clock shift changes to roll around. Earlier there had been twin flurries of activity. The first concerned the movements around the Amur River, with Defense shooting info probes on what they had from their in-China agents. Unfortunately, their contacts were feeble and most of those were concentrated around Beijing. Nothing solid was coming in from the capital that could give hints of what was happening up along the Manchurian border.

The second was a report through Naval Intelligence of an attempted run on the Seascape One by a PT boat. For about an hour everybody was thrown into a different direction. What was this? An assassination attempt on the leaders down under?

The first report had been terse: vessel designated old U.S. torpedo boat, Elco class, caught in high-speed approach to the Seascape with accompanying gunfire from one of the Aussie frigates. That was all.

It took nearly twenty minutes to get the whole story. With Director Price attending the President, Main Station Chief Rick Alworthy was operational liaison with the conference security via Sydney's Australian Naval Headquarters and U.S. Naval Intelligence.

By one-thirty in the afternoon, Alworthy had the rest of it. The boat had been sunk and its crew killed in an explosion of its fuel tanks approximately seven miles from the hotel. No one knew the purpose of the run, or who had crewed the PT. But everything was now secure. At this news Alworthy breathed easier. A potential close one. He turned his main attention back to the situation on the Chinese border. Then, just before four, he was hit with another bomb.

It had first entered the FBI network as a low-priority request from San Diego Communications Center for a trace on a man named Jack Stanford. FBI records indicated that a Jack Stanford had once worked for the Drug Enforcement Agency at stations in Europe and Southeast Asia. He had been a good agent, his file actually showed duty commendations. Then, two years before, he had simply disappeared somewhere in Thailand.

At first he was thought to have been killed by drug lords. In response the DEA had pushed some hard counter strikes by the Thai government. Drug areas were raided, a few secondary runners arrested. No sign of Stanford had been uncovered. Then reports began filtering in which claimed he'd been sighted both in Europe and Hong Kong. Interpol addendas seemed to link him with drug trafficking in the Golden Triangle.

The FBI had dutifully returned the trace request to San Diego's Comm Center and, as an afterthought, relayed a secondary ID probe to Langley. There it might have lain for weeks except for a frantic call which came into the agency at 3:39. It was from a Captain Clifton of San Diego's CC.

He refused to talk to anyone but the director. The call was passed to Alworthy. Clifton didn't waste words. ''I think we may be looking at a missile attack on the President's meeting,'' he blurted.

Taken aback, Alworthy snapped, ''Who the hell am I talking to?''

Clifton identified himself and gave his station clearance code number. Alworthy typed the number into his PC. A few seconds later, a verification came through while Clifton continued ranting on.

''All right, hold it,'' Alworthy cut him off. ''You're the one who requested ID on a Stanford, Jack. Correct?''

''Yes.''

''So what's this shit about a missile?''

The captain explained. After receiving the FBI's report, he had contacted NI with the entire message from the *Indonesian Spring.* But there he'd run into a stone wall of security and had been shunted to Langley, since the CIA was prime coordinator involved with the President's personal security.

''Okay, read it to me,'' the station chief said.

Clifton did. Alworthy frowned, shifted in his chair. A Chinese missile? Hurriedly he signaled one of his aides to come on-line.

"I'm here," the man's voice cut in immediately.

"What do we have on a Chinese rocket launch?"

"I'll scan," his assistant said.

'Come on, man," Clifton shouted.

"Just hold it."

Alworthy's assistant returned quickly. "There's a Chinese rocket carrying a U.S. and Swiss weather satellite set to go from their Xchiang pad site four P.M. our time. It's probably lifting off right about now."

Alworthy's neck began to prickle. "Run up the IDR on FBI log number"—he checked his book—"00785."

A moment later, Stanford's CIA file splayed across Alworthy's monitor. He scanned it quickly, seeing data similar to the FBI's. Except for the latest update entry:

TRANS-SOURCE: MANILA, PI///8-12-90**STA: 177 STANFORD, JACK ID WITH MANILA POLITICIAN/LAW-YER AGUINALDO BABIYAN TWO DAYS BEFORE AB AS-SASSINATION . . . STANFORD, JACK ID WITH SEA VESSEL DES FLYING SUN STA LISC HONG KONG (FILE: 8695867) OWNED BY KNOWN AFFILIATE OF GREEN TIGERS TRIAD ORGANIZATION

Triads! That made twin Chinese links. Alworthy's spine was touched with ice. He immediately shunted Clifton to his aide. Within thirty seconds he was on the line with Naval Intelligence's Admiral Kitchner's office, got a captain named Garza.

As he ran through what he had, his mind was shooting probabilities. Was there some connection between this and the intruding PT? Could it have been testing the Aussie patrol defenses against a missile attack? Sounding out range and guidance data?

Apparently Captain Garza had also been probing the same territory. "Jesus Christ, Alworthy," he cried.

"You think there's a possibility a Triad assassination attempt is in the works down there?"

"I don't know. God, I don't know. But you'd better roust Aussie Naval and get your people down there jumping." He felt a powerful throb in his temples. He glanced at his watch. It was two minutes after four.

"I'm on it," Garza said and was gone.

Alworthy slammed down his receiver, bellowing, "In here, in here. Status Red!"

The bunker's mainframe computer clicked through its time scan with galactic speed. Outside, the heavy generators dropped in volume as the power came off. At the console bank, Gallaudet was frozen, only his blazing eyes showing motion.

A display on his right which had been quiescent now came to life. It was showing his radio probes searching for access of the shut-down satellite's command system along with the positional data off the bunker's tracking dishes. So far these showed that the dormant vehicle was still holding to normal glide trajectory.

Clothed in Xchiang MC's command code, his automatic radio impulses were ranging at 6000 megahertz, while his receivers remained tuned to the vehicle's transmission frequency of 4192 megahertz. A second passed, then another. The satellite wasn't responding.

Moreover, his tracking data was showing that it was beginning a slight pendulum distortion within its trajectory due to the resonance effect of the plasma vibration. Its orbit was gradually beginning to deteriorate. If allowed to continue, the vehicle would eventually tumble out of orbit, possibly before reaching the exact position for controlled reentry.

But Gallaudet had foreseen both possibilities. The vehicle's command platform was discarding his signal probes because their source angle was different from that of the Xchiang MC. He keyed an override command which ordered the satellite to switch from Xchiang control to the frequency and code designation of a new tracking station assigned Delta. This was the bunker, with a new frequency band at 6418 megahertz and earth coordinates of 136:40 E/05:43 S.

More seconds passed. He knew that the on-board redundancy system was now analyzing his command. Moreover, it would also be trying to deal with its own ERD data showing its wobble and deteriorating orbit trajectory. Like a prowling, hungry dog on the verge of dying, the arbiter's emergency guidance command system would be desperate for resolution and therefore would home to the logical command to switch control base angles.

A single line of *kanji* characters suddenly splayed across the display on Gallaudet's right. Instantaneously routed through the Coors-Hashigawa transcriber, it was secondarily relayed into English. It read: Accept sig 6418 MHz, Delta Comm co-od: 13640 left/0543 down. Right behind it came a rush of data as the command platform sent its situation status and a demand inquiry to what it perceived as its new command track station.

Gallaudet's hands now flew over his keyboard. Momentarily interjecting an override to his own guidance program, he manually took over assignment of all incoming data and went to his mainframe for calculation of the precise time-position of the vehicle.

Within fractions of a second, the huge computer had tabulated data analysis and fixed the time-set for relink with his pre-programmed guidance sequence, which would then control the satellite in its reentry state and precise impact arc coordinate. Initiation position showed at 47.05 seconds.

He punched up a command for transmission of the new guidance package. Instantly the entire program went out on his outgoing frequency band. Exactly 14.33 seconds later, his vehicle display registered: "COMMAND RECEIPT COMPLETE."

He tested it. Within the new guidance command he had earlier placed a single byte of extraneous, absurd information at the very end of the programmed se-

quence. Now he questioned the vehicle's guidance
command to see that it had completely absorbed and
integrated the entire reentry sequence.

He typed: ??? dimensions of Jean's penis . . .

Instantly came back the answer: Penis (erectile
state): 225 mm (length)//53 mm (width) . . . Purpose
point ???

Stanford, who had crept up and was leaning over
Gallaudet's shoulder following his gaze, read the incoming data. "What the hell is that penis crap?" he
snarled.

Gallaudet cried triumphantly, *"D'accord! C'est ma
salope petite."*

He quickly extracted himself from manual control
and keyed to automatic sequencing. Time to initiation
of reentry procedure showed 16.81 seconds and running.

In the momentary pause the Frenchman had a violent urge for a coke hit. It spread over his body like
the warm flush that precedes orgasm. He was aware
of every sound and minute tentacle of air. Smelled
Stanford's breath close, the sour tang of gastric juices
wrapped in rum sugar; heard the sough of distant surf
ripple over the mechanical-electronic whispers of his
machinery.

Time to reentry sequencing 4.00 seconds . . . 3 . . .
2 . . . 1 . . .

The vehicle data display signaled: "REENTRY SE-
QUENCE STARTED . . ."

One hundred and fifteen miles in the sky, the Chinese vehicle sailed leisurely through the soundless void
of space, a compact blue and gold cylindrical canister
brilliantly lit by the sunlight. The forward portion of
the vehicle, behind its nose cone of super-insulating
tiles made of silica fibers and coated with borosilicate
glass, was the main telemetry and command packet,
itself heat-protected by a foundation structure of
carbon-carbon.

Just below the TC platform were the scanning instrument units of the U.S. and Swiss pod arranged concentrically around a power source isolated within a tungsten-nickel-copper sphere. Below that were the multiplexers, input-output filters, command receivers, and de-spin shelf.

The main body of the vehicle was composed of the solar array, strips of Fiberglas and foil with the azulene hue of morning glories. Here solar energy was transformed into electrical impulses which were then stored in internal nickel-cadmium batteries.

Aft of the array was the power segment. Its main housing carried the ring of maneuvering-position and axial jets which controlled pitch, roll and yaw movements, along with the earth and sun sensor horns and the power electronic stack. Below this assembly was the booster adapter-shield which housed the apogee motor, and between the two distinct housings were packed the deployment chutes to be used during recovery.

As Gallaudet's new guidance program took over, electronic pings and the soft bursts of the hydrazine maneuvering jets broke the silence. Slowly, in a controlled swing, the vehicle began to turn one hundred-eighty degrees on its central pivot point. Tracking by sun-earth angles, it continued swinging until its axial line returned to the original flight path but now with the apogee engine facing forward. The maneuvering jets stabilized it.

Keying off the guidance command, the apogee motor started up two seconds later. It held to a three-second burn before shut-down. The vehicle began decelerating sharply, dropping under 17,000 miles per hour. Its arc trajectory began to steepen as it responded to the slight increase of gravitational pull.

This was the critical point of the entire reentry procedure. If the vehicle came in at too high an angle, it would ricochet off the thicker atmosphere and go back out into space, overshooting Gallaudet's calculated entry point. If the angle was too steep, however, the vehicle would get sucked into the atmosphere too quickly, before it had time to reposition itself with its tile heat shield forward.

But the Frenchman's guidance timing was perfect. As the vehicle dropped past an altitude of 110 miles, the maneuvering jets again blew minute adjustment surges. The vehicle swung on its pivot point, slightly slower now due to the thickening atmosphere, until the heat shield was once more pointed forward.

Altitude was now 105 miles with the descent angle steadily increasing as the earth's gravity pulled harder and harder on the mass of the vehicle. At the same time the atmosphere's increasing density was bleeding off velocity, which now stood at 15,500 miles per hour. . . .

The outgoing current had picked up slightly as Bonner headed for the after-anchor chain. Below him, the swirl of sand in the clearings of the reef had become thicker, whirling along crevices and then forming clouds out over the rim of the escarpment. The sunlight had become white and brilliant as it came down through the struts and outer foundation beams of the hotel, forming strange shadows on the bottom and vivid, dancing shafts and curtains of light. In them he saw the dull silvery flash of mullet schools riding the current, looking like strips of foil caught in a breeze.

He descended strongly, arms drawing in masses of water, legs knifing rhythmically. Before the dive he had oxygenated himself to the verge of dizziness, and now his tissues and cells responded with clean, smooth energy.

He reached the anchor piling. Gripping it with one hand, he let the current pull his body out while he readjusted the satchel in order to get to the ring of the firing wire. Without hesitating, he yanked it off. Instantly there was a little hiss as the timer broke its vacuum seal.

He had sixty seconds to reach Liz's satchel, place it on the base of the forward anchor chain, trigger it, and get to the surface and out before the concussion of the first charge blasted through the water.

Propelling himself away from the piling, he shot for the bottom. He swam with all his strength, gliding close to the reef face, taking advantage of the current as it angled and deflected off the coral. Now and then he gripped an upthrust and flung himself forward.

Four hundred fifty feet away, the other anchor chain was silhouetted against the sunlight. Behind him, the timer on the first charge buzzed softly, clicking off the seconds: 51 . . . 50 . . . 49 . . .

23

Teddy Weaver's cigarette never got lit.

For the past seven minutes he had been tracking the Chinese satellite. As he turned away from the main tracking panel of the Smithton Station to pick up his fag, his eye caught a jittery movement within a series of numbers on the display screen loop-linked to the ST grid.

Frowning, he slipped the cigarette behind his ear and sat down in front of the screen. The numbers were altitude and trans-arc coordinate radar fixes on the satellite. Until a second ago they had been registering smoothly as the space vehicle glided in low orbit. But the arc numbers were slowing and the altitude read indicated a fractional decrease. They were tiny divergences, yet Weaver instantly realized that something was wrong up there.

"Arlo," he yelled over his shoulder. "Have a gander at this."

His co-watchman sauntered over and leaned down. "What?"

"That bleedin' chinkaroo satellite's in trouble. It looks as if it's losing AAT stability."

Both men watched for several seconds. The arc track slowed even more, indicating a downward movement of the vehicle. Altitude was near 100 miles.

"Holy shit!" Teddy whispered. "That little bitch is coming out of orbit. Quick, run a check on our gear. Maybe we're off."

Arlo darted away to the tracking console. A few seconds later, he yelled back, "Nope, everything's clean and on key."

Weaver was on his feet, staring wide-eyed at his display. AAT data was showing rapidly increasing descent. "Get Pakillen on the horn." John Pakillen was Chief Meteorologist for the Australian Weather Bureau.

"Right."

Teddy seated himself at another console, a big-frame unit used to calculate movement of weather fronts. Fingers flying, he linked into the rocket tracking grid and ran off a projected estimate of the footprint, the ground area of probable impact of the satellite's fragmentation debris should it actually reenter the atmosphere.

He came up with a swath three miles wide and one hundred miles long running across the eastern portion of Cape York from Thursday Banks all the way down to Princess Charlotte Bay north of Cooktown. He swung around and glanced at the AAT console, eyes focusing on the altitude track. It showed the space vehicle had reached 91 miles.

"Teddy," Arlo shouted at him. "Pakillen, on three."

Weaver scooped up his phone and jabbed the lighted button. "Sir, we've got a bloody disaster on our hands." He quickly explained what his track indicated.

Pakillen swore. "What's impact time estimate?"

"Hold." Teddy quickly ran off an estimate parameter. "Eight minutes, fifty-three seconds."

"I'll raise AN headquarters. You lay up the Grenville, Melville and Cooktown watch stations. Order them to issue an emergency procedure alert through local police immediately."

"Yes, sir."

There was a pause and then Pakillen cried, "Jesus Christ, I just realized something. That Seascape One's dead center in the impact footprint."

Teddy was jolted. Before he could say anything, Pakillen was gone. He threw his phone receiver away and scooted back to his main console. Impact time-fix was now reaching eight minutes, thirty-one seconds. . . .

Bonner's lungs were burning, a fire that felt as if it were incinerating tissue. He had put out too much energy streaking across the reef, and now carbon dioxide residue was drawing up the tannic acid in his muscles, corrupting the long smoothness of his stroke.

At last, with a final thrash of his legs, he reached Liz's satchel, scooped it up, and headed for the chain. A covey of sergeant-major fish darted up from a crevice in the cement piling, their striped sides streaking across his face.

He reached the anchor and rammed the satchel charge in between the bottom link and the piling anchor half-link. His eyes were stinging fiercely. He opened the satchel, felt for the timer and adjusted it for a fifteen-second detonation.

During the dash through the water he had tried mentally to count down the seconds of the first charge's timer. The mental calculation helped keep his mind off the need for oxygen. But halfway across, he'd lost track, and now he had no idea how long it had been.

He glanced back at the after anchor and knew instinctively the charge was about to go. He had to get out. If it went with him in deep water, the concussion would burst his eardrums, most likely knock him unconscious. Cursing silently, he left the second satchel unarmed and shot for the surface.

He had no sooner broken through, catching a split-second glimpse of the dock where they'd caught Liz, than the first charge exploded. Floundering to keep his upper body above the surface, he felt the concussion lash at and past his legs. A hard, slamming rush and then a peculiar sensation through his muscles, as if tissues were being compressed and then rapidly expanded.

The explosion was a deeply muffled volcanic rumble that went on and on. Then a massive volume of water blew upward at the other end of the hotel. The deluge slammed into the corridors and catwalks of the structure, roaring like a waterfall. Within the sound were other reverberations: the tearing of metal, an almost chimelike ringing from the flotation tanks, a deep thunder as the hotel structure, beams and foundation struts lurched heavily.

As the concussion riffled off, Cas oxygenated and went under. He was instantly immersed in a thick cloud of bubbles. It was as dense as a heavy snowfall, and he heard a violent, gigantic hissing like a thousand steam pipes releasing pressure. He drove through it, heading for the bottom.

Twenty feet down, he broke out of the cloud. Off to his left he saw what was causing it. The underwater tube which linked the main structure with the outer tennis courts and restaurant had been torn away as the hotel swung in the current without the anchoring effect of the after chain. Pressurized air was erupting from the nearer end of it as from a giant fire hose. Mistily he saw objects within the tunnel—human bodies!—being blown out into the ocean.

For a fleeting moment he wondered, Dear God, am I right? Is there really a rocket coming? But he didn't have time to debate the question. He had reached the second charge. All around him the water was filled with galactic sound. He hooked the timer ring with his forefinger and pulled it.

Somersaulting, he planted his feet against the piling face and catapulted his body back toward the surface.

Five minutes earlier, CIA Director Price had felt an insistent tap on his shoulder. He was standing at the arched entrance to the Seascape One's main dining room, watching the closing ceremonies of the formal meeting of the heads of state. A seven-piece band played the national anthems of each nation represented, flags were unfurled by blue-uniformed Australian soldiers looking absurdly like Boy Scouts at a jamboree. Price turned to find the ashen face of his chief adjutant, Mike Olmstead, staring at him. "What's the hell's the matter?" he snapped.

Olmstead leaned in close to his ear. "We've just got a high-priority message from C-2. They think a missile attack on the hotel is coming."

The director drew back in shock. Hotel? What hotel?

"It just came in, sir," Olmstead whispered.

Price shot one glance toward the President, standing with his hand over his heart while the final strains of the Chinese anthem blared across the dining room. Then he grabbed Olmstead's arm and propelled him back across the lobby and into one of the elevators.

An operator dressed in a bright red uniform quietly asked their floor. "Weather station," Price barked. The door whispered shut. There was a tiny jolt and they headed upward.

"What the hell is this all about?" he growled.

"Alworthy said there was a relay from a—"

Price hissed, silencing him, suddenly realizing the operator was there. The man's eyes slid over and stared at them. The director forced a smile.

A few moments later, he and Olmstead burst through the outer door of the weather station. The room was filled with CIA men, prowling around in ridiculously colored shirts and shorts. Price took hold of arms and huddled everyone near a coffee urn.

One of the agents gave him an update. He listened, his gaze flying around the room. When the man finished, he blurted, "Goddammit, does Alworthy have a solid verify on this?"

"Just what I said, sir. He thought the coincidence of Chinese reference too—"

"A Chinese missile? Here?"

The agent was about to answer when something impacted the floor. Another jar. Everybody automatically looked down as a general whisper of astonishment scattered around.

Then the floor violently shifted. Price felt his hip slam into the edge of a console desk. Around him aloha shirts were flung sideways. One man sprawled across the tile.

Still wincing from the pain of his collision, Price lifted his head and bellowed, "The President! Get to the President!"

"You have to believe what I'm saying," Liz pleaded. But Angus Porter merely glowered. They were in a small office on the main floor of the hotel. "I know it sounds crazy, but it's horribly true."

"How the bloody hell did you get out here?" Angus barked.

"Aboard a PT boat that—"

Angus's eyes widened. "Jesus, you're part of it!" He swung around to Jocko. "Get Security down here fast."

Jocko hurried away.

Liz touched Porter's arm, about to speak, when suddenly a sharp, rolling surge of energy came up through the soles of her feet. Angus blinked twice, rapidly, and then whirled around. Liz yelled at him, her voice croaking: "Oh, God, it's starting!" But he was already racing through a side door.

By the time he reached the back access hatch down to the foundations of the hotel, he realized something was drastically wrong. The whole building was moving! Like a skier going into a side skid, he could actually feel the horizontal motion.

The Seascape had lost anchor!

He took the stairs four at a time. As he burst through the lower deck door, he ran into a solid wall of water that knocked him to the deck. It was coming from a pressure break in one of the forward flotation tanks.

He thrashed around within the deluge, trying to find the doorsill. As his hand touched it, he felt another powerful jolt go through the structure. Big, heavy blow, felt in the kneecaps.

Fighting against the raging water, he regained his

feet, pulled himself through the door, and tumbled onto the outer catwalk. He hit the bottom, elbows screaming against the metal deck. But that was drowned out by the thought screaming inside his head: *Somebody is dynamiting my hotel!*

Gallaudet's urge for a coke fix was getting partially compensated for by the flash of data on his display. The numbers appeared like needles of light that were absorbed by his eyes, creating a maniacal high. Satellite altitude was now 84 miles and dropping. Extrapolating from the data, he projected images of what was happening up in near space.

The vehicle was plunging into the uppermost atmosphere, pushing its molecules aside with enormous speed. Its friction was increasing as kinetic energy turned into heat energy, the temperature along the forward tile face increasing to 2,500° Fahrenheit.

From outside the vehicle came the slowly rising whisper of rushing air. It grew louder as the satellite was engulfed in a soft red glow. As gravity increased, the sound of the rushing air became a howl. The glow, created by molecular compression, turned orange, then a rosy pink that became almost white. The velocity, due to the increasing friction effect of the densifying atmosphere, had dropped to 12,500 miles per hour.

With altitude at 80 miles, guidance command retrofired the hydrazine maneuvering jets, all pointed forward to increase deceleration. But still the atmosphere was being rammed so violently ahead of the tile face that electrons were being stripped from the air molecules. Within seconds an electromagnetic cone formed around the vehicle, and it entered the area known as the Zone of Exclusion, where no radio or radar could pierce the cone. From now until it reached an altitude of 35 miles, it would be invisible to tracking stations on earth.

In the bunker this was signaled by an abrupt halt of infeeding data off Gallaudet's screens. After a few hundredths of a second, they came on again. Only now the data was back-reeling as the machines tried to pinpoint the cause of the data loss.

Stanford let out a howl: "Shit, we've lost her."

The Frenchman ignored him. Instead he swiveled his chair around and fumbled for a syringe and tiny vial. Before he could draw up, Stanford was on him, trying to grab the hypo.

"No, you don't, you bastard," he screamed. "Get that satellite back."

Growling viciously, Gallaudet grabbed Stanford's shirt and hurled him back with astounding strength. Before the American could recover, Jean had drawn up a hit, flexed his forearm, and jabbed the syringe home.

With a tiny burn like a beesting, the drug hit his veins, the clean, hot blow of pure power. His head lifted, then his body, arms, legs were singing. He laid down the syringe and looked at Stanford, grinning cheerily. "Not to worry, *mon cher,*" he cooed. "The little one is still ours."

He eased his chair around again and stared at his main console screen, waiting. Stanford roared around the bunker, threatening to disembowel him. But he didn't touch Gallaudet again.

The world of Admiral Elliston Hardie, Chief of Australian Naval Operations in Sydney, had been turned upside down over the past eight minutes. First he had received a red-hot communiqué from U.S. Naval Intelligence, Washington, that there was substantial reason to believe that a missile attack might be mounted against the Seascape One.

The prospect of such a thing so stunned the ANO commander that for a moment he was completely at a loss as to what to do. Then he came roaring to life and people scattered, hurled away by his rapid outpouring of commands.

The Americans had said that the missile was Chinese. That meant that it would be either a land- or sea-based firing, since the Chinese had no long-range air force to deliver a missile. He automatically assumed that a Chinese missile meant a Chinese coup attempt. The political ramifications of that he simply put out of his mind for higher-ups to figure out. He hurriedly went over his maps, plotting ranges for known Chinese ordnance.

Meanwhile, in the outer office, his people were scanning the data banks which registered all sea traffic within a five-hundred-mile radius of the hotel in an effort to isolate any ship that might be a possible launching pad. The search covered sea space out across the Coral Sea and westward into the Malacca Strait.

Next, the mainframe ANO computers also surveyed recent photos of the scatter islands within that quadrant for any unusual ground clearance which had been photographed over the past three months but had not yet been analyzed.

Last, Hardie began marshaling his military defense contingents. Here he found a frustrating snag. The base at Grenville, where the heads of state had first landed on Australian soil, was essentially a coastal watch operation. It contained only a squadron of slow twin-engine PS—140 patrol aircraft and a few helicopters. His nearest attack squadrons were at Croker Naval Air Station north of Darwin, and at Bundaberg AAFB near Hervey Bay on the Queensland coast. Even under scramble condition red, the aircraft from these sources, Harriers and FA-18 Hornets, could not arrive on-site the Barrier Reef in less than twenty-two minutes. Nevertheless, he ordered them into the air to begin fan-recon runs along the northern and eastern coasts of Australia.

His final line of defense was the four station frigates which had been patrolling the waters near the Seascape. Unfortunately, only the lead ship of the squadron, a revamped U.S. Coast Guard frigate of the Island class rechristened the *ANS Wallongong*, possessed ship-to-air anti-missile capability. Aboard her was the "Hip Pocket" launch setup, which contained the rather outdated Chaparral launcher with passive engagement and infrared threat acquisition components and dual-mode Redeye missiles.

The Redeye, utilizing a passive radar and infrared guidance system, could knock down an incoming cruise missile. But its range was limited to a ten-mile radar pickup, a thirty-thousand-foot ceiling, and it could only track incoming missiles traveling less than Mach 1.3 speed. It was also known to have a tendency to stray off its target.

Just as his command for Status Red Alert: Missile with contingent defensive deployment of the patrol squadron was relayed to the *Wallongong*, Hardie had his second shock. Word had been received from the Australian Meteorological Office that a satellite was being observed in what appeared to be an aborted orbit. ANO claimed that impact footprint would occur alonga three-hundred-mile corridor of the Queensland coast.

Hardie almost lost it on that one. After a few juicy obscenities, he ordered all coast watch stations to put out an emergency order for people within the footprint area to seek shelter immediately, and set up coordination with his headquarters to the main police barracks which oversaw the entire York Peninsula at Cooktown.

Then, with a brusque prayer that pieces of that godforsaken satellite didn't end up in somebody's bedroom, he returned his full attention to the missile threat. Hovering over his radio operators, he watched and listened as the Hornets and Harriers, now airborne, streaked toward the Seascape. The *Wallongong*'s relays were also coming in as she took up position, her emergency situation missile search-scanning the western horizon and clicking through her computerized threat library for warning of an approaching missile.

Cas never quite made the surface near the little dock. He got lost in the bubble cloud and slanted off to the left. Instead he came up under one of the main flotation tanks. He pulled himself up and frantically scrambled around until he reached a catwalk barrier.

When the second charge went off, the impact was horrendous, lifting him right off the railing and back into the water. It was filled with a wild roaring. Then he was lifted by a massive surge. For a few moments he found himself whirling and tumbling within a churning mass of heated water.

At last he struck something solid and held on. He was on a flotation beam, water cascading back down all around him. Dazed and hurt, he listened to a horrible screeching of metal. The entire hotel seemed tilted at a sharp angle. Directly below him was a thick rumbling, while inside it came a high-pitched, siren-like sound of metal under unbearable tension.

Suddenly something snapped, an explosive crack that sounded like the discharge of cannon. A fraction of a second later, something huge crashed through the flotation tanks. Grinding metal blew, pressure lines hissed. The whole world seemed to be colliding. From a corner of his eye Cas saw several huge chain links plow through the sheet metal of a nearby tank, folding it inward as if it were tin foil.

Groaning with terror, he clung to his beam.

Forty feet above him, Liz was wandering around in near panic. After Porter had taken off, leaving her alone in the office, she had at first started after him. Then realizing that the explosion must have been Cas's charge, she turned and tried to retrace her steps down to the foundations of the hotel, hoping that she might still be able to retrieve her satchel and set off the second charge.

She went down a flight of stairs, but it ended against a wall. Retracing, she came to a door, listened, then pushed it open. She found a large room with a window that faced toward the main lobby. It was filled with people and computers. Everybody was standing, looking at one another with open-mouthed immobility.

When the second charge exploded, she felt the floor

surge upward as if the explosion had been right under her feet. People cascaded against typewriter stands and PC consoles. Liz was propelled right off her feet, went straight up and then down again.

Her gaze shot to the front window. The lobby was filled with all sorts of bizarre sights. A man in a red jacket was thrown into an ice sculpture of a bounding stag. Elevator doors opened and closed rapidly, out of control. A wall light tore loose, nearly smashing down onto a waiter. Beyond, in the main dining room, people were dodging about, grabbing at tables which tilted, sending plates and flower arrangements sliding.

As the floor beneath her tilted sharply to a grotesque angle, she had to hold onto a desk. A moment later it went sliding wildly away and collided with a woman in spiked heels. She was lifted bodily, screaming, and Liz felt her come back down hard on her lap, felt the sharp edge of corset against her legs.

"Go, Casimir," she whispered into the woman's red hair. "Do it!" Then she and the woman sailed across the space between two desks and into a cabinet.

The satellite blew through the height of 35 miles in a final flaming burst of yellow-white light flecked with streams of lavender and green. Filling the sky all around with its brilliant glow, it sundered the tropical air with a chain of three sonic booms as violent as ammunition dumps exploding. Its velocity, however, had now slowed to 7,000 miles per hour and was continuing to drop.

The emergence of the vehicle out of the Zone of Exclusion instantly threw data back onto Gallaudet's displays. The Frenchman leaned in as his computers calculated new fixes and projected time frames and impact coordinates. Everything was running precisely on the knob.

At present descent rate, with the increasing retardation effect of the atmosphere, sea impact was fixed at thirty-two miles northeast of the Seascape One. In order for Gallaudet to send the vehicle into the proper target frame, he had to maintain a descent velocity of no less than 1,200 miles per hour. This would shallow the descent arc and bring the impact fix to the exact coordinates of the hotel.

However, he did have a tolerance vector to his targeting. As long as the vehicle struck within a radius of two or three hundred yards, the violence of the collision would create an energy and sea wave powerful enough to turn the Seascape One upside down, killing everyone within it.

As Gallaudet watched his data feeds flashing rapidly, he entered a parabolic overlay to the track line of the descending vehicle. Instantly his mainframe gave him back a proposed interject command for apogee motor burn time and initiation which would change the trajectory arc of the satellite to fix on the exact center of the target frame. It specified a three-second burn with initiation command holding at 7.003 seconds.

The satellite had now reached an altitude of 28 miles, velocity down to 3,000 miles per hour. Under normal reentry-recovery operations, guidance command would have soon triggered the release of the two drogue chutes to slow the vehicle sufficiently for the three main chutes to be deployed. But Gallaudet's guidance program had already killed the chute deployment sequence completely.

He entered a command for automatic apogee motor firing and burn. This was the one command over which he had maintained manual control, since any descent arc trajectory divergence was unknown during the period when the satellite was in the Exclusion Zone.

The mainframe fixed the automatic sequence and began a countdown: 4.890 seconds. It snapped through thousandths of a second click-offs. 2.190 seconds . . . 1.356 seconds . . .

Apogee motor ignition. The mainframe clocked burn time.

Shut-down.

Gallaudet's eyes snapped to the tracking displays.

Altitude: 25.119 miles . . . velocity: 1,542 mph . . . declination parameter: 0.12% per second.

"Violà, mon poule!" he yelled, making Stanford with his rum bottle jump. Gallaudet's eye swung to a new number sequence which snapped onto his screen.

Time to impact: 1 minute, 30 seconds . . .

24

Down under the hotel, everything was going off at once: the screeches of ripping metal; sharp explosions as electrical conduits broke open, sending hot wires up against the overhead; the hissing of shattered pressure lines; and the low, thunderous rush of water pouring into the forward flotation tanks.

The girder Bonner was clinging to was now sharply tilted and getting worse as the Seascape's southern side slowly lost buoyancy. It heaved suddenly and a wall of water came up through the catwalk tunnel, rolled into and past Cas. He tried to fight against it, but it was useless. Like a papier mâché mannequin, he was swept off his perch and back through the honeycomb of walkways and tank girders.

At last he managed to grab a railing as the wave petered out, finally blowing out through the opposite end of the hotel. All around him water was cascading into the ocean, and when he looked down, he found it shimmering with oil scum, opaque with bubbles and foam. But he recognized that the water was very deep now, for the half-light through the foundations faded out twenty feet below into blue-black depths. The hotel was no longer over the reef but had been pulled by the current out beyond the main escarpment.

He had little time to rejoice over that. He pulled himself over a railing and fell onto a small catwalk. Again the structure ponderously shifted and the ocean started rising sharply, welling up like a great bubble.

Ten yards away, a portion of a tank rumbled and then broke from its heavy retaining straps. It rolled in the surge, exposing its bottom intake vents, which were covered with streamers of seaweed. The baffle networks had been smashed and twisted like the blades of a power mower that had been run over solid rock. With a hollow clang it smashed into the catwalk tunnel and wedged there.

Bonner's blood was pounding crazily as he pulled hand over hand along the railing, struggling against the water pulling his legs. His gaze roved about the upper level, looking for an escape hatch. All he could see were hanging clusters of pressure lines and high-voltage conduits. They were still intact, but he knew that soon they too would be ripped out, sending down massive electricity through the metal decking.

At that moment he heard voices, faint, throaty bellows. Pausing, he glanced toward the north end of the structure. Three men had come charging out of a side walkway and were running around in the deepening tilt of the substructure, peering at strut beams and tank housings with large flashlights. One was a short, barrel-chested man who seemed to be screaming orders.

Suddenly he spotted Bonner and swung his flashlight toward him. "There's the bloody barstid!" he screamed. "Get 'im!" All three men came slipping and sliding along their catwalk toward him.

Cas waved wildly at them, yelling, "Go back. There's hot electrical lines down here."

They ignored him, coming on. One man had a spear gun which he had scooped off a nearby bulkhead. He cocked it as he ran. The barrel-chested one lost his footing and slammed against a tank bulkhead. Right behind him, the one with the spear gun stopped, braced himself on the railing, and fired.

With a tiny blow of compressed air the spear shaft, thick as a finger with a dark, barbed head, zipped straight at Cas, its trajectory arcing slightly. With a soft groan of shock, he twisted away from it. An in-

stant later, he felt a sharp pain slice his left shoulder
as the spear ricocheted off him and then collided with
the corner of the walkway. He saw a splash of blood
come off his shoulder and roll down his chest.

He took one quick glance back. The barrel-chested
man was up again, face contorted with rage. The other
had taken one of the spare shafts off the gun's compression tank and was recharging the weapon. He
brought it up.

Cas plunged into the water in a knife dive, stretched out,
his shoulder burning like fire. He saw the second spear
shaft shoot past him. Then, for a heart-clutching moment, he felt himself being *lifted!* Huge bubbles surrounded him as another portion of a tank gave way,
expelling its trapped air up through the bottom vents.

The upsurge carried him back past where he'd
been, forming itself into another wave. Vaguely he
saw the men going down in it, their legs and arms
whirling. Then he was dropped sharply as the receding
water equalized.

He swam, arms and legs gouging and slamming
against the water. A few seconds later, he popped
through the bottom turbulence like a chip of wood
hurled out of a whirlpool. Below him, the ocean went
way down, dark as midnight velvet with a crazy quilt
of light shafts piercing it and then fading. In those
depths he saw the pale, shadowy forms of sharks moving, drawn to the wild cacophony of the disintegrating
hotel.

Unnerved, he looked up. Above him the structure
was a mass of air pockets and clouds of bubbles, everything silvered by the diffused sunlight. Forty feet
to his left was the massive forward anchor chain, its
weight pulling it straight down. Also hanging out of
the turbulence were long strings of broken cables,
swaying loosely in the current like the tentacles of a
man-of-war jellyfish.

He headed for the front side of the hotel. As he
neared it, he made out the dark face of the reef escarpment, nearly a hundred yards away. A huge cloud

of coral dust churned up by the satchel explosions and the ripping of the chains as they were dragged off the reef smoked through the channels and curled over the edge like mist from a waterfall.

The viewing tube was visible too, pinioned in bright sunlight, lying on the bottom like a giant eel waiting for prey. He bumped into something and jerked away from it. It was a corpse in a pale shirt, slowly twirling in a deathly pirouette.

The front of the hotel was tilted sharply, submerged nearly up to its front entrance. Furniture, curtains, sodden flags floated above what had been the main stairway. Along the small grassy concourse the tiny Samoan palm trees were sunk up to their top leaves and long strips of sod snaked through in the current, forming clumps like little sargasso islands.

He swam up through the debris and came out of the water on the upside of the main portico. Through the entrance he saw people running around frantically, yelling and shouting. He glanced back at the spot where the hotel had been anchored. It was about two hundred and fifty yards away. Beyond, the outer restaurant and tennis courts lay in sun-sparkled serenity. But some twenty people were lined along the crushed walkway which had led to the viewing tube. They too were shouting and waving, wildly pointing toward the sky.

He lifted his eyes and scanned the deep blue beyond the slanting top of the hotel. There was an object up there, clothed in white with pieces of flame and fluorescence torn from it trailing away in a wide tail that seemed to fill the whole sky. It was so high it appeared motionless.

His heart turned to ice: *There it is!*

Four hundred miles to the northwest, Jack Stanford was also watching wide-eyed as the impact time flashed off. In the stillness of the bunker, broken only by the clicks of Gallaudet's machines, he beheld his dream playing out. It was a heady experience, seeing his life's triumph racing to fruition.

He wondered with boyish glee if he could actually see the satellite coming down if he went outside. Making fire in the heavens. But he chose not to move, remained sunk into silence, deliciously creepy and tingling. Beside him, the Frenchman was still a stone statue.

Both were staring at the same countdown clicking off as the mainframe threw updated track calculations of the satellite's position. It now read: Time to impact: 59.30 seconds . . .

The *Wallongong*'s sonar sensors had picked up the detonations of both satchel charges. As it passed a mile to the west of the Seascape, the first had thrown the ship's Combat/Intelligence Center into momentary confusion. Analysis instantly fixed the parameters of the explosion, a low-yield charge with depth fix at thirty feet and bearing line right through the hotel.

Captain of the ship, Commander Quinn Hill, huddled with his XO, Ensign Billy Walsh, behind the sonar panel. What the hell had it been? Part of the opening ceremonies? Walsh suggested. But nothing on Hill's schedule from ANO indicated any pyrotechnics were to be used.

Then the second explosion came. Hill actually saw its effects splay across the panel in a sharp little smear of light. Again analysis showed underwater detonation of a low-yield charge. Hill hurried back to his position beside the helmsman and glassed the hotel.

For a moment he couldn't believe his eyes. The structure looked as if it were tilting. His scalp prickled as he realized that it was! "Raise Seascape Watch!" he shouted without lowering the binoculars. "And get the other boats in there, fast. Something's gone bloody wrong."

He quickly considered turning his ship toward the hotel too, then belayed that order. He had to remain on missile watch, laid out in firing position with his

Chaparral launcher tubes already scanning azimuths above the western horizon. He shouted for the engine room to ease off to four knots and steady up for launch speed. The quartermaster rang down the command, and the *Wallongong*'s deck tilted slightly as they slowed.

In the next moment he heard three clear but muffled sonic booms as the satellite penetrated the lower atmosphere. And then a quick, yellowish flash snapped past the ovals of his binoculars as if a strobe had just flicked across his vision.

"Jesus, sir, what the hell was that?" the helmsman croaked.

Jerking away his binoculars, he whirled around and stared at his CIC panelmen. All three were bent forward, intently studying their displays.

The overhead speaker suddenly boomed: "Conn, Deck, we have a fireball in the sky. Port side, eleven o'clock high." Right behind it came a shout from his electronic ranging panelman: "I have target on J-band. Bearing zero-eight-nine degrees true, incoming. Range on outer rim, twenty-nine miles and closing. Speed Mach 2 plus."

Hill felt his bowels heave. As he gripped down on his sphincter, he bellowed, "Give me analysis." Around him, men were stiffening, moving in suddenly agonized slow motion.

Two seconds passed before the ER panelman reported, his voice squeaky with tension: "Conn, non-analysis read on target. No infrared signature on SISS. Velocity Mach 2 and holding."

"Range on H and I bands," he yelled.

Two seconds flashed by. "Still non-analysis and negative IR signature on H and I read."

Hill was desperately trying to find something on which to focus his training parameters. Mach 2 plus velocity? No infrared signature? What the hell was coming at them?

As the satellite descended enough to come within the Chaparral's passive engagement system range, the firing-control panelman began shouting data from his own radar acquisition probes. "Conn, FC, I have target alarm. Fix, bearing zero-nine-three degrees true, range 22 point 4 miles and closing. Negative ITAVS status. Negative IR on SPS-10 search."

"Impact fix?" Hill snapped.

Automatic-tracking data reeled in. "Time to impact estimate is on 53 point 25 seconds."

Ensign Walsh's voice cracked through the clicking half silence of the CIC. "Conn, do we release for automatic tracking?"

Hill had remained dazed. Then something flicked across his consciousness. Could this phenomenon be merely a diversion for the real missile that would soon be coming out of the western horizon? Yes, of course! "Negative," he howled. "Subvert present SPS reading and hold scan 270 through 360 degrees. Stand by for incoming missile target and AF command."

He jammed the binoculars back to his eyes, swept with fingers shaking slightly, squinting out at the clean pastel blue of the sky that lay over Australia, looking for that tiny dot of a missile that he knew was already airborne. . . .

A minute before, Teddy Weaver had leapt clean out of his console seat when the new coordinate calculations came up off his big box. It had just fixed the precise impact point of the plunging satellite from its velocity and projected descent arc.

His eyes darted to the little slip of paper Arlo had shoved beside his panel, hoping desperately his memory was wrong. The chit contained the exact coordinates of the Seascape One, which his co-watchman had found in a recent scientific magazine. 142:34 E/ 012:44 S. His eyes lifted to the console readout.

The two fixes were precisely the same.

In one mad sweep he had the phone receiver to his ear. Punched in 333, the Emergency Weather Dispatch System code number for eastern Australia. The soft, sensuous voice of a woman came on: "You have EWD, Sydney. Please press zero for voice intercept. Now."

"Shit!" Teddy screamed and jabbed the zero on his receiver.

Almost instantly a man said, "Station One, Feyne."

"Get me a clear line to ANO headquarters."

"What's your ID and priority?"

"Listen, you bleedin' asshole, this is Smithton Station 4. I've tracked the aborted satellite. The fuckin' thing's gonna come right down on that Seascape hotel."

A millisecond of shocked silence. Then: "Say again."

"Fuck say again. Get me ANO."

There was a click. Teddy turned and looked into Arlo's pale face. Another click. A stiff voice said, "Australian Naval Operations, Level 2, Lieutenant Edwards."

"This is the Smithton weather station. We've got an aborted Chinese satellite coming down. It will impact on the Seascape One hotel."

"What the bloody hell?"

"It's homed to the Seascape One, you barstid. An' you've got less than a bleedin' minute to intercept it."

There was a slight pause, and then an avalanche of clicking followed by a steady buzz. He'd been disconnected. Teddy stared into Arlo's eyes. They were unblinking, wide with shock.

Admiral Hardie's vehement voice sounded as if he were right there on the *Wallongong*'s bridge. "It's an aborted satellite," the admiral screamed. "That's the attack! Locate and kill it. Dear God, kill it."

Before the last echo of Hardie's voice was gone, Hill himself was roaring, "Retrieve SPS track and go to AF command *now.*"

The order was relayed, double voices cracking: "SPS retrieval, going to AFC, immediate, aye. Stand by for launch."

Hill's gaze whirled past open mouths and homed

onto the Chaparral launcher on the foredeck. Instantly the apparatus swung around nearly one hundred and eighty degrees, jiggling as its radar tracker homed to the incoming satellite.

Three seconds later, there was a blow of rocket smoke, thick as an erupting volcanic seam as the twin Redeyes went out. The flames and hurled smoke hit the deflector pads and sprayed out. A jolt went through the bridge, along with the odor of hot metal and the acetate-like stink of rocket fuel.

The fire-control panelman called out, "RAM one and two out and hot." Hill closed his eyes as the consoleman's voice droned on: "RAMs tracking clean . . . I have laser guidance click on . . . anti-bloom TV functioning and reading up . . . "

Hill opened his eyes. He turned and looked aft into the CIC, noted that his XO's mouth was hanging open too. Stupid look, asinine. Then he heard the FC man swear.

"What?" he cried.

"Conn, I have diverging track."

"Oh, God!"

"Divergence passing through eight degrees . . . twelve. I have GMAS in chaotic state."

Defeated, Hill gave a long sigh that bespoke a fatally blown assignment, a ruined career. He vaguely heard the panelman calling the increasing divergence. The twin Redeyes had just lost homing fix on the satellite and were now arcing up there in the sky like a pair of confused hunting dogs trying to relocate a scent trail.

Gallaudet lifted himself delicately off his console seat and walked out of the bunker, leaving Stanford standing there.

"Where the hell are you going?" Jack cried.

"It is done," the Frenchman said simply.

"No, you stupid shit. Come back here."

"It is done," Gallaudet repeated, his voice trailing

off. He giggled. ''I find need to immerse myself naked in the sea.''

Stanford let him go. He swung back to the console, crept closer. The time display was jittering through its phosphorescent delineations. Time to impact: 9.005 seconds . . .

He sucked air, found it dry, and tilted his bottle to let a rush of fiery rum down his gullet.

4.000 seconds . . .

He blinked as the liquid burned his throat.

1.500 seconds . . .

He watched the last numbers click off, down to 00.000.

Impact.

The satellite smashed into the sea exactly one hundred and forty-three yards west of the Seascape One's original anchor point, beyond the outer restaurant and tennis courts. Its 989 pounds of mass had been quadrupled by its velocity of Mach 2.

The initial collision created a dish blow that lifted out over the reef. Instantly a twenty-five-foot wave, followed by smaller waves, rolled away from the impact point in an expanding circle. Debris from the satellite sailed with it, chunks of the heat shield and body mass carrying the same velocity as ultrasonic bullets.

Within a fraction of a second the main wave front swept over the outer restaurant and courts. The tidal force lifted large sections of roof, rubberized asphalt and fencing into the air along with human bodies that made jerky contortions in the sunlight. But the solid mass of pilings and cement base broke the wave front as a pier or breakwater will sunder a tsunami. The shattered wave then extended outward, away from the destroyed structure in an ever expanding *V* as it swept on toward the main hotel, now drifting nearly six hundred yards from the satellite's impact point.

Mega-tonic forces still remained within the plunging, disintegrating satellite. As it drove through the thirty feet of water over the reef, compression heat turned the ocean into steam around it. Instantly violent expansion explosions erupted, sending up clouds of superheated moisture. This too dissipated energy from the collision.

Nevertheless, there was still a tremendous amount in the driving hunk of deformed metal that had once been a technological piece of work. It struck the reef and bore into it, forming an astrobleme, an impact crater, eighty yards across and fifteen yards deep.

Shock waves went out through the soft limestone and coral, and a high lip was thrust upward around the hole. Within the depression, heat and the pressure of five thousand atmospheres chemically changed seawater and silicate components into glass. Free calcium molecules merged with dissolved nitrogen and chlorine to form tetrachloride gas, purple as royal ermine and explosive as gunpowder.

As the violent forces began to dissipate in the vast expanse of ocean, the core of the impact was flooded with inrushing water. In new explosions, steam and gas shot three hundred feet into the air. As the impact crater became filled, the water behind the initial deluge whirled together. The confused turmoil of sea coiled back onto itself, thrusting powerful energy in an expanding circle, forming a new wall of water that hurtled away from the impact zone at eighty miles an hour.

Bonner had been shocked into immobility at the sight of the incoming ball of fire. Like the biblical prophet's apparition, Stanford's missile was alive in the heavens. Then his body circuits hit all at once, hurled him forward and through the main entrance.

"Get out!" he screamed. "It's coming!"

The great blue rug of the lobby was soggy under his feet, covered with water seepage. As he rushed in, people flicked a wild glance at him, then twisted away. Only one started toward him, a dark, heavyset man in a black suit. He had a shotgun in his hand, no longer than his forearm. He looked like a Russian peasant out after stag.

As Cas turned toward him, he saw the man's face open in shock. Following a fraction of a second later was a horrible explosion from outside, the blast so powerful that it compressed the space between it and Bonner's ear and seemed to erupt just behind his back.

A nuclear-like concussion wind blew every glass window inward, lifted the heavy curtains at the dining room entrance straight out. Shards of glass and slivers of metal sill whipped through the air. Cas was lifted and thrown forward. Blue carpet skimmed past below him. Around him other bodies were rolling in the air grotesquely. He collided with a man in midair, and together they smashed into the closed door of an elevator. The other man's body took the full impact, and blood spewed out of his mouth. Cas crumpled to the floor, dazed. The sound of the explosion receded deeper into the hotel, echoing through narrow passageways, howling up elevator shafts.

He lifted his head and looked out through the glassless windows of the main entrance. His vision danced and shimmered as if he were looking at a mirage. Just outside, the sea lay glistening in sunshine. But six hundred yards out, a gigantic cloud of dense white smoke was boiling off the surface. Silhouetted against it was the outer restaurant, like the pencil sketch of a building blocked out on foolscap.

His heart lurched. Out of the boiling smoke came the first impact wave, as tall as a hillside. Its front fumed smoke like surf on an arctic coastline. It engulfed the restaurant, which instantly blew apart as if blasted by dynamite. The impact shattered the wave front and sent explosions of water upward. As it swept past and its side portions closed in, the wave was smaller. But it kept coming, straight for the Seascape One.

The surge of sheer self-preservation rose in him. Groaning incoherently, he lurched to his feet and headed for the entrance, for the ocean. He would find sanctuary out there, his mind told him, down deep, below the turbulence.

He had covered ten feet when a thought crystallized amid his panic. Liz! Christ, I forgot about Liz! He glanced wildly around him. People were beginning to lift up off the floor, their eyes quivering at what they saw coming. He bellowed her name, then turned and sprinted across the lobby.

A man was cowering behind the main desk. He was whimpering, like a child left in a dark closet. Above his pathetic murmur Cas heard the incoming wave hissing and roaring, a wind plunging through canyons.

He darted past the crouching man and through a door. The room beyond was small, filled with coats and filing cabinets strewn over the floor. He called Liz's name over and over, but his voice was lost in the increasing din of the approaching wave. Spotting a second door, he lunged through it into a narrow corridor with metal stairs at the far end. In the confined space the wave sound became compacted, seemed to make the walls and deck shake.

The wave hit.

The collision was so violent that it wrenched him off his feet, sent him sprawling on his face. Then the whole building was tilted upward. He slid down the corridor and rammed into an after bulkhead, rolled over, and immediately crashed into the stair railing. The hotel was heeling sharply, shifting lumberously sideways as it weathervaned into the face of the wave.

Up the corridor, the door he had come through slammed open and a deluge of water shot through. It rolled down the narrow space and struck him, momentarily pinning him against the railing. Gradually the weight of it eased. Cas groped upward until he cleared the surface. His head, in darkness, was four inches from the ceiling.

Something went by, the upper half of a wooden desk. It twisted and banged hollowly against the ceiling, responding to a reversed flow of the water. He clung to its edge. The water was rapidly emptying out of the corridor, back through the doorway, and he and the desktop were sucked with it. The top jammed against the door frame. He ducked under it and re-emerged into the small room, in five feet of water.

From the lobby he heard screams mingled with men roaring in confused rage and terror. He lost his footing in the rushing stream and skidded out to the area where the main desk had been. It and the whimpering man were gone. In the lobby the water was over his head. Furniture, palm trees, dead fish floated and spun in whirlpools. Here and there men thrashed the surface, trying to find solid ground. Then he spotted Liz. She was curled behind one of the main I-beam struts that held up the dome of the lobby, struggling feebly to extricate herself. He swam over to her and touched her hair. She turned her head and stared at him, her face stark. Then she began to talk and cry in a rush of words: "Oh, Cas, I thought you were dead. It hit, it hit."

He gently lifted her free. She clung to him. "It's okay," he shouted into her neck. "It's over now."

It wasn't.

Hearing the isolated roar of engines and a powerful, metallic rapping, Cas lifted his eyes. The huge blue body of the helicopter which had been chained to the roof of the hotel now crashed into the flooded portico with the resounding collision of boxcars smashing together. Its huge blades sliced across the entrance, broke apart, flinging out chunks of cement and iron. There was a fleeting second of almost vacuumed silence and then the copter exploded. A ball of flaming fuel blew through the windows.

Reflexively, Bonner jerked away from it, hauling himself and Liz down under the water. Even submerged, he felt the heat sweep over them. The explosion sound faded, echoing.

He came up. The entire lobby was burning, the ceiling and walls coated with flaming fuel, and large pools of it turning the water into a fiery mass. Away from it he swam, his right arm brushing flames aside, his other hand pulling Liz's body.

They were approaching the door to the small filing room when, as if the floor had dropped out, the water was sucked away, leaving small fish and a single black sting ray flopping helplessly in the remaining six inches. Cas rolled to his feet and pulled Liz up. He cupped her face in his hands, shouted down into those wide, frenzied eyes: "Are you hurt?"

She shook her head, choking.

"We've gotta go up!" he shouted. Liz stumbled to her feet and they went through the corridor door. Like the room, it was already filling with smoke and the stink of burning fuel. The lobby flames threw sharp etchings of yellow and orange against the bulkhead opposite the doorway.

And a new hissing sound came with it.

They ran for the stairway. Water was erupting out of the lower stairwell, coming up in periodic surges that burst open, releasing the sounds of massive things colliding. The hotel seemed to be settling. Yet it still rocked ponderously, like an ocean liner in a hurricane.

Cas headed up the stairway, going three at a time with Liz coming right behind him. They reached a landing where the stair curved back on itself, then a dead-end landing that abutted on a yellow door with a fire bar on it. He grabbed the bar. It was scorching hot. The fire had already reached the second level.

"Shit!" he roared, turned and started back down again.

The second wave struck.

This time the impact had a different character to it. The hotel lifted sharply but there was no lateral movement, since the first wave had turned it parallel with the second. But it trembled cumberously, the bulkheads cracking with strain with reports like rifle shots. Beyond that they heard, as if they were on the edge of a tornado, the wave blowing into the lobby with a roar.

Bonner leaped around Liz and jumped the remaining steps to the corridor. He raced to the door and tried to haul it shut. The hinges were sprung, he couldn't move it. As he turned back from it, a wall of water smashed into him and drove him back. He curled his body into a ball, the instinctive reflex of a surfer riding hard turbulence. Again he struck the far bulkhead, this time with such force that it felt as if his body had shattered, a glassy dismembering that pounded the breath out of him. He whirled about, blackness coming and fading and coming again.

The next thing he knew, someone was holding his head up to air. He sucked in, gorging his lungs. But the darkness still remained, only faintly lit. A dark object bobbed up into his vision. Liz's head, masked with hair streaming down. Embracing, they did a wild waltz in the water, hitting walls, twirling, twirling.

A shaft of light shot through the darkness. Smoke filled it like moonlight. Another. The water was dropping. He felt his leg get sucked against the door frame and locked there. Liz's body pressed against his. He could feel the entire contour of it, from soft breasts to the long line of legs.

A surge of rage hit him. "This is bullshit!" he thought. "Bull-fucking-*shit!* Locked in a metal cocoon like a fly in a friggin' jar. *No!*

The door suction increased, pulling them down. Swift as leaves sucked into a storm drain, they went down and through the door, popped up on the other side in the little room and into a world of flame. Long tongues of fire lashed at them, blast-furnace heat that curled the ceiling wood. They huddled in a corner beside a hat rack in the wall, treading water. Beyond the outer door the lobby was a caldron. But through the flames they could see the ocean.

"Cup your hands and take deep breaths," he shouted at her. "Hurry, before the oxygen's gone."

She obeyed, her eyes staring at him over her fingers. Inhaling stinking air into his own lungs, he studied the distance to the main entrance, calculating their route. His head was buzzing, the blood pounding like hammers against his temples.

He swung back to her. "Put your arms around my neck and lock your fingers."

"What are you going to do?"

"We're going out."

"Through that?" she cried. "We'll never make it."

The rage in him was peaking. If he could have stood free he would have raised his arms and roared to the sky. Instead he grabbed Liz's hair. "We *will*, goddammit."

She grimaced, twisted away from him. He felt her arms come around him. He took one last breath and went under. Crazy currents surged against him. He lashed out his legs, found the wall. Coiling, he thrust himself forward, feeling the heavy weight of Liz's body like a brick-filled backpack. He stroked, pulling water to him in an even, rolling rhythm.

The water was misty, a smoky green color that contained flitting iridescent flashes and sudden patches of bright orange etched in acetylene blue where fuel pools burned. Under these they swam, feeling the heat coming down through the water like scorching rain.

He struck a pillar. It was tilted, protruding out of the lobby floor. He went around it and right into a man's face. It was ghostly gray and back lighted, its features screaming in open-mouthed silence. He shoved it aside and went on.

His chest was beginning to burn with sharp muscle surges that flared through his chest. His legs were starting to feel leaden. Objects evolved out of the mist, fell away. He collided with a wall. He felt down it to the floor, then up, his fingers clawing at sculpted cement. He found a windowsill, then jagged glass that sliced his hand. Beyond it was a matrix of green: palm branches. He tore through them, out into water suddenly clear and dancing with sunlight.

They surfaced fifteen feet from the submerged main entrance. Beside them protruded the broken stub of a helicopter blade. Away stretched the rocking ocean patterned with long streamers of foam. The sharp prow of a frigate, rolling sharply in the turbulence, blocked off the sky. Grappling lines were strung from it to the hotel like spider silk, and a single sailor in a boatswain's chair was pulling himself across the abyss. Beyond the ship, small Zodiac boats were skimming, sailors in the prows riding bow lines, pointing.

Cas whirled in the water. Liz's arms came up off his neck, dragged his head inward. Her mouth was a blubbering, icy impression against his lips. He held her and then threw up his arm, twirled it in the platoon leader sign: "Converge on me."

Fifty yards away, a sailor yelled, and then his Zodiac spun around and he came boring in toward them.

Afterscene

Aboard a Navy E-2C Hawkeye electronics aircraft headed toward Pago Pago, the president of the United States listened to constant updates from the Pentagon and Aussie military headquarters while he scratched at the bandage over a deep gash in his foot. He had received it during the mad rush up to the helicopter pad on the roof of the hotel.

In the pandemonium he had been shoved and herded by his frantic security men as stark faces zipped past. Everybody was running upward, yelling unheard comments.

The explosions in the main lobby blasted through the fleeing men like a wind through a wheat field. Somebody heavy threw himself onto the President's back and they hit the floor, the man shielding him. "Stay down, sir," he heard him whisper. Then they were up again, running.

At last they reached the top of the structure. Everything was clothed in hot sunlight, with the ocean bizarrely filled with floating debris and churning turbulence. Streaking toward them were the Aussie frigates, hurling water off their bows.

Black smoke was billowing up the face of the Seascape One. The President turned to someone near him. "What the hell's happening down there? Is this thing sinking?"

"The chopper exploded," the man answered, then quickly added, "sir."

The sound of another helicopter's blades tore up the momentary silence. The craft came down, swaying back and forth, adjusting to the movement of the deck. Its wheels hit solidly and the rap of the blades died down. Arms lifted the President and set him gently on the copter's corrugated deck. It was wet and he cursed, rubbing the blood off his ankle.

With a groin-whirling lift, the aircraft went up sharply. The hotel fell away, becoming smaller and smaller, a little rectangle filled with scurrying men like worms on a corpse.

Word of the events on the Reef crammed through the Beijing military network radios. Gradually stations all over southern China started getting data too. Soon loudspeakers out on Tiananmen began broadcasting the incoming news reports.

The city stopped. Citizens on their way to work milled together in tight, whispering clots. Traffic bunched up along the man boulevards, and soldiers stood around in stunned silence. Even tank crews, who ordinarily never dismounted in public, crawled out of their vehicles and stood looking up at the speakers as their echoes crackled across the breathlessly waiting populace.

Only the cadre of conspirators moved. In his office, Minister Litung was monitoring his secret police comm network, issuing brusque position orders. His men were already outside government buildings, ready to begin arresting Sichen's people. They waited only for Litung's word, which he continued to hold back until a definite verification that the premier was dead came in through the jumble of southern communiqués.

Meanwhile, General Hsien, utilizing Chairman Zao-bang's forced acquiescence, was gearing up for implementation of martial law. Around him was gathered the hardest of the hard-line generals, whom he had called in from their units.

But then a totally unexpected thing happened. It started with a low murmur down in the square. Like a wave, it spread through the soldiers, into the groups of civilians. Out on the roads, people got out of their cars, surged toward the square. Within minutes the sound had become a single roaring voice surging out of Tiananmen. It became a chant, thousands of feet stomping time: "Sichen Zian . . . *bauchou* [revenge] . . . Sichen Zian . . . *bauchou* . . ." Assuming that the death of their premier was due to foreign assassins, the people had, in a spontaneous explosion of outrage, melded into a single mass around their fallen hero.

On the outskirts of the gigantic crowd, citizens began picking out foreigners and attacking them, pummeling them to the sidewalk. Gunfire sounded from somewhere near the People's Hall. Soldiers, responding, shot into the air.

Inside the government buildings surrounding the Forbidden City, officials went into renewed shock. And then the emotion from the square swept through the doors, a hysteria that infected everyone. Even the most ardent reactionaries who had fought against Sichen's policies now joined the call for national revenge. Litung's own secret police left their stations and joined the surging throngs.

To the tiny coterie of conspirators, however, this upwelling for Sichen struck with a jolt. As they watched, awed and immobilized, their neat plans for a coup disintegrated. Military commanders, ministers, and high governmental officers who would have been sympathetic to their purge were now forming impenetrable ranks with Sichen's supporters.

Then Chen Jann's body was found. Further work of foreign agents, people cried, probably working with internal dissidents. Next, Chairman Zaobang defied Hsien's men. In a panic they released him. Thirty minutes later, General Hsien and the three hard-line generals were placed under arrest, ironically by Hsien's own CMC forces. At the same time in Kunmintang, General Yeh Son committed suicide.

At 6:58 A.M., word finally came that Sichen was still alive. Both he and Markisov were at an Australian military base. Instantly setting up a communications command there, Sichen began broadcasting orders to Beijing. Martial law was immediately instituted throughout the country, only this time under the military governorship of Sichen's most trusted commander, Senior General Zheng Guangmei of the Northeastern Bureau.

In the suddenly isolated sanctuary of his office, Minister Litung listened to the incoming messages off his monitor link with CMC comm. He paced about the room, head down, trying to reach meditative serenity. Yet he could not escape the thoughts of doom as he realized his dream of empire had just ended.

At last, however, he found *jijeng*. Breathing slowly, deeply, mind focused on the white dot of concentration, he moved to his desk and took out the pistol he had used on Chen. Hefting it in his hand, he paused before his window. Down below, a sea of people surged and roared, yet he heard only a soft rumbling through the thick glass. He waited.

At 7:36, he heard boots thundering outside his door. Someone pounded on it. Litung turned slowly. The door was smashed open with rifle butts. Soldiers rushed in, bayonets fixed on their weapons. Behind them came a tall officer with the blue insignia of an Air Force Group captain.

"Stand to, Minister," he shouted at Litung. "You are under arrest by order of Chairman Zaobang."

Litung looked at him with his snake's eyes, black and blazing. Then he snapped up his arm and pointed the pistol at the group captain's head. Instantly the bullets of three weapons blew him back and over his desk.

It took Stanford over an hour, hovering over Gallaudet's radios, to untangle the frantic reports from the Reef and realize that his monumental plan had misfired. The rocket had missed and all the world leaders were still alive! He slumped to the floor and sat there, head shaking.

Then he sprang up in terror. "Lui!" he croaked. Within hours the Unicorn would be back, and Stanford would become bloody chunks scattered across the bunker. He ran around like a crazy man, his rum high vanished. Finally, regaining some semblance of control, he grabbed his gear and headed out the door.

Down on the beach, Gallaudet was lying naked on the sand, his skinny white body looking like a survivor from a concentration camp. Without pausing, Stanford turned and headed into the jungle, a solid wall of green which sucked him in. He drove on, soaking wet in seconds, whimpers pumping out of him as he projected terrifying images of crocs and snakes and tattooed Chinamen into the underbrush ahead.

Bonner nearly fell asleep in the hot shower. He was in a hotel room in Cooktown where two Australian Intelligence officers had deposited him for the night.

After being rescued, he and Liz had been taken to the base hospital of the Greenville AAFB. There, identified by Angus Porter, they were arrested. Intense sessions with Australian and American intelligence officers followed. At first nobody believed them. But as more information came in, the elements of their story began to fit together, particularly since their message to the *Indonesian Spring* had created a documented backup.

Cas turned off the water and dried, then stepped from the shower and lit a cigarette. It tasted terrible and he flicked it into the toilet. He studied his face in the mirror. It looked haggard. His shoulder was bandaged and his entire body was bruised and aching as if he had been in a violent fistfight. Now he heard music coming from the outer room. He opened the bathroom door and peered out.

Liz Forsythe was sitting on his bed. She had on a yellow shirt with the emblem of the Australian Northern Air Force on the breast. Yellow sweat pants were thrown on the floor. With a towel wrapped around his waist, he walked across the room. She watched him.

"Did I ever tell you you look sexy?" she said. "Even with all the black and blue."

"No." He sat on the side of the bed.

"You do."

"So do you. Where're your guards?" Although technically still under house arrest, they were to be released in the morning.

"Out in the hall. They're good mates."

"Mates?"

"I promised them I wouldn't tell if they let me in." Her eyes went bright, her mouth slightly turned down. She reached out and touched his mouth, ran a finger around the curve of it.

He kissed her.

"Your breath smells of cigarettes," she said.

"My soul smells of cigarettes."

She surged up to him. He held her, felt her breasts through the shirt. He slipped his hand under the cloth, ran a nipple between his forefinger and thumb. She sighed and lifted her head.

She cried out when she reached orgasm. Her body trembled convulsively and tears glistened in her eyes. She whispered against his neck, little soft, disconnected words. He took her repeatedly with a fiery, lustful exhilaration until his own paroxysm sang through his nerves.

Afterward, she curled into his arm. Running a finger down his belly, she asked, "What are you going to do?"

"Make love to you again."

"Wonderful, but I meant later."

"Go back to work."

She cooed. "Guess what?"

"Mm?"

"I just spoke to my editor, the uptight little bastard. He said offers are flooding in for me to do a story. Lots of bucks."

"Nice."

She was silent, then kissed his ear. "How much does a sailboat cost?"

"What kind?"

"One like the *Napah*."

"About seventy thousand."

"You've got it."

He lifted his head, looked askance at her. "Whoa."

"I'll buy it for you."

"No."

"Why not?"

"I'm not a kept man."

"Oh, bullshit." She licked his mouth. "Okay, then, how about I hire you to crew for me."

"To where?"

"Well, let's see. Tahiti?"

"You pay good?"

"The going rate. With perks."

"Yeah, we might work something out."

She chuckled deep in her throat and slipped on top of him. "Tahiti, here we come."